Praise for

BEST AFRICAN AMERICAN FICTION
2009

"A treasure trove of discovery . . . Readers across
racial lines will find reason for delight in this debut of
what is intended as an annual series."
—*Kirkus*

"There hasn't been an anthology of such talented African-
American literary figures since Marita Golden's *Gumbo,* and
the result is a masterful bouquet of literary flowers, some grand,
some subtle, but none shrinking . . . With something for every
reader's taste, this is a collection not to be missed."
—*Publishers Weekly*

"This engaging collection . . . shows the incredible range of
talent and focus of fiction written by African Americans."
—*Booklist*

"These short stories, excerpts from novels, and thoughtful essays
cover a broad range of subjects, experiences and perspectives from
many of the best writers working today."
—*Sacramento Bee*

Best

African
American
Fiction

2010

ONE WORLD

BALLANTINE BOOKS • NEW YORK

Best

African

American

Fiction

2010

GERALD EARLY, SERIES EDITOR

NIKKI GIOVANNI, GUEST EDITOR

Preface and compilation copyright © 2010 by Gerald Early
Introduction copyright © 2010 by Nikki Giovanni

Published in the United States by One World Books, an imprint of The Random House Publishing Group, a division of Random House, Inc., New York in simultaneous hardcover and trade paperback editions.

ONE WORLD is a registered trademark and the One World colophon is a trademark of Random House, Inc.

Permissions credits are located beginning on page 312.

978-0-553-80690-8 (Hardcover)
978-0-553-38535-9 (Trade paperback)

Printed in the United States of America

www.oneworldbooks.net

2 4 6 8 9 7 5 3 1

Book design by Diane Hobbing

For my good friend, Chester Himes, who told wonderful tall tales of Harlem

—Nikki Giovanni

In memory of E. Lynn Harris (1955–2009), a novelist and an entrepreneur who inspired many

—Gerald Early

Preface

One reason I embarked on the enterprise of editing *Best African American Fiction* and *Best African American Essays* was to learn something very elementary. In the first instance, I was quite sure about what I would learn: a great deal about black writing and who is writing what about race these days in provocative, even beguiling, and skillful ways. For someone who teaches literature, the fiction volume is even more important in this regard. Who are the good young black writers, or the good young writers, dealing with race in fiction these days was a question that, for me, has become more acute as I grow older, because as one grows older the present seems to recede ever more stubbornly from one's grasp or comprehension.

This might come as a surprise to those readers who may think that, as a professor in an African and African American Studies Program, I would rather naturally know what is going on in the realm of today's literature. But college professors are a great deal like physicians. They specialize in small corners of their fields, acquiring a remarkable expertise that is marked by sharply defined limits, in the hope that they may make up in depth what they lack in breadth. As one of my colleagues once humorously put it, "We all know more and more about less and less." More often than not this approach has much to commend it: It is better, from a scholarly perspective, to know every bit of minutiae about a cell than to have a casual, passing acquaintance with a continent, better to have the native's inherent knowledge of small rites than the tourist's guidebook grasp of big systems.

I do not specialize in recent or, as it is called, contemporary African American literature. Because I also teach in an English Department and for an American Studies program, I frequently teach material that is not African American–oriented. Sometimes I do not teach literature at all but rather subjects of broader historical and sociological significance, like the Korean War or social thought in the 1950s. Thus, it is easy to lose track of what is going on in the literary world now. In this way, a professor can seem out of touch to his or her students, as they are, rightly, enthralled with now, the works that are being produced at this moment, which, after all, are meant to speak directly to their experience as they understand it. As the years go by, one does not mind appearing to the students as a crusty sort of ancestral presence (it encourages filiopietism), but not as a sclerotic relic who ought to remain obscured by the fog of his irrelevant obsession. Also, to become too hidebound, too limited to one's area of specialization, means losing the perspective that allows one to connect what one knows about how blacks saw and wrote about the world in the past with how blacks see and write about it now. Specialization can provide enormous insight and rich understanding about a particular problem or situation or period, but it can also hermetically bind one's thinking. How can you ever really be sure that you understand what you know unless you can find ways of testing it against what other people think?

Literature grows and changes, as it is written under different political, social, economic, and even technological conditions. It is not static and it cannot be captured through the study of one era or one school of thought or one particular author. Students are sometimes right that we professors, in our efforts to preserve and understand our subject, may very well be killing it, as Stein did his butterflies in Conrad's *Lord Jim*, nailing creativity to a wall in order to study what creativity is, when it has, of course, ceased being creative because it has ceased being alive.

Obviously, having now been involved in making selections for two volumes of *Best African American Fiction*, I have learned a good deal about black writers and the current literary scene, much more than I would ever have known otherwise. Just as I hope these books have made me a better, more informed teacher, I hope they have informed and engaged the reading public, making readers aware that the world of black authorship consists of more than just the few big names who win mainstream literary prizes or are regularly assigned in ethnic literature classes.

But that accomplishment, necessary as it is, is only part of the story. I have become aware not just of names and titles of works but of fissures, shifts, and different audiences for the works included in these fiction volumes. Literature is a complex sociological phenomenon insofar as it involves understanding who is attracted to it, as both creators and consumers, what it is expected to do *for* its audience, and what it does *to* its audience. Literature is meant to entertain, to be sure, and the audience for so-called minority or ethnic literature craves distraction or escape as much as any other. But literature is also burdened by the expectation of conveying some sort of truth that combines both a sense of practical problem solving—how do characters deal with unfairness, dysfunction, defeat, and the like—and a claim to moral authority—do characters behave in such a way to elicit the approval and admiration of the reader. I tend to see the fiction volumes, at this stage, as, to use Kenneth Burke's phrase, "equipment for living." Reading good fiction tells us how to live and what to expect from life. But different people live differently and it is striking how we can all read the same plot and meet the same characters but interpret the story in which they are found so differently.

Amina Gautier, a professor at St. Joseph's University, and one of four writers to have appeared in both the 2009 and 2010 fiction collections, read the story that appeared in the earlier volume at Washington University in St. Louis where I work. In fact, as she was a post-doctoral fellow at Washington, it was easy enough to arrange the reading as a way of advertising the book and her talents as well. She was a bit surprised by the variety of people who turned out—sorority sisters, students both graduate and undergraduate, colleagues ranging from political science to performing arts, but more surprised by how people engaged the story in such varied ways, far different from her own views. Surprisingly readers and listeners take characters as real people facing real choices, not as constructions of a writer's imagination. Of course, writers expect this, but it is still slightly surreal to confront in person how much readers need and want to see what they think is there. Then fiction writers discover that their writings serve not a whim or an enigmatic fondness but a primary function in modern human existence.

This 2010 volume has a range of writers from the renowned, like John Edgar Wideman, Colson Whitehead, and Edwidge Danticat, to the lesser known, like W. David Hall, David Nicholson, and Amina Gautier (although, I daresay that Amina will not be a lesser known talent for very much longer). There is also a mix of styles here, highly avant-garde stories like "Bread and the Land" by Jeffery Renard Allen nestled side-by-side with pieces like "Night Coming" by Desiree Cooper, which is much closer to what is called urban literature. I am pleased once again as in the 2009 volume to feature young adult fiction: an excerpt from Laurie Halse Anderson's extraordinary novel about a young slave girl, *Chains,* and an excerpt from the classic 1959 novel about school integration, *Mary Jane* by Dorothy Sterling, who, before her death in 2009, made important contributions to African American letters throughout the course of her professional life.

I am much indebted to my guest editor, Nikki Giovanni, for her work on this volume. Ms. Giovanni is a poet who emerged during the Black Arts Movement of the late 1960s, which gave us writers like Larry Neal, Amiri Baraka (the father of this movement), Don L. Lee (Haki Madhubuti), Carolyn Rodgers, Etheridge Knight, and Sonia Sanchez, magazines like *Black World* and the *Journal of Black Poetry,* and such publishing houses as Broadside Press, Jihad Press, and Third World Press. It seemed as though every young black person I met at the time wanted to be a creative writer, and that being black itself had become, in our collective imagination, a creative act. Ms. Giovanni was one of the most noted of the Black Arts Movement writers and some of her work from this period is still fondly remembered and requested whenever she gives readings. But she is no "oldies" act. She has continued to write poetry, as well as children's books, essays, even album liner notes, while becoming a bestselling author. She occupies a place in American letters not unlike that of Maya Angelou, a foundational figure who marked the transition of African American writing from one stage to another. I am sure that many of the authors selected for this volume were particularly pleased to have had their talent recognized by Ms. Giovanni.

There is no attempt here to present this volume as writings from the black world, if there is such a thing, or any kind of monolithic concept of an imagined reality. This is rather the second volume in what might be called varieties of literary experience. If there is a black world, there are worlds within that world, worlds that include people who are not black, that include the living and the dead, the past and the present. It might be better to say that there is a black cosmos of a sort, within which are a complex set of worlds that sometimes collide and sometimes converge. This volume is meant to invite readers to experience in some measure that un-predictable, sometimes volatile, but always spellbinding dynamic.

Gerald Early
St. Louis, Missouri
June 2009

Contents

Short bios of all the contributors to *Best African American Essays 2010*
and *Best African American Fiction 2010* can be found at
www.randomhouse.com and at http://cenhum.artsci.wustl.edu

Introduction:
On the Edge of Comfort

A couple of hundred thousand years ago when humans were sitting around the fire preparing to close up the cave for the night, someone took notice of the eyes shining just beyond the warmth. Or maybe in the African rain forest as the elders sat singing praises to the gods, telling the stories of defeat and triumph, a rustling in the leaves turned all eyes toward a creature who seemed in need of community. Since they were tree dwellers they had no particular reason to fear this creature, so they continued their activities and went on to bed. Or, rolling the boulder to protect against big predators, the fire was not doused but banked for the night. Both communities found essentially the same thing in the morning. The garbage had been eaten and a creature and his family had found a home on the edge of comfort.

Or maybe it was when the castles were being built, leaving those without castle funds in thatch-roofed houses, or maybe on the Western Plains with homes that were dug out, or maybe even just a campfire next to the covered wagon carrying food supplies while the cowboys slept on the cold hard ground that the creature offered warmth and became our friend.

We named him Wolf.

And he and his followed us and ours throughout our travels. He eventually evolved to become the dog. Giving proof that God loves us.

But humans are not a good species. Yes, we liked the comfort a dog offered, but we didn't like the freedom those we still called Wolf had. Just as we liked the speed of the mustang but would try, are trying, to destroy the free horse so that the thoroughbred we created can be raced to their deaths. But that would be another story.

However old Earth is, and however we came together, to avoid ugly discussions that might lead to curses and bloodletting, when each community began its tale of how the family blended to become a community, instead of trying to date the encounter of the Hatfields with the McCoys, as it were, we say "Once upon a time." A great beginning, right up there with "Good morning"; "I love you"; "Paid in full." We humans have always had a need to tell our story, to show how we arrived at Point B from Point A. And our trusty companion, the Wolf, has made this journey with us. It's amazing to me that we have so demonized the Wolf. The lovely story of Rome would make no sense if Romulus and Remus had been suckled by a sheep or a cow. No one could believe it. No. It had to be a Wolf who turns out to be the mother of one of humankind's greatest cities. Then why do we have that despicable cliché: Keep the wolf from your door. Why do we blame the Wolf for the foolishness of Little Red Riding Hood? She should have listened to her mother and stayed on the beaten path. Who are The Three Pigs that they should, instead of inviting the Wolf in, scheme to kill him? Pigs don't eat wolves and wolves certainly helped them to see they needed better housing. But living things are rarely grateful. It seems everyone wants something to demonize.

Not a good idea.

But what I like about humans is Hope. There is always the idea that we can and we should get better. The question is, of course, how shall we go about improving ourselves? Easy. We improve by hearing heroic tales of those who struggle, as we do yet, to find a way to do the honorable thing: Break against our political party to help a young president save our nation's economy. Resign from a tainted Senate seat. Be Alan Shepard and John Glenn and sit on top of a controlled hydrogen bomb explosion and be shot into space and orbited around Earth. Be Harriet Tubman and shepherd hundreds of enslaved Africans to freedom. Be any of the tall tales such as *John Henry* or *Shine* or *Ulysses*. Be who you want to be in your imagination.

We tell tales to change our hearts and minds, to educate and delight.

We sit by the campfire of our hearts, with our loving and trusty dog at our side, and we read. These stories are among the *Best African American Fiction*. Quilt across our knees. Check. Glass of wine. Check. Munchies. Check. Dog at our feet. Check. Short stories. Check. This is good.

Nikki Giovanni

Best

African
American
Fiction

2010

The Ariran's Last Life

Maria Eliza Hamilton Abegunde

When the first big boats arrived, I had not yet married. Along with all the girls in my age group, I was learning what I would need to know to go to market, court a mate, and, for me, initiation. For months I had been told to be patient as my parents worked hard selling herbs and woven cloth every four days to traders. Every morning after prayers, they both instructed me in things I should know about the history of our village and our family lineage. Sometimes, they would let me help in the weaving of cloth that would be used in the ceremony. I liked, especially, the white with gold threads at the hem. My mother was a master weaver and sewer, and every *lappa, bouba, shokoto,* and *gele* had a small fish on the inside hem to let it be known it was she. There were three of us to enter the *egbe* right before the festivals started. We were excited, but frightened and curious. We had heard only of what was done but couldn't believe it.

In the village, the wind blew warm air through the tops of our homes. We lived in a compound surrounded by outer walls, which had two doors. Between the walls and our homes was six feet of space where warriors were always on guard. A family lived together in one area with several connecting rooms. If a man had more than one wife, then each wife had her own room and kitchen for herself and her children, but there were common areas where everyone ate and talked during the day. You saw everyone once you stepped outside. It was better that way. When one of us needed something, we asked the person nearest. Not like I see the world has developed where you have to travel miles to reach another family member, or where you suffer in silence because you do not trust the person next door. In the compound, I knew who my aunts and uncles were, which ones would chide me or let me get away with something. We didn't always agree with one another, but we did not go to bed angry.

When the wind blew, the dirt in the compound covered everything. When it rained, we moved our pots to the back room and sat inside to talk. The chickens and goats found shelter where they could. There was not ever the silence of loneliness or fear as there is now.

The girls in my age group all worked together. We were really young *obirin* then, some of us being taller than our parents. Some of us had already filled out in our bodies, and we had started *ase*. I seemed to be taller and bigger than everyone and my mother began speaking to me of marriage, but I was not interested. We learned many new things every day. How to cook, sew, make our own containers, and how to care for ourselves. How to weave and bargain a good price for what we sold and bought. We learned how to bead so we could make our own belts and necklaces or do our hair. So many centuries have gone by that I do not remember all. I only remember wanting to learn because I saw what joy it brought my family.

The day the first big boat arrived, I was sitting on a ledge above the water. I had finished my morning duty of straining herbs to be used in medicine. When they were ready, my mother would show me the next step of forming the compound. If I was lucky, she'd let me watch her work and assist as I had on other occasions. I had swept out the front room where my mother, father, and I gathered at night with my aunts and uncles. I had rolled our mats and placed them in a corner of the main room. My father had no other wives, so my tasks were simple but many.

I wanted to be away from everyone. We were between the coast and nearest inland village. It took me half a morning to walk there, and half the afternoon to walk back. I did not always come so far, but that day I had longed for the water. My parents did not like me going to the sea, and whenever I mentioned the water they looked at each other and said nothing. In fact, they seemed to increase the speed of whatever they were doing at that moment.

That day, the first boat came in slowly, just enough so I could see it meant to stop here. The sails were white with red crosses. There were three. From where I sat, they could not see me. After a while, men climbed down ropes thrown over the side. They rowed to shore in the smaller boats. I ran home thinking I had seen ghosts leaving some type of coffin. My feet were hurting from the long sprint and I was out of breath when I reached the front of my house.

"Ago, Baba!" I called to my father.

"Wole!" He answered, and I ran inside quickly.

"Hear what I have seen, Baba." I was talking too fast to get out all the words I was thinking.

"Slow down, Abi," my father said and came to rub my back. He was smaller than my mother but strong. He often made me laugh when he pretended to be unable to carry anything and would begin piling things in my mother's hands or on her head while he bent over and held his back as if in pain. His hands were twice the size of mine and I enjoyed the warmth on my back as he continued to calm me. The inside of his hands were almost the same cocoa color as the outside. "Seen what, Little One?" He smiled when he called me this, like it was our private joke.

"Big boats, Baba. Boats with red marks and *oyimbos* climbing—"

He had called my mother before I could finish. She ran to meet him from the back bedroom and they both left heading toward the *Babalawo's* house. I ran after them, dodging women's pots and children's sprawling bodies. They waited outside.

"Ago, ile, Baba."

"Wole." They entered and I followed.

"It is time, Baba. We have a few days," my father said after saluting and embracing the *Babalawo*. My mother sat quietly. They looked at me without looking at me directly.

"Has everything been done?"

"Beni, Baba," my mother responded softly.

The *Babalawo* stood up and looked at me very sadly. "Now would be good."

At once, both my mother and father grabbed my hands and pulled me farther into the *Babalawo's* house. They covered my head in a dark cloth so I could see nothing. They sat me on the ground and told me to wait and to keep my eyes closed. Had these people been other than my parents I would have cried out for help. But, I remembered they always joked me about "being prepared" at any time.

But, I was scared. The boats. The *Babalawo*. What about the other girls? I heard feet move around me. One pair shuffled. Another set walked hard around me. Then someone came and put down a mat, and asked me to sit on it. The cloth over my head was dark but I could see a little out the edge. I opened my eyes and looked down. There were more people now. I heard them greeting one another and then sitting down.

Suddenly, I was picked up and moved to another room. My head was uncovered but I was told once again not to open my eyes. My *lappa* was torn from the bottom up. My head was shaved quickly and closely. What happened next knocked the breath out of me but someone kept telling me to breathe. I was then moved to another room and redressed. The cloth against my skin was soft, but unhemmed. It was not something my mother would have made or given me to wear.

I remember standing for a long time, not knowing if I was being watched or whether I was alone. I was afraid to open my eyes in case someone was there. I tried to focus on where I was standing.

"Why are you here?" It was the voice of the *Babalawo*.

I did not know. Someone leaned over my shoulder. My mother's voice whispered in my ear. All night, I was tested on things I had been learning. The hardest things to remember were the sacred stories. When I stumbled, someone helped me. I recognized the voice of my father, other priests from the compound, and my aunts and uncles. There were voices I did not recognize, but they were kind and encouraging.

Finally, after what seemed like hours of standing, I was moved again to another room. On the way there, I smelled chicken roasting. I had not eaten since before seeing the boats. Someone guided me toward the floor and I was told to open my eyes.

"So you will remember who you are and never forget us, even in the face of iku, even as egun." The *Babalawo* leaned over me and finished the last part of the ritual. I was then brought out to my elders, who did not applaud. They stood quietly around me; some were crying. Others did not look at me.

One of the women I did not know led me to the back room. "Sleep the best you can," she said, pointing to my body. "It may be difficult, but the marks will heal in time."

I settled on the mat, careful how I placed myself. There was silence. Everyone seemed to have disappeared more suddenly than they had arrived. I turned to face the wall, still afraid and wondering if the other girls would join me soon.

I am standing on the beach by myself. The moon is high and the reflection casts a long path from the water straight to me. I move to dance in the light, not caring if anyone sees me.

Then, I am not sure how I have gotten here. I am in a small boat being held down by men who are speaking things I do not understand. My eyes are covered tightly with cloth. I cannot breathe. The edge of the cloth presses down hard on my nose.

They are tying my feet, and with all my kicking, I cannot stop them from tying my feet with rope and then sitting on top of me. We are moving slowly on the water. Some of it comes through the bottom of the boat and I am certain I am going to drown because the more they sit on me, the more the boat sinks. I begin screaming because they have not covered my mouth. I cannot stop screaming.

"Abi, Abi," my mother and father yelled. "Get up. You are dreaming."

I did not move from the mat. My body felt heavy and I began to struggle again. My mother stepped back from holding me. "You were only dreaming," she said and walked away.

"Baba, there were men tying my feet and carrying me away."

"Don't worry, Abi, everything will be OK." He walked to my mother, held her hand, and then gently squeezed it.

I shook my head and tried to get up, but my body hurt very badly. My mother rushed to help me up.

I do not remember all that happened the rest of that day. I ate well. My mother fixed all my favorite foods and let me sleep during the day. I did not have to complete chores. But no one came to visit. For a period of time after initiation, you were kept quiet. I had been told this gave the young initiate plenty of time to think about what had happened and how your life was now different or would be different. From the beginning when I was called, I had made up my mind that I would do as asked, and began learning from my parents immediately. I realized early that there was a lesson in everything, and never wasted a moment playing when I could accompany my mother to market or a patient, or sit at my father's feet as he recounted the *pataki* or remembered things he had seen as a boy.

At the end of the day, the *Babalawo* came to the door. "Ago!" He shouted this in a rather harsh way as if demanding entry instead of asking permission out of respect.

"Wole, Baba." My father's response was slow and tired.

I approached the entrance of the room. The *Babalawo* stepped in, and then behind him, two *oyimbos*. "Baba," I whispered, "what are these *oyimbos* doing here?"

Instead of answering, my father gently pushed me away and walked to the *oyimbos* and began talking. I turned to run to the back of the house, but my mother put out her hand and stopped me. It was then I looked down at my feet and remembered the dream. I did not move. I turned to face my father and the *Babalawo*. I had no idea they could speak the language of the *oyimbo*. My father turned and put his hand out for me to come toward him. I looked up at my mother, who gestured with her chin that I should go.

It was only now that I became more frightened than the night before and more frightened than I had been in the dream. There was an odd silence in the compound. It was midday and yet there was no noise outside as if everyone had vanished. There was no wind, yet dust was everywhere as if the strangers themselves churned the air. As I looked at the window, another *oyimbo* appeared but this time with a gun.

"Iya! Do not let them take me!" I fell on the ground and began pulling her *lappa*. I knew what was to happen. I had heard stories of villages disappearing or families losing a member to strangers who took them away. Sometimes there was an attack. Or worse, yet, sometimes the chief or family sold a prisoner or someone who was too much trouble, or because the village was starving. Usually, the ones sold or disappeared were not family, but someone who had been bought or captured from another village during war. We always seemed to have enough to eat. We were not at war. We did not live inland.

Had I been too much trouble? I began screaming and running around the room, trying to find an exit, but there was someone at every doorway. "Baba, please, do not let them take me. The dream, Baba! They will take me away!" I fell at my father's feet and held on.

"Forgive us, Little One." My father reached down to pick me up. Our faces were together and I could see where he had lost the back teeth on the right side of his mouth. His breath smelled like the mint root he chewed every day after eating. "But you are the one who must go. You will be the only one who will live to tell the story. It is the only way to save what will be left."

I beat his chest so that he opened his arms and dropped me. My mother did not come to help me up. Instead, she leaned over and pressed a small piece of gold into my hand. She placed my beads on my neck and knelt in front of me. My father put his hand in mine and lifted me.

"You will be taken care of. It has been divined as so. You will survive. You will not forget."

The moment the *oyimbo* touched me, I knew the world was inside out. Even in our dry, hot climate, his fingers were cold through the fabric on my arm. Yet, he was sweating and his skin had turned a pink or brown in certain places. He pretended to be gentle so my father would send me. Baba held me in his arms as if he were sending me off to be married in a strange village instead of sending me off with strangers. He did not know, like my mother knew, that women suffered differently at the hands of strangers.

The *oyimbo* took my hand and guided me out. The compound was quiet, but I could see elders looking at me from inside their homes. I wanted to run back, but every time I turned around, I saw my father indicating that I should go. My mother did not join my father. She ran to the back of the house and tore her clothes. After a while, my father left the doorway.

Once outside the walls, I began to cry. My mother tearing her clothes from her own body meant only one thing: she was already mourning me.

As I turned to look back, hoping someone would come to help me, the *oyimbo* slapped my face so hard that my neck snapped to the front. He uttered something from his mouth with spit. He kicked my left foot from underneath my body. I hit the ground, and landed hard on my right arm, but managed to hold my head up. Blood was warm on my lips. I struggled to stand. My foot throbbed where he had kicked me. Before I could stand completely, he dragged me up and pushed me against a tree. His mouth was directly at my forehead. I kept my eyes down not knowing what else to do. I could fight. But it was apparent my parents, maybe the village, had made a bargain. They would not take me back.

His hands pulled at my *lappa* until it was off, and then he pulled everything else off except my beads and the small gold chain I had tied to them. He did not touch me as I had feared. Instead, he took a heavy rope from the sack that he was carrying. The other two *oyimbos* watched. The one with the gun stepped closer and said something and then they all laughed. I tried to cover the front of my body. I could see that this amused them and the one who had kicked me bent my hands up and pulled my arms down. The other *oyimbo* who had been silent came and pushed me away from the tree, kicked my legs apart. The kicking-*oyimbo* bent down and tied my feet with the rope and then brought it upwards to wrap my wrists. When that was done, he took out a metal collar and locked it on my neck.

They stood back and watched me. I put my head down because I was too ashamed of being naked and tethered like a common animal by strangers who could not speak my language. In the back of my head, I decided to keep focused on my feet. I could not think about the compound. I could not even think about what was going to happen to me. Just as I was beginning to feel that I would be planted like a tree and left to die, gun-*oyimbo* pointed the rifle at me and then in front of me. Kicking-*oyimbo* pulled me, and they began to talk among themselves as I was led through the forest.

Even if I wanted to recall now what I saw on the way I couldn't tell you. I did not see much except my own tears. Every time I looked at something other than my feet, there was nothing but water. Each time I breathed, the metal around my neck tightened. The heat around my neck at times was searing and the only reason I stopped crying was that I became certain the clamp around my neck would choke me to death if I even whimpered.

I heard nothing except the changes in the voices that might indicate they were going to do something to me. And silence. No matter that the wind blew. Silence protected me from believing what was happening.

After about five days we met a large group of other *oyimbos*. I was led into an area that contained at least a hundred people, all tied like I was. I was pushed toward the females where I was connected by my collar to another woman, making me the last in the line. When the *oyimbos* walked away, she turned her head left as far as it would go, and smiled. It was a welcome, I knew, but I could not feel welcomed here. When I did not return the smile, she stepped back a little, pulling the other women with her, and rubbed her foot on top of mine. She turned and smiled again. This time, I nodded.

I was exhausted. I had not eaten since I had left the village. The bottom of my feet had been torn open and I could feel small rocks and twigs trapped in my heel. I was afraid of infection but could do nothing about it. My wrists had bled the first two days from the rope, then stopped. I could no longer remember how to get home even if I could escape.

I was grateful for the woman in front of me. It was not much comfort to know other human beings had met the same fate, but at least, someone had thought enough to smile. When she stepped back, the other women did not appear disturbed at the movement. It was as if they had an unspoken agreement that someone would connect with the new ones brought on. I noticed the men doing the same thing. None of these people looked like my people. This meant no one spoke the same languages or they understood only a little of maybe one or two languages. We could not help ourselves because we could not understand each other. But, the *oyimbos* understood one another, making them already more powerful because they could communicate.

I had not been standing long, when we heard the sound of chains and whips. I looked cautiously in the direction of the noise. There were at least ten men and four women being dragged by those who looked like us. They resisted movement, but every time one did not move, one of the *oyimbo* fired his gun at his or her feet. This did not make them move any faster or even out of the way, and I suspected that they wanted to be hit. However, the bullet always missed their feet. The whip and chains, however, did not, so that when the *oyimbo* had emptied his rifle, he took up the whip and chain and began beating the backs of their legs.

As they walked past us, I recognized 'Bunmi, a younger cousin from my mother's aunt's house. My throat was too parched to whisper, so I looked at her hard, hoping that she would turn, but she did not. Her body was covered in dirt and she was thin. Her lips were cracked and her wrists bled where the ropes had been tied too tightly. There was blood on her legs. Her village was at least a five-day walk from my own. Suddenly, she stopped moving. The whip snapped across her back and with it a sound like a heavy branch breaking during dry season. Instinctively, I moved to help the cousin I had once bathed in the river. My body was instantly pulled back into line. The woman in front of me turned, this time without a smile.

They beat 'Bunmi hard. When the *oyimbos* finally stopped, she did not move. They disconnected her from the line and tossed her body to the side in view of everyone.

I cannot tell you what I was feeling at that moment. Even now, as I recall it, there are so many things going through my mind. I cannot grasp one long enough to speak about it. For a long time, things were like that: moving like waves and wind through my head. Everything too fast at one time. As quickly as something happened, even more quickly a heavy dullness settled over my mind. I could not speak. And then with whom would I speak?

We stood for a long time after that doing exactly what they wanted us to do. We looked at 'Bunmi's body and reminded ourselves that we should live. An *oyimbo* began walking down the line with two pails and a cup. He tipped our heads back at the throat with the butt of his rifle, and we opened our mouths to gulp down water and mashed yam. Afterwards, they watched as we struggled to eliminate what our stomachs didn't want without watching or dirtying each other. We wiped ourselves with what leaves we found. When all this was done, they lined us up again and began to march us into the forest.

On the way out, each of us looked at 'Bunmi's body once more. Leaving her must have been too much for one of the men who had come with her and before we finished our silent prayers, he lunged at the first *oyimbo* he saw, taking his chained companions with him. He pounded the man and wrapped his chains around his neck. Soon the other men joined him, taking any *oyimbo* standing near them. The one who began the attack stood at least a full head higher than all the *oyimbos* and clearly had the advantage. The other *oyimbos* not involved looked on amused for a while, then one I had not seen raised his gun and fired. The big man stopped, looked at his chained companions, and fell over. Another shot was fired and the man next to him fell.

Not one of us moved. And those who only a few minutes before had been eager to fight, stepped back as the two dead men were removed. They joined the coffle silently. But I could see they were waiting for another chance.

As we began walking again, I did not want to look at the two dead men, one bleeding from the heart, the other from the eye. We were not allowed to bury them or 'Bunmi and would never know if the forest took them back or whether some animal had eaten them. Worse yet, I feared some unsuspecting neighbor or family member would walk here on another mission only to discover the horror of their bodies, bloody and twisted, left for everyone to be reminded that we were now strangers in our own land without protection.

From the number of times the sun rose and set, I knew we had walked another five days by the time we arrived at our next destination, a small outpost where more of us were exchanged. Although most of the women in front of me were unchained and hurried along to a tent, I remained where I was. I did not dare look around, afraid I would see more than my soul could store.

After a while, though, your only concerns are when you will stop walking, when and if they will give you water, if they will kill or rape you, when the whip will cross your back. If you will ever stop to eliminate instead of doing so while walking. And how to walk without falling. The woman in front of me walked too slowly. As if her pace would give the situation a chance to change itself. Instead, I tripped every few steps. My badly bruised feet could not heal and each time I stumbled, a closing cut reopened.

The second day after leaving the first stop I, like many others, was limping from the pain of holding stones and branches inside our cuts or between our toes while they bled. I was certain that my toe was broken. The first night out I had tripped over a large stone. Every step I took was a tentative one, putting my feet out until I could feel the proper placement. But that night, the *oyimbos* were in a rush and made us run in the dark with only a lantern in the front and back to guide themselves and their horses.

As I moved forward, I felt my right toe hit something the size of a coconut, but harder. I could not stop as the woman in front of me had missed it and kept running. I stumbled, but did not fall down. Instead, my entire big toe placed flat against the sole of my foot, like someone would fold over a piece of cloth. The next morning, I could not step on my toe or the inside of my foot. Each time I placed pressure on the toe or the ball underneath it, the pain moved up my ankle and into my knee. There was no swelling. Just pain and a little darkness around the toe where I could tell a bone had been chipped.

Had I been in the village, my mother would have used this time to show me what herbs to use. She would have also continued her practice of teaching me the ways of the healer, the kind that she was who could mend broken bones, draw out illnesses, or set spirits at rest so they wouldn't trouble a particular person. I knew enough to use my hands, but could not remember the herbs and plants that would benefit. I did not yet know all the prayers and how to use them.

The woman who had been in front of me remained as we began to walk again. I remember her not only because I tripped over her feet. She was silent. She did not cry when they beat her. She did not murmur when I whispered something. Her eyes were unforgiving, distant—like so many of the other women. There was no place for comfort.

I had begun to feel as if all my tears had abandoned me after leaving 'Bunmi's body for the animals. I felt them rush to the rims of my eyes then suddenly pull back into a tight sack like a small udder right beneath my heart. Sometimes, it was as if they were caught between my heart and my rib cage. When I breathed, the pressure made me feel as if my heart and ribs would break at the same time.

After leaving 'Bunmi, we had been herded into two lines and this is how we traveled. Men on the left, women on the right. The men were tied with their arms behind them, a rope or chain extending from one wrist to the neck of the other, all the way until the last man had his chain held by one of the horse-riding *oyimbos*. Any misstep, any sign of trouble and the chain was pulled hard. This automatically tightened the neck rings, choking everyone and making them stop. Then, the men were beaten for stopping.

The women were linked by neck collars alone. Our hands were free to allow some of us to carry baskets of food and water gourds from one place to another. Every few hours, the weight on our heads was shifted back. The woman in front passed her bundle to the woman behind. The last woman, who was me, had her bundle taken by an *oyimbo* and passed back to the front. In this way, we were equally beaten and tired.

✳

My children, I tell you, I was afraid of the life that was about to be given to me. Something worse than death, without preparation, choice, or ritual for the transition. I cannot tell you that I spent much time thinking about the reasons I was suddenly sold away from my home. I did not. At the start and end of each day I was too tired to do anything but move or rest. And it would only be after I had lived for many years in my new life that I was able to allow myself to believe what had happened.

I am ancient now. I have lived that life and many others. But it is the life of the young girl, sold without an explanation by the man she loved and trusted most that haunts me unresolved. For a long time, I wished I had not been born. For longer still I wished my father had never been born. And then I made myself forget him.

But even my anger fades. These last twenty to thirty years as ancestor to several who have returned to some of the ways I knew as a girl, I feel my heart softening as they salute my family and ask for healing to begin.

Dying does not free you. Without the body and the attachments to those things that keep you alive, the spirit changes. But sometimes, your anger and an unfinished destiny trap you. The anger is like a spirit itself, surrounding you, seeping from you and into those you care for. Sometimes, if you are unable to release it before dying, it takes hold of you and you find yourself forcing it on others being born or too weak to resist.

If you die angry as you are completing your destiny but death finds
you of *iwa pele* and *suuru,* good character and patience, your elevation is
sometimes easier. You rely on the ones after you to recognize and acknowledge your life so that you may be freed from the box of hatred and
anger that binds you—and sometimes has trapped them.

✳

During the horror, I did not think of anything except my own exhaustion.
After the last exchange, more of us traveled. We did not know where we
were going. We seemed to be moving in circles to the edge of the coast,
then away from it. Unlike me, many had come from the interior. Had
never seen the sea. I had never seen so many people. I would catch sight
of tents and boats as we passed on higher ground. But except for short
stops to restock our supplies, we never stayed long enough to rest. Usually, one of the black hires and one *oyimbo* went to trade. The supplies
were really for the *oyimbos.* They seemed to tire and thirst very quickly
and assumed that we, the natives of the land, did not. I would come to understand, however, that they did not care whether or not we were tired or
thirsty. They wanted only for us to make the final point. And their black
helpers did not care either. For all of them, we were gold, reals, pounds,
livres, brandy, cloth, and other such things that would make them and
their descendants wealthy over centuries.

When we did stop, I sometimes heard gunfire in the dark, uncertain if
it was an animal or one of us that had been spared this new life. Always,
the morning told which. If food roasted, then they feasted. If, instead, the
end of a rope hung to the ground, we knew that it was one of us, headless
for some minor infraction.

They thought they knew everything about all of us. Kill and dismem-
ber us to teach the rest a lesson. If they had known, that kind of killing
only makes a spirit wander. Makes it angry and bitter so that as long as it
can't reach home it will terrorize everyone responsible for its sacrilegious
death. For as long as it took to make it right. But, they did not ask us about
our rituals and the proper way to kill or bury an unwanted enemy so he
did not rise up centuries later to seek revenge, or be reborn through some
unsuspecting line.

Instead, they cursed the world with a despair and hatred that has no apparent root cause. They decimated a race of people for acres of land that
belonged to no human being.

Yes, there were those who stayed and married us, or served kings and chiefs. But what kind of man leaves his own home and resides in another just because he can have more wealth and more women who do not speak his language and do not even respect him. If they had known what would become of all their comfort in the coming centuries and how bloody the fight to keep it, they would have left us alone. Perhaps. All men are greedy. No matter what land claims them. They will go to the ends of the world—all the way to Africa even—to get what they want.

On the day we reached what would be our final stop before the boats, I saw it everywhere. Greed. Cowries exchanged hands like water pouring into sieves. All over the sand, tents were pitched with different flags. There were black men and *oyimbos* unloading canoes. There were other men giving orders. There were men with guns shoving lines of men, women, and children onto small boats or through doors.

I was pushed with the rest of the women into a doorway. Before entering, I could see that the place we were to enter was made of stone, with one set of floors above our entrance. Cannons jutted out of every section of the wall it seemed. A flag, which matched one of the tents, flew from its highest point. There were bars on the bottom windows with faces looking out, crying and frightened.

Inside the black men with guns stood on two sides at the end of the pathway. On either side, there was little light. One pulled the first woman to the right. The other shoved the first man to the left. This is how they divided us. The men were handled first.

Being the last one in the line, I could see the men struggling and those who did so got whipped with the butt of the rifle. There were rings attached to the wall. One of each pair was attached to this ring by his collar. When the rings were full, the next man was attached to the next available man. Their leg irons were then fitted with a heavy ball between them. As I walked past, I could see the room was full. Flies covered some of the men who had been there longest. One man who could not get out stooped in the corner to relieve himself.

The entrance to the women's room was farther down. We walked about twenty steps to a door, then stepped down into a long passageway. There were no rings here, just women squeezed tightly. They unchained us, and we all stood silently for a moment, looking.

My eyes moved slowly over the crowd. Women crouching down hid their faces in shame. Young girls combed the hair of older women with their fingers. Some sat in the corners like tight fists, crying. One laughed out loud and walked the tight spaces between us. I looked and they stared back, the ones who were not ashamed to search for the same thing. We did not recognize each other.

"Abiodun." I pointed to myself, and slowly spoke to indicate my village, and my lineage. There was a shuffle, but no response. Then very quietly, I heard someone say, "Iya, ba wo ni? 'Dele." She pointed to herself.

"Dele. Da da ni."

I walked toward the voice to find a young woman my age sitting in the corner. Her legs were pulled close to her body, and blood was dry on her thighs. I sat down next to her, afraid to look at her, but without thinking, I touched her shoulder. She grabbed my hand, pulled herself close to me as I have seen newborn monkeys do.

Not long ago, she would have been someone with whom I might have played or entered an *egbe*. Her hair had been shaved off. I noticed for the first time that a number of the women were also clean shaven. Her shoulder blades jutted into the palm of my hand, making me uncomfortable and forcing me to release her despite her reluctance. But, it gave me a better opportunity to study her. Her feet bled, especially from the heel and her ankles, where metal had cut down to the bone.

When I took the right foot in my hand, I could see that the big toe was black. She would certainly lose it if nothing was done. And nothing would be done because as long as we could walk, we could be used. I opened my hands, placed them on her foot. She clung tighter still. Since no one came to feed us, we slept like this: me listening to her rasping until I could no longer keep my eyes open, and until the pain of what was ahead flowed from her feet into my hands and completely overwhelmed me.

I was awakened by the sound of thunder and by rain pelting through the barred windows onto my head. I was stiff as I tried to get up, and one of the women came and gently unfolded us. They were looking at me and looking at her feet. As a woman came forward, we heard the door open and the yelling of the *oyimbo*, which I could not decipher, being in the back. But, I noticed the women stand up and begin jumping up and down, and then gradually the line began to move out. The woman who had slept in my arms all night encouraged me to do the same.

At the passageway, the men had set out buckets of lime and black soap.

I followed the women as they each dipped their hands into the bucket and pulled out as much soap as they could gather. They washed themselves and I knew I was to follow their lead.

When it was my turn, I put my right hand into the bucket, pulled out a handful of liquid black soap. I divided the soap into a smaller segment by pouring some into my left hand. I then dropped the soap onto my body at different sections so that a little was everywhere.

I was fortunate to be near the end of the line again. I began with my *ori*. In small tight circles I moved my left hand across the crown of my head until I reached my face. If this was my destiny, I prayed, give me strength to complete it. I prayed for a clear, cool head, even as I felt blind and angered and frightened. I washed behind my ears, asking that I be made alert to hear what could not normally be heard. I washed my eyes, my nose, mouth, all with the prayer that I be given senses that protect me from dangers, seen and unseen.

I noticed that the other women were nearly finished, and hurried to wash my feet. My hands rubbed my toes and the spaces in between gently. I massaged the soles of my feet, allowing the soap to seep into the cracks that had not healed, and ignored the burning. As I touched my broken toe, I held my hands over it longer, spitting in my palms and rubbing the mixture hard into the toe, all the time praying quietly. I could feel the warmth flow from my hands into my toe, and then up to my ankle.

As quickly as I could, I then soaped the rest of my body, crouching as low as possible when I washed between my legs. I felt a slight cramping in my abdomen and was alarmed that in a few weeks' time I would begin bleeding with no way to cover myself.

When I stood up, the women nearest me were staring. As I caught each of their eyes, they lowered them respectfully. One *kunled*, touched her right hand to the ground and then brought the inside of her hand to her mouth to kiss it. Another brought her forehead to the ground quickly. I shook my head sharply and she stood up.

We were then herded farther into the rain where we were allowed to wash off. The soap ran into my eyes and into my mouth, but I did not care. I had not bathed since I had been taken from home, and I welcomed the sting and bitter smell of the soap we used for healing and washing away the unwanted.

Today would be the beginning and end of my life, and for a moment I stopped washing myself and looked at the women around me. Some had found the courage to wash each other. Others just stood in the rain, looking at the water and boats around them. One began to run toward the water, but the two women next to her pulled her back, held her briefly, and then let her go. They stood quietly around her, moving intermittently to not attract attention.

The woman I had held all night came gently to me and washed my back. Her hands were warm and rough, and she was careful not to break skin where I had been hit with the whip several times. She began slowly rubbing my scalp.

The sack that had stored itself under my rib cage floated to the center of my chest, up my throat, and finally, I felt it in my mouth, my teeth opening so as not to puncture it. But my tongue could not move out of the way fast enough and before I could turn to offer the same kindness, my tongue began moving furiously around my mouth, uttering and shouting and spinning me until the women gathered around me. They formed two circles. The outer circle continued to wash themselves, letting the rain fall onto their backs. But, in the center, there were other women, older than I, holding me, rocking me between them and singing, "Orisa, do not abandon your daughter now," until I could no longer hear myself. Until their songs had calmed my shouts into a humming. Until I could stand straight trembling, half carried back to the room where the woman I had held all night held me.

After that, the women began their mornings by each coming to my feet and saluting me. No matter how many times I tried to dissuade them, they would not stop. In the corner that I had taken, they began leaving small pieces of food on the ground. They would take my hand and put it over the food, then sprinkle it with water.

In the evenings, the ones who could not walk or whose backs had been torn open, placed themselves at my feet again, lying or sitting down. At first, I was uncertain of what they asked. But then, the woman who had remained at my side since the rain, took my hands and put them on her feet. Her big toe was brown now, and she did not limp. I did not limp. And by the time we were ready to be moved into the boats, not one of the women limped, and their scars had healed without infection.

The woman who had laughed to herself the first few days of my arrival was quiet. At each meal, she set aside a portion of her food and her water for me. And every night, she slept standing up, leaning against the wall closest to me and making herself a barrier between me and anyone or anything that would dare walk toward me at night.

Three Letters, One Song & A Refrain

Chris Abani

This Red String Is for You, Mama

Dear Mama,

This is a kind of letter, though I am writing most of it in my heart, for you, for me, for a time when I can speak it. This torn and bloodied sheet should be enough, but words bring clarity.

My first thought after it happened was that I should wash the sheet. I should take it home and wash the shame from it. But something stayed my hand. I was afraid to take the sheet at first, afraid of him. For what seemed like a long time, I couldn't look at him. But it couldn't have been that long because his shadow on the floor didn't move. When I looked, his eyes didn't meet mine. I guessed he was about forty. Maybe it was his greying hair. There are many stories in the camp about men like this. Ordinary men who because we are at their mercy here in Thailand, far from our home in Burma, take advantage of us like this. A rage blacker than any mud I have seen came over me, and I grabbed the sheet. At first I meant to strangle him with it but hesitated when I saw him stir, saw the hate in his eyes return. Instead I swallowed the bitter taste in my mouth and stuffed the sheet into the small raffia bag I had brought. You must take me back to the camp now, I said. You must take me home.

On the ride back, I sat shakily on the back of his motorcycle; the wind was like ice on my skin. I knew it wouldn't be long before the rain came. I had nothing to cover myself with. The man was wearing a yellow rain slicker that ensured he would stay warm and dry. I had no choice but to wrap myself in the sheet, I thought. I pulled one end of the bloodstained cloth out of my bag. It fluttered in the wind like a red sail, and I felt revulsion for myself and the man fill me. But I couldn't use it as a wrap. It would have felt more like a funeral shroud. I stared at it for a moment. There were two loose threads tickling my wrist. When I got home, I plucked them. One red string I tied around a flower and hid in the bamboo rafters; the other I tied around my wrist. This is the old way, Mama.

As we rode on that unstable motorcycle, I shoved the cloth back into the raffia bag and instead wrapped my arms around the body of the man who had just raped me. For balance: for safety. The first drop of cold wetness hit me, and I thought, let it rain, that is better than wrapping death around me.

It is still raining, Mama. The way it does here. One drop first and then sheets all at once. I used to play as a child in the rain back home. Do you remember? There is something primitive about this rain. It feels right.

I know we are Christians now, but if I had money, I would set a date for the great sacrifice and have the priest kill a boar and a white chicken as I confess my sins to the Lords of Land and Water. But I can tie my wrist. I still remember what you taught me, even here, even here without you. This red string is for you.

Letter to a Vengeful Angel

Dear Boy,
I don't know your name otherwise I would use it. So I call you boy, because that is what you are. A child: no different from me and also, like me, one who carries the burden of our people's hate. I think of you as an angel because from the bottom of that ditch where we hid from your patrol, a line of soldiers not far from me, the sun, bright through the rain, looked like an angel's wing spread over them. And you, the

youngest one, followed a few steps behind. You stopped when you saw me, and there alone, framed against the fan of sunlight, you looked like an angel. I knew you could see me; I knew because your gun was pointed at me and you were crying. I never knew soldiers could cry. But you were crying.

That is why I am writing this unspoken letter in my heart to you, and believe that because you were crying you will hear me. I have often wondered why you spared me. Was it to spare yourself the consequences of my death? Or was it because you looked deep enough into my eyes, and saw something that kept you from pulling the trigger?

I feel pity for you even though soldiers like you have treated us like animals because we are Karen. I am Karen, my mother taught me to say even as a child. To say it like this—ko ren. Like the fish? I asked; and she said, Why not? Our ancestors crossed the Gobi, the river of running sand, to come to our homeland.

It was raining when the first soldiers came, raining and night darker than water in a well. At first we thought the mortars were thunder, the flash of tracer bullets lightning. But it was soldiers like you, and soon everything was noise and fire and smoke. People running, screaming, as bullets cut through us like sticks through wet rice paper. That's when I lost my mother. I saw my father begging for our lives as we ran out the back of the hut and into the jungle. I saw as they cut him down like a weed. And then I ran deep into the rain and the dark wet steaming jungle and lost both of them.

And in the morning, I walked out of the jungle into the burning skeleton of my village. Most of the villagers were back, and they had buried nearly all the dead. I walked to the edge of the hill, the one that falls down into the valley. From up there I used to pretend I could see the whole world, and a river whose name I have forgotten. That morning, it was just a deep ravine with a river.

I couldn't find my parents or our house at first and probably never would have if I hadn't found our neighbor's son, twelve like me, sitting on the floor by the remains of his home. Both his parents were dead, too, leaving him with his baby sister. I forgot myself at this sight. I tried to take the baby from him, but he fought me, so all day I sat next to him as he rocked her, letting her suckle at his nipple. Together we stared into the distance. It was hours before I realized the baby had died. Later, before dark, the elders gathered the survivors, and we all left for the safety of the jungle, sure the soldiers would return.

I cannot remember much about that time in the jungle hiding. Only little things, like a bird flashing by, red and rude against the jungle walls so green and dark they could have been the face of night. Staring with surprise at my reflection in a clear pool: eyes that held irises so black, a square face that made me look like a boy, and a smile that my mother used to say was like a butterfly landing on her palm. I can't find that smile anywhere, anymore.

One morning, a few days into the jungle, I woke to a woman wailing over her dead dog, and it wasn't long before other mourners joined her. They weren't crying for her dog, though. Many had lost family and their own pets. And they were crying not only because it was safe to mourn this way but also because they loved their pets. It is a sad sight: a rainy dark jungle and a woman crying over a dead dog.

I remember pulling leeches from my skin with a joy that was hard to describe. When they popped off they left a bleeding wound, red against my dark olive skin, a wound that stung. It felt good, that stinging. It felt good to feel something. We ate what we could find: worms, grubs, bananas, and even insects, but no meat. It was always raining so hard we couldn't cook anything.

We couldn't even make a fire to keep us dry, to keep warm by, and soon, our clothes began to rot on us. As they rotted, we got rashes and sometimes sores. By the third week we had all lost our shame. We went to the toilet within sight of each other, men and women. It was simply safer—or felt safer—to be no further than a quick glance from each other. My period came on that trek through the jungle. I had no rags to staunch it like I had seen my mother do, so I let it run down my leg.

The rain took it all.

My mother used to say that rain here pours like a blessing, like a thick veil that parts to reveal the bride's face. But nearly every day, when this rain parted, it was not a bride's face that was revealed but a long line of soldiers, like you, like death, marching toward us, and we would always scatter with a practiced silence and hide. Six weeks after we first went to hide in the jungle, we were found by a group of Karen guerillas. They led us out of the jungle. Warned us about the paths and showed us how to avoid the mines. They led us to a refugee camp.

I feel bad because I pity you—boy, soldier—because it feels like a betrayal of my people, and of my dead parents. But maybe this is how I will relearn my beauty. If you are still alive, boy, I hope you find yours.

A Song for the Camp

Sing with me.

Camp: rickety shelters we would never have put our animals in, packed in tight rows like the pretend houses children might build; hunger; narrow streets running through this shantytown, each a river of filth and shit even the dogs avoid; hunger; scavenging the already barren countryside by the river for food; hunger; sickness, diarrhea; hunger; rain and more rain; hunger. It is hard to hold on to all that we were before we came here.

Sing with me.

I was so young when my mother left me, but I can remember the verse of Karen poetry she sang as she cooked, mixing her grief in with the food. Perhaps this is why I remember it so well:

> *God took the foam of water*
> *It becomes banyan's flower*
> *Foam of water god's taking*
> Keh taw weh ler kler ah klee
> *It becomes a banyan's seed*

Sometimes I want to be the banyan seed, to hold all of Buddha's enlightenment in my heart. I heard about Jesus and the angels in this camp, and sometimes I want to be an angel. When I see hungry children like me wandering around, shoulder blades sharp as wings, I want to fly. Between my house in this camp and the one next to it is just enough space for me to spread my arms. Every day I place my arms against the wood beams of the two houses and hold them there, pushing up against each beam with all my strength. When I step out and hold my arms down, they rise into wings by themselves, and it feels like flying, and I love it because it is the best secret ever, like an angel. And I can be free, but not afraid.

A Letter to My Rapist

> *Dear Rapist,*
> *I wasn't afraid when you came on your motorcycle to hire someone to*
> *clean your house. I wasn't afraid because I was hungry. I had heard sto-*
> *ries of men like you, men who prey on the weak and needy, but I wasn't*
> *afraid because whatever else you might do to me, it is better than wait-*

ing for the slow death of starvation here. And there is always the chance that you will be a good man, that you will have work and food for me.

I try to tell myself that it wasn't my fault. That if death comes to you wearing a safe face it is hard to run. We rode for a long time until we came to a hut in the middle of some rice fields. You parked your motorcycle and pulled me off. I am coming, I said, running to catch up. I had brought a small brush and rags in my raffia bag to clean with. It was a small hut and I would do a good job and be paid well. I was saving to go back to school. Once inside the hut, you pushed me onto the small mattress with a dirty white sheet in the corner and tore my clothes. I didn't understand until I felt the pain.

Surely you must have seen my fear in my eyes. I was barely thirteen; I had almost no breasts, no pubic hair; and I had been bleeding for only a few months. You must have seen the child I was in my eyes. How were you able to turn away?

I want to curse you. I want to curse you until your manhood shrivels up. I want to curse your unborn children and your wife and your mother and your father and your life. I want you to die. This is true. No one will ever see it on my face, or hear these words from me, but I want you to die.

It rained the whole ride back to the camp. I felt it on my head, and I bent back and felt the cool water run off my face like tears, and I thought that in the end this is what it is like to be a woman here. We are seen only when men want the banyan seed between our legs; until then, we are composed of shadows. Nothing more.

Did you know that I had enough rage to kill you even as I held on to you to keep from falling off your motorcycle? Did you feel the power of my eyes in your back? Perhaps not. I am not very expressive. Like my mother before me, I have learned to hide everything deep in my heart.

You dropped me off in the mud pit that is the entrance to the camp. Before you roared off on your motorcycle, I reached out and scratched your face. A deep red line appeared. I did it to mark you, so that you would not forget me. You stopped, a shout on your lips, but you hesitated. I followed your gaze. By the river to the left I saw a line of women bent in the rain like a long sad caterpillar. I knew what they were doing. Searching for food, for some root they somehow missed the day before or the day before that. They rose as one, like a wave behind *me, their eyes locked on you. You fled before all those ravenous eyes, ready to devour you.*

    I will be free of you.

    I am free of you.

Refrain for My Mother

Hear me sing.

    I must wash this sheet, Mama.

    I return to the gate of the camp, days later, sheet clutched under my arm. The line of women are there again, bent to their labor.

    I pluck a red string off the sheet and hold it up to the wind. Here, Mama, take the red string, I say. And then I walk toward the women who are always by the river, wondering if I look like a ghost as I move through the grey light. The women look up for a minute as I approach; then, as one, they dip back to the ground, fingers sifting the mud.

    They don't look up as I walk into the river.

The Headstrong Historian

Chimamanda Ngozi Adichie

Many years after her husband had died, Nwamgba still closed her eyes from time to time to relive his nightly visits to her hut, and the mornings after, when she would walk to the stream humming a song, thinking of the smoky scent of him and the firmness of his weight, and feeling as if she were surrounded by light. Other memories of Obierika also remained clear—his stubby fingers curled around his flute when he played in the evenings, his delight when she set down his bowls of food, his sweaty back when he brought baskets filled with fresh clay for her pottery. From the moment she had first seen him, at a wrestling match, both of them staring and staring, both of them too young, her waist not yet wearing the menstruation cloth, she had believed with a quiet stubbornness that her chi and his chi had destined their marriage, and so when he and his relatives came to her father a few years later with pots of palm wine she told her mother that this was the man she would marry. Her mother was aghast. Did Nwamgba not know that Obierika was an only child, that his late father had been an only child whose wives had lost pregnancies and buried babies? Perhaps somebody in their family had committed the taboo of selling a girl into slavery and the earth god Ani was visiting misfortune on them. Nwamgba ignored her mother. She went into her father's *obi* and told him she would run away from any other man's house if she was not allowed to marry Obierika. Her father found her exhausting, this sharp-tongued, headstrong daughter who had once wrestled her brother to the ground. (Her father had had to warn those who saw this not to let anyone outside the compound know that a girl had thrown a boy.) He, too, was concerned about the infertility in Obierika's family, but it was not a bad family: Obierika's late father had taken the Ozo title; Obierika was already giving out his seed yams to sharecroppers. Nwamgba would not starve if she married him. Besides, it was better that he let his daughter go with the man she chose than to endure years of trouble in which she would keep returning home after confrontations with her in-laws; and so he gave his blessing, and she smiled and called him by his praise name.

To pay her bride price, Obierika came with two maternal cousins, Okafo and Okoye, who were like brothers to him.

Nwamgba loathed them at first sight. She saw a grasping envy in their eyes that afternoon, as they drank palm wine in her father's *obi;* and in the following years—years in which Obierika took titles and widened his compound and sold his yams to strangers from afar—she saw their envy blacken. But she tolerated them, because they mattered to Obierika, because he pretended not to notice that they didn't work but came to him for yams and chickens, because he wanted to imagine that he had brothers. It was they who urged him, after her third miscarriage, to marry another wife. Obierika told them that he would give it some thought, but when they were alone in her hut at night he assured her that they would have a home full of children, and that he would not marry another wife until they were old, so that they would have somebody to care for them. She thought this strange of him, a prosperous man with only one wife, and she worried more than he did about their childlessness, about the songs that people sang, the melodious mean-spirited words: She has sold her womb. She has eaten his penis. He plays his flute and hands over his wealth to her.

Once, at a moonlight gathering, the square full of women telling stories and learning new dances, a group of girls saw Nwamgba and began to sing, their aggressive breasts pointing at her. She asked if they would mind singing a little louder, so that she could hear the words and then show them who was the greater of two tortoises. They stopped singing. She enjoyed their fear, the way they backed away from her, but it was then that she decided to find a wife for Obierika herself.

✳

Nwamgba liked going to the Oyi stream, untying her wrapper from her waist and walking down the slope to the silvery rush of water that burst out from a rock. The waters of Oyi seemed fresher than those of the other stream, Ogalanya, or perhaps it was simply that Nwamgba felt comforted by the shrine of the Oyi goddess, tucked away in a corner; as a child she had learned that Oyi was the protector of women, the reason it was taboo to sell women into slavery. Nwamgba's closest friend, Ayaju, was already at the stream, and as Nwamgba helped Ayaju raise her pot to her head she asked her who might be a good second wife for Obierika.

She and Ayaju had grown up together and had married men from the same clan. The difference between them, though, was that Ayaju was of slave descent. Ayaju did not care for her husband, Okenwa, who she said resembled and smelled like a rat, but her marriage prospects had been limited; no man from a freeborn family would have come for her hand. Ayaju was a trader, and her rangy, quick-moving body spoke of her many journeys; she had even travelled beyond Onicha. It was she who had first brought back tales of the strange customs of the Igala and Edo traders, she who had first told stories of the white-skinned men who had arrived in Onicha with mirrors and fabrics and the biggest guns the people of those parts had ever seen. This cosmopolitanism earned her respect, and she was the only person of slave descent who talked loudly at the Women's Council, the only person who had answers for everything. She promptly suggested, for Obierika's second wife, a young girl from the Okonkwo family, who had beautiful wide hips and who was respectful, nothing like the other young girls of today, with their heads full of nonsense.

As they walked home from the stream, Ayaju said that perhaps Nwamgba should do what other women in her situation did—take a lover and get pregnant in order to continue Obierika's lineage. Nwamgba's retort was sharp, because she did not like Ayaju's tone, which suggested that Obierika was impotent, and, as if in response to her thoughts, she felt a furious stabbing sensation in her back and knew that she was pregnant again, but she said nothing, because she knew, too, that she would lose it again.

Her miscarriage happened a few weeks later, lumpy blood running down her legs. Obierika comforted her and suggested that they go to the famous oracle, Kisa, as soon as she was well enough for the half day's journey. After the *dibia* had consulted the oracle, Nwamgba cringed at the thought of sacrificing a whole cow; Obierika certainly had greedy ancestors. But they performed the ritual cleansings and the sacrifices as required, and when she suggested that he go and see the Okonkwo family about their daughter he delayed and delayed until another sharp pain spliced her back, and, months later, she was lying on a pile of freshly washed banana leaves behind her hut, straining and pushing until the baby slipped out.

✳

They named him Anikwenwa: the earth god Ani had finally granted a child. He was dark and solidly built, and had Obierika's happy curiosity. Obierika took him to pick medicinal herbs, to collect clay for Nwamgba's pottery, to twist yam vines at the farm. Obierika's cousins Okafo and Okoye visited often. They marvelled at how well Anikwenwa played the flute, how quickly he was learning poetry and wrestling moves from his father, but Nwamgba saw the glowing malevolence that their smiles could not hide. She feared for her child and for her husband, and when Obierika died—a man who had been hearty and laughing and drinking palm wine moments before he slumped—she knew that they had killed him with medicine. She clung to his corpse until a neighbor slapped her to make her let go; she lay in the cold ash for days, tore at the patterns shaved into her hair. Obierika's death left her with an unending despair. She thought often of a woman who, after losing a tenth child, had gone to her back yard and hanged herself on a kola-nut tree. But she would not do it, because of Anikwenwa.

Later, she wished she had made Obierika's cousins drink his *mmili oʒu* before the oracle. She had witnessed this once, when a wealthy man died and his family forced his rival to drink his *mmili oʒu*. Nwamgba had watched an unmarried woman take a cupped leaf full of water, touch it to the dead man's body, all the time speaking solemnly, and give the leaf-cup to the accused man. He drank. Everyone looked to make sure that he swallowed, a grave silence in the air, because they knew that if he was guilty he would die. He died days later, and his family lowered their heads in shame. Nwamgba felt strangely shaken by it all. She should have insisted on this with Obierika's cousins, but she had been blinded by grief and now Obierika was buried and it was too late.

His cousins, during the funeral, took his ivory tusk, claiming that the trappings of titles went to brothers and not to sons. It was when they emptied his barn of yams and led away the adult goats in his pen that she confronted them, shouting, and when they brushed her aside she waited until evening, then walked around the clan singing about their wickedness, the abominations they were heaping on the land by cheating a widow, until the elders asked them to leave her alone. She complained to the Women's Council, and twenty women went at night to Okafo's and Okoye's homes, brandishing pestles, warning them to leave Nwamgba alone. But Nwamgba knew that those grasping cousins would never really stop. She dreamed of killing them. She certainly could, those weaklings who had spent their lives scrounging off Obierika instead of working, but, of course, she would be banished then, and there would be no one to care for her son. Instead, she took Anikwenwa on long walks, telling him that the land from that palm tree to that avocado tree was theirs, that his grandfather had passed it on to his father. She told him the same things over and over, even though he looked bored and bewildered, and she did not let him go and play at moonlight unless she was watching.

Ayaju came back from a trading journey with another story: the women in Onicha were complaining about the white men. They had welcomed the white men's trading station, but now the white men wanted to tell them how to trade, and when the elders of Agueke refused to place their thumbs on a paper the white men came at night with their normal-men helpers and razed the village. There was nothing left. Nwamgba did not understand. What sort of guns did these white men have? Ayaju laughed and said that their guns were nothing like the rusty thing her own husband owned; she spoke with pride, as though she herself were responsible for the superiority of the white men's guns. Some white men were visiting different clans, asking parents to send their children to school, she added, and she had decided to send her son Azuka, who was the laziest on the farm, because although she was respected and wealthy, she was still of slave descent, her sons were still barred from taking titles, and she wanted Azuka to learn the ways of these foreigners. People ruled over others not because they were better people, she said, but because they had better guns; after all, her father would not have been enslaved if his clan had been as well armed as Nwamgba's. As Nwamgba listened to her friend, she dreamed of killing Obierika's cousins with the white men's guns.

The day the white men visited her clan, Nwamgba left the pot she was about to put in her oven, took Anikwenwa and her girl apprentices, and hurried to the square. She was at first disappointed by the ordinariness of the two white men; they were harmless-looking, the color of albinos, with frail and slender limbs. Their companions were normal men, but there was something foreign about them, too: only one spoke Igbo, and with a strange accent. He said that he was from Elele, the other normal men were from Sierra Leone, and the white men from France, far across the sea. They were all of the Holy Ghost Congregation, had arrived in Onicha in 1885, and were building their school and church there. Nwamgba was the first to ask a question: Had they brought their guns, by any chance, the ones used to destroy the people of Agueke, and could she see one? The man said unhappily that it was the soldiers of the British government and the merchants of the Royal Niger Company who destroyed villages; they, instead, brought good news. He spoke about their god, who had come to the world to die, and who had a son but no wife, and who was three but also one. Many of the people around Nwamgba laughed loudly. Some walked away, because they had imagined that the white man was full of wisdom. Others stayed and offered cool bowls of water.

Weeks later, Ayaju brought another story: the white men had set up a courthouse in Onicha where they judged disputes. They had indeed come to stay. For the first time, Nwamgba doubted her friend. Surely the people of Onicha had their own courts. The clan next to Nwamgba's, for example, held its courts only during the new yam festival, so that people's rancor grew while they awaited justice. A stupid system, Nwamgba thought, but surely everyone had one. Ayaju laughed and told Nwamgba again that people ruled others when they had better guns. Her son was already learning about these foreign ways, and perhaps Anikwenwa should, too. Nwamgba refused. It was unthinkable that her only son, her single eye, should be given to the white men, never mind the superiority of their guns.

Three events, in the following years, caused Nwamgba to change her mind. The first was that Obierika's cousins took over a large piece of land and told the elders that they were farming it for her, a woman who had emasculated their dead brother and now refused to remarry, even though

suitors came and her breasts were still round. The elders sided with them.
The second was that Ayaju told a story of two people who had taken a
land case to the white men's court; the first man was lying but could speak
the white men's language, while the second man, the rightful owner of
the land, could not, and so he lost his case, was beaten and locked up, and
ordered to give up his land. The third was the story of the boy Iroegbunam, who had gone missing many years ago and then suddenly reap-
peared, a grown man, his widowed mother mute with shock at his story:
a neighbor, whom his father had often shouted down at Age Grade meetings, had abducted him when his mother was at the market and taken him
to the Aro slave dealers, who looked him over and complained that the
wound on his leg would reduce his price. He was tied to others by the
hands, forming a long human column, and he was hit with a stick and told
to walk faster. There was one woman in the group. She shouted herself
hoarse, telling the abductors that they were heartless, that her spirit would
torment them and their children, that she knew she was to be sold to the
white man and did they not know that the white man's slavery was very
different, that people were treated like goats, taken on large ships a long
way away, and were eventually eaten? Iroegbunam walked and walked
and walked, his feet bloodied, his body numb, until all he remembered
was the smell of dust. Finally, they stopped at a coastal clan, where a man
spoke a nearly incomprehensible Igbo, but Iroegbunam made out enough
to understand that another man who was to sell them to the white people
on the ship had gone up to bargain with them but had himself been kidnapped. There were loud arguments, scuffling; some of the abductees
yanked at the ropes and Iroegbunam passed out. He awoke to find a white
man rubbing his feet with oil and at first he was terrified, certain that he
was being prepared for the white man's meal, but this was a different kind
of white man, who bought slaves only to free them, and he took Iroegbunam to live with him and trained him to be a Christian missionary.

Iroegbunam's story haunted Nwamgba, because this, she was sure,
was the way Obierika's cousins were likely to get rid of her son. Killing
him would be too dangerous, the risk of misfortunes from the oracle too
high, but they would be able to sell him as long as they had strong medicine to protect themselves. She was struck, too, by how Iroegbunam
lapsed into the white man's language from time to time. It sounded nasal
and disgusting. Nwamgba had no desire to speak such a thing herself, but
she was suddenly determined that Anikwenwa would speak enough of it
to go to the white men's court with Obierika's cousins and defeat them

and take control of what was his. And so, shortly after Iroegbunam's return, she told Ayaju that she wanted to take her son to school.

They went first to the Anglican mission. The classroom had more girls
than boys, sitting with slates on their laps while the teacher stood in front
of them, holding a big cane, telling them a story about a man who transformed a bowl of water into wine. The teacher's spectacles impressed
Nwamgba, and she thought that the man in the story must have had powerful medicine to be able to transform water into wine, but when the girls
were separated and a woman teacher came to teach them how to sew
Nwamgba found this silly. In her clan, men sewed cloth and girls learned
pottery. What dissuaded her completely from sending Anikwenwa to the
school, however, was that the instruction was done in Igbo. Nwamgba
asked why. The teacher said that, of course, the students were taught
English—he held up an English primer—but children learned best in
their own language and the children in the white men's land were taught
in their own language, too. Nwamgba turned to leave. The teacher stood
in her way and told her that the Catholic missionaries were harsh and did
not look out for the best interests of the natives. Nwamgba was amused
by these foreigners, who did not seem to know that one must, in front of
strangers, pretend to have unity. But she had come in search of English,
and so she walked past him and went to the Catholic mission.

Father Shanahan told her that Anikwenwa would have to take an English name, because it was not possible to be baptized with a heathen name.
She agreed easily. His name was Anikwenwa as far as she was concerned;
if they wanted to name him something she could not pronounce before
teaching him their language, she did not mind at all. All that mattered was
that he learn enough of the language to fight his father's cousins.

Father Shanahan looked at Anikwenwa, a dark-skinned, well-muscled
child, and guessed that he was about twelve, although he found it difficult
to estimate the ages of these people; sometimes what looked like a man
would turn out to be a mere boy. It was nothing like in Eastern Africa,
where he had previously worked, where the natives tended to be slender,
less confusingly muscular. As he poured some water on the boy's head, he
said, "Michael, I baptize you in the name of the Father and of the Son and
of the Holy Spirit."

He gave the boy a singlet and a pair of shorts, because the people of the

living God did not walk around naked, and he tried to preach to the boy's
mother, but she looked at him as if he were a child who did not know any
better. There was something troublingly assertive about her, something
he had seen in many women here; there was much potential to be har-
nessed if their wildness were tamed. This Nwamgba would make a mar-
vellous missionary among the women. He watched her leave. There was
a grace in her straight back, and she, unlike others, had not spent too
much time going round and round in her speech. It infuriated him, their
overlong talk and circuitous proverbs, their never getting to the point, but
he was determined to excel here; it was the reason he had joined the Holy
Ghost Congregation, whose special vocation was the redemption of black
heathens.

Nwamgba was alarmed by how indiscriminately the missionaries flogged
students: for being late, for being lazy, for being slow, for being idle, and,
once, as Anikwenwa told her, Father Lutz put metal cuffs around a girl's
hands to teach her a lesson about lying, all the time saying in Igbo—for
Father Lutz spoke a broken brand of Igbo—that native parents pampered
their children too much, that teaching the Gospel also meant teaching
proper discipline. The first weekend Anikwenwa came home, Nwamgba
saw welts on his back, and she tightened her wrapper around her waist
and went to the school and told the teacher that she would gouge out the
eyes of everyone at the mission if they ever did that to him again. She
knew that Anikwenwa did not want to go to school and she told him that
it was only for a year or two, so that he could learn English, and although
the mission people told her not to come so often, she insistently came
every weekend to take him home. Anikwenwa always took off his clothes
even before they had left the mission compound. He disliked the shorts
and shirt that made him sweat, the fabric that was itchy around his
armpits. He disliked, too, being in the same class as old men, missing out
on wrestling contests.

But Anikwenwa's attitude toward school slowly changed. Nwamgba
first noticed this when some of the other boys with whom he swept the
village square complained that he no longer did his share because he
was at school, and Anikwenwa said something in English, something
sharp-sounding, which shut them up and filled Nwamgba with an in-
dulgent pride. Her pride turned to vague worry when she noticed that the

curiosity in his eyes had diminished. There was a new ponderousness in him, as if he had suddenly found himself bearing the weight of a heavy world. He stared at things for too long. He stopped eating her food, because, he said, it was sacrificed to idols. He told her to tie her wrapper around her chest instead of her waist, because her nakedness was sinful. She looked at him, amused by his earnestness, but worried nonetheless, and asked why he had only just begun to notice her nakedness.

When it was time for his initiation ceremony, he said he would not participate, because it was a heathen custom to be initiated into the world of spirits, a custom that Father Shanahan had said would have to stop. Nwamgba roughly yanked his ear and told him that a foreign albino could not determine when their customs would change, and that he would participate or else he would tell her whether he was her son or the white man's son. Anikwenwa reluctantly agreed, but as he was taken away with a group of other boys she noticed that he lacked their excitement. His sadness saddened her. She felt her son slipping away from her, and yet she was proud that he was learning so much, that he could be a court interpreter or a letter writer, that with Father Lutz's help he had brought home some papers that showed that their land belonged to them. Her proudest moment was when he went to his father's cousins Okafo and Okoye and asked for his father's ivory tusk back. And they gave it to him.

Nwamgba knew that her son now inhabited a mental space that she was unable to recognize. He told her that he was going to Lagos to learn how to be a teacher, and even as she screamed—How can you leave me? Who will bury me when I die?—she knew that he would go. She did not see him for many years, years during which his father's cousin Okafo died. She often consulted the oracle to ask whether Anikwenwa was still alive, and the *dibia* admonished her and sent her away, because of course he was alive. Finally, he returned, in the year that the clan banned all dogs after a dog killed a member of the Mmangala Age Grade, the age group to which Anikwenwa would have belonged if he did not believe that such things were devilish.

Nwamgba said nothing when Anikwenwa announced that he had been appointed catechist at the new mission. She was sharpening her *aguba* on the palm of her hand, about to shave patterns into the hair of a little girl, and she continued to do so—*flick-flick-flick*—while Anikwenwa talked about winning the souls of the members of their clan. The plate of breadfruit seeds she had offered him was untouched—he no longer ate anything at all of hers—and she looked at him, this man wearing trousers and a rosary around his neck, and wondered whether she had meddled with his destiny. Was this what his chi had ordained for him, this life in which he was like a person diligently acting a bizarre pantomime?

The day that he told her about the woman he would marry, she was not surprised. He did not do it as it was done, did not consult people about the bride's family, but simply said that somebody at the mission had seen a suitable young woman from Ifite Ukpo, and the suitable young woman would be taken to the Sisters of the Holy Rosary in Onicha to learn how to be a good Christian wife. Nwamgba was sick with malaria that day, lying on her mud bed, rubbing her aching joints, and she asked Anikwenwa the young woman's name. Anikwenwa said it was Agnes. Nwamgba asked for the young woman's real name. Anikwenwa cleared his throat and said she had been called Mgbeke before she became a Christian, and Nwamgba asked whether Mgbeke would at least do the confession ceremony even if Anikwenwa would not follow the other marriage rites of their clan. He shook his head furiously and told her that the confession made by women before marriage, in which, surrounded by female relatives, they swore that no man had touched them since their husband declared his interest, was sinful, because Christian wives should not have been touched *at all*.

The marriage ceremony in the church was laughably strange, but Nwamgba bore it silently and told herself that she would die soon and join Obierika and be free of a world that increasingly made no sense. She was determined to dislike her son's wife, but Mgbeke was difficult to dislike, clear-skinned and gentle, eager to please the man to whom she was married, eager to please everyone, quick to cry, apologetic about things over which she had no control. And so, instead, Nwamgba pitied her. Mgbeke often visited Nwamgba in tears, saying that Anikwenwa had refused to eat dinner because he was upset with her, that Anikwenwa had banned her from going to a friend's Anglican wedding because Anglicans did not preach the truth, and Nwamgba would silently carve designs on her pottery while Mgbeke cried, uncertain of how to handle a woman crying about things that did not deserve tears.

Mgbeke was called "missus" by everyone, even the non-Christians, all of whom respected the catechist's wife, but on the day she went to the Oyi stream and refused to remove her clothes because she was a Christian the women of the clan, outraged that she had dared to disrespect the goddess, beat her and dumped her at the grove. The news spread quickly. Missus had been harassed. Anikwenwa threatened to lock up all the elders if his wife was treated that way again, but Father O'Donnell, on his next trek from his station in Onicha, visited the elders and apologized on Mgbeke's behalf, and asked whether perhaps Christian women could be allowed to fetch water fully clothed. The elders refused—if a woman wanted Oyi's waters, then she had to follow Oyi's rules—but they were courteous to Father O'Donnell, who listened to them and did not behave like their own son Anikwenwa.

Nwamgba was ashamed of her son, irritated with his wife, upset by their rarefied life in which they treated non-Christians as if they had smallpox, but she held out hope for a grandchild; she prayed and sacrificed for Mgbeke to have a boy, because she knew that the child would be Obierika come back and would bring a semblance of sense again into her world. She did not know of Mgbeke's first or second miscarriage; it was only after the third that Mgbeke, sniffling and blowing her nose, told her. They had to consult the oracle, as this was a family misfortune, Nwamgba said, but Mgbeke's eyes widened with fear. Michael would be very angry if he ever heard of this oracle suggestion. Nwamgba, who still found it difficult to remember that Michael was Anikwenwa, went to the oracle herself, and afterward thought it ludicrous how even the gods had changed and no longer asked for palm wine but for gin. Had they converted, too?

A few months later, Mgbeke visited, smiling, bringing a covered bowl of one of those concoctions that Nwamgba found inedible, and Nwamgba knew that her chi was still wide awake and that her daughter-in-law was pregnant. Anikwenwa had decreed that Mgbeke would have the baby at the mission in Onicha, but the gods had different plans, and she went into early labor on a rainy afternoon; somebody ran in the drenching rain to Nwamgba's hut to call her. It was a boy. Father O'Donnell baptized him Peter, but Nwamgba called him Nnamdi, because he would be Obierika come back. She sang to him, and when he cried she pushed her dried-up nipple into his mouth, but, try as she might, she did not feel the spirit of her magnificent husband, Obierika. Mgbeke had three more miscarriages, and Nwamgba went to the oracle many times until a pregnancy stayed, and the second baby was born at the mission in Onicha. A girl. From the moment Nwamgba held her, the baby's bright eyes delightfully focussed on her, she knew that the spirit of Obierika had finally returned; odd, to have come back in a girl, but who could predict the ways of the ancestors? Father O'Donnell baptized the baby Grace, but Nwamgba called her Afamefuna—"my name will not be lost"—and was thrilled by the child's solemn interest in her poetry and her stories, by the teen-ager's keen watchfulness as Nwamgba struggled to make pottery with newly shaky hands. Nwamgba was not thrilled that Afamefuna was sent away to secondary school in Onicha. (Peter was already living with the priests there.) She feared that, at boarding school, the new ways would dissolve her granddaughter's fighting spirit and replace it with either an incurious rigidity, like her son's, or a limp helplessness, like Mgbeke's.

The year that Afamefuna left for secondary school, Nwamgba felt as if a lamp had been blown out in a dim room. It was a strange year, the year that darkness suddenly descended on the land in the middle of the afternoon, and when Nwamgba felt the deep-seated ache in her joints she knew that her end was near. She lay on her bed gasping for breath, while Anikwenwa pleaded with her to be baptized and anointed so that he could hold a Christian funeral for her, as he could not participate in a heathen ceremony. Nwamgba told him that if he dared to bring anybody to rub some filthy oil on her she would slap them with her last strength. All she wanted before she joined the ancestors was to see Afamefuna, but Anikwenwa said that Grace was taking exams at school and could not come home.

But she came. Nwamgba heard the squeaky swing of her door, and there was Afamefuna, her granddaughter, who had come on her own from Onicha because she had been unable to sleep for days, her restless spirit urging her home. Grace put down her schoolbag, inside of which was her textbook, with a chapter called "The Pacification of the Primitive Tribes of Southern Nigeria," by an administrator from Bristol who had lived among them for seven years.

It was Grace who would eventually read about these savages, titillated by their curious and meaningless customs, not connecting them to herself until her teacher Sister Maureen told her that she could not refer to the call-and-response her grandmother had taught her as poetry, because primitive tribes did not have poetry. It was Grace who would laugh and laugh until Sister Maureen took her to detention and then summoned her father, who slapped Grace in front of the other teachers to show them

how well he disciplined his children. It was Grace who would nurse a
deep scorn for her father for years, spending holidays working as a maid
in Onicha so as to avoid the sanctimonies, the dour certainties, of her parents and her brother. It was Grace who, after graduating from secondary
school, would teach elementary school in Agueke, where people told stories of the destruction of their village by the white men with guns, stories
she was not sure she believed, because they also told stories of mermaids
appearing from the River Niger holding wads of crisp cash. It was Grace
who, as one of a dozen or so women at the University College in Ibadan
in 1953, would change her degree from chemistry to history after she
heard, while drinking tea at the home of a friend, the story of Mr.
Gboyega. The eminent Mr. Gboyega, a chocolate-skinned Nigerian, ed-
ucated in London, distinguished expert on the history of the British Empire, had resigned in disgust when the West African Examinations
Council began talking of adding African history to the curriculum, because he was appalled that African history would even be considered a
subject. It was Grace who would ponder this story for a long time, with
great sadness, and it would cause her to make a clear link between education and dignity, between the hard, obvious things that are printed in
books and the soft, subtle things that lodge themselves in the soul. It was
Grace who would begin to rethink her own schooling: How lustily she
had sung on Empire Day, "God save our gracious king. Send him victo-
rious, happy and glorious. Long to reign over us." How she had puzzled
over words like "wallpaper" and "dandelions" in her textbooks, unable to
picture them. How she had struggled with arithmetic problems that had to
do with mixtures, because what was "coffee" and what was "chicory,"
and why did they have to be mixed? It was Grace who would begin to rethink her father's schooling and then hurry home to see him, his eyes watery with age, telling him she had not received all the letters she had
ignored, saying amen when he prayed, and pressing her lips against his
forehead. It was Grace who, driving past Agueke on her way to the university one day, would become haunted by the image of a destroyed village and would go to London and to Paris and to Onicha, sifting through
moldy files in archives, reimagining the lives and smells of her grandmother's world, for the book she would write called "Pacifying with Bullets: A Reclaimed History of Southern Nigeria." It was Grace who, in a
conversation about the book with her fiancé, George Chikadibia—stylish
graduate of King's College, Lagos, engineer-to-be, wearer of three-piece
suits, expert ballroom dancer, who often said that a grammar school with-

out Latin was like a cup of tea without sugar—understood that the marriage would not last when George told her that it was misguided of her to write about primitive culture instead of a worthwhile topic like African Alliances in the American-Soviet Tension. They would divorce in 1972, not because of the four miscarriages Grace had suffered but because she woke up sweating one night and realized that she would strangle George to death if she had to listen to one more rapturous monologue about his Cambridge days. It was Grace who, as she received faculty prizes, as she spoke to solemn-faced people at conferences about the Ijaw and Ibibio and Igbo and Efik peoples of Southern Nigeria, as she wrote commonsense reports for international organizations, for which she nevertheless received generous pay, would imagine her grandmother looking on with great amusement. It was Grace who, feeling an odd rootlessness in the later years of her life, surrounded by her awards, her friends, her garden of peerless roses, would go to the courthouse in Lagos and officially change her first name from Grace to Afamefuna.

But on that day, as she sat at her grandmother's bedside in the fading evening light, Grace was not contemplating her future. She simply held her grandmother's hand, the palm thickened from years of making pottery.

Bread and the Land

Jeffery Renard Allen

I hear my train a comin'.

—Jimi Hendrix

Black flutter, Mamma flashed about the room, workbound, her shiny knee-length black leather boots working against the wood floor like powerful pistons. Up, down, up, down. She stopped and looked at the space around her. I have everything, she said. The hem ends of her long black dress flared like wings.

Yes, you do, Hatch said. He waited patiently on the bed edge, warm, his snowsuit packing him tight in heat and sweat, all of him sausaged inside puffy outer skin.

She put herself before a full-length mirror, flexed a black hat onto her plump head, and slipped inside a black fur coat. The hat was real fur, but the coat, some imitation material.

You look dashing, he said.

Thank you.

He watched her with hot pride. She was heavyset but pretty. Even with her second chin, she was ten times prettier than the mother of any classmate at school.

The phone rang on the faded brass nightstand next to the bed. Uh. Who could that be? People always call you at the wrong time. She lifted the receiver to her ear. Hello. Her eyes widened. It's Blunt, she said.

Oh, he said. My grandmother. He didn't like his grandmother.

You must go to work, he said. Tell her. Be frank.

Words chirped in the earpiece. Mamma brightened. The preacher's dead, she said.

Oh, he said.

The preacher's dead.

That's good, he said.

She gave him a hard look. Placed her hand over the mouthpiece. Don't get smart.

He didn't say anything.

Put those things in Mamma's bag, she said.

A small duffel bag lay unopened on the bed.

Okay, he said. He picked up her rubber gloves, pulled the fingers, and let them snap.

She looked at him. You know not to make noise when I'm on the phone.

Fine. He crammed the gloves, a white smock, white rubber-soled shoes, deodorant, and a bar of soap into the bag, which spread at the sides, stuffed like a holiday turkey.

Yes, Blunt, Mamma said. Okay, Blunt. I understand.

Blunt and the preacher lived in New York City, in Harlem, point of origin for a nationwide chain of funeral homes. Just around the corner from where Hatch lived, a Progressive Funeral Home entombed an entire street, the name spelled out in square orange blocks lit from inside, like supermarket letters. A man-high wrought-iron fence surrounded and secured the parking lot, four redbrick columns for corners, each topped with a white globe at the end of a long stem-slim black metal pole.

Blunt and the preacher own that, Mamma liked to say.

Yes, Blunt. My grandmother.

Snooping, he had found two other Progressive Funeral Homes listed in the local telephone directory.

Name and deed, Blunt traveled through his mind like some inky substance. He had never spied the photograph first—Mamma had burned all existing images many years before he was born—or heard her voice. Once a month, Mamma mailed Blunt a letter with his most recent portrait, and Blunt mailed her a letter—typed, always typed—with a check.

Why doesn't Blunt send us more money?

She sends all she can.

How much is that?

Whatever she sends.

Fine.

Good-bye, Blunt, Mamma said. She hung up the phone. Turned to Hatch. Smiled. Hatch, come here.

What? he said.

Come over here to Mamma.

Is this something frank?

Yes.

What?

Blunt's coming to live with us.

Nawl.

Don't use that street language.

I'm not.

Choose your words carefully.

Who's coming to live with us?

Blunt.

My grandmother?

Yes.

Why is she coming to live with us?

Because the preacher's dead.

So?

The preacher's dead, so now she can come live with us.

How come she didn't come live with us when the preacher was alive?

You know why.

No, I don't.

Don't talk back. And don't talk countrified.

How come she never visited us?

You know why.

I don't know why. Tell me. Be frank. Good people are always frank.

I am being frank.

You ain't.

Watch your language and stop talking back.

I ain't talkin back.

Mind your mouth.

How did the preacher die?

Suddenly.

Oh.

You know that the preacher had a bad heart.

Who had a bad heart?

Be a good boy for Mamma.

I am being good.

Then we'll let Blunt stay in your room when she comes.

Nawl. I don't want her around me. He liked his small room, high above the world, a third-story nest to which he flew for refuge.

We're going to move your things into my room so that Blunt can put her things in your room.

Nawl.

It'll only be for a little while. Blunt has lots of money now, and she wants to buy us a house, and we'll all live together, and you'll have a big room.

She lyin.

Watch your mouth. You get worse every day.

I do not.

And stop talking back.

He said nothing.

You can sleep in my room when she comes.

Nawl. I'll sleep in the kitchen *if* she comes.

What did I tell you about talking back?

I'm not talking back.

She *is* coming.

Fine.

Okay?

Fine.

You'll be a good boy for Mamma when she comes?

Fine.

She knows how smart you are.

Fine.

✳

The train screeched around the curve, the passengers firm and erect in their seats like eggs in a carton. Hatch checked flight conditions. The El was a strong, sprawling nest erected over the city. Safe, Mamma beside him, he looked down on the world far below. Wormlike people wiggled through snow. Habit, they often rode like this, all day on Sundays. Mamma wanted him to memorize every route. He would touch the map like his skin.

Car to car, the train pulled into the station, a flock of magnetic migratory birds. They quit the bright metal insides and, hand in hand, pushed through the rushing crowd. His snowsuited legs rubbed together and made a noise like that of an emery board against fingernails. He kept his eyes low, sighting varied shoes and boots flopping like fish across the wet concrete floor, his blind forehead colliding with belted or fitted waists. His sight lifted to bright lights perched, pigeonlike, in the high conical roof.

Some fabled creature waited near the checkpoint to gate 12. Human, beast, and fowl. Feathery white mink hat and coat, red amphibian jump-suit (leather? plastic?), and knee-length alligator boots. She was tall and wide like a man, and carried a white suitcase in one hand, a black guitar case in the other.

Mamma swallowed. That's Blunt, she said.

The creature called Blunt spotted Mamma and strode forward without hesitation, strode full of life. She halted two feet shy of them and set down the suitcase and the guitar case with equal care. Extended her hand. It was big. Mamma took the big hand into her own.

Hello, Joy, Blunt said.

Hello, Blunt, Mamma said.

Blunt released Mamma's hand. Seemed to think twice about it and gave Mamma a quick peck on the cheek. Studied Hatch. So this is my little Hatch, she said.

He studied her back. She was butt ugly. A net of wrinkles drew her skin tight. Her dark face masklike, coated with rouge. A flat pug nose some fist had mashed in. And long protruding jaws and lips, like a stork's mouth. Nothing baby about her face. Nothing. Thinking this, he was forced to admit that she had pretty eyes. Green.

Come give your granny a hug, she said. Spread her arms wide. He didn't move. She bent down and hugged him tight, forcing his constricted lungs to breathe in her perfume. Strawberry pop. He didn't like straw-berry pop.

She released him and rose back to her full height.

Where's your other suitcases? he asked. Mamma pinched him. She only pinched; she would never strike him. She'd had two stillbirths; he was her only child.

What? Blunt asked.

Where's your other suitcases? Mamma pinched him again. If you're coming to live with us, then where's your other suitcases? You can't put nothing in no one suitcase.

Blunt gave him a fierce cold look, eyelashes so stiff with mascara, they resembled tiny claws. Now, you're a smart little boy, so you know I'm having the rest of my things shipped.

I don't know nothing.

Mamma looked at him, hard. Blunt green-watched him. Such a pity. You look so cute in that snowsuit.

They left the station for the taxi stand. A storm had set in; snow sprayed his face, white, wet, and cold. Blunt walked over to the lead cab, a fat yellow block, and roused the driver, a short man with short thick legs.

How you today, ma'am?

Just fine, Blunt said.

The driver placed her white suitcase inside the yellow trunk.

She opened the passenger door, slid the guitar case on the floor, then held the door wide. Mamma motioned for Hatch to get in. He did. She followed. Blunt held her hat with one hand, ducked inside the cab, and seated herself. Mamma hadn't held her own hat. Blunt shut the door. The motor roared to life. The driver slammed the taxi into gear. Where to?

Mamma told him.

Enjoy your ride.

They rode to the dull hum of the busy engine, the heat full blast, Hatch damp, his body boiling inside the meaty snowsuit. He studied Blunt's reflection in the driver's rearview mirror. She sat very stiff, green eyes staring straight ahead. Glad that he didn't have to sit next to her.

Easy motion and casual heat, they cruised in bubbled metal. No one moved. No one spoke. Three monkeys, deaf, mute, and blind. They rode on past Hatch's school, Andrew Carnegie Elementary. Mamma gestured to Blunt. Blunt nodded and smiled. Traffic started to thicken. The driver took cautionary measures, dodging around the El's pylons, only to get pinned between a pylon and some stalled cars.

Move this thing, sir, Blunt said.

I'm doin all I can, ma'am.

Well, move it.

I'm sure we'll be moving soon, Blunt, Mamma said.

Look, I'm paying you good money! Blunt watched the driver with her green eyes.

This will go much better if we all jus relax, the driver said.

Hatch peered through the frosty cab window. Thickly clothed people hurried by with their heads tucked against slanting wind and snow.

Sheltered inside a doorway, a musician vied for attention. He was seated on a footstool, acoustic guitar angled across his body, strumming the strings and tapping an athletic-shoed foot, an empty coffee can a few feet in front of him. His voice rose above snarling traffic and honking horns.

> *If you don't wanna get down wit me*
> *You can't sit under my apple tree*
> *Say, if you don't wanna get—*

One passerby tossed him a coin. Hatch felt all twisted inside. He caught Blunt's face in the rearview mirror. She too was watching the musician, effort in her looking. All the anger seemed to have left her. She saw Hatch seeing her and gave him an icy look.

She faced the driver. Driver, get this cab moving, she said.

He did, foot on the accelerator to race down lost time. The Progressive Funeral Home soon blinked by. Against Hatch's expectations, both Mamma and Blunt sat oblivious. He grunted. That Blunt! She ain't look at it cause she don't want me to know she ain't nothin but a phony.

They braked to a quick stop, bodies thrown forward and back. Blunt pulled rolled bills from a jumpsuit pocket, unfolded them, and licked her thumb and forefinger to catch the crispy edges. She paid the driver and tipped him five dollars. You don't deserve a tip, she said.

He smiled. Thanks anyway, ma'am. I'm gon get yo suitcase from the trunk.

Mamma frowned at his vocabulary.

Only if you're capable, Blunt said.

He's using that countrified language, Hatch said. The driver shot Hatch a glance. Mamma pinched him. But he speakin street. Mamma pinched him again. Stung, Hatch's arm was hot and hurt in the snowsuit. Hand on the door handle, he tried to make a quick exit. The door refused to budge. Frozen, perhaps. Blunt leaned across Mamma and opened it. She smiled. Hatch gave her a mean look.

They quit the cab, snow crunching underfoot. The short driver hoisted the suitcase from the trunk while Blunt pulled the guitar case from the floor.

All y'all have a nice day, the driver said. He shot Hatch another glance and grinned.

Mamma shook her head at the diction. Hatch gave the driver his meanest look.

Blunt passed the driver another five-dollar bill. Learn how to drive, she said.

Yes, ma'am. Thank you. He got inside the cab and sped off.

Three flights of stairs spiraled a challenge to the apartment above. Mamma started up, Blunt following—the suitcase in one hand, the guitar case in the other—and Hatch following her. At the top landing, Mamma leaned her tired weight on the banister, sucking for air. Seem like the *fourth* floor, she said. Blunt said nothing. Chest rising slow and easy. Hatch believed himself an excellent judge of age and had concluded that Blunt was *very* old—she was so ugly—but, having witnessed her feat on the stairs, he was now uncertain.

You got a nice apartment, Joy. She looked the kitchen over with her green eyes.

Thank you, Blunt. It's small but comfortable.

Well, don't you worry about that.

Mamma smiled.

Would you like some breakfast?

I sure would. Where do you keep your pans?

No. You must be tired from your trip. She lowered her eyes. Do you eat meat?

Blunt looked Mamma full in the face. Yes, Joy.

Well, let me show you to your room.

My *room,* Hatch thought. He was shaking, either from cold or heat—he couldn't tell—his arm still hot from the pinch.

Mamma looked at him. Go into the bathroom and get out of that snowsuit. She and Blunt started for Hatch's room. He watched them.

Joy, let Hatch keep me company. Blunt stopped her body like a truck and waited for a response.

Mamma didn't say anything for a moment. She turned and looked at Hatch. Hatch, hurry out of that snowsuit and come keep Blunt company.

Hatch watched Blunt, hard. Wind and snow had smeared the makeup around her eyes, the talon streaks of some huge bird.

Mamma came forward and gripped his hand. Be good, she whispered. Don't be mean and selfish like your father. She had been frank about his father. Normally, these words about his bad father would have settled him. He struggled to free his hand.

Be good, Mamma said.

He knew she would not hit him. No matter how angry she became. Mind working, he stared through the distance at Blunt. Formed a plan. He would pretend he liked Blunt. Alone with her, he would give her a piece of his mind. Choice words. All right, he said.

Mamma gave him a hard look that said, *Be good*. She pushed open one of the French doors that separated her room from his, then headed for the kitchen.

Hello, Hatch, Blunt said.

Hello, Blunt.

Blunt removed her coat and hung it in the closet. Her arms were thick inside the sleeves of the red jumpsuit. She removed her hat before the dresser mirror, intent on her reflection. Hair spilled gray and long about her shoulders. With her back to him, she began unpacking the one suitcase, now open on the bed. She turned and smiled. Hummed low deep waters in her throat. *You can't fool me*, he thought. Puffy in his snowsuit, he watched her unpack and searched for the correct way to phrase what he wanted to say.

✳

I mean, all that happened twenty-five, thirty, years ago. Blunt chased him out of town with her straight razor. Red, they called him, though I never saw him myself. Clay colored. Bowlegged. A midget. A bad man. Like your father.

Blunt kept his ten-dollar Sears Roebuck guitar and taught herself how to play it.

Then Blunt married the preacher-mortician. I was ten by this time. They'd known each other all along. We moved into his funeral home. It was like a castle, enough rooms to sleep fifty people. Plenty places to wander and get lost.

The preacher always spoke his mind. Children make me nervous. This is what he said. I got a bad heart, and people like me, with bad hearts, also have bad nerves, if you see my meaning. I did. So I kept fifteen feet away from him. Fifteen feet. Measured it.

He was the most disliked colored man in the Rains County. He kept a stable full of horses he had never learned to ride. (His bad heart.) And he had dainty ways like white folks. Always wore a suit and tie in the blazing heat, and walked with his head up high, and breathed like a rusty well pump, and sweated like a fountain. He would place his napkin in his lap when he ate and sweat down into it. He had been in a car accident that scarred up his face pretty bad. (You should have seen it. Unbelievable.) And he never ate meat, since it aggravated his scars. This is what he said: God saw to it to give me the accident, and with it, scars and a bad heart.

The accident had given him the calling to be a preacher, but his sermons put people to sleep. (Christ is fire and water insurance!) That was what led him into the mortuary business. Preachers must eat. He was the picture of success. (They often wrote him up in the newspapers.) With the dead in your corner, you can't fail. Not that he didn't have his problems. Rumor had it that he disrespected bodies placed in his care. (I never saw him myself.) He carved tic-tac-toe on skin. He stuffed hollow cavities with marbles. He drained insides with a garden hose. He embalmed with shoe polish. These accusations turned away no customers. He was cheap and allowed payment by installments and gave a free vase of flowers to the family of the deceased and guaranteed his caskets to resist rust and rot for fifty years.

Then this man—his name always escapes me—took things one step further. I was sixteen. One Sunday he entered the chapel shouting and screaming and cursing and woke the snoring congregation. He voiced his charges: The preacher had removed his wife's neck and put a short log in its place. And the preacher had wrapped that log in a pretty pink scarf to hide the evil deed. (I did see the scarf.) He pointed a sharp finger at the preacher. Your tail is mine, he said. And I got something fo that hefty woman of yours too.

The preacher's nerves took over after that. He would not let Blunt leave the house. And when he went out into the street, he took me along with him as his eyes and ears. He would look in every direction at once, scars twitching. Then he would put one hand over his heart, desperate to calm it. But the hand would jump every few seconds, like it had been given an electrical jolt. Then the wheezing would start, and I would guide him back to the parlor. This went on for about a week; then he and Blunt grabbed their hats and coats in the middle of the night and caught the first thing smoking.

I heard what you did, Hatch said. I know what you did. Mamma had always told him to respect adults, to speak when spoken to, but Blunt deserved no respect.

She stopped what she was doing and turned to him with her green eyes and wild mascara. Her big shoulders tense and her big hands stiff. What did you hear?

You know.

You tell me.

No, you tell me. Why did you do it? Why? Speak up. Be frank.

She studied him for a moment. Sometimes it just be's that way.

Fine, he said. Neither understanding nor caring to understand, he freed himself from the snowsuit and went into the kitchen, where Mamma was.

Were you good? she asked.

Yes.

Then why are you frowning?

I don't know.

You'll have to try harder to be good.

Fine.

Okay.

Fine.

⁂

A burly foreigner under an ugly red hat explains to a primly dressed man behind a desk why he wants a Liberty Express card: In our country, it is forbidden to wear fur hats or ride speedboats. The white man issues him the card. He zooms offscreen in a long red speedboat. The camera zooms in on the ugly red hat, buoyant on the water. Bubbles carry it under.

How many times had he seen that commercial over the day's slow course? They had sat in continual silence, no catching up on lost time, no planning for the found future. Mute monkeys.

Joy, why don't I prepare dinner?

No, don't trouble yourself. I'll do it.

Why don't we both do it? Blunt smiled.

You don't have to.

It'll be fun. We'll do it together.

I would like that, Mamma said. But why don't I cook and you stay here with Hatch and let Hatch keep you company?

Blunt hesitated. That's a good idea.

Mamma went into the kitchen. Blunt and Hatch watched the television.

Quiet day, Blunt said.

Yes.

Shadow and light, her face flickered. What's yo favorite show?

The Phony from Harlem.

＊

They sat around the round wood kitchen table, with platters of fried chicken, black-eyed peas, corn bread, and candied yams in easy reach. They sat like quiet spectators, as if waiting for the food to perform. A roach crawled onto the table.

Mamma forced a chuckle. These roaches are about to run us out of here, she said.

Blunt smashed the roach with her hand, as swift as a judge's gavel. Mamma turned her eyes away. Stunned like the roach, Hatch watched Blunt until she rose to wash her nasty hand.

Mamma cleared the table. All three moved into the living room, before the TV, and sat down, not saying anything. Blunt faced Hatch, some half-formed song in her wide throat.

He watched her. When you gon play that guitar? he asked. Blunt was a phony, and he would prove it.

Hatch! Mamma said.

Joy, it's okay. She looked at Hatch. Why don't you bring it to me?

Disbelieving, he rushed over to the guitar—invisible inside its armored case—tensed, stooped down, and lifted it. It was light, weightless. He brought it over and set it down at Blunt's feet. Blunt shifted forward in her seat, crouched over the case, flipped open the latches, and removed the guitar. Clean bright color. Sun and flame. And thick, cablelike strings that hovered an inch above the fingerboard and the sound hole (a deep dark cave). *I bet that's Red's old guitar,* Hatch thought. *Too cheap to buy a new one.*

Blunt plucked the strings with her right thumb—big as a shoehorn—while she twisted the tuning pegs with her left fingers, releasing long scraping vibrations like those of a dragging muffler. Hands working, she tested the strings some more and nodded to herself when she achieved the desired pitch.

And now, for my next tune—

Hatch did not laugh at her joke.

She cleared her throat. Stroked the strings and set them humming. Opened her mouth wide in song.

Sweet daddy, bring back yo sweet jelly roll
Sweet daddy, bring back yo sweet jelly roll
Don't leave me this way
Burdened with this heavy load

Hatch's heart tightened. He rode deep waves of thought and feeling that carried him to some far-off place in the room, where he sat alone, in a small boat, spiraling on a whirlpool of blue water.

Mamma started briskly for the kitchen. Hatch went dizzily after her. Mamma? Where you going?

To do my cleaning.

Come and hear Blunt.

I can hear her from in here.

Come hear. A lasting spray of blue water, cool on his skin.

Come see Blunt play.

You go back and watch her.

He went back. Why you stop? Go on. Play some more.

No. It's late in the evening. Folks trying to sleep. Blunt put the guitar back inside the case and closed lid and latches. Maybe I'll teach *you* how to play tomorrow.

Really?

Yes.

I'd like that.

Mamma came into the room. Hatch, bedtime.

Fine.

Time for bed.

Fine.

Good night, Mamma said. She kissed him.

Good night.

Good night, Blunt said. She kissed him, her big lips wet on his face, her pug nose hard against his cheek.

Good night. Anger dragged him from the room and to a dark thinking place under Mamma's bedsheets.

He lay there for some time, weighing, calculating, then quietly left the bed at the precise moment when Mamma and Blunt would falsely believe him asleep. He tiptoed over to the French doors and put his ear to the cold squared glass.

Please try.

I will.

You know plenty. So please . . .

I understand.

Yes. That's all I'm asking. He's still young.

I will.

Well, I said my piece. Good night, Blunt.

Good night, Joy . . . daughter.

Hatch hurried back into bed and pulled the covers over his head. He heard Mamma enter the room. Felt the opposite side of the mattress sag under her weight. He kept his back toward her as a wall and waited for sleep to come.

✳

I must leave for work.

Why? Blunt said. I see no need.

Mamma seemed to ponder the words. Thank you, Blunt. I'm glad to hear you say that.

No need to thank me. Those bones is tired. It's time for some rest.

I won't argue . . . Well, I better get Hatch to school.

You two go ahead. I'll stay here and get some rest. Still ain't got that train out of my system.

Okay, Mamma said.

Good-bye, Blunt, Hatch said. He smiled up at her.

Good-bye, Hatch. Yall need money for a cab? It's a bad day out there.

That would be nice, Mamma said.

✳

Rubber boots inches above the floor, Hatch floated on the seat, an astronaut in his inflated snowsuit.

Why do I have to go to school today?

Because that's your responsibility.

You got frank with me about Blunt and the preacher and you got frank with me about my father because you want me to be responsible? She had once explained it to him.

Yes.

Is Blunt responsible?

Why do you ask?

She still be responsible if she run away from the preacher?

Good people stick by those who are good to them.

The preacher was good?

Yes.

That's not what you said.

What did I say?

You know what you said.

You misunderstood.

He was good?

Yes?

Why?

He helped her.

Are you being frank?

Yes.

They swung over to the curb.

Be good. She kissed his cheek.

I will. He wasn't sure if she had been frank.

She paid the driver. Driver, could you please wait? I'll be right back.

You got it.

They quit the cab and took the short path to the school.

Be good.

I will.

✳

When school let out, he found Mamma waiting for him in an idling cab. He spoke excitedly about a typical school day. They had a quick ride home, the cab seemingly sliding above the snow like a great yellow sled.

Blunt! Blunt! We're home!

He ran freely through the apartment. Blunt's eyes stopped him, heavy on mind and skin, holding him in place like paperweights.

What happened to your eyes? Hatch asked. They're blue.

I'll show you. Blunt moved into Hatch's bedroom, her large body in blue silk pajamas, hair flowing like a silver wave down to her nape. She returned with a small plastic case resting on her palm. These are contact lenses, she said.

What? Hatch said.

She removed something from the case, raised her hand to her eye. Removed her hand. Now her eye was green. The other was still blue.

How'd you do that?

Contact lenses, she said. She held out the case, full of many colored lenses, painted Easter eggs.

Wow.

Those are lovely, Mamma said.

Blunt smiled with radiant satisfaction. Eager to please, she turned her eye gray, then light brown, then green, then blue again.

✳

Lahzonyah, Blunt called it. Lah-zon-yah. He tried to rise to his feet but found himself anchored to the seat, his stomach heavy with sunken treasure, the long empty casserole dish abandoned in the middle of the table like a beached boat.

Play some music.

Mamma glared at him over the hot coffee at her lips.

Maybe later, Hatch. Let my food digest first.

How long will that take?

Blunt laughed. Do you know that I used to have my own place where I could play music anytime I wanted and where dozens and dozens of people would come see me?

Mamma noisily returned her cup to the saucer.

What did you call it? Hatch asked.

The Red Rooster.

Did it look like a red rooster?

Blunt laughed. No. Like a barn. The only barn in Harlem.

Did it have—

Saturday, we should do some sightseeing, Mamma said. The coffee steamed up into her face. You haven't seen the city.

That'll be fine, Blunt said. How does that sound to you, Hatch?

Fine, he said. Please play your guitar tonight.

Why don't you ask your mother if it's okay with her?

Hatch looked at Mamma.

She was a long time in answering. I don't see why not.

Great. Blunt hammered a beat on the table with her roach-slaying palm.

After some time, she arranged herself in a chair with her guitar.

If you gon walk on my heart
Please take off yo shoes

Said, if you gon walk on my heart
Kindly take off yo shoes
I got miles to make up to you, baby
And I ain't got no time to lose

Bright stringed music radiated from the sunburst guitar and enwebbed the entire room. Job done, the rays recoiled back into the dark sound hole.

Play another one!

Bedtime, Mamma said.

No, it's not.

Bedtime.

It's too early.

Bedtime.

Fine.

Come on.

Fine.

Good night, Hatch. Blunt kissed him.

Good night.

He stalked out of the room. Pounced upon Mamma's bed and clawed the sheets. Voices on the other side of the glassed door tamed his anger.

I asked you.

I'm sorry.

I mean—

I really am sorry.

I explained my reasons.

Yes. He is a child.

I mean, you know plenty. What was that one the preacher liked?

"Unchanging Hand."

Yes. How about that one?

A solid choice.

I've tried. Tried my best. I've been patient. More than patient. I'm not one to cry over spoiled milk.

No, you aren't. And bless you for it. If you put spoiled milk in the refrigerator at night, it'll still be spoiled in the morning.

Yes.

Oh, Joy, I know. You may not believe it, but I know. You see, I ain't much to look at. No feast for the eye. But the preacher chose me.

He wasn't a pretty man himself.

No, he wasn't, but he was a good man . . . Sometimes you had to fish for it. And good fish stay deep. Only the dead ones float on top.

Well, Mamma said, one might look at it that way.

Spoiled milk and dead fish both stink.

That's true.

Good night, Joy. Daughter.

Good night, Blunt. Mother.

The next morning Hatch rose early and watched Mamma wake from the gray paralysis of sleep. She struggled out of bed, her hands positioned at her chest like a gloved surgeon's, careful not to touch anything or let anything touch her. More than once he had watched her sore hands soak for hours in a deep tub of warm water and Epsom salt.

Mamma?

What?

Is Blunt sad?

What makes you think that?

Is she sad because the preacher died?

I don't know.

Is that why she can sing and stroke and make—

Don't talk that way.

I'm being frank.

You aren't being frank. Don't talk like that.

How come she likes to—

That's enough. Get ready for school.

They bathed and clothed themselves, then entered the kitchen, the table set and breakfast prepared. Blunt followed her sweet heavy perfume into the room, tight leather jumpsuit and tall leather boots slowing and constricting her movement, and her makeup so thick, she struggled to keep her chin up.

Good morning, Blunt.

Good morning, Joy.

Good morning, Hatch.

Good morning, Blunt. Blunt bent down—her eyes gray—and kissed him, then drew herself straight. In that space of time he glimpsed something in her face.

They all sat down at the round wood table.

Why are you dressed so early? Mamma asked.

I'm going out to buy some new guitar strings.

Mamma didn't say anything.

Maybe I'll even buy a new guitar.

Can you find your way around?

Sure. I'll take a cab.

Mamma, let Blunt take me to school today.

Remember your place.

No, Joy. It's okay.

No, it's not okay. He's too smart for his own good.

That is so. How bout I take him to school today—if it's okay with you.

Mamma hesitated. Looked at Blunt. Looked at Hatch. Looked at Blunt again. Perhaps that would be good.

Blunt smiled.

I'll write down the address. Just show it to the driver.

Of course.

✳

Blunt sat next to him, like a big block of ice in her white fur coat. The weather had not changed. For the first time, he was glad to be inside the padded snowsuit. Kind. The two of them all plump, like fresh pastries on display. But he found it hard to keep still in his seat, victim to the stab of wondering. Should he confront her about what he thought he'd glimpsed in her eyes? Confront her about what he'd overheard last night? Something about dead fish, spoiled milk, and funky smells. *Maybe she is a phony. Maybe she jus playin and singin to make me like her.* His curiosity caused him to sight down the guitar's polished neck, fret by fret—railroad ties—to the ragged paper edge of a brown grocery bag; and to continue down the bag's side, to a bottom corner and Blunt's black boot wedging it in place. Why had she not brought the case along? Surely Mamma had noticed. Should he—

How do you like school?

Just fine.

Of course you like it. You're a smart boy, and you're doing so well. I'm proud of you.

Thank you.

I was real proud when you graduated from kindergarten.

Hatch said nothing.

That beautiful picture Joy sent me.

Yes.

And now we're all together.

Yes.

I'll buy that new guitar and play something nice for you this evening.

Fine. Will you play—

Maybe. Let's wait and see what your mother wants to hear.

Why did you put yo guitar in that bag?

Blunt didn't say anything for a moment. Why, didn't I jus tell you? I plan to sell it.

Why you leave yo case at home?

I don't need it.

Why you ain't jus throw yo guitar away?

Some people are needy.

You want to help the needy people?

Yes.

So you want needy people to have yo guitar?

Yes.

Why?

Because—

Let me have it.

Oh. You don't want this old thing.

Why not?

It barely plays.

I thought you said you gon teach me how to play.

Yes.

Then I can use that old thing.

I'll buy you a nice new one.

Fine.

But—

Fine.

Wouldn't you like a new guitar?

Sure, he said. *But you ain't gon buy it,* he thought.

Enjoy school, Blunt said. She kissed him on the cheek.

I will, he said. Her pug nose looked like a big beetle stuck onto her face.

Good-bye, Hatch.

Good-bye, Blunt.

✳

Where's Blunt?

Plumed exhaust rose from the idling cab.

She hasn't returned. Mamma spoke from the dark cavelike inside.

She was sposed to pick me up.

Mamma blinked nervously. Did she say that?

No.

Well.

I thought she was gon pick me up.

Watch your mouth. Those kids at this school are a bad influence.

She was sposed to pick me up.

Get in this cab.

He got inside the cab. The driver pulled off.

How come we can't take the train? He spoke to the moving window, the moving world.

We have no reason to take the train.

I'm being frank.

Please be quiet.

He obliged. Quiet and caught, the living moment before him and behind. He tried to imagine Blunt's face and received the taste of steel on his tongue. He let his violence fly free like the soaring El cars above, a flock of steel birds rising out of a dark tunnel, into bright air, the city shrinking below.

The cab slowed and felled his desires. Slim currents of traffic congealed into a thick pool up ahead. The taxi advanced an inch or two every few minutes. The El's skeletal structure rose several stories above them. An occasional train rumbled by and shook the cab and mocked his frail yearning. He looked out the window to vent his anger. A good ways off he could discern a woman standing in a building doorway, a guitar strapped to her body and a coffee can at her gym-shoed feet. Coatless, in a checkered cotton dress, her bare muscular legs as firm as the El's pylons in the bitter cold. She kept rhythm with one foot, while some lensed smiling face rose or fell with each stroke of the guitar.

He shouldered the cab door open and started through the street, his boots breaking through snow at each step, and traffic so thick he had to squeeze between the cars. Wind tried to push him back, and the fat snowsuit wedged between two parked cars. But he freed himself from the moment and thought of his mother and thought of his father and thought of the preacher and thought of Blunt and fancy clothes and contact lenses and lahzonyah and smiles and promises.

Hatch! Mamma shouted after him, her voice distant, weak, deformed, small, dwarfish, alien. Intent on his target, he moved like a tank in his armored snowsuit, smooth heavy unstoppable anger. Close now. Blunt framed in the doorway, his face trained on her guitar. Her hair was not long and flowing and silver but knotted in a colorless bun. Her eyes were not green or blue or brown or gray but a dull black. She shut them. Aimed her pug nose, arrowlike, at the El platform. Snapped open her mouth.

Baby, baby, take off this heavy load
Oh, baby, baby, lift up my heavy load
Got this beast of burden
And he got to go.

Quick legs, he stepped up onto the curb and almost tilted over in the heavy snowsuit. He kicked the coffee can like a football, coins rising and falling like metal snow, then crouched low and charged like a bull. He felt wood give under his head and loose splinters claw his face. He fought to keep his balance, loose coins under his feet, and in the same instant found himself flailing his hands and arms against Blunt's rubber-hard hips and legs. Gravity wrestled him down. Dazed, he shook his head clear, gathered himself in a scattering moment, and looked up at Blunt. Her lined face. Her pug nose. Her stork mouth. And the strapped guitar that hung from her body—broken wood, twisted wire, useless metal—like some ship that had crashed into a lurking giant.

His eyes met hers, black, stunned. Wait, she said. You don't understand. She shook her head. You don't—

I hate you! he screamed. I hate you! Concrete shoved him to his feet. I hate you! Brutal wind pulled him into motion and led him as if he were leashed. Down the sidewalk, beyond the El's steel pylons, through warped, unfamiliar streets.

Body and Soul

Wesley Brown

There was a small group of musicians waiting for Coleman Hawkins when his ship docked in New York City. Coleman had been away in Europe for five years. But with war simmering to a boil, he knew it was time to get himself on the first ship steaming back to the States. The welcoming committee included two of his oldest friends, Benny Carter and Jimmy Harrison. After the glad-handing was out of the way, they started signifying to make him feel at home.

"Hey Bean, you looking as trim as your mustache," Jimmy said.

Leave it to Jimmy to draw first blood. Something Coleman was known for when they were in the Fletcher Henderson Band together. Nobody had called him Bean since he left the country. Early on, Coleman gained a reputation for having a mean "bean" of a brain that allowed him to do just about anything he wanted on the tenor saxophone. He kept tight-lipped about how good he was, but the name stuck and he answered to it.

"I guess if you got a lot of trim over there in England," Jimmy said, "you more than likely gonna stay that way yourself."

He enjoyed the laughter that followed but didn't join in. That was always his way. Stay close to the mix of what was going on, but don't get too familiar with it. Laughter continued bouncing around in everyone's shoulders. And Coleman remembered Jimmy was also called "bean," but only the kind that went with the word "string." He was still all arms and legs, his skinny limbs like rubber, connecting him to the trombone when he played.

"So who's who and what's what?" Coleman asked.

Heads swiveled toward one another to see if everyone got his drift.

"It didn't take you long to get down to business," Benny Carter said.

"What business might that be?"

"Bean! You've gotten even more slippery than you were before you left. But you just gonna have to wait 'cause we don't wanna spoil the surprise!"

They all piled into Benny Carter's Cadillac and headed uptown. Benny always impressed Coleman with how he held his own in any musical setting. He wasn't intimidated by reputations, whether they preceded his or came after, making him someone who could play with the best and never let anyone play him cheap. This made them do their best when they challenged each other on saxophone or clarinet years before in the Henderson Band. Benny still had that barrel chest, easy laughter, and eyes that soaked up anything worth paying attention to.

"So Bean, tell us about all the 'fine dinner' you had while you were gone," one of the other musicians said.

"You got me all wrong. The reason I came back so trim was because I traveled light and ate the same way."

"Man! You as much of a tightwad about giving up any info on all your overseas chippies as you've always been about holding on to your money!"

"I'm sorry fellas, but I follow the old saying that those who tell don't know."

"You don't need to worry none, Bean. We can't cut in on your time with ladies who're way over on the other side of the ocean."

They had that right, since no one cut in on Coleman's time with women more than he did himself. He was known to play gigs all night and then find jam sessions that lasted late into the morning. This steady diet of playing fed him creatively but starved his first marriage. Coleman's wife, Gertie, always greeted him with a ready-made breakfast and a sweetness that only wanted to please. To be honest, he had to accept his share of the responsibility for that. There was more than a little calculation in how meticulous he was about his appearance—from double-breasted Gibraltar-shouldered suits and long spike-collared shirts to the slim trim of his mustache and cut of his nails. He knew the stylishly dressed figure he cut while playing the Glenn Miller Band's hit ballad "Wishing (Will Make It So)" would have more than a few women rushing up to him afterward, hoping to convince him how anxious they were to please. And he was more than happy to have them try—which was how he first met Gertie. What he hadn't figured on was how wanting to please got old when the thrill didn't cut both ways. It would've been better for both of them if Gertie had done what she probably really wanted to do—which was to get up in his face about his late hours and demand that he spend more time with her. That's what Coleman lived for: the opposition he got from other musicians who took each other's best shots and came away from the fray with the only kind of companionship that made sense to him.

The day after Gertie finally left, Coleman looked around the nearly empty apartment. Whatever home they shared, she'd made and taken it with her. Coleman felt no loss for what was gone and saw nothing of himself in what remained: a bed, a table, and a few chairs. The only thing that mattered stood upright on a stand in a corner, gleaming like it had been washed in a burst of light from the sun. Coleman often wondered if he could ever be with a woman who needed, as much as he did, the opposition that was the same as friendship. Good question.

Coleman continued to take the ribbing that tightened the squeeze of bodies on either side of him. They could have all the fun they wanted, since there were more pressing matters on his mind, like the surprise Benny said was waiting for him later that evening. The conventional wisdom was that any advances in the music were a young man's game. He looked at his reflection in the rearview mirror. The streamlined mustache that curved upward just short of his nostrils had no traces of gray and still received compliments from women on how it made his mouth fuller and more expressive whether he was playing or talking. Since he was only a few months shy of thirty-five, his hairline had receded a bit, something he would fix by keeping it cut short. Could it be that he might've stayed away too long, and would be unable to keep pace when challenged by these young upstarts who were eager to expose him as a has-been? But being a little anxious didn't mean he was fearful. He'd spent too many years honing his musical chops to believe there was anyone so good that he wouldn't have answers for whatever they had to offer.

Coleman had come a long way since his youthful days in the early 1920s, when he was given top billing as the "Saxophone Boy," with Mamie

Smith and her Jazz Hounds. He never mentioned this period of his life because it froze him in a time he wanted no part of. Coleman was even close to the vest about his birth, saying his father was a merchant seaman who met his mother on the Cape Verde Islands, where they married. He was born at sea on a merchant ship heading back to the United States. So there was no record of the actual date or year of his birth. The here and now was all that interested him. On the rare occasions when Coleman dwelled on the past at all, it usually related to music he was thinking about at the moment. He recalled the advice of his mother, Cordelia, whose voice hammered into him the importance of finding something constructive to do that few people, colored or otherwise, could do, and then to do it better than anyone else. She told him, he'd be surprised how many people would flock to be near him once they were aware of how special he was. His father took a second job to pay for a cello and lessons for their only son.

One of the first things Coleman learned about playing the cello was the amount of breath needed to play it. Pressing himself against its wooden body, it surprised him how much he'd taken breathing for granted. As his breath breezed along with the groans plucked and bowed across the strung ribs of the cello's chest, he realized that every breath he took gave his fingers, hands, and arms the strength to bring another sound to life. But nothing prepared Coleman for his first sight of a saxophone in a music store window, glistening like a golden goose whose beak and keys, running down its spine, awaited fingers and a mouth to make it sing. He could only marvel at an instrument in which breathing mouth to mouth was at the heart of making it live. He tried out the various voices of the saxophone and chose the tenor, whose size nestled comfortably in his arms and against his already broad chest, and whose tone was closest to the range of his voice, which had a maturity beyond his twelve years. But the one thing that convinced Coleman that he had to play the saxophone, and made him laugh out loud whenever he thought about it, was the fact that he could blow into the mouth of this long-necked bird of a horn and hear his breath burst out of the other end, which looked like the place where the sun didn't shine!

Coleman tuned in and out of the talk going on in the car and found himself hearing his father's voice, as it sounded when he was a child. William Hawkins was a man of few words. But when he spoke to Coleman, it usually took the form of a story. One of his favorites was about the legendary outlaw Jesse James, who was shot dead in 1882 by Robert

Ford in St. Joseph, Missouri, the city where Coleman was born. According to family lore, Coleman's grandmother had once let James hide out in her home while he was on the lam from the law. William Hawkins never bought into the stories of James robbing the rich and giving to the poor. Like most of the colored in St. Joe, James came into the world with very little but did more harm than good while he was in it. If he had any saving graces, the one Coleman's father took to heart was James's philosophy of how the world worked. Those who had the best of everything in life made sure that other people paid for it, which is what the rich did. And the only people who paid for everything were those who could least afford to. His father made it clear that this never justified stealing, even from those who were thieves themselves. So Coleman embraced his mother's view that he deserved nothing less than the good life, with all the trimmings worthy of his gift. By 1923, he found, in Fletcher Henderson, a bandleader who was more than willing to pay for his young virtuoso's expensive tastes in clothes, food, liquor, and fancy cars.

In 1936, while performing in Switzerland, Coleman received a letter from his mother that his father had died. A newspaper article, included with her letter, reported that William Hawkins, age sixty, stood on the bank of the Missouri River around noon, lit his pipe, adjusted his glasses, buttoned his coat, and walked calmly into the river. Witnesses who saw him said his body floated on the surface for some minutes before it disappeared. Coleman couldn't remember feeling much of anything afterward. The fact of his father's death seemed less important than the way he took his life. Aside from walking into the river, he did nothing that was a departure from his daily routine. It wasn't his father's way to draw attention to himself. He went about his business without making a big fuss. And when he decided that the price for living his life was more than he was willing to pay, he calmly got out of a world that didn't allow him to live in it the same way he was leaving it. Coleman learned the lesson of his father's life very well and didn't feel there was any reason to grieve. He'd found his own way of separating himself from the world. But instead of getting out of this life by taking his own, Coleman left his waking life by making another out of his own breath.

Fingers snapped Coleman out of his reverie.

"Damn, Bean," Jimmy said. "You ain't been back an hour and you already off somewhere else."

"String Bean! You got anything better for me to think about until we get to the Savoy?"

"That'd be difficult to do, since you ain't never allowed anyone to get much of a peep inside your head."

"It's all there for anybody to hear when I play."

"Things've changed since you been away. Folks want a lot more from musicians they're paying their hard-earned money to see. You know what cats were saying about you when you left?"

Coleman didn't press Jimmy to answer his own question. Why should he care one way or the other what anyone said about him?

"The word on the street is that you wouldn't give a damn or a dime to see the Statue of Liberty doing the 'Lindy' on the Brooklyn Bridge at high noon!"

He had to give it to Jimmy. That wasn't bad. And by the time they reached the Savoy, everyone's throat, including his, was sore from coughing up a load of laughter. It was several hours before the ballroom opened to the public, but musicians from several bands had already gathered. There were a few double takes and mouths opening in surprise before outbursts of "Hawk!" and "Bean!" echoed everywhere, followed by a round or two of needling to see if the years away had made it any easier to get underneath his skin. As the group around Coleman drifted away, he spotted a chunky, fat-cheeked man with a trumpet under his arm, giving him a grin that stretched out to a whole upper row of teeth. A smile creased Coleman's cheeks but didn't go any further than that. It was Rex Stewart, a trumpet player who'd been in the Henderson Band. The last time he'd seen Stewart, there wasn't even peach fuzz on his face. Coleman remembered him as someone who had difficulty figuring out the keys that many of the band's arrangements were written in. Sight-reading was second nature to Coleman. Thinking back on it, he wondered if he should've been more understanding of what Stewart was going through. But he was only twenty-one at the time, not much older than Stewart, and found ways of messing with band members, especially those who weren't able to keep up with him musically. Stewart was one who fell into that category. Coleman had gone into the dressing room early before a gig and rubbed some itching powder into the collar of the shirt Stewart was going to wear. During a high point of the night, when heat was rising up off of dancers on the floor, Stewart stood up to take his solo. The itching powder mingled with his sweat, and it was all he could do to keep his jerking head from flying off the handle of his neck. He was too old for that kind of foolishness now. But it was still funny as hell.

"What are you smiling about?" Stewart asked, no longer grinning.

"Just thinking about all the laughs we used to have in Fletch's Band."

"You mean the laughs you had!"

Stewart was no longer that kid who gripped his trumpet so tightly that he strangled the notes in his throat before he could get them out. He lifted his trumpet slowly to his mouth and gently pressed it against his lips. The sound came out in short bursts at the tempo of a high-stepping march. It was strangely familiar. It took a few seconds before Coleman recognized Stewart's slow-motion version of reveille. He dipped his shoulders from side to side, strutting in time with his trumpet jabs snapping Coleman's head back. Stewart was serving notice that he was fully awake; and if Coleman put a deaf ear on this wake-up call, he had better be a praying man because that was the only way he would get any mercy. Coleman was impressed by the brashness Stewart added to his trumpet. And he liked the way Stewart called him out, not with a lot of blowhard and bare knuckles, but with a gloved fist, just loud enough for him to feel the punch. But he wasn't worried. Stepping over to Stewart, Coleman heard his voice crackle with laughter as he slapped him on the back.

"You think what I did was funny?" Stewart asked, unsure of how to take Coleman's good cheer.

"No, Rex. If I did, I'd have slapped my knee and not your back."

Benny Carter had arranged to take Coleman to a number of nightspots, so musicians around town could welcome him back. When they arrived at the Famous Door, a midtown Manhattan club where the Count Basie Band was appearing, guests that included Billie Holiday, Ella Fitzgerald, and Jimmy Lunceford took up several tables. Hands reached out to touch Coleman. Words jumped out at him from every direction but were cut to shreds by slashing sounds from the Basie Band. He was never at ease in large gatherings unless he was playing. And as far as small talk, forget it! Coleman ordered a double scotch. Benny leaned over and whispered that his money was no good for the rest of the night. He downed the scotch, ordered another, and waited for the liquor-coated comfort to take hold. By the second double, Coleman was cut off from everything except the Basie Band, with his ears tuned into the two tenor players: Leon "Chu" Berry (who'd taken the other tenor chair left empty when Coleman's old adversary, Herschel Evans, died earlier that year) and Lester Young. Basie opened up with an old standby, "Jive at Five," playing a stingy five-note intro followed by the trombonist, Dickie Wells, setting a medium tempo, with mouth rumblings of someone shivering from a chill. The big-as-a-tub Chu Berry took a leap into the cold, gripping the saxophone in a choke hold. He was husky-throated and shouted into his horn until it did what it was told. Before Young took his solo, Coleman watched this large, soft-bodied man cradle his saxophone in his arms like a sleeping child. Standing up, he held the sax in his trademark fashion, cocked to the right as someone would while playing a flute. Those sad-sack, heavy-lidded eyes looked out beyond the bandstand; and then the sound, like slippers, soft-pedaled around Berry's rough edges with an easy-does-it, no-sweat attitude, sliding over the beat like a skater on ice.

Benny poked Coleman in the ribs, and other musicians around the table eyeballed him to check his composure. This must've been the surprise he was promised. The baiting began just as the band entered the stretch run to end the tune.

"What do you think, Bean?" someone asked.

"About what?"

"About what you just heard."

"You can't beat the Basie Band!"

"What about Chu and Prez? Can you beat them?"

"I just try to play up to my own standard."

"Will that be enough when you go up against Lester like you did at the Cherry Blossom Club in 1933?"

That was always brought up. The night in Kansas City when he took on Ben Webster, Herschel Evans, and a newcomer named Lester Young. He'd gone to the Cherry Blossom to see if Young was everything people said he was. And he was. All that scuttlebutt about his quitting when his wailing on tenor couldn't get Young to spit the bit was never worth the breath it would've taken to give his version of what went down. Coleman believed his playing gave the best account of what he'd done. And since the numbers of people continued to grow who claimed they were there in that closet-sized club the night of the jam session, the less said about it the better.

Coleman tried to ignore the taunts, but it was impossible to block out the voices, bending his ears with shouts. He wanted to kick back and take it easy after such a long day. But as he glanced around, no one in the club was having any of that. No one except Lester Young, whose teabag-lidded eyes lifted to catch Coleman looking his way. And before Young blinked, something in his eyes told Coleman that he wasn't that hot to trot to give the audience what it wanted either. Coleman reached under the table for his saxophone case, got up, and squeezed his way up to the band-stand. By the time Coleman joined Young, a hush snuffed out any other sound. Lester spoke to Coleman just above a whisper.

"Looks like we got a lotta edge-of-the-seaters out tonight looking to see a cruise where somebody gets bruised."

"Looks that way," Coleman said.

"You down for that?"

"The question is whether we're up for it."

"Where's your head at on that?"

"Same place yours is," Coleman said.

Cracks of restlessness were heard in the silence that held the audience captive.

"What you cats gonna do—" a man shouted, "dribble or shoot!"

"We might just pass," Lester said, shooting his arms forward like a two-handed toss of a basketball.

There was a smattering of laughter, but the uneasiness remained.

"Bean! You got the time?" Lester asked.

"Thanks, Prez. I appreciate that. Everybody else in this joint just wants to tell me what time it is without asking."

"Maybe 'cause they don't know."

"Could be."

"So you wanna take it from letter A on 'Jive at Five'?"

Coleman nodded and roared out of his horn as fast as breath and fingers could carry him, with Lester no more than half a leap behind. The audience was up in arms with yells and whistles. But before they had a chance to get a hold of the speedy groove, Coleman let out a high-pitched whinny, raising his saxophone up like a thoroughbred being reined in until it slowed to loping along. Lester followed Coleman into something sounding like "Home on the Range," where the buffalo roamed and deer and antelope played without butting heads, and where there were no discouraging words or showdowns that left the skies cloudy all day. When Coleman and Lester were done, people began filing out of the club, not knowing quite where they were, using their hands to guide them, like someone walking in the dark. Only the musicians seemed not to be confused by what they'd heard. Some shook their heads with smirks on their mouths.

Coleman caught sight of Lester near the door of the club and went over to him.

"I guess we'll get to do what everybody's waiting for another time," he said.

"Yeah, as long as we both got the time," Lester said, giving a two-finger salute against the wide brim of his flat crown top hat, and then turning on his toes and sliding out the door with the same ease that he played.

Coleman ordered another double scotch, returned to his table, and found Jimmy Harrison in a fit of uncontrollable laughter.

"Bean! You and Prez gotta be the most contrary Negroes I've ever seen!"

"Why you say that?"

"You just can't give folks a good time the way they want you to."

"I give them myself. That should be a good enough time for anybody."

"What would it have cost to give them the show they wanted to see?"

"I can't speak for Prez. But it would've cost me my need to do what everyone didn't expect."

"Yeah, like the time we were playing baseball in Fletch's Band, and you showed up wearing a Panama hat, a tuxedo, and patent leather shoes. And when you took the field to play shortstop you had on a first baseman's mitt!"

"I had to protect two of my most important jewels," Coleman said, holding out his hands.

"What were you protecting up on the bandstand?"

"The element of surprise."

The club continued to thin out, and Coleman was surprised when Louis Armstrong came over to greet him.

"It's solid having you back on the scene, Bean."

"Good to be back, Pops!"

"You're still one clever son of a gun."

"How so?"

"What you and Prez pulled tonight will make the bread you get for the real showdown smell even better."

"Well, you must be doing something right because you're looking as prosperous as ever."

"I got no need to be kicking."

Armstrong didn't linger, and Coleman felt no desire to say more. Aside from his unmistakable gravel throat, Armstrong was laid-back without any of his usual fun-loving joshing around. Truth be told, Coleman never cared much for Armstrong. His first impression when the New Orleans wonder joined the Henderson Band in the early 1920s was that this thick tongued–talking young man, wearing clodhoppers with long johns showing at the ankles below his high-water pants, didn't square with the trumpet phenom he'd heard so much about. During his time with Mamie Smith, Coleman went through a period of looking country and smelling funky before he was set straight on how to present himself properly. He wasn't proud of it, but as a younger man he fancied himself as somewhat of a peacock. So how could he take this Armstrong fella seriously? But his head, like everyone else's in the band, was spun around when he heard him trumpet a story as old as Adam and Eve, but swinging with the sweetness and stink of a new century. Coleman remembered the night Armstrong played ten choruses of "Shanghai Shuffle" at Roseland Ballroom in New York City. He worked the crowd up into such a frenzy that several men carried him out into the street on their shoulders like a conquering hero.

Armstrong was that one-of-a-kind performer, who burst the seams keeping an audience cooling their heels and roused them with sky-high trumpet howls that stormed the heavens and sang with grunts from deep down in the belly of the earth. There were few who could command the stage even without an instrument in hand. That night at Roseland proved to Coleman that he wasn't one of them. But Armstrong's performance made him see his own strength in the undivided attention he gave to the saxophone, playing not to the audience but for himself. Like Armstrong, Coleman was not a big man. But with a chest like a pot-bellied stove, he could blow thick slices of sound that slapped together, making his own size and everything around him seem larger.

Coleman watched Armstrong leave the club. And he had to admit his fondest memory of him came when he opened his mouth, not for a hot trumpet solo or vocal, but to give Fletcher Henderson his notice. Armstrong was a bit tipsy after a night celebrating his decision to return to Chicago and form his own band. He was saying good-bye to everyone and approached Henderson to thank him for all his help. As Armstrong spoke, his stomach heaved, and he threw up all over the bandleader's suit. Coleman couldn't stop laughing, especially when the unflappable Henderson thanked Armstrong, as though expressing gratitude for what Satchmo had just done to him. It wouldn't have surprised Coleman if Armstrong had never forgotten the incident and who laughed the loudest and the longest.

Coleman rented an apartment on Central Park West and began playing gigs on 52nd Street and going to after-hours jam sessions in Harlem. There was great anticipation among musicians and devoted followers of the music for the eventual showdown between Coleman and Lester Young. But the main event was delayed by would-be contenders who Coleman believed were supposed to keep him so busy carving them up during the nightly cutting contests that he wouldn't be ready when the real test came. They would often arrive, sit quietly, and try to unnerve him by never touching their instruments. At other times they hid their horns inside their coats, then pulled them out and began playing in the hope of catching him off guard.

Coleman enjoyed all the attention but wasn't surprised by it. He'd recently gone to see the movie *Stagecoach* and was quite taken by an early scene where a stagecoach, traveling through Indian territory, was stopped in its tracks by a gunshot. Through a camera trick, the man who fired the shot was zoomed out of the distance into a close-up that took up most of the space on the screen. The cowboy holding a rifle and a saddle was played by John Wayne. And the camera singled him out as someone to be reckoned with. A jolt rushed through Coleman that he usually felt after downing a double shot of scotch. He knew something about being front and center, and he'd be damned if he was going to give that up!

One night Coleman appeared as a featured guest soloist at the Famous Door with the Lionel Hampton Band. Waiting to take his solo on the opening tune, he shuffled his feet and bobbed his head like a bronco rider about to be let out of the chute. He'd been thinking about what Chu Berry and Lester Young played that first night of his return. Coleman stepped into the spotlight and blew a path that stretched out beyond what he'd heard. He took a bit of Berry's rough-edged sputter and Young's slippery glide, mixing them into a ride that had the bumps of rusty roads and the dizziness of flying floors. He nodded his appreciation for the applause from the audience. They'd obviously enjoyed the ride. But it was different when he performed at ballrooms. This was something Coleman noticed in Europe, where he played many more club and concert dates than dances. When folks hit the dance floor during his years with the Henderson Band, it wasn't so much playing for them as it was with them. It would begin with the band leading the charge that kicked the dancers into gear, as they scuffled to match their steps to the tempo. But that could change in an instant, when the dancers hit a stride that turned the band into bystanders, taking their cues from the swinging stuff being played by the flash of feet. On the best nights at the Savoy or Roseland, the band and dancers would take turns huffing and puffing and blowing each other down.

The exchange of air at clubs in Europe and that night at the Famous Door was much quieter. And Coleman had become attuned to what he was getting from the people who came to sit and listen. He could tell, from the slightest rise and fall of their shoulders and chests, who was with him, breath for breath, and who inhaled what he'd blown and then exhaled it back at him when he took another breath. Coleman took it all in: the bobbing heads, the fingers drumming on tabletops, the patter of feet on the floor, the mouthing of words and sounds that were not, and the eyeballing, some of it reckless.

After any set, Coleman was never eager to step out of the time and tempo of the music and back into what he left behind. Well-wishers, wanting to talk, crowded around him. There was desperation in the way many reached out to him, their eyes pleading for some other piece of himself, in a word or a touch, that was more lasting than what he'd played. His mother hadn't warned him about this part of having a gift that people wanted to be near. Coleman couldn't help but be sympathetic. He needed what they wanted from him even more than they did. But he could only offer it while playing. Afterward, he needed to protect it and himself. So he let them buy him as many rounds of drinks as they wanted.

The much-anticipated shoot-out between Coleman and Lester Young was delayed because the Basie Band was on the road and wouldn't be back until sometime in September. In the meantime, Coleman contented himself with swatting away the unsatisfying challenges from pretenders, big and small alike, buzzing around him like flies. He became bored by the predictable outcome of these encounters but perked up when an offer came to feature him on a recording of several tunes and backed up by an eight-piece band. On the afternoon of the recording session at the Radio City building, he walked past a newsstand with the headlines on all the papers warning of a possible German invasion of Poland. The date also caught his eye, September 2. Coleman wasn't one to keep close tabs on the news of the day. But this date reminded him of the following day in September ten years earlier, when the stock market crashed. Normally, this would have meant very little, except that it convinced him he'd been right to keep his money close at hand rather than in the money-changing hands of a bank.

The other musicians were in the studio when Coleman walked in and a few started to snicker.

"Bean? Was it running out of ladies that got you here on time?" one of them asked.

"Don't you worry about it. Just remember, it's more important to play in time than to be on time."

"You hear that? Bean listens to a different beat from the rest of us."

One of the men in the sound booth called out over a loudspeaker.

"If we don't start soon, we won't have enough time to lay down the tracks of all these tunes."

The band settled in, and the first tune was recorded without much difficulty. The second, "Fine Dinner," was written by Coleman and was one of his favorites. The trumpet and alto saxophone opening gave voice to the tastes that were in their mouths, as they bounced on top of the bass player's finger-plucking that carried them along breezily. The horns took the tempo up a notch and sounded out a "wow!" as if they'd spotted a woman who wasn't satisfied to be served up like dessert on the sidewalk, but stayed on the go, just out of reach, and let it be known that her swivel hips were for her to show and a precious few to know. The brass and reeds hollered for Coleman to size her up. His solo gave her a juicy big buildup, filled with pulp and seeds. But he begged off getting underneath her crust, as if to say, he only handed out those goodies when he had a "fine dinner" all to himself.

The band took a break before doing "She's Funny That Way," and Coleman talked to the singer, Thelma Carpenter. His eyes lingered on her a while. She couldn't have been more than eighteen, but she seemed eager enough.

"So! You're what's up and coming?"

"I don't know how up and coming I am. But I am a singer."

"Being a singer is more than carrying a tune. You have to want the song to carry you. If you can do that, then you can treat it like someone you have a thing for but don't really know. But the more they get next to you, you just can't get enough of their smell."

"Mr. Coleman, I don't mean to be disrespectful but . . ."

"Just hear me out. . . . So you start living in every corner of that song to find all of its hiding places, and let it do the same to you. And when your nose is wide open and you're about to bust from holding in all that sweet sweat, nothing can stop you from letting out all that joy and trembling."

She was perspiring and didn't like it.

"Mr. Coleman? What are you talking about?"

"I'm talking about being a singer!"

The band cleared the way for her to enter "She's Funny That Way." Coleman's advice kick-started his hope that her sweat would offer up a secret, which would surprise them both. He coaxed her under, over, around, and through the lyrics and heard some Lady Day in her voice. But what young singer didn't. She had a ways to go, though, before her tongue put enough mischief in her mouth to make her voice "funny" in the way the song needed it to be.

The band prepared to play the last tune of the session, when the recording engineer called out to Coleman.

"Why don't you do 'Body and Soul' to finish up?"

"I had something else in mind."

"We can do that another time. I heard you do 'Body and Soul' in a club once, and I think it'd be good to have a recording of it."

Coleman shrugged in agreement.

"Give me an intro to start off," he said to the piano player.

He laid down a light drizzle of notes. Coleman took a breath and spewed out something gruff, from deep in his chest. For some reason, he still didn't want to play this tune about the two halves of one person that were often at war, just like the world was about to be. Coleman felt the weight of his legs holding him down. And the steady beat of walking feet from the bass and the drummer's whispering brushes against the snare weren't enough to take the floor out from under him.

"Could we do another take, Coleman?" the engineer asked afterward. "The sound levels were a little bit off."

"We'll have to do it another time. I'm done for the night."

Coleman left the studio by himself, since all the other musicians wanted to listen to what they'd recorded. He walked down the hall toward the elevator and passed an open door to another studio. Pausing to glance inside, he saw a raw-boned, slick-haired man kneeling down over an opened long narrow suitcase. He reached inside and pulled out a wooden dummy dressed in a tuxedo. The man impressed Coleman with his stylish double-breasted suit and stickpinned collared shirt behind a checkered tie. He lifted the dummy into a sitting position and, very carefully, straightened the white bow tie, attached a monocle over the right eye, snapped open a top hat, and placed it on the head. This had to be that guy on the radio, Edgar Bergen, and his smart-mouthed sidekick, Charlie McCarthy. Coleman started listening to the show shortly after he returned to the

States. At first, he couldn't understand how a ventriloquist act could work on the radio. But he got such a kick out of Charlie McCarthy's wisecracks that it didn't matter how good Bergen really was at making his voice sound like it was coming out of the dummy's mouth.

"May I help you, sir?"

Coleman was a bit startled when Bergen spoke to him.

"I'm sorry. I didn't mean to disturb you. I just finished a recording session down the hall, and I was on my way to the elevator. You're Edgar Bergen, aren't you?"

"Yes, I am."

"I enjoy listening to your show."

"Thank you."

Bergen looked at Coleman's instrument case.

"What do you play?"

"Tenor saxophone."

"I guess you could say we both live our lives out of what's in these cases."

"You'll get no argument from me on that."

"Of course, Charlie has told our listeners that I've got the whole country fooled because I move my lips when he talks."

Coleman raised his instrument case.

"I move my lips too when I make this talk. But I guess the important thing is what Charlie McCarthy and my saxophone are saying when our lips are moving."

"I appreciate you saying that. What is your name, sir?"

"Coleman Hawkins."

"I'm pleased to make your acquaintance."

"Likewise."

"I have a feeling Charlie would like to meet you too."

He pulled over a chair, sat down, and put Charlie on his lap. His mouth opened and a squeaky voice, unlike Bergen's, came out.

"I thought he'd never let me talk. Bergen sometimes forgets that without me he's a body without a soul."

Coleman shot a stare at Bergen.

"Don't look at him, Mr. Coleman. This is me talking!"

Bergen's lips didn't move, and Charlie's voice seemed to be coming right out of his own mouth. Coleman directed his eyes slowly back to Charlie.

"Why are you so surprised? I only tell the listeners that Edgar's lips move, so he'll get some of the credit for my sharp mind and quick wit. But when we're not in front of an audience, we don't have to fake it."

Coleman looked at Bergen again, hoping he would explain.

"Charlie has a very vivid imagination," he said, moving his lips for the first time since Charlie began to speak.

"Of course I do!" Charlie shot back. "I'm no dummy!"

"So if Mr. Bergen doesn't do the thinking for you, how'd you get to be so smart?" Coleman asked.

"Only God could explain it."

"And only a double scotch could make me believe it," Coleman said.

"Bergen! I think W. C. Fields left some of his strong medicine in a drawer, the last time he was on the show. Would you pour us a drink?"

With his free hand, Bergen pulled open a drawer and took out a flask and a shot glass. He poured in two fingers worth and handed it to Coleman.

"Hey Bergen! What about me?"

"Nothing for you, Charlie," Bergen said.

Coleman downed his scotch and shook his head.

"Are you all right, Mr. Hawkins? Why don't you have a seat?" Charlie said.

Coleman settled into a chair, not sure of what he was seeing or hearing. Then Bergen stood up, holding Charlie from behind with one hand.

"So, Mr. Coleman, as a musician, are you paid exuberantly?" Charlie asked.

The scotch kicked in, and Coleman, feeling a little giddy, gave his complete attention to Charlie.

"As a matter of fact, Charlie, I play exuberantly, but the pay is never exorbitant."

"You hear that, Bergen! Mr. Hawkins is quick on the draw, even when he's sitting down."

"Yes, he is, Charlie," Bergen said.

"Mr. Hawkins. Would you be interested in a job as my mouthpiece?" Charlie asked.

"I use one, but I don't want to be one."

"I'm glad to hear that," Charlie said. "Because I don't want to be one either. But I wonder if you're as good on your feet as you are sitting down?"

Coleman glared at both Bergen and Charlie, who gave him back the look of seasoned cardsharks, refusing to show their hand until he played his. They'd gotten his juices flowing, and he welcomed the sweat soaking his underarms, just as it did right before he went toe-to-toe with a worthy challenger in a club or after-hours joint. He'd been waiting to feel like this since returning from Europe. And it was hard to believe that a ventriloquist playing second banana to his wooden buddy would've made mischief in their voices that he'd been hoping to hear from other musicians. Coleman opened his saxophone case, pulled out his horn, and stood up. He tightened the mouthpiece, put the strap attached to the sax around his neck, and nestled the lower body of his horn against his stomach. Standing shut-eyed and not giving a thought to what he would play, Coleman heard a rumble rising up from his belly to his throat, which came out in a growl that he recognized as the first few bars of "Body and Soul." He flashed on what Charlie McCarthy said about Edgar Bergen not being much more than a soulless body without him. Coleman wondered whether it was said deliberately to see how far he'd go to prove that whatever Bergen did to throw his voice into Charlie's was nothing compared to what he made come out of a saxophone. But he quickly lost interest in that and began tasting his tenor for the labor of his life from mind to mouth. And with each breath, he sucked into his gums and between his teeth a world tumbling into deep trouble. He was hot with fever; and his fingers burned against the keys, making the skin feel like it was melting into the metal of his horn. Coleman opened his eyes, sweat streaming down his face. Bergen and Charlie were a blur, blending into each other, bone to wood. He played the final notes, letting out a sigh that quivered like the flame on a candlewick before it went out.

"I don't think anybody could've explained how I tick any better than that. Don't you think so, Bergen?"

"Absolutely!"

"But I have to ask you something, Mr. Hawkins," Charlie said. "Since it was you who explained everything about me, did having that drink help you believe what you played any more than if God had done it?"

A fistful of laughter punched its way out of Coleman's mouth. And he almost choked, stopping another one coming right behind the first. Coleman nodded. Charlie's comeback was worthy of anything Lester Young could've hit him with. He tried to sidetrack the question by playing a nursery rhyme about Little Bo Peep watching her sheep and falling asleep.

"It's a little early for me to be turning in, Mr. Hawkins," Charlie said. "Bergen and I still have a show to do."

Bergen glanced quickly at his watch.

"You're right, Charlie. Mr. Hawkins, I'm sorry, but we're due in the studio for tonight's show in five minutes. I know I speak for Charlie . . ."

"Don't even think such a thought, Bergen."

"Charlie, I was only going to say how much we enjoyed our lively conversation with Mr. Hawkins."

"Oh! I'll go along with that. Mr. Hawkins, you have definitely kept me on my toes. W. C. Fields won't know what hit him when he runs into me again."

"I have a W. C. Fields that I'll be tangling with soon. But after going a few rounds with you, I'll be ready for him."

Bergen extended his hand to Coleman.

"It's been a pleasure, Mr. Hawkins."

"The same goes for me," Coleman said, shaking his hand. He then took hold of Charlie's hand and shook it. "You take care of yourself, Charlie."

"You too, Mr. Hawkins. And when we come back to New York to do another show, maybe you could show me a few things on your saxophone."

"I'd be happy to."

"You know, Charlie," Bergen said. "It's wonderful that Mr. Hawkins has agreed to give you some pointers on playing the saxophone. But I think you should do something for him in return."

"Well, let me see. Oh! I know what! I can show you something even Bergen doesn't know I can do."

"What's that?" Coleman asked.

"When we come back to New York, I'll meet you without Bergen tagging along."

Coleman shot a glance at Bergen, wondering where this was going.

"There you go again, Mr. Hawkins," Charlie said, "looking at him, instead of listening to me. You don't believe I can get along on my own without Bergen, do you?"

"What I believe, Charlie, is that Mr. Bergen would have more trouble getting along without you."

"What makes you say that?" Bergen asked.

"Because like you and Charlie, *this* is what I am wherever I go," Coleman said, lifting his saxophone lengthwise like a baptized child.

"Hey fellas, I got a news flash for you," Charlie said. "You may be joined to us at the heart, but not at the hip."

A smile wormed into Bergen's mouth. Coleman could tell that he was having a great time listening to Charlie give him a lot of grief. This was probably how he prepared for the knockdown, drag-out, sharp-tongued fisticuffs between Charlie and W. C. Fields. It reminded Coleman of his own struggles with the saxophone when he tried to play things he'd only heard in his head. Without these tugs of war between himself and his horn, he would've never built up a full head of ideas and the stamina to take on all comers during those wee-hour jam sessions. While Coleman waited on the elevator, he watched Bergen carrying Charlie down the hall to the radio studio. Charlie's head turned to Bergen, and he spoke loud enough for Coleman to hear.

"You know Bergen, those last few words we just had with Mr. Hawkins make me wonder if I might be better off doing my act as a solo."

Night Coming

Desiree Cooper

Why doesn't the key fit?

Nikki hesitated for a second in the early dusk, wondering if she was at the right house—whether the hundred-year-old, rambling Tudor was really where she lived. She put down her briefcase, and looking around nervously, laid her black leather purse down beside it so that she could try the key with both hands.

Nikki had left work early hoping to avoid just this kind of meeting between herself, a locked door, and sundown. The spiral topiaries flanking her front door stood mute. She flinched as a squirrel darted across the damp cedar mulch.

"Damn!" she said out loud, jiggling the key impatiently in the swollen lock. "Damnit all!"

It was stupid, she knew, but suddenly she wanted to cry. Maybe it was the tension that had built up during the desperate rush home to meet Jason, only to see that he hadn't made it there yet, the house disappearing into blackness, the porch cold and unlit.

Maybe it was because she didn't really want to go with him to the Diaspora Ball after all. They went to the benefit for African American art at the museum every year. She was tired, feeling nauseous. Couldn't they skip it, just this once?

Stemming easy tears, she gathered her things and clomped to the back of the house, her sleek pumps crushing the brittle leaves in her wake. The motion-sensitive lights along the side of the house blinked on, holding her startled in their beams.

Entering the backyard, Nikki scanned it quickly: the brick barbeque pit, the teak outdoor furniture, the star-white mums offering a last bloom before frost.

No one was there.

Of course no one's back here, she thought, sniffling courageously. *This neighborhood is safe.*

It was as if the house had been waiting for those magic words, for her hands to turn the key with patience, for her clammy palm to push open the door, for her feet to tread cautiously into the warmth of the kitchen.

"Whew," Nikki blew, immediately flipping on the light and locking the door behind her. Putting the briefcase down, she kicked off her pumps and rolled down her panty hose, which, of late, seemed to be even more confining.

Hungrily, she opened the refrigerator. It was typical of DINKS—couples with double income, no kids. Leftover Chinese, a bottle of Fat Bastard chardonnay, fruit-on-the-bottom yogurt, Diet Coke.

Nikki eyed the wine but thought the better of it, slamming the door. Instead, she took out a box of Cheerios from the pantry and munched to quell her nervous stomach.

Just a few handfuls, she promised herself, glancing at the clock. *Jason will be home soon and we'll eat dinner at the party.*

She dialed him on his cell, but got his voice mail. Shrugging, she picked up her purse and briefcase and went to the front of the house to turn on the lights.

Five thirty. It wasn't like Jason to be late without letting her know where he was—especially these days. Nikki paced before the leaded-glass windows of the living room, her mind racing.

Maybe there's been an accident, she thought. *Maybe he'll never walk again. Maybe he's . . .*

"He's just running late," she said out loud, her voice echoing around the vaulted ceiling. She tried Jason's cell again. No answer.

Making her way across the marble foyer to the den, she turned on the lights in each room as she passed. The quivers returned to unsettle her stomach. Her muscles drew taut like a cat's. Placing her briefcase on the coffee table, Nikki plopped on the leather sofa. She tried to concentrate on the paperwork she'd brought home, but stopped after only a few minutes. It was futile. The words had no meaning. She felt like an actress, improvising busyness for some invisible audience.

Every once in a while, Nikki touched the back of her neck where her short black hair lay in soft curls against her chai tea skin. Had she imagined that swift puff of air—a stranger's warm breath?

She thought about Jason's bottle of wine chilling in the refrigerator and was tempted to dash back through the empty house to take a sip. Instead, she picked up the remote, turning on the design channel. But soon she found her attention shifting from the flat-screen TV to the neighborhood security truck outside, its yellow patrol lights splitting the night.

✳

"You'll love it in Detroit," Jason had said about his hometown.

That was five years ago, only weeks after they'd graduated from Emory's business school. Nikki remembered the wide grin on Jason's handsome chestnut face as he'd flapped open his offer letter from General Motors. She'd thrown her arms around him, her heart clutching. Her mediocre grades had left her without similar options.

Nikki's mother had cried when she'd found out her baby girl was moving from Atlanta to Detroit, of all places. Nikki had cried, too, as she'd followed Jason to the Motor City, red-eyed and rudderless.

The newlyweds had sublet a loft in the Cass Corridor next to Wayne State University that first summer. Jason had convinced her that it would be a hip place to live, a place where the hookers coexisted with organic bakeries and socialist bookstores.

For Nikki, Detroit had been her first real adventure. Raised by a black middle-class Atlanta family, she'd walked on the debutante stage at sixteen and graduated from Spelman University at twenty with a marketing degree—the third woman in her family to attend the historically black women's college. She'd applied to Emory to assuage her parents, who'd kept asking, "What are you going to do now?" Her performance at Emory was lackluster, reflecting both her ambivalence to business school and her waning interest in marketing. But when she'd met Jason Sykes, a well-heeled Detroiter who had a way with numbers and women, she decided that her investment in graduate school would pay off in one way that she hadn't predicted. She married him after their first year.

She'd been immediately seduced by the side of Detroit that never made newspaper headlines. There was the large, tight-knit black upper class, with their galas and vacations on Martha's Vineyard. In addition, there were the unbelievably long July days when the sun didn't set until after 9:00 p.m. During her first summer, the city seemed to be in permanent celebration with endless concerts, happy hours, ethnic foods, and festivals.

Maybe Jason was right, Nikki had thought. *Detroit just gets a bad rap.*

But being from Atlanta, she had no way of knowing that she was experiencing only a seasonal euphoria. As summer turned to fall, a paralyzing darkness encroached upon the city. By December, it seemed to cut the afternoons in two. Nikki found herself leaving the house in the morning and coming home at night without ever seeing the sun. For months on end, the drag of winter circled from gray to black, then back again.

Thankfully, she'd landed a position as a private banker with a suburban boutique bank that first fall. The high-powered job helped rescue her mood.

Their second year, they'd bought in the exclusive Palmer Woods, the same integrated, ritzy neighborhood where Jason had grown up. Despite her privileged upbringing, Nikki had a hard time comprehending the wealth that the stately homes represented.

"The Archbishop of the Detroit Archdiocese lived there," Jason had said, pointing to a sprawling estate that looked more like a castle than a house. "Then one of the Pistons moved in—can you believe it? And that's the old Fisher mansion."

Fisher, she realized, as in Alfred Fisher, the auto baron. As in one of the many car moguls who blossomed in Detroit in the early twentieth century. Jason was full of stories like that, stories that made her think of the neighborhood of stone mansions, carriage houses, and English gardens as something out of a fairy tale.

"During World War II," he said, "people had to wall off entire sections of their homes to save energy. Neighborhood patrols went around at night and knocked on people's doors if any light was showing through the windows. Some people filled their attics with sand in case the roof caught on fire." When Nikki looked at him quizzically, he added, "Air raids."

Their own house had only three owners, the last of whom had sealed the drafty milk chute and turned the maid's quarters into an exercise room. But it was the back staircase—the one that went from the maid's room to the kitchen—that had given Nikki pause.

"Why would we need that nowadays?" she'd asked as they considered putting down an offer.

Jason had looked at her and shrugged. "I don't know. A secret escape route?"

It had been just a joke, but many nights since, Nikki had been lying awake imagining herself scampering down the back stairs, away from an intruder. Or worse, an intruder creeping up the hidden staircase to where they lay sleeping.

Nikki had quickly filled the den, dining room, and master bedroom with furniture from mail-order catalogs—the working couple barely had time for grocery shopping, much less interior decorating. They left the rest of the sprawling Tudor echoing and empty. On weekends, she and Jason spent Sundays trolling for antiques to accent the other rooms in the century-old house.

But deep down, Nikki worried that escape would be harder when weighed down with useless things.

✳

Outside, a car pulled up in the driveway, the headlights forming prison shadows through the blinds.

Jason! Nikki thought. But before she could get up, the car backed out, then headed in the opposite direction down the winding, elm-lined street.

She sighed heavily, pushing aside her briefcase, hating herself for being so clingy. She'd rushed out of her suburban office at 5:00 so that she could beat the Friday afternoon traffic and meet Jason at home. She was always tired these days, and had hoped they'd have a couple hours to unwind before getting to the Diaspora Ball by 8:00.

Now it was nearly 6:30, according to the dull green readout on the cable box. *I guess I should get ready,* she sighed.

Her footfalls made the refinished wood stairs creak. She laughed at herself for wondering—if only for a second—whether the sounds were coming from someone else lurking inside the old house.

She went into the bathroom, with its white pedestal sink and claw-footed tub. Running the hot water, she slowly took off her navy-blue knitted suit. She couldn't help but notice the slight bulge of her stomach, which made her self-conscious even though it was easily hidden beneath her straight-cut jackets.

She hated being vulnerable in the bathtub with only the sounds of the settling house to keep her company. She thought about turning on the television in the master bedroom, or putting on some Miles Davis, but what if someone tried to break in and she couldn't hear?

Jason will be home soon, she thought.

The warm water was like a baptism. She breathed in the lavender aroma of the suds, and let her shoulders relax. Sometimes she could be so silly, she knew.

When had she become a woman afraid to stay alone in her own house?

It was the news. The constant stories of carjackings and murders. The endless stream of black men in mug shots, or bent low with their hands cuffed, getting into the back of police cruisers.

No, it wasn't just the news, it was the way the different social classes bumped up against each other in Detroit. In Atlanta, this house—all 5,000 square feet of it—wouldn't come with a neighborhood, but with horses and a long, gravel driveway. And even if it came with neighbors, it wouldn't come with poor ones.

Nikki added more hot water to her bath and closed her eyes. She remembered her first Halloween in Palmer Woods. How she'd gone and bought three bags of candy, even though she'd seen very few children in the neighborhood.

That Halloween had been particularly cold, and she'd wondered how the children were going to show off their angel wings and Superman capes if they were bundled up like Eskimos. She'd just come home from work and barely had a bowl of soup before the doorbell rang.

She'd put on her witch's hat and run to the door, expecting to see tiny tots hollering, "Trick or Treat!" Instead, there were adults and teenagers, most with only a half-cocked attempt at a costume—the stark white face paint of the "Dead Presidents," or a terrifying Freddy Krueger mask—holding out a pillowcase for candy. They came in droves all night, kids tumbling out of buses and church vans, and the hungry adults vying with them for the best candy.

The enormity of it had shocked and depressed her. As she opened the door, some of them peeked inside. "You have a nice house," they'd said and she'd blushed, Marie Antoinette doling out her little pieces of cake.

Within an hour after sunset, she'd given away all of her candy and had started combing the kitchen for bags of chips, apples, anything. She'd finally closed the door and turned off all of the lights, trembling. And still, the footsteps came.

This was Detroit. A city where there was no place to hide.

"Nikki? Nikki!"

Suddenly came her husband's voice on the stairs—the front stairs—his keys jangling in his hand. Nikki felt a wash of relief. "I'm in the tub getting ready. Where were you?"

"On an international conference call, couldn't get away to call you. Sorry."

Just like that, there he was grinning in the doorway, his teal silk tie setting off his russet complexion.

"Is that what you're wearing?" he asked, his eyes lingering on the bubbles glistening against her amber skin.

In his presence, the noises of the house silenced themselves. Her fears shriveled.

"Stop playing," she said. "Get dressed."

✳

There's no such thing as *a little bit pregnant.*

Nikki was surprised at how true the old adage was, how completely pregnancy had changed everything, though she was only nine weeks and barely showing. Even now, as Jason helped her into her plush, vintage Mouton coat, she felt a tip in the balance between them, something she hadn't known in their five-year marriage.

"Careful," he said, as he tucked her into the Cadillac.

Nikki noticed how her own senses had become heightened, almost feral. As they walked up the marble steps to the Detroit Institute of Arts, the cold spotlight of the moon caused her to squint. She could almost hear the clacking of the brittle limbs overhead as the autumn wind tossed the branches. Jason's cologne—the bottle she'd bought him on her last business trip to New York—was suddenly overpowering. She thought, too, that she could sense something uneasy in the way he guided her by the elbow into the Diaspora Ball.

No, she thought. It was her own insecurity. The long-coming surprise of a baby after two years of trying. The kind of doubts that a child can raise in even the most prepared couples.

Jason had been less than accepting when Nikki had presented him with the blue plus sign on the plastic stick. Maybe he'd been going along with her quest for a child because he'd come to believe that they'd never conceive. But the positive pregnancy test had called his bluff.

Suddenly, he'd been full of reasons why they shouldn't have a baby: he traveled too much; they didn't have enough savings; in Detroit, they'd have to commit to twelve years of private school, not to mention a nanny.

Nikki had listened to his rational arguments and smiled. At least he was thinking like a father, even if he wasn't sure he wanted to be one. Maybe what both of them needed was time to get used to the idea.

Since then, the baby had floated in the silent sea between them.

"Julie!" came Jason's greeting as he planted the customary kiss on an acquaintance's cheek. "Julie, you remember my wife? Nikki . . ."

Nikki smiled and offered a limp handshake. There was an effort at conversation—the Pistons, the mayoral election, the coming auto show—then on to another couple. Sipping club soda with a lime twist, Nikki soon found herself wandering away from Jason's salesman-like energy. She needed to breathe.

She found herself where she always ended up whenever she visited the art institute, even when she came there for Thursday night jazz or Sunday Brunch with Bach.

The N'konde, a nail figure from the Congo.

It was like no other artifact in the African collection. Standing nearly four feet tall and carved out of ebony, its features were oddly un-African—a jutting chin, sharp nose, and bony cheeks. Against the palette of the smooth, smoky wood were the figure's half-moon eyes, as white and dazed as a mummy's. Nikki hadn't noticed the cowrie shell belly button before. Suddenly it seemed to gape open rawly, like the figure had just been yanked from an umbilical cord.

What always drew her to the N'konde was its torso, jabbed and jammed with rusted nails, screws, and blades. According to the placard, when two parties reached an agreement, they'd drive a nail into its body to seal the oath. If anyone broke the promise, the N'konde's spirit would punish him.

This N'Konde's body was a garment of promises, spikes sticking horribly from its chest, belly, shoulders, and even its chin. The figure's mouth was partially open in a punctured surprise, its jagged teeth guarding a deeper darkness.

Nikki gazed at it in horrified fascination, wondering how the parties had decided where to impale the figure to seal a deal. What were they doing now, their contracts hijacked to this glass case, their promises forgotten and unaccounted for?

The din of the party nearly evaporated as Nikki stood there, entranced. The figure seemed to want to tell her something. She was suddenly aware of the low-grade nausea that was her constant companion. Her head started to swim.

Then came the sound—a man's familiar laughter echoing in the empty exhibit hall.

"What *else* do you want me to do to you?"

Low murmurs. A woman's muffled giggles.

Nikki thought she had heard that same sexy bass in her own ear many times. "Jason?" she whispered, as the N'konde stared, eyes hard white.

Her heart began to pound. Spinning around, she saw no one nearby. Wobbling, she wondered if she'd dreamed the voices. She fought to tamp the bile gathering at her throat. Heading into the crowd, she hoped to make an escape. She was nearly to the door when someone grabbed her arm.

"Nikki? I didn't know you were here!"

It was her sorority sister, Terry Hines, dressed, as always, in shades of pink and green.

"Hey, Terry," Nikki managed foggily.

"Girl, are you okay?"

Nikki blinked twice. *Try to get it together.* "I—I'm pregnant."

As soon as it left her lips, she regretted the slip. Detroit was a small, big town. People were constantly cross-pollinating. Gossip took root quickly.

"WHAT???" Terry shrieked, her garnet lips shimmering against her dark honey skin. Then, lowering her voice conspiratorially, she asked, "How far along are you? Do you need to sit down?"

Before she could answer, Jason was at her side. "There you are," he said, exasperated. "I was wondering where you'd wandered off to!" He sidled up to her, lovingly planting a kiss on her cheek.

"My God, Jason, Nikki just told me!" gushed Terry, not catching the look of foreboding in Nikki's eyes.

Jason glanced from Terry's exuberant face to Nikki's miserable one, sizing up the awkward pause.

"The baby?" Terry prompted.

Jason was taken aback, but tried to conceal it. "Oh!" he said, smiling uneasily. "Yeah! Imagine me—a dad!"

"We're not really telling people yet," Nikki said. "It's still early, you know . . ."

Terry's eyes grew large and she covered her mouth as if to cap a secret. "Of course," she said. "But I just know that everything will be fine."

"I'd better get you home," Jason said. "You look a little pale."

Nikki nodded, letting him lead her toward the door, his hand firm around her waist. Her body went limp against his, seeking forgiveness.

Outside, the night air had turned frosty, the flat moon giving the ground its luster.

"It slipped," Nikki said finally, as they waited for their car.

Jason nodded, but said nothing.

While they rode home, she glared at the sights along Woodward, the strange people with their nightshade business, shivering in the cold. She was tired, her bones heavy.

Jason noticed her trembling and turned up the heat. The fan only blew the freezing air harder and she reached up to close the vents. She could feel his eyes on her, but he said nothing to lighten the mood. The moon, yellowing as it rose, followed them home.

His silence humiliated her, and she wondered how he'd managed so quickly to turn the tables. Wasn't it he who'd just backed another woman against a display case and fondled her? Wasn't it he who'd suddenly been unable to come home on time like he used to, who always left her waiting, who wouldn't return her calls?

He pulled the Cadillac into their driveway, got out of the car, and walked around to her side to let her out. On the porch, he was about to put the keys in the lock, but instead he turned and looked at her.

"I don't want a baby," he said.

He stared at her, his eyes accusing her of ruining everything. But she stared back, her feet planted and steady, the queasiness fading into resolve.

"I do," she said back, the shivering now ceasing. "I do."

He lowered his eyes. For a long moment, he didn't speak. "It's cold out here," he said finally. "Let's talk inside."

He leaned to put the key in the door, but like a dark invitation, it swung open by itself. His eyes shot her a question: "Didn't you lock the door?" But it was too late.

Inside the house, the night moved.

Ghosts

Edwidge Danticat

Pascal Dorien was living in Bel Air—the Baghdad of Haiti, some people called it, but that would be Cité Pendue, an even more destitute and brutal neighborhood, where hundreds of middle-school children entering a national art contest drew M-16s and beheaded corpses, and wrote such things as "It's not polite to shoot at funeral processions" and "I'm happy to have turned in my weapons. What about you?" Bel Air was actually a mid-level slum. It had a few Protestant and Catholic churches, vodou temples, restaurants, bakeries, and dry cleaners, even Internet cafés. For a while, there were no gang wars; there was just one gang, whose headquarters were in a large empty warehouse, painted with murals of serpents, lions, and goats, and Haile Selassie and Bob Marley. The two dozen or so young male inhabitants of the warehouse called it Baz Benin, for reasons that only the person who came up with the tag knew for sure. That person, Piye, was killed when a special-forces team shot several bullets into the back of his head as he was lying in bed one night. The shooting was in retaliation for a series of fatal kidnappings, some of which the Baz Benin men had committed and some of which they had not. (The men of Baz Benin gave themselves the monikers of Nubian royalty, which also happened to suggest, in Creole, menacing acts—*piye,* for example, means "to pillage.")

Pascal's parents were shop owners and restaurateurs in Bel Air. They had a slightly larger yard than most of their crammed-in neighbors, so they had closed it off with sheets of rusty corrugated metal, and there, at four long wooden tables beneath a string of lightbulbs, which dangled from a second-story clostra-block window, they served up to thirty customers per night, if the turnover was fast. They sold rice and beans, of course, and fried plantains and cornmeal, but their specialty, for a long time, was fried pigeon meat.

Pascal's parents had moved to Bel Air at a time when the neighborhood was inhabited mostly by peasants, living there temporarily so that their children could finish primary school. But as the trees in the provinces vanished into charcoal and the mountains gave way, washing the country's topsoil into the sea, they, like the others, stayed and raised their two sons and at least a thousand pigeons, which, over the years, they sold both alive and dead.

Pascal's father had been a pigeon breeder since he was a boy in Léogâne. He'd stopped briefly in the early eighties, when some soldiers came and collected his birds because it was rumored that he was breeding carriers to send messages to armed invaders in the Dominican Republic. But when the dictatorship finally collapsed—without any help from his pigeons—he started again. Then most of his customers were nervous young men who wanted to perform a ritual before their first sexual encounter: they'd slit the pigeon's throat and let it bleed into a mixture of Carnation condensed milk and a carbonated malt beverage called Malta. Sometimes their fathers would come with them, and, after the sons had held their noses and forced down the drink, the fathers would laugh and say, as the pigeon's headless body was still gyrating on the ground, "I pity that girl."

It was a ritual that Pascal's parents didn't approve of. But for each bird that was killed this way they were paid enough to buy two more. They quietly mourned the days when people had bought pigeons as pets for their children. Then they began missing the days of the fathers and sons, because suddenly their customers were beefy young men who had gathered themselves into what were at first called "popular organizations," then gangs. The gang members, who were also called *chimès*—chimeras, or ghosts—were, for the most part, former street children who couldn't remember ever having lived in a house, boys whose parents had died or been murdered during the dictatorship, leaving them alone in a lawless and overpopulated city. Later, these young men were joined by deportees from the United States and Canada and by some older men from the neighborhood, aspiring-rap-musician types. The older local men were "connected"—that is, ambitious businessmen and politicians used them to swell the ranks of political demonstrations, giving them guns to shoot when a crisis was needed and having them withdraw when calm was required. Sometimes, before these demonstrations, so many men came for the milk-Malta-pigeon-blood mix that Pascal's parents were tempted to close the business for good. How had they become the people in whose yard pigeons were tortured and massacred? Finally, they released their last two pigeons. For a while, the birds kept coming back to nest, then someone in the neighborhood must have got to them, and Pascal's parents never saw that last pair again.

Still, with the money they'd made from the pigeons, Pascal's parents were able to expand their menu. They bought the house next door and added a few more tables. Pascal's father bought a pickup truck, which he drove back and forth between Léogâne and Port-au-Prince daily, packed with people and livestock. He was always at the restaurant, however, for the busiest time, from 7:00 p.m. till midnight, when the gang members, many of whom had by this time abandoned politics for the drug trade, took over the entire establishment. Watching these boys drift from being sellers to users of what they liked to call "the white man's powder," watching them grow unrecognizable to anyone but one another, Pascal's parents were disheartened and disgusted, but they kept the restaurant open, because, as they often acknowledged, the blight that had destroyed the neighborhood that had once been a kind of haven for the poor was allowing them to prosper, to send their children to school with the heirs of the country's tiny middle class. Although they could not afford the luxurious extras—holidays at the resorts of Jacmel and Labadie, or summers abroad with émigré relatives—their children were making contacts that might one day help them get good jobs and marriages. In order for their children to leave one day without ever having to look back, the Doriens had to stay.

Jules, Pascal's older brother, had already fulfilled this promise. For a long time, he had dated a girl whose parents were in Montreal. The girl had vowed that as soon as her visa came through she would marry Jules, so that she'd be able to send for him once she got to Canada. In the meantime, the government had turned over again, and the United Nations had come to train yet another police force. Jules had joined up, even though he was scrawny—barely five feet tall—and had a disproportionately large head, a distinctive family trait that had gained him the nickname Tèt Veritab, Breadfruit Head. But Jules had found that he couldn't be a policeman and live in the room he shared with Pascal above his parents' restaurant in Bel Air. Every time a neighborhood gang member was arrested, Jules was blamed for it. So he had moved in with his girlfriend's aunt and uncle for a few months, then married and left the country. Pascal had stayed, of course, and once Jules was gone no one bothered him or his parents.

When he wasn't helping out at the restaurant or going to computer-programming classes at a vocational school, Pascal worked as a news writer for Radio Zòrèy, one of the country's most popular stations. Having grown up in Bel Air and witnessed the changes there firsthand, Pascal imagined himself becoming the kind of radio journalist who could talk about the *geto* from the inside. An idea came to him one night as he was walking from the small concrete-block kitchen his parents had built next to the street—to tempt passersby with appetizing smells—to the table where Tiye ("to kill"), a one-armed, bald-headed gang leader, was nursing a beer and a massive cigar. Tiye was wearing his plastic-and-steel artificial arm under a long-sleeved white shirt and was expertly raising and lowering his beer with the shiny metal hooks of the prosthesis. Surrounded by three eager "lieutenants," Tiye was laughing so hard about the way he'd once slapped a man, back when he'd had both his arms—sandwiching the man's head between his arms and pounding his ears—that he had to dab tears from his eyes. Pascal, eavesdropping, wished that he had a video camera, or at least a tape recorder. He wanted the rest of the country to know what made these men cry. They cannot remain *chimès* to us forever, he thought. His show at Radio Zòrèy, if he was ever given one, would be called *Ghosts*. It would be controversial at first, but soon people would tune in by the thousands. A kind of sick voyeurism would keep them listening, daily, weekly, monthly, however often he was on. People would rearrange their schedules around it. They wouldn't be able to stop discussing it. "What are the people in the slums up to now?" they'd say. Then they'd be encouraged to figure out ways to alleviate the problems. Also featured on the program would be psychologists, sociologists, and urban planners.

Pascal's friend Max liked his pitch for the show. Max was a middle-class boy who lived in another type of neighborhood, one perched between affluence and despair. Max was not rich, like most of the children his mother taught at the Lycée Dumas, in the hills above Port-au-Prince, but. he was also not historically poor, like Pascal; you could tell this from the small gold stud earring that he always wore in his right ear. Max had started at the station as an afternoon d.j. when Kreyòl rap—hip-hop from the slums—was just beginning to make it to the airwaves. Sometimes, Pascal would slip Max a CD from one of Baz Benin's aspiring rappers, and Max would play it on his hour-long music program.

"I'm feeling everything you're saying, but the management won't buy it," Max said. He was keeping Pascal company while Pascal translated that day's newswires into conversational Creole for the announcer to read. "Who'd sponsor a show like that?"

"The government should sponsor it," Pascal said. "I'd be offering a public service."

But, just as his friend had predicted, the station's director turned him down. A few weeks later, while Pascal was typing that afternoon's news script, he overheard the news manager, a stuttering man who had been an inept police spokesperson, discussing a program called *Homme à Homme,* or *Man to Man.* The program would consist of a series of in-studio conversations between gang members and business leaders. "They'll hash out their differences," he heard the news manager say, "with the help of a trained arbitrator."

The first program paired the owner of an ice factory that had been broken into at least once a week over the past six months with a gang leader from Cité Pendue who was believed to have organized the "raids."

"What do you expect?" the gang leader told the owner. "You're chilling in all this ice while we're in Hell."

The arbitrator, a Haitian-American F.B.I.-trained hostage negotiator, then suggested the obvious—that the businessman find some way to sell his ice at a lower price to the people who lived near his factory, and that the gang leader respect the property of others.

Pascal was not at the station during the taping, but he heard part of the show on the radio at home. He could not hear the whole thing because he was helping at the restaurant that night and the taunting of both guests on *Homme à Homme* by Tiye and his crew was too loud. Many of the gang members had known about Pascal's plan—he had coyly approached some of them as possible guests for his show—and, as he served them their beers, they teased him, saying, "Man, they stole your idea." A few of them tried to grab him as he put the bottles on the table—as if to squeeze out the anger that they knew was building inside him. The more they laughed, the angrier he got. They could see it in the layer of sweat that was gathering on his face. Tiye was still laughing when he said, "Pascal, bro, I didn't like the way that *masisi* said that the guys in Cité Pendue had to leave the ice alone. I should find him and kick his ass."

"That's right," one of the lieutenants chimed in.

"Pascal," someone else said. "You should kick the ass of the guy who stole your show."

Just then Pascal's cell phone rang. It was Max.

"Man," Max said, "that guy stole your idea, and when I tried to call him on it do you know that he fired me?"

"You shouldn't have said anything," Pascal answered. "Now that you've lost your job, I'll probably lose mine, too."

Tiye and his guys were chanting, "We've got to kick his ass."

"The truth is," Pascal told Max, while passing an empty tray to his exhausted father, who was piling the last of the night's food onto a plate for himself, a cigarette dangling from his lips, "I've already put it out of my mind. *Homme à Homme* is not the show I wanted to do. I wanted to do something closer to the skin, something more personal."

After he got off the phone, Pascal waited for Tiye and his crew to leave. His mother and the neighborhood girls she'd hired were working on the dirty dishes. He asked if he could help, but they refused. His mother's stern face, darker than the bottom of the burned pot she was scrubbing, never really changed. It was as if the heat of the kitchen had melted and sealed it. Even if she never worked again for the rest of her life, whatever beauty she'd had when she first met his father would not come back.

That night, he persuaded his mother to go to sleep a little earlier than usual, before going to bed himself. In his room, where two cots faced each other from opposite walls that he and his brother had painted bright red, he felt Jules's absence in his gut. If he were younger, he might have started crying, the way kids cry for their mothers.

Leaving had been easier for Jules than anyone had expected. Because gang members had threatened him when he was a policeman, he'd filed for political asylum in Canada as soon as his wife's papers came through.

Now Jules was living in Montreal while Pascal was sleeping by himself in this ridiculously red room, his clothes hanging from nails that he and his brother had hammered into the walls. Jules called only once a week, on Sunday afternoons, though he could easily have called more often. Pascal and his parents all had cell phones now, and kept them charged and filled with usable minutes, waiting for him. Sometimes, as his mother fanned away the vapors from the food she was cooking, she'd let out a big sigh before saying, "I wonder what Jules is doing now." The truth was that Pascal was always wondering what Jules was doing. He was even thinking of asking Jules to find some way to send for him. If he were gone, he thought, his parents might finally give up the restaurant and move back to Léogâne, where they could breed pigeons again, freeing the birds in the morning and watching them return safely at dusk.

Pascal went to bed with all these thoughts swirling in his head, stirred up, he knew, by his disappointment over his show. Now it would be much harder for him to pitch the idea to another radio station. The programmers could always say, "But *Homme à Homme* is already airing. We don't want to give these gangsters too much of a platform." He fell asleep thinking that he'd have to redefine his idea, sharpen it up a bit. Maybe he'd add music to it. Max could help with that. They could play throbbing, urgent-sounding, reggae-influenced hip-hop, and, in between songs, he would let his neighbors speak.

He was still asleep the next morning when a dozen policemen with balaclava-covered faces, members of the special forces, knocked down the front gate of his parents' house, climbed up to his room, blindfolded him, and dragged him out of bed. He was not allowed to change out of his pajamas, even as his mother wailed uncontrollably and his father shouted that a great injustice was taking place.

By the time he arrived at the nearest commissariat, a small crowd of print, TV, and radio journalists—including his boss—were waiting for him. The night before, the police spokesperson, a shrill-voiced woman, explained, there had been a shooting at Radio Zòrèy. Four men with M-16s and machine guns had been seen jumping out of the back of a tan pickup truck. They had shot at the gates and windows of the three-story building, killing the night guard. The police had arrested Tiye, the notorious head of Baz Benin, and he had named Pascal as the mastermind of the operation, the person who had sent him and his men to do the job. Pascal was not allowed to speak at the press conference. He was simply forced to stand there, like a menacing prop, surrounded by the still-hooded special-forces team, with his chafed wrists handcuffed behind his back.

The box of a room where he was taken to be questioned was hot, with the stench of fresh vomit in the air. In addition to the rusty metal chair on which he was placed, with his hands still cuffed, it had a fluorescent light whose flickering beams penetrated the black cloth that covered his eyes.

During his questioning, he was repeatedly punched on the back of the neck.

"Do you know Tiye?" one of his interrogators asked, sucking on a cigarette and blowing the smoke in his face.

"Yes," Pascal replied, coughing. His lungs seemed to be closing down. The constriction forced pieces of last night's dinner onto the front of his pajama top and, when he was allowed to bend his neck, down to his lap.

The questions continued. "How do you know Tiye?"

"He lives in my neighborhood and often eats at my parents' restaurant," he stammered.

"You're a big man, huh? Your parents have a restaurant in the slums. I'm hungry now. Feed me. Feed me."

The officers were laughing even as he hiccuped and sobbed. To his ear, there was no difference between their laughter, their taunting, and that of Tiye and his crew. They could all have switched places, and no one would notice.

"How much did you pay the crew from Baz Benin to shoot at the station?" someone else asked.

"Nothing . . . I . . ."

"So they did it for free?"

They threw freezing water in his face. Panicked, he tried to rise from the chair, but several hands shoved him back down. Between the smoke, the vomit, and the water, he felt as though he were drowning.

After the questioning, he was left alone in a dank cell. That afternoon, his mother and father came to see him. They were allowed to kneel next to him on the floor, where he was lying in a fetal position, and remove his blindfold.

"Pascal, *chéri*." His mother wept quietly, while his father supported her with one hand beneath her armpit and the other firmly pressed against her back.

"Pascal, could you have done such a thing?" his father asked. He sounded stern, as though scolding his son.

Pascal shook his head. His throat ached, and he could taste the vomit still lingering in his mouth. His father, he knew, needed a denial from him in order to proceed with his fight.

"They're not beating me too badly," he said, to fill the silence. "Not yet, anyway. You see I have no blood on me."

The mother raised his filthy pajama top to look for cuts, wounds.

"The lawyer we got for you," his father said, "her cousin is a judge. She says she's going to try to move things along very fast."

Years earlier, under the dictatorship, Pascal's father had had a facial tic—a quick batting of his eyes and an involuntary twitching of his mouth. Now it had returned. Pascal had not seen it in such a long time that he had almost forgotten about it.

"They'll probably take you to the court, to Parquet, this afternoon," his father continued, despite the spasms in his face. "Then you might possibly go to the Pénitencier, to jail, for a few days, until we get you out."

From Montreal, Jules had told his parents what to say and do. Jules had called the lawyer, who'd successfully represented many of his old police buddies in corruption cases, and was paying her himself. He had also phoned many of his police friends and his former bosses, including the secretary of state, on whose security detail he had briefly worked. Then he had called Tiye's people, telling them that Tiye must have misunderstood. Pascal would never have asked them to shoot up the radio station. If they had meant to do him a favor, they'd failed.

Everyone Jules was able to reach, including Tiye's second-in-command, told him to stay calm. The case against Pascal was a *lamayòt*, a vapor. Nothing was going to stick. Give it a few more hours. Let it cool off.

✳

Pascal was on a fast track, it seemed. After his parents left, a black-robed magistrate came in and informed him of the charges against him. Later that afternoon, more charges were filed. Now he was said to be not only the mastermind of the radio-station shooting but someone the police had been seeking for a long time. In him they'd found a scapegoat for a whole tally of unsolved crimes.

Because of the additional charges, the lawyer asked for more money. They should consider paying off a judge, she said. Twenty thousand dollars. American.

"This is a kind of kidnapping," Jules hollered on the phone from Montreal. Jules had not eaten all day. In despair, he was trying to deprive himself as well. He was expecting his brother to rot in an overcrowded cell at the Pénitencier or simply to disappear before he got there. Pascal's parents were preparing to sell their business to buy Pascal's release. That evening, having slept through the dinner hour in his cell, with his face pressed against a cool groove on the floor, Pascal saw a line of black shiny boots marching toward him. He was blindfolded again and thrown into the backseat of a police jeep.

"Who does he know?" the officer who put him there asked. "What are they going to tell people?"

"That they made a mistake," another voice answered.

He was dumped in front of his parents' restaurant at ten that night.

✳

Tiye, it turned out, had made some kind of deal with the police for his and Pascal's release. Rumor had it that after he became the head of Baz Benin, Tiye had collected highly incriminating drug-related dirt on everyone, from the lowest street cop to Supreme Court judges. Whether it was true or not, it was said that he possessed a slew of records, from videos and audiotapes to copies of contracts and bank statements, which were being held by relatives of his in Miami. The day he was killed—or convicted of a crime—they were supposed to send the records to a certain reporter at the Miami *Herald*, who would publish everything.

Later that night, Jules cheered on the phone. "Mamman and Papa will have to leave now," he said.

But Pascal wasn't sure where they would go. "Back to the countryside?" he wondered aloud to his brother. "To the hills? To you?"

These were all possibilities, Jules told him. "Urgent possibilities," he added. "Home is not always a place you have trouble leaving."

Pascal, now showered and clean, was lying in bed as his parents hovered, handing him water, juice, creams for his skin. It was nearly midnight. His mother had not cooked that evening, but her customers had still come for cigarettes and drinks and to offer their sympathies over Pascal's arrest and their congratulations on his release.

When Pascal got off the phone, one of the girls from the kitchen came up to say that Monsieur Tiye was downstairs and wanted to see him.

"We'll go first," his father said, the tic returning in a milder version.

His parents filed out dutifully, their bodies tense with a new level of worry. What could Tiye want now? Did he want to be paid?

In the yard, Tiye and his lieutenants were already settled at a table, with drinks provided for them by the girls.

"No need to pay tonight," the father said.

Tiye had a few extra guys with him for protection. They listened with rapt attention as he described what he'd been through. "I was afraid they were going to shoot me," he was saying. "You know how they take some of the guys out to the woods in Titanyen and put them down. I was afraid that was going to happen to me."

He said this casually, almost matter-of-factly, with a kind of amused air that indicated that, if this had happened, it would not have been a big deal. This was perhaps how Tiye and his guys faced the inevitable, Pascal thought. Crossing the yard on shaky legs, he realized that he shared this with them. This was perhaps what Tiye had tried to teach him by turning him in and then rescuing him. One day, they would all be shot. Like the night guard at Radio Zòrèy, like Tiye's predecessor, Piye. Like almost every young man who lived in the slums. One day, it might occur to someone, someone angry and powerful, someone obsessive and maniacal—a police chief or a gang leader, a leader of the opposition or a leader of the nation—that they, and all those who lived like them or near them, would be better off dead.

Pascal stopped at Tiye's table and held out a hand to him.

"No hard feelings?" Tiye said, pounding his fist on his chest, near his heart, in greeting.

Pascal noticed, and not for the first time, that Tiye's gums were bright red, as though he had a perpetual infection or had been eating raw meat.

"Did they jack you up?" Tiye asked Pascal.

"Wasn't so bad," he said.

Tiye wasn't wearing his prosthetic arm, and the sleeve of his bright-yellow shirt sagged. With his good hand, he motioned for the guy who was sitting next to him to get up so that Pascal could sit down.

Pascal looked again at the space where Tiye's missing arm would have been. He thought he saw something white, as though a polished piece of bone were protruding. He tilted his head to see it better, while trying not to seem obvious. He almost checked his own body to see if anything was gone.

In his dreams, Pascal had imagined beginning his radio program with a segment on lost limbs. Not just Tiye's but other people's as well. He would open with a discussion of how many people in Bel Air had lost limbs. Then he would go from limbs to souls, to the number of people who had lost family—siblings, parents, children—and friends. These were the real ghosts, he would say, the phantom limbs, phantom minds, phantom loves that haunt us, because they were used, then abandoned, because they were desolate, because they were violent, because they were merciless, because they were out of choices, because they did not want to be driven away, because they were poor.

It was his mother who brought the last beers to the table, and for the first time in his life he could see between her furrowed eyebrows a disdain for those she served. She avoided their eyes as she lifted the bottles from her metal tray and placed them between the coconut-shell ashtrays on the hibiscus-patterned plastic tablecloth. Pascal waited for her to return to the kitchen before raising his drink toward Tiye and clinking the top of his bottle with his. Tiye's bottle struck his with force. Pascal saw a brief spark, and the top of his bottle broke apart, leaving a jagged gap in the glass. A shard landed on the table with a splash of beer; another fell to the hardened clay floor at his feet.

Tiye flashed his bright-red gums and pointed his intact beer bottle in Pascal's direction. "You wanted to know what it's like for us," he said. "I just thought I'd give you a taste."

Tiye filled his mouth with beer and swished it around loudly, as if he were gargling with mouthwash.

"Don't worry," he added to Pascal, but also, it seemed, to himself. "As long as I'm here, nothing will happen to us tonight."

Been Meaning to Say

Amina Gautier

Leslie Singleton awoke to the unexpected drone of a lawn mower. It was late November and he and his neighbors had long since stopped cutting the grass. He'd fallen asleep on the couch again and as he rose a cramp stiffened his neck. With Iphigenia now gone, no one threw bedspreads over him, nudged his shoes off, slipped pillows under him, or did anything to make him more comfortable. The remote was on his lap, the *Philadelphia Inquirer* was folded on the end table by his side, and the TV was on, but he couldn't remember what he'd been watching before he'd fallen asleep. Now, without Iphigenia, such a simple thing as that had become difficult for him to do.

Joey Leibert was outside in the neighboring yard doing the edges with his cordless grass trimmer. Every so often, he'd get too close and the line of cord would slap against the metal stake of the fence and he'd have to bump the feed head to continue.

"You're either too early or you're too late," Leslie called, standing between his open door and screen door.

The lanky white man looked around for the voice. When he saw Leslie, he waved. "How ya doing Mr. Singleton? Just giving her a little trim." He switched the trimmer off.

"You should let the lawn alone, Joey. It'll be snowing soon enough."

"The agent's bringing a family by tomorrow. I wanna make it look nice for them." He winked. "With any luck, this will be my last time."

"They're going to look at a house on Thanksgiving?"

"That's the plan."

"Good family?" Leslie asked.

Joey Leibert shrugged. "If they've got the down payment, they're good enough for me."

Leslie laughed with him. "How's your Ma doing?"

Joey Leibert kicked at the guard protector to knock stray cuttings loose. "She's great. Just great."

"How's she like the place?"

"Oh she likes it just fine." Joey Leibert raked the yard. "She won't have to worry about maneuvering up and down these steps come winter. That can be real hard on the knees when you get to be old."

Leslie tapped his leg and smiled grimly. "I know."

"Come on, Mr. Singleton. You're not that old."

"Getting there."

"Your Carole's years behind me. How's she doing anyway?"

"Coming for Thanksgiving. Bringing the husband and the boy."

"Hah," Joey said. "Sounds like you're all set."

The phone rang inside and Leslie excused himself to Mrs. Leibert's son, which was how he always thought of Joey, even after all this time.

✳

They could not possibly come and stay with him for the short break, his daughter said. Carole spoke to him in a no-nonsense voice, as if she were talking to one of her undergrads and not her own father. She was on her cellular phone and Leslie wanted her signal to go in and out as it sometimes did so he would lose the last of her words.

It cut him that she would spend the holidays with her husband's family and not him. Especially when she'd promised. He remembered it clearly. A week after the funeral, she'd called to check on him. When he heard her voice, so like her mother's, he'd started to weep into the phone. It was then that she'd promised to bring the family to stay with him for the Thanksgiving break, her way of soothing a grieving old man. It was May then, and she'd had to cancel her students' finals and give them take-homes in order to be in Philadelphia for the wake and funeral. She and her husband were sending their son to camp for the summer since they had gotten some sort of grant to do research in some sort of humanities center. She'd given him some long story about junior faculty productivity and procuring tenure, which was supposed to explain why he wouldn't see any of them that summer. Their next break was Thanksgiving, and she'd promised she'd bring her family to stay and it would be just like old times, except without Iphigenia. Now she said she couldn't stay, but they might drop by for a few hours on Thanksgiving Day, which wasn't the same at all.

He told her so.

She said, "Dad, you have to be reasonable. Martin's parents—"

"—Is it because—" He had cut her off, but he couldn't continue, couldn't say the words.

"Because what, Dad?"

"Just give me the truth. Why don't you just say it?"

"Say what?" she asked. Then: "Fine. It's not the same anymore with Mom gone. We really don't want to stay the night."

"Why?" he asked her.

Never one to pull punches, his daughter said, "I don't want my son growing up like I did," she said.

"What was wrong with your childhood, honey?" he asked, wondering if he'd ever left her alone with an uncle or male cousin.

"You were."

"Me?" he said. "Me?"

"Don't act so surprised, Dad. You. Yes, you and your attitude."

"Attitude?"

"Are you going to repeat everything I say? Amir, leave that alone honey before you break it," he heard her say. "Fine. Then put it in the trunk for Mom, okay? Thank you. Martin, take that away from him." Then she was back again. "Dad, you've always been very unapproachable. Mom was always there to smooth things over after you'd fluffed them. Mom always had to pick up the slack. She had to do extra just to make up for you. Now there's no one to cover for you."

"It wasn't like that," he said.

"I call them like I see them, Dad," she said. "I was there too, you know. Excuse me a second, Dad. Amir—" He heard the sounds of traffic before she placed the phone against something so he couldn't hear her.

He never thought of himself as having deficiencies or of his wife having to compensate for them. Not his Iphigenia. She was just a loving and generous woman. A keeper of the peace. It was in her nature to make things right.

Everything began and ended with Iphigenia. It took Leslie almost three years of marriage to her before he got up the courage to ask her about her name. He'd thought it an uncommon name, especially for a black woman born in the 1930s. Before her, he'd met his share of Esthers and Eunettas, Anna Maes and Audreys, Marians and Mabels, names that were old-fashioned even back then. His good buddy Roland had set him up on his first date with Iphigenia. Leslie had never before met an Iphigenia and he'd been impressed before he even saw her legs. It wasn't every day a man met a woman with a name like that and he strove to be worthy of her. He'd made a vow to himself that he would not become one of those husbands who shortened his wife's name out of convenience. He would preserve his wife's name in its entirety, never referring to her as Ginny or anything other than Iphigenia.

Iphigenia, sacrificed for favorable winds.

"I'm back," Carole said.

"Can you at least let the boy stay over, even if it's just one night?"

"Dad, the boy is my son. His name is Amir."

"I can't remember all the time."

"There's nothing wrong with your memory. You just don't want to say his name and give my son the respect he deserves. Maybe it would be better for us not to come."

"Respect? Since when do eight-year-olds get respected? Besides, I just don't like saying those mumbo jumbo names."

"It is not a mumbo jumbo name, Dad. It's Arabic. It means prince. Ruler. We've gone over this before."

Arabic or not, Leslie thought his grandson's name sounded just as silly as the names he'd been hearing slapped on children lately. It seemed that every time he turned around, children were being named after cars, medicines, and condiments. "Neither you nor Martin is Muslim. Why's he need an Arabic name?"

"We wanted something with meaning. Something that reflected our pride in our African heritage and culture."

The way he saw it, Carole was a generation too late for names with meanings. Her generation had gotten all of the real African or Arabic names. Iphigenia had wanted Carole to be named Naima because it meant tranquil and benevolent. Naima sounded too much like Naomi to him and Naomi sounded too much like somebody whining. So they named her

Carole since she was born on Christmas Eve. It seemed to him that the generation that had purposefully chosen African and Arabic names as symbols of pride had given way to a newer generation of illiterate parents willing to slap anything on a child and call it a name. It wasn't safe to have a meaningful name anymore. People were liable to confuse the meaningful and the made-up. "Meaning," Leslie said. "Not something like Carole, you mean. I guess being named after the birthday of our Lord Jesus Christ can't compare to being a Muslim prince."

His daughter sighed as if she'd been waiting for him to say exactly that. "And you wonder why I'm not bringing him over?"

Leslie went back outside after Carole hung up, but Mrs. Leibert's son was already gone. The Leiberts' lawn was short and manicured now, no ragged edges, no unsightly exterior to warn away a prospective buyer.

Overbrook was still a good neighborhood. The Leiberts in the twin next door were the last white family to move off the block. Mrs. Leibert had been having trouble making it up and down the stairs for four years before her son the pharmacist finally convinced her to move into an assisted living facility. For three months, Leslie had been watching the agents and potential buyers go in and out of Mrs. Leibert's house. The Leiberts had been living there when he and Iphigenia first moved in, long before they ever had Carole. He'd never been inside, but he could guess at the peeling paint on the bathroom's water-stained ceiling, the old white tile, the Formica kitchen, the living room's wood-paneled walls identical to the inside of his house. The Leiberts' son Joey was a full ten years older than his own Carole. Joey was a good boy, even though he had moved his mother out of the only house she'd ever known. He'd come every other Sunday afternoon to mow the little patch of grass in front of the house, and twice a week in the winter to shovel the snow and salt the steps. In the fall, he'd bag the fallen leaves and set them on the curb. Still, it must have been a lot for a man to do when he had his own family and his own leaves and his own grass and his own snow, his own seasons to cultivate and his own winter to beat back with the force of his shovel.

With Iphigenia there, their house had pleased him. The slow deterioration of it had not gone unnoticed. The paint on the ceiling was chipping and the windows needed new caulking, but who had time for those things? It was hard work, keeping a house. Things had a way of slipping through, coming undone. But they were too busy getting on with the business of life. They put off the household repairs to take a line-dancing class. To have friends over for Bid Whist, then a few hands of pinochle.

Now, with Iphigenia gone, he did none of those things alone, and the house mocked him. It had never been the money so much as the time. You needed time to fix a house. Time to let someone come in and do the work. With Iphigenia around he'd had none. Now he had more time than he could stand. No longer could he pretend the house's disrepair was the sign of a busy and happy couple rather than that of an old man himself in need of repairs.

Soon, in the seasons to come, he'd have to pay a stranger for his up-keep. There would be no one to trim his grass and rake his leaves when he could no longer do it himself. Leslie didn't have a Joey. He only had a Carole.

✳

Back in the kitchen, Leslie placed a frozen turkey in a basin of cold water and hoped it would thaw in time. Iphigenia had always made the Thanks-giving dinner, but he had been willing to try. He would have split the wishbone with his grandson, pretending to have no strength so the boy would pull off the larger part.

He wasn't asking for much. They wouldn't even have had to spend that much time with him. Everyone would have had their own room. As al-ways, there were the three bedrooms upstairs. His and Iphigenia's master bedroom at the front of the house, above the enclosed porch. Carole's room at the back of the house, over the kitchen and mudroom. The mid-dle room, smallest of all three, had never belonged to anyone, but slowly, over the years, Iphigenia had come to claim it for herself. She'd had the reclining chair brought up there. He didn't remember getting it up the stairs but somehow he must have because it was there, right by the radia-tor, just like she'd wanted it. She'd had him put her console sewing ma-chine in there, too, though she kept the machine folded under so the whole thing looked like a small table. She'd used it to set her drinks and reading glasses down. The room was cluttered with things that had mean-ing only to her and, except for the slippers, he'd left it exactly as it had been the last time she'd sat in the recliner, the night he'd found her dead.

He would have given the boy Iphigenia's room. There was no bed in there, but there was a serviceable cot in the basement that he could have brought up. He'd have liked it, Leslie knew. Though small, the room was inviting.

Those slippers were the only things he'd disturbed. Her very last pair of house slippers. He'd bought them for her so she'd stop wearing his. His were dark leather, with strips that crisscrossed over the toes, the kind you could buy in any discount store. His Iphigenia would slip into his too large slippers and wear them all through the house, the backs flapping along the floor without the weight of a man's heels to ground them.

Leslie waited a month after she died before he took her slippers from the middle room. Carrying them one in each hand as if to prevent each slipper from knowing its fate, he brought them into the master bedroom. He knelt by Iphigenia's side of the bed and placed them there. There they waited. She needed only to return, slide out of bed, and slip right back into them.

They were god-awful ridiculous-looking slippers. Boudoir slippers made of lavender satin with short heels and a bit of fluff across the bridge of the toes. The kind of slippers women wore in the movies he'd grown up watching. Women with thinly drawn eyebrows and shoulder-length beveled curls and Cupid's bow mouths. Women with vanity tables and silver-backed brushes. Women clad in long silky negligees with matching robes with fur at the collar and cuffs. And slippers. Women wearing the daintiest matching slippers. Those lavender slippers had cost him thirty-eight dollars before tax, eight times the price of his own and Iphigenia hadn't even liked them. She pretended she did, but he had known by the half-hearted way she'd pranced when she modeled them. He could still hear her forced enthusiasm, "Look at me. Dorothy Dandridge! Ms. Lena Horne! Watch out, Greta Garbo! Move over Lauren Bacall."

Loneliness was inevitable without her. He missed his wife, to be sure. Her presence and smell and the way she never rolled her hair at night tight enough to keep the small hard pink and yellow rollers from slipping off and rolling under him. He missed getting up to close the window because she'd gone to sleep with it open even though he warned her about catching colds. He missed the way she said "Mmmhmm" right before going to sleep, knowing it meant I love you. He missed working with her. Arguing over their daughter's faults. Iphigenia thought Carole could do no wrong, but he thought she'd outgrown them, relying too much on what was in a book rather than what she knew to be so. She believed anything she read and now that she was a professor at a college he'd never heard of she got paid to read more of those books and write articles about what she'd read.

Whenever he and Carole argued, Iphigenia had been there to smooth things over, to keep the peace. To remind them that the reason they quarreled was because their temperaments were so similar. "Headstrong," she'd say. "The both of you are just two mules and I've got all the carrots."

Maybe Carole was right. Iphigenia had been sacrificing herself a little each day to smooth his way over and keep his paths clear. Maybe that was why she passed before him. Perhaps she had just grown tired of looking after him. He'd always thought he'd be the first to go.

More than anything he missed her being there with him, missed the presence of a spouse, missed having her know him so well he could turn to her and say, "Isn't that right?"

They'd gotten spoiled, he and Iphigenia. They'd had only each other for so long that he sometimes thought of their daughter as a presence intruding on their routine. They'd been childless for fourteen years before Carole came along, so it was hard not to think of Iphigenia as someone he had all to himself. He was old enough to be his daughter's grandfather. Maybe they *had* left Carole out. They'd been so used to just each other for so long that, once their daughter came along, they didn't know what to do with her. He'd treated her like a guest, a relative come to stay just until she could get back on her feet again, the way Carole didn't want her son to be treated.

He could try, but he could not promise. There were times when he would look at his grandson and think what a fine boy he was, sometimes even getting teary enough to wish he could live to see the boy graduate from college. There had been times when he and the boy would be in the living room together and he would mean to reach out for him, to encourage him or pat his shoulder, but as often as he thought it, Leslie stayed in his chair and watched the boy playing on the carpet, running his truck around in circles in the area between the TV and the coffee table. He spoke only when the boy did things he thought children ought not do. "Back up some from the TV," he'd say. "You're going to strain your eyes like that." Not what he'd been meaning to say at all.

He'd call his daughter and apologize. He'd cook Thanksgiving dinner anyway and hope to convince her to bring her husband and the boy. They could go back to Martin's parents' house afterwards. All he wanted was a little time with them.

Carole didn't answer. His call went straight to the voice mail. He wondered if she'd turned her phone off just so she wouldn't have to speak to him. "Carole honey, it's Dad. I'm sorry about what I said. I didn't mean any of it and if you bring your family over tomorrow I promise I'll try and do better. All right, that's all I have to say. 'Bye now. Hope to see you real soon."

Leslie put the bird in the oven early the next morning, not trusting the instructions on the plastic. He made the stuffing on top of the stove. He made the stuffing from a box and got his string beans and cranberry sauce from cans. His biscuits he'd bought frozen. There would be no pies and he had never liked collard greens.

He had been watching the parade on TV when he heard a car door slam outside his house. He looked out of the enclosed porch's window, but it wasn't Carole. A white woman and a black family emerged from the car.

The couple dressed neutrally, casually, the way they'd probably learned to dress in case the owners were at home and not as well-to-do. Their clothes were unlabeled and understated, yet expensive. The woman's dreadlocks were a lighter shade of brown than the unlocked hair at her scalp; the man was bald. They each carried a young child, but Leslie couldn't tell if the children were twins or not.

The agent entered the code into the lockbox and removed the key. She opened the screen door, unlocked the front door, and motioned them to enter. Before they did, the woman re-clipped her daughter's barrette and kissed the top of the little girl's head. The husband followed after his wife, pretending to bump the daughter he carried against the door's frame. The girl's surprised giggle followed the family into the house, where Leslie could not see them.

There inside, the agent would convince them.

Don't buy it! Leslie wanted to shout. Not just because you have those children and you think this is a better environment for them to grow up in. Not just so they can play safely in their own yards. Not just to keep them from the riffraff. Don't buy this house for them. They will grow up and they will leave it. They will leave you. They will scorn what you have saved for. They will want apartment complexes with personal parking spaces. They will not want to wake up each day and set garbage cans out on the street just to protect their parking space until they get home. They will want central air. Hardwood floors will not move them. Once they are no longer children they will not find joy in sliding across a waxed floor in their socks, pretending that they are ice-skating. Instead they will want to cover that floor up with thick, plush carpet. Your son will say Berber like it's the name of his mistress. Your daughter will shop for fixtures the way your wife shopped for lingerie.

He did not wait for them to return to their car. He will meet them after closing. After they reach settlement, he will see them slowly moving in. He will wend his way around their two daughters who will not keep to their side of the steps. He will see them when he comes out to sweep his front yard clear of the snack bags and straw wrappers their daughters leave behind when they go down the block to jump rope. By that time, they will see in him only an old man, crotchety and disgruntled, bothered by the smallest things, unvisited and alone.

Maybe his daughter will make friends with the wife. Maybe his family and their family will smile at each other over their grills, folding chairs, and coolers when they barbeque on the Fourth of July. Maybe his grandson will torment those two could-be twin girls and they will run to him for succor, but he would give them no satisfaction. He'd take his grandson's part and shoo them away, reminding them that boys will be boys.

When Leslie poked the turkey with a fork, the juices ran bloody.

It was too much for a man to have to do. He turned the oven off on the underdone bird. He would not wait for them to come. He sat at his dining room table, stiff and upright like a guest. He ate his side dishes straight from the pots. He ate methodically, taking small bites to make the meal last. Leslie Singleton ate with unwavering vigilance, for, if he relaxed, he'd soon move to the couch in front of the TV. He'd switch from the parade to catch a little of the Eagles game. Next thing he'd find himself nodding off. Then he'd awaken to that funny sour morning taste that said he'd slept too long, that thickness of head and tongue that let him know he'd drifted off. From there, it would be nothing to convince himself to head on up to bed. Upstairs he'd have to pass that middle room and see Iphigenia's recliner and the empty space at the foot of it where her slippers had been. It would take everything in him just to make it to his bed and climb over the pair of slippers he dared not sacrifice.

The Torturer's Wife

Thomas Glave

But in the earlier days, these deadwomen are saying (sitting in a circle, in a muddy field far from any homes or people, long after dark)—*in the earlier days,* they are saying, *she truly* had not *known. No. Of course not,* they say. *A young laughing girl like that, as she had been when she first came to* Him, He *to her? And what a figure she'd had!* one woman says, sighing out of what remains of her face. *A gorgeous young thing, she was back then, even while falling in love with* Him. *What do you mean "even while"?* asks another. (The Lost Whore without Arms, they call her. She is remembering now the feelings on her fingers of rings. Her fingers, like her arms, now somewhere at the bottom of the sea.) *Especially while, you mean to say. O yes, well,* He *had that effect on her. On every woman,* another says, known among them as the One Who Never Stops Sobbing. (And it is true—since her death twenty-nine days ago, she hasn't. Sobbing now and still wearing the necklace of blood that He had given her.) *On every woman who survived* His *attentions, you mean,* says an old, toothless one, bent over to the point that what remains of her forehead touches the ground before her. *Yes, and the same for every man* He *favored also,* laughs another. They all laugh. And laugh some more. But they soon grow quiet, knowing that they will not be here long—for they are dead, after all, just a bunch of deadwomen with scars over their rotting flesh and amputations in a few places. If this is a dream—and tonight it is, once again, as always, her bluewashed dream of them—who can stand to gaze upon them for long?

In complete darkness, they all are sitting in a circle, in this field whose ground lately has become muddy; that changes color minute to minute from brown to black to blueblackbrown; that changes color, moves beneath the body, and sucks at the private parts.

Those who still have complete faces try, from time to time, to look at each other.

Soon, all of them will feel a terrible, stabbing pain in their breasts (in what remains of their breasts, for a few). The pain will sear out of their decaying flesh to consume them utterly. The flames will come then—bright orange licks that will roast them unto blackest ash. They will scream, will feel unimaginable pain—worse than the pain that, in one of the secret places underground, had finally killed them—but how can they know that the flames that will finally incinerate them will, at least in this dream, be the direct rage of the dreamer? How can any of them know how much she, even while feeling their deaths and obliteration, hates them? Hates them *because,* she dreams, *even while He had electrified some of them in the secret underground place hidden from all vision, then defingernailed them, then watched His uniformed minions sew their eyelids shut with the coarse thread commonly used* (now twitching; grasping at the nightdark air that thickens her bedroom; feeling herself choking on black water in the dream, but still unable to awaken)—*even through all that, especially through all that, He had always loved putting His hands on them. In them. Had loved, between electric shocks to their inside parts, pushing Himself into them and then watching His uniformed minions do the same. Zippers and flesh opening as the minions did the same, sometimes with gloved fists, the entire ritual enhanced by muffled screams beneath urinesoaked gags as the manacles had clack-clacked about those many slender wrists and the single burning lightbulb above had continued to glare.* (She dreams. Twitches. Chokes on the rage that refuses to awaken her. *Because it is true,* she dreams: *He had always been handsome, even beautiful: still was.*) *So many dying and deadwomen beneath a naked lightbulb suspended far beneath the ground. The women who are gathered there now in complete darkness, sitting in that circle.*

The women who try from time to time—those who still have complete faces—to look at each other.

Being a witness is never easy, one of them thinks.

They return frequently. (She tosses on the pillow. Lying next to Him. Listening, in the deepest passages of her dream, to the sounds of His breathing next to her. He is there. Do the deadwomen now watching her chest rise and fall, and her tossing, quail before the sight of Him?) Frequently, among many other voices. Yes.

She truly had not known. Hadn't known, when, younger, she was still the laughing, glowing creature, about all those secret rooms. Twisted limbs. Eyelids sewn shut. Lighted cigarettes pressed into—but O my God, I just can't take it anymore, one of them screams out. (She tosses on the pillow. He breathes. She registers His breathing. She tosses. Where, right now, can there be an actual space for her hands?) *And so the laughing, glowing creature she had been had soon disappeared over the years, hadn't she, as the knowledge slowly, inevitably, became more, more . . . more inescapable, she herself came to think on the heels of all those increasingly thick-blue-dreamed nights, those hours lying beside Him . . . hours filled with listening to Him breathe. In. Out. Wondering what it would be like to hear Him breathe no longer. In, out.* The soughing words once known only by deadwomen and deadmen (and who knew how many deadchildren) had finally been carried into her nights even by the things she had trusted for so long: the reliable evening breezes, seasonal rains, and the spreading sea that she had so long believed to be her friend. But at last even the sea had betrayed her—reviled her, when, on that afternoon not so long ago, in an hour when she had sought its caresses against her tender skin, it had thrown out to her from its depths that sightless chorus of mermaids. Those voices obsessed with

"falling,"

they had sung, gazing directly at her out of those sightless eyes,

"and planes."

But do not blame her, one of the deadwomen beseeches the others, even as she begins, with them, to feel the first fire licking at her flesh. *For who can know exactly what she will do when, soon enough, that rainfall of most secret parts clatters, in moonlight, upon her roof? How will she feel about the sea then?*

And about Him, the others murmur as the flames, in the field and beyond it, begin to roast their flesh—

*And So Once Again Hating (But Really Fearing) Moonlight. With Difficult
Breathing, and Skulls*

Yes, it is true. She abhors the moonlight.

Lying next to Him, breathing in His night scents and the sweat glistening on the back of His neck, she does her best to close her eyes against it.

It frightens me, she thinks, *the way it shines so brightly, insistently, on
skulls.*

(*The skulls that return every night,* she dare not think.)

It terrifies me, she thinks, *the way it exposes all those skeletons out there in
the garden—in the garden,* she thinks, *where all those skulls are or soon will
be. Out there,* she tries so desperately not to think, *where I know all those
hands lie waiting. Waiting—*

(But tonight is still weeks away from the time she will send the principal maid out there to sweep up that most unbearable rainfall of hands.)

The moonlight, she knows, reveals skulls. Gleaming. Grinning. Skulls
of bodies dumped "somewhere out there," she thinks, "in the secret
places that everyone pretends don't exist." The moonlight reveals
"teeth," she thinks (but trying so hard right now not to breathe Him in),
"that all the truncheons knocked out. Scattered like dice. And fingernails," she thinks (but how can she bear to think of *that?*), "—that all the
men, working down there, in all those secret rooms everyone says don't
exist, wrenched out. With pliers," she thinks, screwing shut her eyes,
clenching her fists, "and other tools. Hammers—"

Moonlight, she thinks, listening for the clattering of the first skull's
teeth outside, surely, in the front garden. One of them will soon come.
One of them always, in the dream-hours, comes. Hangs. *Hovers. Moonlight,* she thinks, *reveals too much. Like the most vulnerable kind of face,* she
thinks, *capable of hiding nothing.*

Song (but from a Chorus of Mermaids). The Madwoman, in Flight

But now here: of an afternoon in a place that she will insist is part of another dream, although today she actually is here: a long, narrow beach of
sand and salt, salt everywhere (so she dreams, insists she is dreaming,
right now): salt and all that water, that so-enormous water she had once
(but why?) believed to be her "friend," she had mused, and somehow
"protector"—pulling her legs down. *Down.* It is here, in what she has
managed to convince herself is this afternoon's dream, that she will refuse

to see them. Refuse to see the women whom she had seen long ago in the bluegreengray waters of so many other dreams. The same women whose bodies, this afternoon, will shortly surface and surface again from beneath that sea's curling waves. She is here, alone (and so happy for once to be alone—out in the sunlight so much is easier)—on this beach: not the dirtier, more dangerous public beach accessible to all, but this private one where she and people like her can come without care to bathe, to laugh; to delight in the unexpected pleasures of an afternoon, which at its best, quickly becomes the joy of life itself. A beach surveilled, sometimes unobtrusively, by His uniformed men. A place where women, women like herself, even alone, can feel safe: no catcalls, no ogling, nor (but she will not think of it) anything worse. It is an unlikely day even for someone like her, a woman of relative leisure, to visit the beach—a weekday. But only two hours ago or so she had ventured forth from His house (their house) so high up above the city, to "escape," *yes, it had definitely been an escape,* down to the beach to bathe in this surf that, as she will later recall (though right now still completely unsuspecting), had, on her arrival, so blithely licked its lips, and beckoned her with those soothing if slightly odd refrains of *Return Come Return*. She lies on her back now on the blanket she has brought—feeling something sublime; feeling actually vaguely "happy," she thinks; noting the freewheeling dives and swoops of seabirds as, her eyes just barely closed against the moody in-and-out sun, she recalls the faces of her children—the faces she will see again in only a few hours. And so in this repose she is at peace, she thinks: *I am at peace, I am nobody. I am alone . . .*

Who will ever know exactly how she knew to sit up so abruptly in the next moment as she did? If the sky had any idea, it discloses nothing now to the sand and the water so far below. It continues to gaze down at her with a blank, impassive face. Gazes down at her as she jerks to her feet with a cry, because she *does see them,* she thinks, *but how can they be here?* All those women out there, in the surf. Out there looking directly at her but as if they are blind. All of them, rising up out of the waves and standing. Standing there. Dripping. Naked. Sightless. Clutching their breasts, she sees: clutching the places where their breasts should be. Crying. No, singing. A tuneless song. A chorus of blind mermaids singing

> *"About the planes," they sing,*
> *"the planes, so full of us, and counting,*
> *laden with bodies and counting,*

drugged bodies and counting,
bodies dying, unmoving,
    parts twitching, soon to rest
       as they lifted off and up, *the pilots,*
         with us all inside and counting,
        took off to bank sharply out over the sea,
          always at night, the darkest hours,
      the time when (yes, it is true) some were pulled—
      pulled out,
      out
      from their homes,
    blindfolded,
   gagged,
 manacled and bound,
along with others to whom that all had happened long ago,
  then loaded into the (yes, into the planes)
        (counting)
    the fingers of a few officers on board even then diddling more
    than a few of our

          cunts,
          drugged cunts,
   deeply asleep, unspeaking cunts,
           unanswering-back cunts,
   officers' cocks dipping into drugged flesh for one last
   (yes, with all of us)
      before they took their final count and
      dumped us,
    pitched all of us, some still living,
  still breathing (though drugged),
into the so-far-below sea.
  The planes, the planes, " they sing,
    "and us falling beneath the waves.
     So far down beneath the waves.
        Those waves—"

But then her absolute refusal. Refusal to admit that, before their sight-less eyes, clasped hands, and all those lacerations, that scream at last ex-plodes out of her; impels her feet beneath her; provides her with (but who would have thought it possible?) the speed that hurtles her so fast so far from them from the song from the waves from the soldiers guarding the sands the red sun red sun red red beach. Away from all of them still standing there naked, sightless but seeing her somehow (yes, she knows it) and holding each other's hands above the curling returning waves *O all that foam* as she flies, as she: *Because no,* she insists, flying, *No. I never saw them.* As she had screamed and screams now. *In the beach in the dream but today. No,* she insists now (*what is the way out—?*). *I was never there.*

Her eyes tightly closed. Screwed shut. Locked. Because of course some of the mermaids hadn't washed up headless. Handless. Headless and handless to elude dental records, fingerprint tracing. O but how very clever, she dare not think. How impossibly clever of Him, His coverups. *How invincible* (but she is not thinking this, she tells herself) *the machetes of His soldier minions.* Ah, but the sun. How it still shines, she sees: now yellow, not red. How the trees flare green, gold. How the day—in dreams, in actuality— still beckons. Life, she thinks, then mouthing the word, "Life": something perhaps still possible, as—not entirely to her surprise—she runs. Feels herself running. Still. And faster still. Racing—

Later, gathered in market squares beneath retreating light, or plaiting their children's hair while daydreaming about the whirr and secrecy of hummingbirds, assorted watchers in the small town that is not far from that sea (a place soothed in twilight hours by the sea, by its croons, by those same curling sighing waves and their perpetual calls of *Return, come, stay*) will recount to each other in hushed tones that afternoon's vision they all had shared: that sight of the madwoman racing through their midst, screaming what had sounded to them not like a scream but a toneless song. *Like a song of long ago,* one of them will say. *Long ago, no,* will say another. *As new as the last hour's whispers.* A song without tone of deadwomen standing before her there and still so red, she had screamed, in the surf. A chorus of dead mermaids baring before her and the waning afternoon the evidence of their lacerated breasts. A chorus singing of what had happened to them in secret hours of blindfolds and handcuffs and (of course, she had guessed: interrogations), and most of all what had been done to them as they had lain drugged in the planes—*the planes,* she had screamed, running. What had been done to them that *He,* only *He,* she had cried out, could have arranged. Out of the sky, into the sea, to form a redchorus of once-were-women, with missing parts. Once-were-women with too much shame, she had screamed to the retreating sky, or none at all.

The Country Itself. But Also She

As a place of beauty? But unparalleled, of course. A place of dark, lean-flanked mountains with sturdy shoulders, more than willing to accept the sea's reliable fawning at their feet. A country busy with trees, birds—birds of which there are many thousands, even millions, all of which (perhaps having received news of the excesses of the evening patrols) make certain to sequester themselves in the most unlikely places after dark.

Beauty and majesty in this place in every type of flower, every sort of butterfly, and in the most fantastically designed insects known to inhabit the sphere. Lushness in rolling hillocks everywhere, and meadows only too pleased to preen beneath the sun that adores their wide-open bellies. A guaranteed rainy season, and—for at least the past two hundred years—none of the devastating betrayals of volcanoes. Nor those of earthquakes. Broad fields ripe with crops whisked quickly enough to the teeming capital, and a surfeit of cracked hands only too willing to work them. Better roads than ever before. Telephone service in almost every village.

And freedom—for the country is, certainly, a free one. So free, so filled with so many choices (flee or remain; survive or die; remember or forget; laugh loudly in daylight, or sob in deepest darkness until a fearsome pounding at the door, accompanied by the growling of waiting jeeps and the clicking of long rifles). So many choices that none of the citizens need even believe in freedom, and in fact are encouraged by those presiding not to do so. Why entertain the need to believe in it, this thing called "freedom," when it so clearly abounds? the citizens are asked. You might as well believe in air, they are told, or in light; you might as well believe in the passing of time, as if such belief would make any significant difference. You need not *believe* you are alive when you so clearly are. Do snakes *believe* that they possess scales, fish *believe* that they sport fins? Does the sea *believe* in its perpetual embrace of the shore?

Similarly, those presiding remind the nation, one need not believe in things that simply are not true, and which, here, have obviously never been true: that in this, our beloved and gorgeous country, extrajudicial executions are regularly carried out in secret; that innocent people are kidnapped nightly from their homes, to emerge from other places sometime later as assorted hands, legs, feet, and arms in small black plastic bags; that more than fifty secret mass graves litter the country, especially the lowland rural areas and the more remote mountainsides in the north; that the most promising soldiers in the nation's sleek army were trained abroad in an infamous school in the most ingenious practices of "detainment" and "innocuous interrogation"; that the very young children of those allegedly kidnapped people—infants and toddlers, mostly—have occasionally been sold on a so-called black market as "orphans" to childless couples; and that He—known in most quarters simply as He—in His splendid uniform, an official of awesome rank just below our cherished President, is, with our President and so many lieutenants, commanders, generals, and soldiers, "behind" it all. "Behind" that which, of course, never occurs.

He: as everyone knows, of magnificent shape and height. Promoted to his rank only five years ago, at a still-useful age, after sixteen sterling years in the illustrious armed forces. (No, of course He hadn't worked for the secret police during those years. How could He have done, when— remind yourself now, please—such a thing has never existed?) He: blessed with a house of enviable design and size, flanked by an Elysian garden, well up in the palatial suburbs high above the teeming capital, with that ever-matchless view of the boundless sea. Blessed, too, with His children: two adorable dumplings, who, naturally enough, resemble Him, and whom, laughing heartily, He bounces frequently enough on His knees; and blessed most noticeably with His superb wife—known by many as She, but more commonly, among many, by her actual name. A lovely name. A name that brings to mind swaying bluebells, lilacs, and the scent of roses glancing off lithe trellises in sultry-houred afternoons. She who had first encountered Him in her earlier days when still a young, laughing thing. As a girl at that time bedazzled by His beauty and His force—as, shortly thereafter, He, gazing upon her, swiftly enchanted by the lively glow she had invariably brought in those times to dulled faces and dim corners alike, had felt rapidly genuflect within Him that thing, that indefinable whatever-thing, that, so tripped unawares within Him, compelled Him whenever in her presence in the time that followed those first gazes, and for years after, to adopt both before and beside her (at embassy parties, at so many required functions of state) the precise adoring position: a sometime (though subtle) bowing of the head, an occasional lowering of the hands, and an always murmuring of her name, followed in His deepest mind by the word "She," He had thought, by the word "Mine," He had thought, and always by

Exactly. By the word "Yes."

He who had had built for them and the children they would soon beget that enormous house so far, *far* up above the city. She who, on His magnificent uniformed arm, lifted high in one easy swing by Him and carried across the threshold, had moved into it with Him and a flock of servants ready for her (surely) imperious command. He who, on so many nights and even during the days, had steadily risen and fallen above her there; had panted and, in earnest desire, conjured her face beneath him; had imagined the conquering and plundering of continents as—though she had not, at the time, felt so—He had in fact conquered her; subdued something in her; quelled her, of course—but had also somehow tenderly come to know some most indefinable and secret part of her, a part not easily given to surrender. He marveling all the while as she had lain beneath Him at what had so unquestionably become, without significant contest, truly His. Spoils. Endless riches. A fertile plain for the planting of much seed, and seed planted again. She who, as He had labored and panted, risen and fallen, had gazed up at Him and clung to Him, her arms about His broad back, in adoration, fulfillment, absolute wonder.

She who had not, at that time, turned her face to the wall in darkness and pondered the flesh of deadmen. No, nor feared the power of moonlight to bear witness.

She who, at that time, had had no fear of skulls or stones raining down upon their (His) roof.

Nor had she felt anything then about what she had not yet discovered: all those other deadwomen who had begun to infiltrate her dreams.

She who, like Him, had always appeared to love the gorgeous, spreading country so completely free it needed not concern itself with freedom. The same she, who, lovely to the eye as she had appeared during those early years, rapidly began to fade sometime in the last . . . but who can remember, in a place where remembering is anyway never wise? Sometime in the last whenever. Began to fade, as if, plagued by unfortunate dreams, she became, at first, slightly—ever so slightly—haggard; then, over time, more so. More thin about the mouth, some thought, and darker than ever in those depthless eyes. O those eyes. And legs. Yes, even now. Even now such overall form. A form still capable of outdressing every other woman in the nation. A form still capable, despite a fuller knowledge of who exactly, in the nation's long history, He has been and continues to be, of grace. Elegance. Style, in spite of all those things brought to her by gradually more insistent dreams, whispers, voices *out there:* secret underground chambers, and blistered testicles set afire before the next round of shouts and punches beneath the naked, dangling lightbulb. Ah, yes, some of the citizens had long murmured and sighed, for years, a model of *haute couture*. Utter aplomb. She.

Garden, Morning Sun; Keeping at Bay Thoughts of Killed Children

But then let her have it: this most secret, nourished hatred. For it is now, after all these years, what she most reliably possesses. What she possesses as, from day to day, pondering her impossible thoughts, she meanders the spreading garden of that house; as she envies the ignorance, simple destinies, of birds. What she possesses aside from her children and insistent thoughts of His "betrayals," she thinks, each of which remain—like everything else—part of Him.

Allow her this private, cherished, solitary time in the beaming garden. He far off in the teeming city at work ("or something," she thinks, feeling the grimace).

Allow her to feel the sun's soft nuzzle along her exposed shoulders, the breeze from the far-off sea carrying to her today the scents merely of sea, not of a redchorus of ruined mermaids.

Allow her, as she strolls, to register that great relief—the relief that comes when, gradually cajoled (seduced) by the sun, she is unable to think. Unable to recall deep-throated dreams. The relief a sojourn that she knows will not last.

Allow her not to summon the very late night, or the very early morning, when she just might—yes, just possibly—murder her children. Murder them perhaps because "that would truly undo Him, wouldn't it," she thinks, and because of that metal scraping somewhere just beneath her breastbone when she thinks of all those women who'd felt his touch . . . *kill her own children,* she thinks, "because sometimes I truly cannot bear looking at them and seeing how very much they so resemble Him," she thinks, and because she so fears, yes, I really do fear "what they might become," she thinks, "carrying His blood." (She will not dare, right now, to look down at her hands.) What they might become "as they grow," she thinks, "and as they—" —but she cannot finish that thought. *What they might finally have in them,* she thinks, especially the boy, who just might (but who really can ever know these things? Who can ever—) —"just might have all of *that* in him from *Him,*" she thinks, shuddering-nearly-trembling in the warm sun. "All of *that* in him," she thinks, "my God. And so much more."

Her head hurts. Too much to think. Too much sun. And no, she thinks, *no:* she has not, absolutely not, lost her mind.

("But even now," she tells the deadman lover who visits her regularly in the hidden room of her most desperate hours, the deadman whose face she can never forget—the deadman who wraps her securely and warmly in what remains of his arms: what the flaying soldiers, before running over his prone body with their jeep, had permitted to remain of his arms, "—even now, sometimes, I really do. I want to—"

"To kill them," he says, stroking her face with a decayed wrist. "Your children. The two of them. Yes. I know."

"I want to kill them not because I don't love them," she says, pulling so hard on his withered cock—pulling on it a way she could never have dared do to Him*— "because, in truth, I do love them. They are my—"*

"They are your—" Pressing ruined lips to her throat.

"My most precious—"

"Your most beautiful—"

"Yes," she whispers, squeezing his mutilated testicles against her belly, "my most precious beautiful gorgeous things."

"Except for the flowers in your garden," he whispers, massaging her breasts.

"Except for . . . yes, but they are the flowers in my garden. They remain so."

"They always will be."

"O yes," she says, moving down to kiss his withered cock. "For all time."

Her children, she does not need to say to him just then. Trundled off to school that very morning. Unkilled.

Years later, the walls of that hidden room of her most desperate hours, the walls of that room filled with the stench of a decaying deadman and the misery of a still-beautiful woman, will remember: recall how, in that next moment, she rose up to climb onto and sit on the shimmering tip of her deadlover's cock. It was there, swaying backward and forward, that she began telling him, through all those tears, what he already knew: how

They are her children,	*"Yes, mine,*
But to have to see, every day,	*"Always,*
His face in theirs,	*"Can you imagine the horror,*
His mouth laughing in theirs,	*"O my God, as if I,*
And His smile, those teeth,	*" 'Close your mouth, children don't smile,' I sometimes tell them,*

And then she can never get out
of her head all those women,

"Of course,

The women who make her
think of the children
who make her think,

"How else could it possibly be,

Think of how much she wants
to obliterate them,

"Eradicate them,

Wipe clean from the earth's face
His *finest creations*,

"Annihilate them,

And kill myself, too,

"Yes, rip open my own throat,

For how frightening it is—is it not?

"Of course it is,

That they, her most precious
somethings,

"Might grow up to be a
something *like* Him,

And that their Father, in addition
to all else,

"Yes, all else,

Betrayed me, lied to me, with so
many others,

"Lied to you, yes, and to
others,

And then there are also the
moments of perversity,

"Of course there are,

Moments when she thinks,

"When I think,

Ah, and now how will You *feel*,

"To come home and find
Your children dismembered,

Your boy's little mushroom,

"Yes, ripped out and stuffed
down his throat,

Your daughter's budding breasts,

"Yes, carved. Sliced. Forced
down into her deepest part,

All because, like those others,

"All those nameless others,

they would not tell,

"They would not tell,

they would not

"O no. To the soldiers. Tell."

So, in the now of today, she once again weeps out the tale to him: the confession, rocking back and forth on his cock: grateful to be able to tell him again *what she had told him so many times before: grateful to be able to tell someone—even a deadman whom, she knows, by the time she comes (if indeed she comes this time), by the time she looks down fully from her rocking and crying, will be gone, gone again: I am bereft, she is bereft, I wanted to murder my children unable to bear the thought of His face growing in theirs, I could not stand the idea that one day they and the boy especially might grow to become like Him and O my God to bring about more redchoruses of mermaids thrown out of planes into the sea and so many daughters incinerated (but first raped) and so many sons raped and carved up their remains fed to the pigs the goats the dogs and so many women, He never told me about that, that in addition to everything else O my God and: but I cannot bear it but he the deadman who always came to me in that hidden room kept every time my hand from striking them down slicing open their throats shooting them in the head as they slept shooting them with the pistol He keeps in the house in that room in that cabinet for our "protection" and: no she thinks I did not kill them I will never kill them I will—she thinks, coming; gasping: holding onto the hips that already are no longer there; holding fast to the cock that has already vanished beneath her and the thighs that already are no more, as the walls of that room that does not quite exist will remember many years from now, as she sobs, sobbing, looking down now to see without doubt that he who on so many afternoons like this one, through so many dreams like this one (but not quite a dream), provided her with both pleasure and comfort even in the midst of his remorseless decay: he who, as so many times before, is "gone," she thinks, slowly sliding down off the mound of her conjure, to lie there once more alone and finger herself in the sorrow that flushed through her coming: "gone," she thinks, "the way he must have gone when His men came and took him away from wherever it was, and took his wife, too, and children . . . the grandparents survived because he had long before sent them into hiding abroad. Gone," she thinks, fingering where a deadman's cock had just rubbed against what He had always half-playfully called her "rose" (ridiculous, she had always thought, what a ridiculous term for a part of the body that was), "and who knows," she thinks, lying there so alone in the room that is now slowly becoming another one, one of light and billowing curtains into which she knows the children she has not killed will soon race, shouting, with news of school and the day, "who knows," she wonders, turning her face away from the billowing curtains and back to her fleeting entertainments of death, "who knows when, if ever, he will come again?"*

Parties; A Smile; Astonishment Regarding the Body That Is Not Hers

But how could she not despise them? All those stupid, laughing women? The women so brightly attired in silver. In gold and diamonds. The women whose hands, at the last shining party, had fluttered like the sparrows' wings that have never, not ever, come to comfort her. Fluttered as their mouths sipped red wine, champagne (imported from "the continent"), and asked in those O so bright voices how she was doing these days, darling, and doesn't she look di*vine?* Divine, darling, and how jealous we all are of you looking so splendid, so lovely with that gorgeous uh huh absolutely *beau*tiful husband of yours. Yes, my dear, you know He is. And in that uniform . . . a few epaulets make all the difference, don't they . . . in the position He's in at His age, and so tall, so grand, well . . . you can only imagine the things He'll be doing in this country in another five years. . . . But then wait. For how could they not have seen? Seen the rage and contempt in her eyes, and the loathing, even though her hands, her very own hands, also had reached for this tray or that one of champagne flutes carried about with perfect balance by the ever-silent, white-jacketed, white-gloved waiters . . . how could they all not have sensed that her whinnying laughter was merely a response to their own? Could they, none of them, not see how much she abhorred not only Him but them, these women who were still alive? "My dear, they look *so* good together—" (yes, well, they always had), "and before you know it, she'll be carrying another one." "Of course, with a man as virile as Him, and those legs and breasts she's got . . ." "*Made* in Paris, my dear, as if she just stepped off the Champs-Elysées, like nothing you would ever see in this country, except at one of our parties, of course . . ."

"But who *is* that woman, standing next to you, smiling like that?"—so she, not quite awake, sitting half-upright in bed, had asked Him one morning on glancing at that photo—O God, not another one!—on one of the newspaper's pages.

Fury, she felt. Thickening in her armpits. Soft rage beginning to scald her eyelids. The woman in the photo had her arm brazenly about His arm, as if . . . and was pressed closely against Him, as if—. And that smile. Smiling, that woman, as if her heart would smash to tragedy without Him.

—Who,—He had half-absently responded. (He had already dressed and inspected Himself, but something had momentarily distracted Him: a button missing, God forbid, from His uniform; a bit of lint on the cuff.)—Why, you, darling,—He told her, laughing, looking down at the photo over her shoulder,—who else? What an odd sense of humor you have sometimes, my sweet.—Bending down His towering form to kiss her. To press His freshly shaven face close to hers. (She had caught the scent of shaving cream: lime, one He liked and had reminded her earlier that morning to make sure and remind one of the house staff to pick up that week; something so *masculine*, she'd thought, not quite permitting her lower lip to curl and disclose the clenched teeth prepared, given the right circumstances, to snarl.)

Me? The word formed without form in her mind. *Me?*

She looked carefully at the newspaper. Blinked. Then, in the photograph before her, regarded her own smiling, if glazed, face. Blinked again, then thought . . . but what she thought she could hardly say. For her thoughts just then formed not words, but colors.

She felt His mouth touch her skin as, still utterly dazed, she sat on the bed amid rumpled sheets and a comforter, her mouth half-open in that way He had always, even from the very beginning, found so "adorable," He'd once told a lieutenant. "Just like her, you know? Always so in her own little world, and still so innocent." Her mouth had hung half-open, suggesting in her face the beginning of the slightly stupid look she had habitually, when taken unawares by it before unexpected mirrors, despised; and her brain—well, "frazzled" had been the only word she'd been able to summon in those moments to describe, accurately, the sensation: "I am 'frazzled,' " she'd thought, "to see myself smiling that way, in that dress that looks so ridiculous, at some embassy party or the other, holding onto His arm as He puts His face next to mine (bending down as always) to plant a kiss on my cheek."

Even with that half-dazed expression still on her face (one of the maids would soon come in to make up the bed and tidy up the scattered nightclothes), she had been pondering—though far behind her veiled eyes—knives. Knives, of course. One or many, right there, in her smooth though trembling hands: one or many to meet and calm the always-there bloodtremble in her hands awake or dreaming or (as was so often the case) someplace restively in between. Any large shining knife that, securely grasped, would complete the necessary task as He slept beside her; as, between shiftings, twitchings, rapid eye movements, occasional teeth-grinding, He called out to the darkness or murmured to it indecipherable things, memories not yet revealed. She envisioned His naked back, so smooth and broad, hairless, as He slept; or, better yet, His chest. His chest into which she. Into which she would. His chest into which she now feels trembling at the thought: trembling over the danger, utter cruelty, *daring*, of the thought. She feels that swift leap of her eyebrows that means *I have transformed*, she thinks, *no longer she but* She . . . but, feeling the slow trembling now quaking throughout her, the trembling that could so easily (*but pretend it isn't so*) carve up her children and rip to shreds the entire world's living fabric, she drops it. Drops the knife that is not there in her hand. Banishes it. Banishes all of them—butcher, cleaver, bread knife. Banishes them to the place where dead lovers disappear, where dead-women and skulls do not, at least not so insistently, call her name. She is startled, of course, when He whom, in this reverie, she had long ago left behind, walks up to her still sitting there on the bed with her mouth half-open ("So innocent! Always in her own little world"), and pats her on the head, does something like kiss her on the head; says something now like

—*Good-bye*—

and

—*Have a good day, I'll see you later tonight*—

as she sees and feels herself lift a hand, an all at once weary and fragile hand, in adieu: adieu, my love, her hands seem to say. The illusion must go on, she knows, like her condemnation: it must continue.

She sits there for some time. ("Not now," she tersely tells the maid who puts her head around the door to inquire if Madam is finished, if she may tidy the room, "in five minutes, please.") She visits, once more, rooms that do not quite exist. Inhales in them the forlorn scents of dead lovers— deadmen who, in the very worst of times, can always be relied on to make ghostly love to her on creaking beds wrenched out of blue (but, thank God, not red) dreams. Sometime later—only minutes later, possibly, or hours—she understands the truth. The truth as to "What I know now," she says in a room that is not quite there. "The simple fact that I am not living in my own body. So that when He kissed me," she says out loud, "or kissed that woman who had my face and was smiling in the newspa-per photo as she held that glittering champagne flute—that woman who might have been one of His, His—His *whores*" (she tastes the filth of the word in her mouth; savors it, hates it, and spits it out)—"I was completely unaware of it because I wasn't there. That wasn't my body," she tells the room that gazes so dully back at her, "nor was it my face, nor my mind be-hind those eyes so full of laughter in the photo. That's why, for so many years now, I have never felt Him when He has touched me, because He hasn't touched me. No, not me.

"Them," she thinks, feeling the knives once again in her hands, "His face so close to theirs, underground beneath a naked lightbulb to the sound of other men's laughter. But not me.

"I live in dreams," she tells the not-there room. "In those dreams (though I would prefer that most of them were different) is where my body, my truest body, truly begins.

"And as for this," she tells the room, looking down at the flesh covered in pajamas—pajamas!—beneath her, "well—

"I do not know," she tells the room. "I do not know who *she* belongs to or even—sometimes, yes, sometimes—what her truest name will finally be."

A Rainfall of Hands, a Nineteen-Day Sweep

PRINCIPAL MAID:
"Well, yes. She did. It's been nineteen days now, and she did ask me on that day, or, no, commanded me, to . . . but wait. I want you to listen. I mean listen carefully. Because—well, because I would never say a word against her. I still love her with all my heart. Yes, I do. I've been with her and the Sir fifteen years, right from the time they got married. (Such a gorgeous bride she was, and He, Oh!—He looked so handsome in His uniform! So happy!) And, well, never in all that time until now—never in all that time did she ask me to do anything so, so—

"So *outrageous*. Yes, that's the word. Outrageous, unbelievable, what you see me doing now. Right here. Always. Alone. In tears.

" 'Come here,' she called to me that morning. And, well, no . . . in truth, she didn't look so good that day. She didn't look like herself. I mean, you know the Madam! She was always made up so beautifully, with her hair just so—everything just so . . . like a true . . . I don't know, majesty, she always was. Perfect, I mean. And the loveliest dresses, and shoes . . . yes, even at eight o'clock in the morning, always when the Sir was ready to leave for the city and the children were packed and ready to be driven by the chauffeur to school. . . . But that day, well—

"All right, then. No, I don't want to say it, but . . . well, it's true. She did look as if she hadn't slept in days. Deep, deep rings under her eyes, there were, and her beautiful skin looking so . . . I don't know. So sickish, sickly, as if she really was sick. And—well, you know, she really was . . . was swaying a little bit. Looking a little unsteady on her feet. But her eyes were bright enough—almost as if she had fever, or something. . . . And so she called me. When she called I always went quick. Why wouldn't I? I loved her. She was the Madam. She . . . yes, I loved her. I still do. With all my heart.

" 'Yes, Madam?'

"She was shaking. I saw that as soon as I got up close to her. But in sickness or health, well—far be it from me to say anything to her, except what I tried to say, which was only:

" 'Madam, is anything—'

" 'I want you to sweep up all those hands outside. Every single one of them, in the garden and on the walkways. There are even some in the— in the *pool*,' she said in that shaking voice, as she covered her face for a minute. Standing there before me, swaying, and looking more sickly than ever. Looking like she was about to be ill.

"I—well, no, I didn't think I'd heard her right. *Hands?* Hands? You mean like *people's* hands? I thought. But I must have misheard her. She must've said 'ants,' or—

" 'Why are you standing there looking at me like that?' she said. Her voice louder. And more—I don't know, like it had a—a pistol in it? Something. Something about to snap, or crack, or—

" 'Madam?' I said, staring at her.

" 'I *said*'—she took one big deep breath then, as if she didn't want to repeat in any way what she had just told me to do.

" 'I. Told. You. To go. To go sweep up. To go sweep up those—those *hands*,' she said, truly beginning to shake then. That was when—O yes, I'm sure of it—I began to get—to get really scared—

" 'Madam—'

" 'There are *thousands* and thousands and *thousands* of hands in the garden!' she began to scream, moving closer to me and stretching out her own hands toward me as if she intended to (but she couldn't have, no; not the Madam. No!) hit me. Hit me! And I—

" 'Hands all over the place,' she shouted, pulling me over to the hallway window. 'Look! Down there! Don't you see them?'

" 'Madam, I—'

" 'Burnt hands. Severed hands. Melted. Hands stuck all over with cigarettes. With lighted cigarettes stuck *into* them. With their fingers broken at the knuckles. And with—O my God, but how could He—how could anyone have—

" 'With their *fingernails* pulled out,' she whispered. Putting her own hands up to her face then and covering it. Shaking, her hands. I remember. Trembling.

" 'Oh yes.' Very quietly. So quietly, she said that. 'Smashed by the hammers they use in that place. By the *wrenches*—' She covered her face again. 'They all fell down last night in the rainstorm.' Talking through the fingers covering her face. 'A rainstorm of hands clattering all over the roof and keeping me up all night. Some of them are already—look, girl, don't you see?—are already becoming, becoming—

" 'Becoming skeletal,' she whispered. 'Down there.

" 'But no,' she finished, turning away from the window and wrapping her arms about her shoulders and squeezing, squeezing herself that way as she began to rock back and forth: standing there in the morning sun streaming in from the window. The same sun that was shining over the garden below, where there were—yes, I'm telling you honestly—*where there were no hands*. Only the forward lawn and the hedges and all the flowers she had always loved so much. And the marble statues. And the pool.

" 'No,' she said, still turned away and rocking herself, 'not this. Not a rainfall of hands. Anything but this. Even the skeletons reaching to me out of the dreams I could take, up to a point. Even the deadmen who wanted me to do all those things to them as they told me one more time what He and His men had done to them, I could take up to a point. But not this. Not hands. Not here. Not in this house. Not where my children— my children . . . *live*. No. *No*,' she said, and—

"She was moaning. Groaning. Sounding as if she needed so desperately to—to sob, cry out loud. But no sobs came. None that I saw.

"I—well, I was so terrified I couldn't—no, honestly, I just couldn't move. I couldn't—

"That was when—well, when I just went up right behind her and tried to—to just—

"To touch her. Hold her. Put my arms around her and say, Madam. Madam, please. Madam, it's all right, Madam. Whatever's bothering you, it's—it's all right, Madam, all right. You don't have to worry, Madam, I wanted to say—yes, so much! I wanted so much to say I'll take care of everything, Madam. You won't have to worry about anything. Haven't I and the others always taken care of everything since you and the Sir brought us here? You just rest now. Yes, rest, Madam.

Prince Valiant
Works the Black Seam

W. David Hall

Junior squinted into darkness as he stood at the edge of the gaping hole they called a coal cave, careful not to let his feet touch the makeshift jimmy track. Men and equipment, picks and shovels, brushed aside his every attempt to get to his father. Of course, the men going in and out were just a small part of the problem. They were only digging and shoveling and making a life from the ground up.

"Hey, Prince Valiant." The voice was gruff with understanding, solid with sensitivity, and layered thick with England. "Real cracka dawn, your fathah is. Jus go straight down. There's a good lad."

Miles. Miles Croier.

Junior stepped aside. Miles' pick *clock-clock-clock*ed as he dragged it behind him. He chucked it into the ground, leaned on the pole handle.

"Jus down that iddy biddy hole there, mate." Miles spat something black into the thick coal air.

Junior rocked on his heels, dancing at the edge of the abyss.

"Ain't gonna gittiny better, there, Princy."

Junior kicked at black soot, his fifty-cent loafers getting scuffed and covered with coal blackness. His mother had told him, when she was watching him pack his few things in the cardboard suitcase, not to get his nice things all dirtied up going to the mine again. *Your father know what he need to know; you jus needs to git yo behind down ta that bus station.* And he had meant to, truly, honestly, but there was time. There had to be. He had to try. Again. She was right. He was getting dirty. But what did it matter? He came from coal and, no matter where he went, no matter what happened at the college, he'd still be just coal and dust. He would always be about the coal.

"You done him a picture, Junior-boy?" Miles understood. He was irritated, but he understood.

Junior nodded, looking at the squat, black British man through still-adjusting eyes. His father said he, Miles, was secretly union, sent from outside the Company to rile up the weak minds who don't want to do a day's work for a day's pay fair and square. *After Matewan, breakers be everwhere ya looks. They come in heah, with they fancy-talk, lookin like wunna us, actin like wunna us, but they ain't wunna us. They ain't starvin like the resta us. Easy enough fo em ta say go slow, start comin in at a decent hour an leavin at a decent hour, start learnin ta read fo youself, start learnin ta say no, not until I'm treated like a mans. They ain't half dead limpin round here, four five six chillen and a roof what ain't no damn good for nothing. Can't even understand him half the time.* Junior's father didn't want Miles at the camp at all, but decency stilled his complaints. After all, where's a black man supposed to find work, especially if he's some foreigner, if not in a mine?

"He's in that new vein you all opened up the other day, Princy," Miles said. "Have an hour or so for they gets enough men down there an he's gone. Best git right on it."

Junior nodded, switched his helmet light on, and climbed aboard a car loading up with tools and miners. He nestled into the unforgiving steel of a nearby seat, jerked as the car moved forward, his eyes now fully adjusted to the no-light.

Now I've Learned My Ay, Bee, Sees

Willie's index finger, his good one, his only one, staggered up one of the capital ay's legs, hurried down the other, tapped the cross bar a few times.

"Ay," Junior said.

"Ay," the older man repeated, slowly, reverently. He was almost afraid to let the knowledge go. All of the book-learning was new enough to confuse him. Many of those little marks, those letters, made words when put together in certain ways, and he had learned many words. It was the uncertain letters and their uncertain togetherness that scared him. New letters, new sounds, new words. Real reading, his son Junior called it. *Ideas will just jump off the page and you can dream of things.* That idea heightened his fear. Would he dream the right things?

Old Willie's finger staggered up the straight back of the capital bee, curly-qued down the two curves on the right side, tapped when it came to rest.

"Bee," said the son.

"Bee," said the father, slowly, reverently.

"Two down," said Junior. "Just twenty-four more to go."

Willie looked at the ay, the bee, the rest of the lines and squiggles standing at attention, a few off base, a few straggling behind, but all reporting for duty. Just like in the war stories.

"I evah tells you bout you granddad and those old boys in tha Virginny regimint?"

"Yes, you did." His son tapped on the page. "Do the next one."

The old man's index finger wavered over the arc. No straight lines here. How would that change the sound? "This here line ah letters remine me ah his story bout walkin ta Fort Boot. Foot Boot, Virginny."

"Yes, Father. Now trace the see."

The old man's finger got dangerously close to the page, then flew up. "Never could figgah out what kinda name Foot Boot wuz sposed to be. Crackers come up with all kinda names, you know? Y'outta axe that teacher of yourn about it. Fort Boot. Best write it down somewheres."

"I'll remember. Trace the letter."

Willie's finger tapped the page and followed the curve of the capital see. Seemed simple enough.

"See."

"See."

"Move to the dee, the next one."

Willie looked at the straight back and curved front. He moved back two letters before, to the bee and its straight back and two curves for a front and shook his head.

"Look like a bee to me, cept it ain't have but one hump."

"That's the only difference."

His father shook his head. There was no such thing as "the only difference." His son was smart enough, alright, but he didn't understand the gravity of "the only difference." You were just as good as any white man, the color of your skin being the only difference. You were just as important as any other American, your way of life being the only difference. You could wield strength and power through the written word just like Denvers, him being the boss being the only difference. Willie shook his head. The only differences were big differences, and the ays and bees and sees probably weren't going to be enough to scale those heights.

He moved to the next symbol, its straight back and three levels—a roof for security, a shorter shelf to rest on, a strong floor—and he felt a bit better.

Paper

"Coupla nigrahs get kilt on accounta they too damn slow be out here hauling coal anyway, gots no biznet in the holes to begin wit, and buncha rich folk up North come swoopin down heah, tryin ta make it like wez all doin somethin wrong." Denvers shifted from foot to foot as he spoke, his neck coiled and taut with anger. "Sos, men, every month I post this here compnee report an evy mont I'll change it jus like they tells me to." Denvers ruffled the page in the slight breeze. "But this heah scrappa paper's all that's gonna change. Work jus like you always do an you'll git paid jus like you always do." He slapped the paper against the rotting notice board, tacked small nails to each corner, surveyed the men once again, and stepped away.

The miner stared at the black straight backs and the curves and dots and lines on the long white sheet. Nobody moved. Then one man reached out, fingers trembling inches away from the page, then withdrew the attempt. Junior knew the fear was wrong but knew what they were thinking: What if the letters were burned onto the page and were still hot? What if, when you touched them, they'd stick to your fingers and your hands and never come off? What if they all just faded away or fell away?

Miles forced his way to the front. "Go head. Touch all ya want. Nuffin's gonna hurt cha." He turned to the page, paused, turned back to the men, rubbed at the brown-rust scraggle on his chin. "Says here, we all gotta meetin up in Washington, dee see, buncha strikes goin on down in Virginia an Maryland. Company supposed ta send a fewa us up there an, if we can't make it, we supposed ta hold a meetin ourselves."

The men all turned to Willie, who shook his head and pointed his one good index finger at the mine's opening. The men donned their helmets, switched on the lights, went to work. Willie weaved against the crowd to stand beside Miles. The breeze picked up and he watched the board. The letters stayed in place. All the marks, with their little nubs at the ends of the lines and curves, remained well-anchored to the notice.

"Dat what this here sheet say?"

Miles nodded. "Every word. It's dated six months ago, though. Time's been moven on."

"Then we's done wif all dis talk . . ."

"No. It just started. Denvers supposed ta change this out every month. We have ta make sure he does."

Willie donned his helmet.

"He'll jus say wez not following tha calendar right an take em all down."

Willie stepped away from the notice board, sliding the pole handle of his pick across his neck and shoulders, resting his hands on either end.

"Yer gonna have ta read this, mate," said Miles. "Read it ta the men every day."

"But it aint gonna change."

"An that's why you have ta read it ta them. Every day."

At lunch break, Willie stood at the notice board and looked at the few words he could decipher.

A.

An.

And.

The.

Coal.

Camp.

Closed.

Now.

Is.

Miles' little speech had rolled around in his head all morning and Willie had finally figured it out. One of the trusted men needed to read this notice over and over to the others. The men would hate to hear that same information all the time and start to grumble. Denvers would have to update the notice. The men would be like the letters he stared at, gathering together with meaning, making noises and sounds that could change their lives. That night, Willie roused his oldest son out of bed and told him to teach him how to read. Tonight. Junior stood in his torn, stained nightgown and blinked his eyes into understanding. "Going to need longer than a night."

"As long as it takes, then."

Coal

Denvers announced Junior's arrival to the company the same day he announced the arrival of some Britisher named Miles. He handed each man a shovel, assigned them to their work crews, and vanished.

They were in the initial details, shoveling loose rocks dumped by the jimmies. They were barely beyond the mouth of the vein, the sunlight seeping through the coal haze, not yet swallowed up by the blackness of the undisturbed rock. But the work was hard enough for beginners. The shoveling had to be fast, furiously so at times. This part of the mine seemed to vomit the bile faster than they could clear out the path. At dinner break, Miles sat off to the side, alone, basking in the sun like the old miners deep inside did. When he made eye contact with Junior, he walked over, knelt down beside the boy, whispered in his ear:

"This is from South America," handing the boy a small, spotted orange.

Junior looked around. Men were gathering helmets and buckets and staggering back into the cave. Miles stood and walked away as well. Junior looked back at the piece of fruit in his hand. If it were from South America, it would have been moved from the tree to a boat and shipped to Texas or Florida and then out on a train to Atlanta, Georgia, then to Baltimore, Maryland, then West Virginia, Parkersburg or Huntington, first, then to Beckley. But it was small and shriveled, which means it was hand-carried from Brazil or Argentina. What it meant was Miles had been places outside the United States. What it meant was that the world was not a torn, yellowing map behind his teacher's desk. It meant the world was real.

He headed back to shoveling, the orange bulging slightly under his coveralls. Denvers grabbed his arm, thrust a pick in his hands, pointed to Willie's work detail. Father and son nodded to each other as Junior joined their ranks and walked behind, deeper and deeper into the cave. The men in front followed a concentrated beam of helmet light along the cave wall and floor, while Junior's light slid all over, the floor, the ceiling, an excited, nervous firefly darting along a black summer's night.

"Bes stop dat fool playin, boy," one of the work crew said. "Yer ol man's bout to learn ya sumpin."

Junior stepped back a few feet as his father's pick stirred to life. The helmet light danced to a side and the pick slammed into the wall. There was a rumble and a rock rolled down, then another, then another, another another another, the solidness of the wall giving up its gold. The other men stopped and stared at this wonder.

"Dat's how it done, boy," the man said.

The crew moved to separate sections and chipped away at the rock bed. Junior settled in near his section, shifting his helmet here and there, looking, searching—

—and finding. There.

A crack in the rock.

He focused his helmet light on the slithering line once twice, tapped the pick edge against it once twice, then heaved the pick over his head, swung down, and sent it home. The force of the blow had been great, not because of what it did to the rock (a small chip plinked to the floor), but because of what it did to his arm. The vibrations shot back along the pick's handle and wobbled his arm, igniting his muscles. Searing pain animated the arm, moving it away from his body, stiffening it, dropping it to his side. He watched himself grab at what looked like his arm, press it against his body. A tap on his helmet and he turned to face his father. Junior wanted to wave him off, willed his arm to be normal again, but nothing worked. The arm was dead. His father signaled and one of the other miners walked Junior out of the cave.

The natural light seemed to increase the pain and reveal the swollen purpleness that was his arm. Miles walked over to him, surveyed the damage, whistled low.

"Got yerself a right good sprain, lad."

Junior nodded. He wanted to speak but didn't want to chance what was going to come out: tears, screams, vomit, fear.

Miles led him home.

Valiant

Junior's mother met them at the door, calling on Jesus as she pulled him by his one good arm and shoved him into a kitchen chair. She slapped a bundled bedsheet on the table, pulled what was left of the ice out of the icebox, set it on top of the sheet.

"Go wan," she said, pointing to the ice. "You jus rest ya arm on that there ice. Feel fine by morning."

The arm was dark purple, stiff, heavy. He lowered it onto the ice, grimacing as it made contact. Pain traveled in jerks and spasms across his chest to his stomach and he grimaced again.

A hand clamped onto his shoulder.

"Blimey. Looks liken it came straight frum them funny pages. This your work, eh, mate?"

Miles sure did move fast for an old miner. He had been in Junior's bedroom, grabbed his notebook, pulled out a page, all within a few minutes. He held a pencil sketch, a young warrior with a page-boy haircut and lion emblazoned on his tunic, sword arm raised back and held high, mighty broadsword at the ready

"You gots talent an loads of it. Hope yer not gonna squander it in some coal cave. No need ta risk hurtin them hands shovlin some wanker's coal again. You outta go to university."

Sword Arm

His mother sat in her rocking chair on the other side of the kitchen table, sewing, keeping vigil over her son hour by hour. She'd found Bible readings on the radio and rocked with the waters of Noah the first day, stitched during the crucifixion of Christ the next. On this day, the pastor talked about the Rapture and she froze, absorbed in every word. Eternity in Heaven with Christ Jesus was the reward. A thousand years of pain and suffering beyond anything man could imagine was the punishment.

"Goin ta be hell here," she said. "Mens gonna be wondrin round, all lifeless-like, acting like ain't nobody inside. Walkin dead. Be all dirty, bugs be crawlin ovah em an suchlike. Best make sho ya's all ready."

Junior was pretty sure he was ready for Heaven, anybody would be, but what he couldn't comprehend was something worse than the lifelessness of the mines. They were overalls and gas masks and goggles and helmets and lanterns and canaries and jimmies and dynamite and byerite and ampelite and lignite and cave-ins and sprained arms but they were not human beings. What could be worse?

This hasn't always been Hell. No, before Miles and the whisper of a strike, it was life. It was Willie up and out before dawn, the kids bathed and in clean clothes, going to school, running all over the coal camp afterwards, eating just enough biscuits and lard to be better off than most before going to sleep three or four in a bed.

But his arm had changed things. His father had stopped the evening lessons with jay or kay or ell, looking at his son's arm more than the letters on the page. The purpleness had faded, as had the swelling, but even two weeks later, the arm was still stiff. Junior could barely grip a pencil without tearing up and that's when fear had taken hold. If he couldn't conjure up Prince Valiant, how was he going to survive?

That was when he noticed Hell. His clothes weren't really clean. The lard and biscuits made his stomach turn. The night songs from the camp that evening droned and buzzed in his ear like mosquitoes. The sheet on his bed, stained from being in some other house or covering up some other boy, wasn't enough to shield him from the biting cold.

After a particularly trying day of the rocking and the preaching and the ice melting and the stiffness, Junior looked at the letters on the page from the night before. He had read the rest of the line to his father, the old man sitting silent, his one good index finger immobile.

"All this ain't gonna do a damn bit of good," was all his father would say, ending the lessons for good.

Junior looked at the letters again. Pain or no pain, he knew and the pencil knew and the paper knew and the lines and curves and shading knew what he had to do. He forced his fingers around the pencil, grimaced through the sting slamming through his hand, and he made a single mark through the letter line. His fingers flared open and he grabbed the pencil again. He slid away from the line to a small, blank corner, and made another mark, then another, and then he was drawing, pencil lead bringing an imagined sword arm, wrapped in chain mail, to life.

Chips

Junior slumped beside Lincoln, the rail driver, a fat man with one eye taken in a rockslide about two years ago. They rocked left right then left again, swaying as a limp extension of the jimmy. The fat man grabbed the brake and the car slowed, stopped. Three miners walked on the track, their faces shining dots of helmet light. The lines of an empty canary cage sliced through one light. The fat man nodded as the men stepped aside and the jimmy lurched forward.

The car stopped short of a group of men chipping away at a wall, the white helmet lights dodging the sharp ends of the picks. Junior climbed out and stumbled to where his father's work crew sledged away. The rock was loose and new here, a day's pile of work in a few hours. Junior wondered how long his father was going to live at this rate, a thought he'd never had before.

"I'm going," Junior said, once, twice, over the *crick-smash-plinkle* of the other picks and shovels.

His father's hand went up, a signal he was close to the breaking point. The other men shuffled back as his father raised his pick over his head.

Junior knew the rest, the kissing of pick and rock, the crashing of coal, the pride of the miners. He opened his mouth to speak again, thought better of it, climbed out of the jimmy, walked away, helmet light scraping the ground, failure dragging his heart behind him.

Out of Body

Glenville Lovell

Phisto remembered it like it was yesterday. The first time he saw a dead body. It was in the embalming room of his father's funeral home. He was almost twelve years old, already bored with school and given to playing hooky, cruising around in stolen cars with his new friends from a Bloods gang that controlled the Baisley Projects.

That day the police had stopped them in a stolen green Caddy on Archer Avenue and had taken the older boys off to jail. He later found out the only reason he'd escaped a trip to the lockup was because one officer had known his old man. Turned out the tough-love cop wasn't doing him any favor by not taking him to jail.

The cop drove him home and he almost bluffed his way out of trouble. But the guy refused to release him without first speaking to his parents. The house was empty that afternoon. His mother had died earlier in the year, and soon afterward, his eighteen-year-old sister ran off with the pastor who conducted his mother's funeral.

The cop took him down to his father's funeral parlor over there on Guy Brewer Boulevard about a mile away from where they lived on 178th Place, a quiet leafy neighborhood of one- and two-family homes dense with Caribbean immigrants like his father who'd settled there in 1960.

Phisto had never visited the funeral home until that day. He knew what his father did for a living. He knew that his father buried people. And made a pretty good living from it, evidenced by the latest appliances and new furniture they had in their one-family brick house, but it was never talked about in his company.

While the officer explained to his father why Phisto had arrived there in the back of a patrol car, his father showed no emotion, merely nodding and shaking his head. Moments after the blue-and-white drove off, his father exploded, displaying a temper that Phisto had heard his mother talk about but had never seen before.

His father took him down into the basement and ordered him to strip. Defiant, Phisto grabbed his crotch, aping the bad-boy posturing he'd picked up on the street. With this bluff, he tried to walk away. His father grabbed him in a chokehold and slammed him to the ground. Phisto was surprised by his father's strength. The slightly built man from the island of St. Kitts, though no more than a few inches taller than his son, was well-muscled with surprising power in his upper body from cutting sugar cane and working construction in his youth. With a piece of electrical cord, he tied his scrawny son to a chair next to the dead body he was preparing for burial and proceeded to rip Phisto's clothes from his body until he was naked in the cold room.

Then the mortician went back to his work. The smell of embalming fluid soon filled Phisto's lungs. The prickly odor knifed through his toughness and singed his palate until he puked all over himself. His father paid no attention to him at all. Singing cheerfully and going about his business, stepping over Phisto sitting there in his own vomit, admiring how craftily he'd restored the young woman's face, mutilated by a jealous boyfriend after he'd killed her.

With nothing left in his stomach, Phisto leaned against the table leg. He was weak and bleeding where the wire chafed his wrist. Slime dripped from the corners of his mouth. From where he sat he could see the blood and fluid draining from the woman's body, flowing down into the waste receptacle.

He glanced at the corpse's face and felt a strange relief, a sort of bonding with something outside of himself. Quietly, as if he'd somehow acquired the facility to remove his spirit from his body, he stared at the pathetic little boy with spittle drooling from his mouth, trembling at his father's feet. He saw himself, the pathetic little boy, rise up and walk over to his father and put his arm around the man's shoulder and whisper, *Thank you.*

Then he headed out of the room, pausing at the door for one final glance at the sniffling kid sitting in vomit.

Phisto stored that dead woman's face in his mind, embracing that stillness characterized by death as a part of himself. By the time his father released him two hours later, the smell of vomit and the sickly odor of embalming fluid had disappeared from his senses. He wasn't even aware of the cold anymore. He could've sat there for another two hours as comfortably as if he were lounging poolside at the Four Seasons in Miami.

Years later, he came to realize that in those two hours he sat in that frigid room while his father worked on that body, he'd formulated the virtue that would rule his life: Feel no pain or remorse.

In 1984, he quit school at sixteen and started selling weed. In three months he had moved onto powder, making as much as $8,000 off an ounce. He struck a deal with some Colombians and by the end of the year was flipping $100,000 a week with rock houses in South Jamaica. In two years, he controlled the large housing projects that dominated the two sections of the southside. But he knew that this game wasn't going to last, so he started taking business classes in sales and real estate. By the time the crack craze was over, he'd amassed a fortune and an army, and while maintaining his stranglehold on the drug trade, exporting to as far away as Texas, he had diversified his holdings into real estate in Atlanta, Miami, and the Caribbean.

People saw him as a drug lord. A gang leader. A killer. A psychopath. He laughed whenever he read those kinds of descriptions in the news. America worshipped psychopaths and other miscreants in the name of business. Just pick up *Business Week* or the *Wall Street Journal* or any major business magazine and you found profiles of men who ran businesses, who on the surface appeared to be legal, but with a little digging were discovered to be looting the companies, stealing employee pensions, and knowingly selling products that killed people. The newspapers and magazines lauded those muthafuckers as visionaries, but condemned people of a similar personality profile like himself, who did business on the margins of society. *Ain't that some shit.*

Was he any different from the CEOs of big corporations in this country? He was just as charismatic, as visionary, as tough as a Steve Jobs. In fact, you could say he was tougher. He had never operated any business at a loss. If his businesses were listed on the stock market, the share values would rise every year. His underlings worshipped him just as shareholders worshipped the Bernie Ebberses or Jack Welches of the world. He did whatever he had to do to get the job done. Just as they did. And just as they were celebrated and applauded by their peers and profit-worshippers for their willingness to take chances, to be aggressive and visionary, so was he by the many people who depended on him for their survival.

There were two codes he lived by. They were ruthless, but effective. His first motto: *Snitches must die.* The silencing of witnesses was the rule he lived by and everyone in his orbit, including all the Baisley Projects, paid heed. Neither the NYPD nor the Feds had ever built a case against him.

The second motto: *Accept no disrespect.*

Which was why he had no choice but to put down Fred Lawrence in view of everyone in the playground in Baisley Pond Park. It was as necessary as any CEO firing a junior executive who disrespected him in public. As much as he liked the youngster, if he let the upstart get away with this, the mystique of being Phisto Shepherd would be destroyed. Forever. The youngster had stepped to him in a way that no one in their right mind should be tempted to do. And bragging on top of it. You disrespect Phisto and walk around bragging? That's asking to be cut down. There's no surer way to commit suicide than to disrespect Phisto Shepherd and brag on it.

When Phisto claimed a woman, she was his for life. Only when he said the relationship was done could the woman walk away. And until such time, all other suitors were expected to wither away, to drop into the gutter like rats running from the exterminator. This young pup, Fred Lawrence, had laid some pipe on one of his women and then told the world that the girl had begged to be his bitch. Said she would give up Phisto and all his money for another night with him.

Phisto had reached a point in his life where he seldom handled disputes personally. There were any number of young guns in his organization he could call on to quash a beef. Of any sort. If the resolution needed to be quick and permanent, he had enough specialists for every day of the week. If gentle nudging or mediation was required in a sensitive matter, there were people who could be trusted to be discreet.

But he had to show the world that he was still Phisto Shepherd. That the Phisto who survived his father's beatdown, who remade himself into a fire-breathing dragon to create the baddest outfit in Queens, wasn't finished, as many were beginning to whisper on the street after word got around that Fred the baller had fucked Phisto's woman. He'd taken on the dreaded Jamaican Shower Posse for turf and sent them scampering back to Miami. He'd ordered the hit on a corrupt cop who tried to shake him down, and he'd gotten away with it. Why hadn't this youngster heeded his warning? When the message was conveyed to the kid, he'd signed his own death warrant with a laugh.

Once in a while, even with the large army at his disposal, Caesar still had to go out and slay somebody to remind his soldiers why and how he became Emperor. This one wasn't a head-cracker. The youngster had to be bodied, and he would do it himself.

Fred Lawrence was a talented young baller who'd just finished his senior year at LSU. Some pundits thought he was sure to be drafted by the NBA. Maybe not a first-rounder, but definitely a second or third. He was that good. Phisto had seen him play and didn't like the kid's game as much as others did. Not enough range on his jumper, but the quick first step and the physical nature of his game reminded Phisto of Stephon Marbury. Fred could have gotten his shot.

That is, had he not come back from Louisiana thinking he could spit in King Kong's eye. Thinking he could steal Fay Wray and not suffer the consequences. Thinking his dribbling skills would get him a buy after dissing Phisto.

Like everyone else who tried to fuck with Phisto's program without considering the consequences, the young man had to pay. The beating and humiliation Phisto took from his father that day in the mortuary taught him never to bluff. Once you bluff you have to back down. And when you back down you lose respect.

His core crew had advised him to let the matter drop. Why knuckle up with this young stud? But he knew they were begging for the youngster's life simply because they were in love with his game. Phisto knew they converged on the park on Saturdays and Sundays, just like everybody else, to watch the muscular youngster play. Everyone on the southside loved this young man, wanted to see one of their own make it in the NBA. Putting the grip on him wouldn't go down well with the residents.

Nevertheless, Phisto's code was his code. The situation reminded him of when his father was shot to death on 121st Avenue during a robbery in 1995. By that time his father had disowned him and he and the old man hadn't spoken in more than ten years. But everyone in the neighborhood

knew this was Phisto's father, and accorded him due respect. Phisto found
the young killer, and in sight of other customers spaded him as he sat in
the barber's chair. Phisto was arrested the next day. But the case never
made it to trial. The man who had identified him to the police was Bobby
Tanner, a retired postal worker. Tanner got a bullet in the back of the
head for his trouble. Word soon got around that Bobby Tanner got tagged
for snitching. The next Sunday, Phisto visited the church where another
of the witnesses worshipped. The bloated man saw Phisto's six-foot, 275-
pound frame blocking the sidewalk and, fortunately for him, fell down in
the street from sheer fright. No one ever appeared in the grand jury to
finger Phisto.

Contrary to what his advisors believed, Phisto didn't actually want to
put the youngster under at first. He would've let the matter go had the
young stud not been stupid enough to woof that he had more dog in him
that Phisto. After that, his hands were tied.

That summer evening, the sun had left a band of endless purple across
the sky. An unusually high wind curled the young tree limbs and stirred
leaves and dust in the park. It blew hard and heavy against the houses on
Sutphin Boulevard, rattling the sign on the Crowne Plaza Hotel on Baisley Boulevard.

A storm was coming. Colored balloons, left over from an abandoned
family picnic, hung from tree limbs. Yet the approaching inclement
weather wasn't enough to delay the fitness fanatics doing laps around the
track, or to arrest the pickup game on one of the three courts behind the
racquetball wall.

The few daring souls on the sidelines that evening who'd scoffed at the
looming bad weather witnessed a near flawless performance from Fred
Lawrence on the court. The perfection of his long lean body, snaking
through small spaces, piercing the tough wind and a tougher defense,
twirling and swerving around defenders with precision, left most people
shaking their heads in disbelief.

Fred scored on a driving, twisting lay-up off the glass, using a classic
crossover move that left his defender flat on his back. The small crowd
screamed. Fred ran back down the court pumping his fist in the air,
yelling, "You forgot your jock, bitch!"

The next time down the court, Fred took a pass on the wing and without breaking stride elevated past a closing defender for a rim-rattling
dunk.

People were whooping and hopping up and down and spinning around in circles of disbelief.

"Did you see that?"

"No he didn't!"

"Replay! Replay!"

"Jordanesque."

"*Better* than Jordan."

Phisto's black BMW pulled up on 155th Street behind a white Explorer. The doors of the truck were open and Jay-Z's latest joint was blasting full force. Phisto wanted to tell the idiot to turn his music down, but decided to ignore the disturbance and walked the short distance across the grass to the courts.

There was a hush as Fred got the ball back on a steal. He veered left and was met by an agile defender. He slipped the ball between his legs and dribbled backward, looking for another opening. Shifting the ball from side to side, through his legs, and then a glance to his left as if searching for someone in the crowd. Everyone knew what was coming. Fred jabbed to the right and the defender bit on the fake. The elusive youngster changed direction and in a split second flew by his defender for another dunk.

Oh, the ecstasy of the crowd. Fred soaked up their response for a full second, posing under the rim.

And then, *praack! praack!*

Heads jerked around. Too loud for a firecracker. Too close to be the backfire of a car. People scattered when they saw Fred stumble and fall to the ground. Even his friends on the court ran and left him.

Seconds later, only five people were left. Phisto handed the .45 to someone in his three-man posse to dispose of it. He walked over to the only person who hadn't run away.

"Do I know you?" Phisto said.

"I don't know."

Phisto took hold of the man's face, digging his fingers through his scraggly beard into his jaws. "Do you know me?"

"Yeah, I know you."

Phisto laughed. "Why didn't you run away like the rest?"

The man hesitated. "Why?"

Phisto's eyes screwed up and he lifted the man's dark glasses from his face. "What'd you say, muthafucker?"

"Why? I didn't think the game was over."

Phisto laughed. "You think you're funny."

"I mean, he was so amazing, the way he defied gravity. I thought he was Superman. I thought he would get up and fly above that rim again."

"He *was* amazing, wasn't he?" Phisto said.

"Yeah. Amazing."

Phisto said, "Did you see anything else here?"

The guy took his sunglasses from Phisto's hand and put them back over his eyes. "What do you mean?"

"Exactly. That's what I mean," Phisto replied, turning away. "You better bounce. Cops gonna show any minute."

"I *am* a cop," the man said.

Phisto turned slowly, his face scarred with a dark smile. "For real?"

The man adjusted his dark glasses and smiled. "Just fucking with you."

Phisto relaxed. "I should kill you for fucking with me."

"Actually, I wasn't. I'm really a cop."

The man opened his jacket. An NYPD detective badge hung from a chain around his neck. Phisto also noticed the 9mm stuck loosely in his waistband.

Phisto gauged the distance between him and the man. "You gonna arrest me?"

"No."

"If you ain't gonna arrest me, what you gonna do?"

"Shoot you between the eyes."

Phisto laughed.

The man wriggled his fingers. "What's so funny?"

"You're gonna shoot me between the eyes?"

"Yeah."

Pointing at the dead baller, Phisto said, "For him?"

"No."

"Is this personal?"

"Remember the cop you ambushed in that crack house?"

"I don't know what you're talking about."

"He had a son. That son became a cop."

"And that son . . ."

"Would be me."

Phisto turned to the member of his crew holding the .45. "Shoot this muthafucker."

Nobody moved.

Phisto made a quick grab at the .45. His hand closed on the grip and that's when he felt a jolt to his chest as if he'd been kicked by a mule. He bounced against the white wall of one of the racquetball courts and slid to the ground on his back.

Phisto had often thought of what this moment would be like for a person. The moment that separated life from death. Was there some brilliant light to illuminate your path into the next world, as some people claimed who'd had so-called near-death experiences? Was there such a thing as coming close to death? He knew what death looked like. His father had made sure of that.

He looked up and saw streams and streams of white clouds. And then he felt a strange relief swell in his chest, a sort of bonding with an energy entering him. A sadness overcame him and he wanted to cry. He saw the faces of his crew and knew that he'd been betrayed. By one or all of them. He also knew it didn't matter anymore. The light was approaching fast.

A Few Good Men

David Nicholson

The way the men in the shop start talking about women that Saturday night is this: The telephone rings once more for Speed, and Lamarr Jenkins, whose shop it is, heaves a heavy sigh of exasperation. Even if Speed were not the newest barber, it would still make sense for his chair to be near the pay telephone and the back room. Since Speed came to work at the shop three weeks before, the telephone has rung for him with the regularity of a factory whistle or the landlord's knock. Always, it is some young girl, a different sweet young voice each time, asking tentatively for Speed. Always, Speed talks to her, his back to his customer, his own voice pitched low and soothing. This time, when Speed finally returns to the head he has been cutting, Jenkins scans the line of men waiting in the chairs underneath the mirrors against the wall. And then, without looking at Speed, Jenkins asks if Speed thinks about cutting hair when he is getting pussy. Speed says no—a man ought to keep his mind on the task at hand. Jenkins says fine—from now on, stop thinking about pussy when you in here supposed to be cutting hair.

After the laughter dies down, old Mr. Perkins, over whose half-bald head Jenkins has been aimlessly wielding his clippers, rouses himself long enough to say, "Boy must be working two or three jobs. Got to be, all them women he got."

Speed grins. A razor-thin man, he has a wicked Ike Turner goatee and a sleek otter's head of slicked-back hair.

"Who you think I am?" Speed asks. "Hubble?"

Hubble, the second barber, ignores it and continues placidly grooming his customer. Hubble is a big man. Though he does not drink, there is a whiskey sadness about him, an amiable alcoholic diffidence. Speed snorts and shakes his head.

"I got one rule," he says, "and one rule only. I live by it. If they don't pay, I don't play."

"Shee-it," says A. B. Prudhomme, a Louisianan known for obvious reasons as Seventh Street Red. "You pay. We all do. One way or another, you pay. Don't nobody give up nothing for nothing. Especially these black gals out here."

"Thass right," Mr. Perkins says over the chorus of assents from the men waiting. Speed says, "You right. Somea these young girls they got out here, you got to be careful. They'll try to game you in a minute."

Doc, an English teacher at the high school, looks up from the newspaper he is reading. "Now wait a minute," he says, taking off his glasses. "What is it you are trying to say? As far as I can see, there is no difference between men and women at all."

"How many men you know got a pussy?" Speed asks.

Doc folds his glasses and puts them in his shirt pocket. He smiles. When the men finish laughing Doc says, "Now you know that is not what I meant. But since you do not seem to understand, I will break it down for you. What I am saying is that there is no *essential* difference between men and women. There are just as many men as there are women out there who are not to be trusted."

Jenkins looks at Doc from underneath his green eyeshade. "Doc," he says, "you wrong when you say there ain't no difference. It's a whole lotta men I wouldn't turn my back on. But I'll tell you one thing—a man might dog a woman, but a woman will give a man the blues for life."

"That may be true," Doc says. "But even if it is, none of it is any worse than what black men have always done to black women."

Hubble lowers his clippers and looks over at Jenkins. "All this y'all talking about got me thinking," he says. "Know who I ain't seen in a long time?"

Speed says, "Your daddy?" and a ripple of appreciative laughter runs down the line of waiting men.

Hubble frowns.

"Speed, I done told you," he says. "I do not play that mess. Now come on now, boy—you might get hurt."

"Hurt?" Speed looked sideways at Hubble. "*Hurt?* Man, you better think twice before you mess with me. I'm the one that whipped lightning's ass and put thunder in jail, drunk all the water out the ocean, and tied a knot in the whale's tail."

Hubble tilts his customer's head.

"Uh huh," he says. "Uh huh."

Prudhomme snickers, and Hubble stands back from his customer, his face a mask of blank disdain. Underneath his blue barber's smock he wears a long-sleeved shirt, the same kind he wears every day, always buttoned at the wrist and the collar no matter how hot it is. For the past twenty-four years, Hubble has worked in a hotel restaurant downtown, first as a cook's assistant, then second cook, then head cook. Two years ago, he became manager. One night every two weeks and one weekend a month, Hubble is absent from Jenkins's shop—those times are reserved for his service in the National Guard. In a year, Hubble will retire from the guard. Five years after that, he will leave the restaurant. He will collect two pensions and still be young enough to cut hair. If he wishes, he can also take another day job. In the fifteen years that he has worked for Jenkins, Hubble has always been on time and seldom sick. He is a good barber. Because of this, he has Jenkins's respect and his own key to the shop.

"You couldn't park in front today, Omar?" Jenkins says. "I didn't see your car."

"Didn't drive. Man didn't have the car ready when I went to get it yesterday."

"You need a ride? Won't be no trouble to drop you off."

Hubble shakes his head.

"Earline picking it up. She'll come for me after nine."

For a few moments the only sound in the shop is the hum of the clippers and the rattle of the old Coke machine. Then Speed says, "Hey, I didn't mean nothing, awright?" He exchanges glances with Prudhomme. "Awright? 'Cause Hubble, I don't know nothing about your daddy—just ask your momma."

"Well, it seemed peculiar to me," Jenkins says, before the laughter can encourage further impudence from Speed. "'Cause I know you can usually find a place in front of the shop."

"Yeah," Hubble says absently, "that's true," and then, "Carver. That's who I was thinking about. What works down at the post office. He still with that young girl?"

"Carver? Lloyd Carver?" Jenkins looks at Hubble and shakes his head. "Omar, where you been, man? They buried Lloyd Carver two weeks ago Friday."

"You got to be kidding me." Hubble considers it. "Come to think of it, last time I seen him Carver look like he'd been sick. But I didn't think he was doing that bad."

"And I'll tell you something else," Jenkins says. "By the time it was over, if it wasn't for the VA, Lloyd Carver woulda been in the street. Yeah, that's right." Sweeping the cloth from Perkins's lap, Jenkins looks to see who is next. Prudhomme rises. Despite his appreciation of Speed's gift for insult and exaggeration, he trusts only Jenkins to cut his hair.

"Now, see, that's just what I been saying," Jenkins says, pinning the cloth around Prudhomme's neck and then leveling his clippers at Doc. "That girl had Carver's nose wide enough open to drive a Mack truck through. And all the time she was fattening him, fattening him just like you fatten a hog for slaughter."

Doc smiles. Like the best bartenders and cabdrivers, men whose chosen profession also requires them to come daily into contact with members of the public, Jenkins is both a storyteller and a philosopher. Doc knows this, and so do the rest of the men present. Whether this is part of Jenkins's temperament and always has been, or whether it is something Jenkins has learned in his years behind his chair of white enamel, overseeing the heads of men, boys, and the occasional woman, Doc neither knows nor cares. He, and the rest of the men, have long been connoisseurs of Jenkins's stories and those that are told in his shop.

"Well, I did not know Lloyd Carver," Doc says. "So I guess you will have to tell me what happened."

"Doc," Jenkins says, as he begins to work the comb through Prudhomme's hair, "what that woman did to Lloyd Carver was a shame. Took everything he had and after she was finished, she just stepped over where he was laying and kept on going. But man, she musta had some good stuff, because as soon as he met her Carver start to act like he in junior high school, and here he was a grown man with more'n forty years at the post office.

"How it started was Carver met the broad in onea them little joints up on Georgia Avenue. Wasn't too long before he ask her to quit her job and come stay in the house his momma left him. Now, it was two things that girl could do, and one of them was cook. Every night Carver come home she got the food on the table, cooked just the way he like it. So when he come home one night and dinner ain't ready and she just sitting there with a long face, Carver know something ain't right. He say, 'What's wrong, darling?' The broad say she want to know do Carver love her.

"Carver say, 'Love you? Of course I love you.' So she say, 'Well, I hope so, because you all I got. And if something was to happen to you, I don't know what I'd do.' Carver say, 'Ain't nothing going to happen to me,' but she keep on, till finally he say, 'Darlin', what you want me to do to set your mind at rest?' And she say, 'Lloyd, honey, would you put your car in my name? That way, if something happen to you, I'd at least have me something to ride around in.' Now Carver had him a Park Avenue didn't have but twenty-eight thousand miles on it. But he just laugh and say, 'Is that all you want, honey? Shoot, I'll do it tomorrow.'

"Few weeks later him and the broad sitting in the living room watching the Redskins and the broad say something, but Carver too busy watching—you remember that game where they kick Dallas ass? That's how come the broad got mad, 'cause Carver wasn't listening. So she got up and turned off the TV and run upstairs crying."

Speed says, "*Turned off the TV?* In the man's own house? Turned off the TV? Shee-it. I'da kicked the bitch's ass in a red-hot minit."

Jenkins lifts the clippers from Prudhomme's head and looks over at Speed.

"Yeah," he says, "I believe you would have. But all Lloyd Carver done was go upstairs asking himself what the hell was wrong. Get in the bedroom, the broad say, 'Lloyd, I quit working 'cause you asked me, and now I ain't got nothing of my own. And I coulda gone back and finished school and had me a good job working for the government.' Carver say, 'Baby, you ain't got to worry about no job. I'ma take care of you.' Broad say, 'But we got to face facts. I know we got us a good long time left together, but you ain't gon' be here to take care of me forever. What am I gon' do after you gone?'

"Carver say, 'Whatchu want me to do?' Broad look at him. Broad say, 'I'm gon' need something to get by. Will you go in tomorrow and make over your insurance to me?' Now Lloyd been paying into that policy the whole time he been at the post office, and you *know* the post office got them a good retirement plan—"

"Wait a minute," Doc says. "Wait just a minute. Do you expect me to believe this? That a man, a grown man, would sign away his car *and* his insurance policy to a woman he met in a nightclub? I'm sorry, but I just cannot believe such a thing would happen."

"You ain't as sorry as Lloyd Carver was, once it was all over," Jenkins says, "and I don't care whether you believe or disbelieve. These are true facts I'm telling you. True facts. The next day Carver went in and changed over his policy. Now, once he did that, you'da thought she'd be real nice to him so she could get the rest of what she wanted. But next time Carver try to get him some, the broad say she feeling sick and ask would he mind sleeping on the couch.

"'Nother few weeks go by and Carver still sleeping on that couch. But what shoulda tipped him off is they been living in that house three, four, maybe five months, and the whole time he ain't never seen her nekkid. Now all of a sudden she wearing these little old shortie nightgowns, leave the bedroom door open and he walk past and she laying there ain't wearing nothing but panties. After a while, Carver start to feel like he gon' go crazy he don't get him some.

"One night, she come downstairs wearing one of them old shortie nightgowns. Come in the living room and say, 'Lloyd, we got some stuff we got to talk about.' Carver say, 'What's on your mind, sugar?' Broad say, 'It's more than thirty years difference between us. Now I know you don't like for me to talk like this, but I got to. You ain't gon' be here for me forever, and it's a mean old world for a woman ain't got no man. You got to do something to make it easier for me if you pass.'

"Carver ain't say nothing for a long time. Then he say, 'Woman—you asked me to put my car in your name. I did it. You asked me to make over my insurance to you. I did that too. What you want me to do for you now?' And the broad, she say, 'Lloyd, it ain't for me. It's for the baby.' Carver say, 'Woman, how come you ain't tell me?' She say, 'I just now found out." The two of them sit there grinning at each other, and then she say, "Now come on upstairs with me, Lloyd. I ain't been as good to you as I should.'

"Afterwards, Carver about to fall asleep, and she say, 'Do it for me Lloyd. Please.' Carver say, 'Do what?' Broad say, 'Put the house in my name. So me and Lloyd Junior can have us a roof over our heads if you pass.' "

"Goddamn," Prudhomme says, and the laughter that follows is rueful and mocking all at the same time, a taunt and an elegy celebrating the recklessness of the late Lloyd Carver and his imprudence in the face of love. Only Speed's laughter is entirely without sympathy. Hubble does not laugh. He frowns, the whiskey sadness heavy on his face. "Shee-it," Speed says again, and Jenkins unpins the cloth from Prudhomme's neck. He snaps it to shake off the hair.

"And then?" Doc says as he approaches the chair. "What happened next?"

"Whatchu mean, 'What happened'?"

"I mean what happened? It didn't just end that way. What happened?"

"Whatchu think happened? Wasn't but a couplea days after he put the house in her name, Carver come home and found two suitcases on the porch. Key didn't work 'cause she'd done had the lock changed. Rung the bell, and she come to the door, didn't even open it. Told him to get his ass off her porch before she call the *po*-lice. And when Carver went to see a lawyer the next day, the man said there wasn't a damned thing he could do."

"He brought it on himself," Speed says, "letting the bitch game him like that. First time she asked for something, he shoulda told her, 'I give you a roof to sleep under, and a bed to sleep in. You want anything else, go get you a job.' "

"That's right," Prudhomme says. "It's all a game, and the sooner you learn that, the better. See, it's like that old man was trying to get next to this young girl, promised her a whole lotta stuff if she just give him some. Girl finally gave him some leg and he putting his clothes on and she say, 'Now, Daddy, don't forget all them things you said you was gon' do for me.' And he just buttoned his shirt and said, 'Baby, lemme tell you some-thing—when I'm hard, I'm soft. But when I'm soft, baby, I'm hard.' "

Speed laughs and takes a cigarette, a Kool, from the pack on the counter behind his chair. He lights it.

"You got to be that way," he says. "Somea these no-good black bitches they got out here will take a man for everything he got, if he let 'em. And it ain't about color. Somea these high-yella and brownskin gals ain't shit neither." Speed blows a jet of smoke out the side of his mouth. "But I still say a real man wouldn't let nothing like that go down. A real man is gon' take charge, a real man know he stronger than a woman."

"Uh huh," Hubble says. "Well, I can see you ain't never been married, son," and Jenkins says, "Doc, what you think?"

"Frankly," Doc says, "I still do not see how a man could be so foolish as your friend to sign away his car, his insurance, *and* his home." Before

Jenkins can reply, Doc says, "Also, I prefer to believe black women are not that greedy, at least no more so than any other women."

"Well, that's a true story," Jenkins says, lowering the clippers. "Lloyd Carver told it to me while I was cutting his hair, down to the VA hospital the week before he died."

The telephone rings. Speed picks it up. A moment later he hangs up and, turning to the counter behind his chair, searches for a new blade for his clippers. Catching sight of himself in the mirror, he leans closer, fingering a blemish on his chin.

"Doc," Jenkins says, "you may have plenty of book learning, but you and Speed might as well be twins because the two of you are still as ignorant about some things as the day you were born. Lloyd Carver just couldn't help himself—that little girl's stuff was too good and her game was just too strong."

"Well," Doc says, when he has finished laughing, "all that may be true. And it may be true that I am ignorant. But there is one significant difference between Speed and me—I respect black women. At least I try to."

Speed turns away from the mirror, one fist on his hip. The ash from his cigarette dribbles onto the front of his smock. "Who don't respect black women? I respect all womens. Long as they respect me."

"All right," Doc says, holding up his hands under the cloth in mock surrender. "But that must be a lot of respect, because we all know you have a lot of women. Mr. Jenkins, for the sake of argument, let us say your story is true. Even so, I still say what happened to your friend is no more than what some black women complain black men have always done to them. And you could even argue that she deserved some compensation for taking care of him."

Jenkins says, "You believe that shit?"

"I certainly do. *I* read. You should too, and not just the sports pages. You might learn something. Or watch TV. Like that talk show in the afternoons."

"Which show? One got that great big old fat broad?"

"She is not fat. Not anymore."

"Huh. Just wait. You'll see—she gon' put it all back on."

"That may be true," Doc says. "But it is neither here nor there as far as what we are talking about."

Jenkins looks at the clock. It is nine, closing time.

"Say, Omar," Jenkins says, "close the door, before some fool can't read come in here. And turn off the sign."

Hubble goes to do it. When he comes back, he says, "I been standing here listening, and I got to say it's been a long time since I heard Negroes this full of shit." He unpins the cloth and dusts the back of his customer's neck with talcum. Sweeping the cloth from his customer's lap, Hubble says, "Speed think Carver shoulda smacked the broad, and I can understand that, 'cause Speed's brains in his dick, if he got any. Jenkins, you think it's all about the woman had a better game than Carver. And you, Doc, you can't understand how a man could let something like that happen. But don't nonea y'all know what the hell you talking about. Y'all ever consider the possibility that Lloyd Carver was in love?"

Prudhomme says, "*Love?* Ain't nobody said nothing about love," and Jenkins says, "Omar, whatchu know about a old man and a young girl? You been married to the same woman twenty-seven years. And I know you don't do no running around on the side."

"Ain't got to. I love my wife. And I got what I need right at home."

"Shee-it," says Speed. "Don't lie. You be too tired. Working as many jobs as you got."

The men laugh, but Hubble says nothing. The chairs against the wall are almost empty now; only Prudhomme, Doc, and one or two stragglers are left. Hubble folds his cloth, hangs up clippers and scissors. He discards an empty bottle of hair tonic, tosses towels and the folded cloth in an orange nylon bag to go to the laundry on Monday. He counts the money he has taken in, counts out the share that is due Jenkins, and counts it again before giving it to him. Finished, Hubble takes a pair of clippers and a small wire brush. He sits down in his chair. He sits for a long time cleaning the clippers, brow furrowed and his mouth pursed, as if closing in on something he does not yet know if he wants to say. Finally, Hubble says, "Long as y'all telling stories, I got me one."

"Go on," Jenkins says, "you think we can understand it," and Hubble says, "It was this man one time loved his wife. Loved her more than he did his momma and his daddy, which is only right, because that's what the Good Book say you supposed to do. Every Friday night this man come home with his money and give it to his baby. She didn't even have to ask.

"Now one day him and his wife decide to get them a little house. He didn't want her working, and the only way they could do it was if he went out and got himself another job. Wasn't like it is now—colored man could only find certain types of work. And times was hard, so hard they was a lot of men couldn't even find *one* job. But this man found him some work washing dishes at night in a restaurant.

"Every morning he get up and go work his regular job. Get off and go wash them dishes till midnight six days a week. Was a whole lotta times he'd come home at night and his baby be sleeping when he get in. A man shouldn't be outside his house like that, not as much as this man was. See, by him being away from home like that, he wasn't able to take care of business. And it was plenty of other men just waiting to take care of it for him.

"One Friday morning, this man getting ready to leave out the house. His wife say, 'What time you comin' home?' He say regular time. And she say she been thinking—bank they been keeping their money in, she been reading the papers, and the money ain't safe no more. She say, 'I want us to take it out. Monday morning we'll find ourselves a good, safe place to put it.'

"He been working himself like a dog for two, almost three years. Had more than five hundred dollars saved up. He say, 'Sugar, you think it's the right thing? I don't like to think about carrying around that kind of money all day like that.' And his wife, she just throw back her head and laugh, say, 'Big as you is, who gon' mess with you?'

"Come lunch time he take all their money out the bank. Walk around all day with them bills folded over in his pocket. Every once in a while reach in his pocket and touch that money, thinking about how he could work so hard and so long and still have so little. Come midnight, he finish washing dishes in the restaurant and get on the streetcar, thinking how he just want to get home and put that money someplace safe.

"Man get off the streetcar and start walking. Almost to his house when he hear somebody say, 'There he is!' and two men jump out the alley. One got a knife. And it's a little man got a handkerchief over his face. One carry the knife say, 'I'ma have to cut you, you don't give it up.' Little one say, 'Yeah, we know you got it.' This man I'm talking about don't even stop to think about what he doing—he knock down the little man closest to him, kick him. Little one yelling, 'Cut him! Cut him!' and the man with the knife bring it down. Man do like this"—Hubble sets the clippers in his lap and raises his arms to cover his face—"and he don't even feel it when the knife cut the back of his arms from his wrist to his elbows. All he thinking about is how he gots to keep that money.

"Knife come down one more time and he grab the man's arm. Knife fall out the man's hand and he pick it up, turn on the little one. Hit him across the face, raise the knife. And hear the little man say, 'Naw, naw, don't do it. Don't you know who I is? It's me. It's me.'

"Man pull down the scarf, and you know what? It was his wife. It was his wife."

No one says anything, and for a moment the men in the shop can hear all the sounds from outside—footsteps on the sidewalk, laughter from the corner by the liquor store, the cars idling at the stoplight on the Avenue. Finally, Prudhomme whistles.

"Damn," Speed says, "that's some terrible shit. What he do, Hubble? Kick the bitch's ass and leave her in the street?"

"Naw. It didn't go like that. This man, he just left and went on home. Couldn't think of nowhere else to go. Got there and the *po*-lice was waiting. She told 'em he beat her. Judge give him six months."

Jenkins turns the chair so that Doc faces the mirror. Their eyes meet, and then both Doc and Jenkins turn to look at Hubble. Neither says anything. Speed says, "*Shee*-it," and puts down his clippers, disgusted. "Now that's what I been telling you. Man let a bitch run a game on him like that, he gon' get what he deserves. He shoulda smacked her a few times, let her know who was in control."

Hubble laughs.

"Speed, trying to tell you something is like trying to preach the Bible to a cat. Yeah, this man I'm talking about, he coulda beat her—he was twice her size, but see, he loved his woman. And while he was in jail, the woman searched her heart and come to understand how wrong she'd been. When he got out she came to find him. They been together ever since."

The telephone rings. Speed hesitates, unable to decide. He wants to set Hubble straight, but there is a little girl waiting. In the end he goes to answer the telephone. Jenkins, still looking curiously at Hubble, says, "Omar, long as you been working in my shop, I ain't never heard you tell no story. Least not like that. Now lookahere—"

Before Jenkins can finish, a car horn sounds outside and Hubble goes to the window. He waves, then turns. "Gentlemen," Hubble says, "y'all gon' have to excuse me, but that's my wife."

As the door closes after him Prudhomme says, "I don't know about y'all, but I don't believe a word . . ." and then he makes the connection, the same connection Doc and Jenkins have already made.

A man can learn many things in Lamarr Jenkins's shop—what to put into a transmission or a motor to keep a vehicle running long past its time; where to get the freshest fish, the cheapest television, the best suit; how to slaughter a hog or raise a sagging roof. And, sometimes, what a man learns may remind him of the true facts—that he can work alongside another man for fifteen years, can know him for that time and more, and still not know all there is to know about him. Prudhomme joins Doc and Jenkins at the window.

The big-bodied Chevrolet is double parked. Hubble walks to the driver's side while his wife slides over. There is nothing remarkable about her—she is a plump, brown-skinned woman with graying hair and a sweet, dimpled face. Hubble gets in and puts the Chevrolet in gear. Doc, Prudhomme, and Jenkins stand watching, long after Hubble has driven off.

Leaning against the wall with the telephone against his ear, Speed shifts the cigarette dangling from his lips and squints past the smoke. "Hey," Speed calls, "whatch'all looking at?"

Jenkins turns, motioning for Doc to sit down so that he can finish and they can all go home. "Never mind," Jenkins says. "Never mind. It ain't got a thing to do with you."

Yellow Moon

Jewell Parker Rhodes

Ten

Dillard University
Friday Late Afternoon

The office was ramshackle. Dimly lit, filled with books, glass paperweights, statues of assorted cultural gods. Isis. Buddha. Vishnu. Skulls—human and chimp—religious medallions, and jars filled with dead specimens—tree frogs, beetles—littered the file cabinets and desk. Cornhusk dolls, rosaries, bottles filled with multicolored oils cluttered the floor, the bookshelves.

Professor Alafin wore a tweed vest in the hot, windowless room. A chain watch dangled from his pocket. He wore a clip-on bow tie and tortoiseshell-rimmed glasses. Gray dreads scraped his collar.

"You're an interesting crew," said Alafin, shaking DuLac's hand.

"Think so?" asked Marie.

"Sure. My friend DuLac, who's never worried, looks worried. Perhaps a bit scared? No insult intended, old friend."

"None taken."

"A lovely young woman." Alafin stepped closer. "Pale. Unsettled. Are you well?"

"I'm fine," she said. Though she'd argued with both DuLac and Parks to let her come. Her body hurt; her head throbbed.

"Are you sure?" Alafin frowned, his brows touching between his eyes. "Wrist bandaged. Dressed to downplay your loveliness in a black T-shirt and blue jeans. And you," said Alafin, intent on Parks, "haven't got the sense not to look like a cop. Or is it a G-man?"

"G-man," said Parks. "I haven't heard that term in a while."

"I'm dated."

"Alafin lives in the present only when he has to," said DuLac.

"And DuLac visits me only when he has a puzzle. Sit."

Parks peered at captive beetles, moths, and butterflies pinned to a mat beneath glass. "What is it you do?"

"A bit of everything. Social anthropology, philosophy, religion—mystics and canonical—cultural history. Folklore. Ethnomusicology."

"Eclectic," said DuLac.

Alafin chuckled. "More like the perennial associate professor. At least according to my department chair. He says my research lacks focus. Significance. Whereas I believe any human inquiry has meaning. And all inquiries loop back to the essential question: Why are we alive?"

"To do good," answered Parks.

"A naive answer."

Parks bristled. "I'm a cop. Not a philosopher."

"I didn't mean to insult you. My own cynicism. Twenty-five years studying, searching, and I wonder whether it's that simple—'to do good.' If your answer is correct, then much of my life has been wasted, hasn't it? My chair thinks my research is a waste."

Marie found Alafin slightly distasteful. Doing good was her foundation.

Alafin sat behind his desk, his hands cupped under his chin, his elbows on his desk. He was a dark man; bright, black, inquiring eyes; medium size. His hands showed his age; years of digging, unearthing mysteries, secrets, and ancient societies had taken their toll. His hands curled like claws, wrinkled and discolored from clay, mud, the earth's minerals. He watched Marie, intent, curious. As if he'd guessed her disapproval.

"You know who I am," Marie murmured.

"I knew you when DuLac suspected you were you."

She looked at DuLac.

"Don't be upset with DuLac. Confirmation. He wanted confirmation."

"You don't even know me."

"I know how you came into being. How history, ancestors, have crafted you. A descendant of Laveau, who descended from a powerful African priestess. See, I have it all here. Five generations." He opened a lineage map, a tree of her female ancestors.

Marie bristled. Part of her wanted to study the tree. To ask questions. Ultimately, it was upsetting that he knew more about her than she him. That DuLac had discussed her with him.

"Don't be upset, *chérie*," said DuLac. "I needed help. With my understanding."

Parks interjected, "We need help with a crime."

"Something to do with the bandaged wrists?"

"A spirit's been draining blood," said DuLac. "Not a spirit called during voodoo ritual."

"But called by music," said Parks. "Isn't that right, Doc? Except Father Xavier's murder doesn't fit the pattern."

"It does," she said. "Check. There'd been a dance class the night he was murdered. Drums in the basement. The room beneath his."

"How do you know this?" complained Parks. "Damnit, Doc—"

"It tried to drain you?" interrupted Alafin.

"I survived." Her left hand covered her bandage.

"Let me see. Please."

She felt Alafin's desperation. Mouth slightly parted, his hands clenched together as if to rein himself in, he could barely contain himself from grabbing, from ripping away gauze.

Marie unrolled her bandage. Layer after layer.

Her flesh was red, as if scalded by steam. Three punctures. Parallel to her bruised veins.

"What did it feel like?"

Marie didn't answer. DuLac was studying her. He wanted to know how she knew about the drums. The music in the basement.

Alafin touched her hole-shaped wounds. *"Wazimamoto."*

He searched his shelves of books. His blue polyester clothes were too big; a ripped pant cuff scraped dirt from the floor. He needed a shave and a haircut. "Here." Alafin grabbed a book, on the far left, from the next to the highest shelf. "Vampires."

"You've got to be kidding," said Parks.

"Quiet," chastised DuLac.

"Not researched much," said Alafin. "Really an unexplored area. One I haven't given much attention. No one has." He flipped through pages, his fingers resting on one particular page. He read silently, the researcher in him forgetting anyone else was in the room.

"What do you know, Alafin?" asked DuLac. "We're among friends."

Alafin lifted his head, focusing on Parks, DuLac, then Marie. He clutched the book tightly against his chest. "I've spent my whole life studying the mystical. Searching for miracles—I've seen things. In Haiti, Brazil, Nigeria, Belize.

"Seen zombies, as you have, Marie. Seen shamans shape-shift. Yes," he said to a sneering Parks. "Seen a man become a cat then a man again. Seen seers predict volcanic eruptions, a woman's labor. All religions, cultures, have their miraculous tales. Christ's image appearing in cloth. The reincarnation of the Dalai Lama. Aboriginal firewalkers. But I've never had the miraculous walk into my office."

"I'm just a woman," said Marie.

"Shame. There's no hope for you then."

Marie stared at Alafin. "Show me," she said. "Show me what you've seen. What you see."

Alafin laid the book on the desk. Black leather, red-trimmed edges on the pages. Leather straps for closure.

DuLac, Parks, and Marie gathered round the book and desk. Alafin adjusted the lamp; the book gleamed.

"Colonial period," said Alafin. "Written when Africa seemed a banquet for Europeans to consume, like a greedy plague."

Marie stroked the cover. She hesitated, knowing that once opened, her life would be forever changed.

Unlike Christianity, with its command not to be tempted by the snake, voodoo proclaimed all knowledge good. Like a snake eating its own tail, renewing itself by shedding its skin, knowledge was infinite, necessary to being human. There was no "two-edged sword." In voodoo, Prometheus would have been celebrated, never chained.

Gently, Marie opened the frayed pages, originally a kind of beige, with red, a reddish-brown, leaking from the edges into the page's interior.

"That's blood," said Parks.

DuLac rubbed the paper between his thumb and fingers. "This page, it isn't flesh, but something close."

"Cowhide," said Alafin. "Seared with elaborate woodblock prints. These, too, dipped in blood. Pages upon pages. All handcrafted. Art embodying the caution. Embodying life and death."

"Amazing," exhaled Marie.

"One of the few books in the world documenting African vampires. It was written by a 1920s missionary. A priest and a village shaman. A unique partnership. Written to warn. Bear witness to humanity's sins begetting sins."

Picture upon picture: African villages, straw-thatched huts, women tilling the soil, carrying infants on their back, children playing by the roadside. Men conversed in small groups, their heads and eyes averted. In the far-left corner, two officers looked down at a splayed body, blood draining from its wrist.

Another: a seemingly unending chain of Africans, each whispering in another's ear. Officers were dragging a man into jail.

Another: moon high and full, a deserted plain. Amid the stalks and high grasses, there were a dozen bodies, emaciated, drained, their wrists blood speckled. A pride of lions ignored them. A soldier with a bayonet, gleaming black boots, counted out coins to a barefoot villager.

"But there's nothing about race here," muttered Parks.

"Are you sure, Detective?"

"The officers are all white, the villagers black. Colonialism. All about race. Class. Part of the psychology. Whites were *wazimamotos*. Colonizers. See, the officers are implicated in the killings. Explicitly, here, they're dragging a man to jail. Everyone knows he won't return. He'll be killed. They'll say: '*wazimamoto.*' "

"It's a metaphor," said Marie.

"Yes. But it's also suspected to be real. Evil takes physical form in the world. The *loas* teach us that. The gods, themselves, can be reflections of hate, jealousy, envy. See this—a small group of black men, wearing badges—men who were probably given power similar to a deputy. They've become spies on their own community. Traitors. Africans, literally and mentally, colonized.

"*Wazimamotos* could be either a white spirit punishing blacks or a colonized, assimilated black—"

"You mean an Uncle Tom?"

"Yes. A black feeding on its own. Similar to African kings who sold their enemies into slavery. That was evil. But a *wazimamoto* can also be someone who commits evil because he identifies with his oppressors, he wants to *be* the colonizer, the master. These black men here are wielding machetes, dismembering this black man—and, by extension, metaphorically dismembering, destroying, their noncolonized selves."

"But a free Africa is still engaging in slavery, brutality."

"I'm not saying, Detective, that evil behavior doesn't exist. It's rampant in all cultures. Throughout history. The Incas' sacrifices. The Romans' feeding of Christians to lions. You need only to read today's paper to know that across the globe, evil thrives. I'm speaking about motivation. Sometimes evil is a product of self-hatred. Learned behavior. When individuals identify with the oppressor. Intraracial, not interracial, prejudice. People feeding off the blood of their own people. Oppressing within their social group to cull favor with the colonizer, the enslaver.

"In these instances, the motivation stems from the legacy of the first evil—a people systematically demeaning, brutalizing, another people."

Marie slammed the book shut. As a physician, she'd seen some of evil's physical results. But she wasn't required to think of the source. For her medical work, it didn't matter; as a *voodooienne*, it did.

The three men watched her.

"Tea?" asked Alafin.

"*Oui,*" said DuLac.

"Scotch," said Parks.

"I have that, too." Without asking, Alafin poured a drink for Marie.

She sipped. The heat in her mouth felt good. "It possessed me. No, that's not right. It was inside me. But it didn't overtake me. I was conscious."

"So it's not a god, not a true spirit *loa*. But other," said DuLac.

"A human creation," said Alafin. "*Waᶎimamoto.*"

"How can that be? It's a monster," said Parks. "Besides, we don't live in a colonized world."

"Are you sure?" asked Alafin.

"New Orleans is the epitome of colonization," said DuLac. "Multiple colonizations taken to their logical conclusion."

"We're all Americans."

"Some living better than others," said DuLac. "Why is it that the more pigment you have, the more oppressed you seem to be," said DuLac. "Not just in New Orleans. But especially in New Orleans."

"Aw, come on, DuLac," said Parks. "New Orleans has a black mayor. Black police chief."

"It also has a legacy," said Alafin, "from the eighteenth and nineteenth centuries. Colonial distinctions detailing the worth of a black—house slave, field slave, a Creole, free colored, mulatto, quadroon, octoroon."

"Who still controls the wealth?" said DuLac. "It's not by accident the majority of Charity's patients are black, brown, and yellow people."

"Look. Can we get back to evidence?"

"In part, I think you're both right," said Marie. "Racism still influences New Orleans. How could it not? A historical port city, home to slavers. Colonizers who owned people as easily as ships, cargo. But the Civil Rights era has happened. African Americans have defiantly staked their claim and right to be."

"*Oui*," said DuLac. "We've always been a proud people."

"Yet racism, colonialism, still brutalizes. Perverts," said Marie. "Like a disease spreading, its power would lie at the source. At the historical nexus when its power was unfettered, rampant. If *wazimamotos* exist, they would exist not as twenty-first-century vampires, but as a remnant from the nineteenth, eighteenth—"

"Yes," said Alafin. "That would make sense. The point of cultural contact. When the conflict in society, within the self, would be at its worst."

"That means—" said DuLac, understanding.

"Our vampire is a ghost. A creature from the past."

"Aw, come on. Speculation is well and good, but I can't convict on theories. Hell, I can't arrest what I can't see. It's like trying to lock up Rudy and JT. The ghosts Doc says she sees."

Marie raised her brow.

"Okay, okay. You see them."

"And?"

"I think I've felt them. That's as far as I'll go, Doc. Shit." Parks downed the scotch. "Okay. I felt them. Ghosts. Invisible dead."

"Don't light a cigarette in here," said Alafin.

"Probably send the place up in flames," DuLac said wryly.

"Have another drink, Parks." Marie poured the shot.

"Shit. Shit. Shit." Parks gulped the alcohol.

Marie leaned forward, reopening the book. A white missionary taught a group of native children.

Parks read over Marie's shoulder. "Reeducation." His scotch-tainted breath was sweet. "Why the multiple languages?" he asked. "They all say the same thing? 'Reeducation'?"

Alafin nodded. "English, French, Portuguese, Afrikaner/Dutch—all of them at one time colonized Africa."

"Just as French, Spanish, Americans did—"

"Enough already," said Parks. "Why the draining of blood, Professor? Murder is murder. Why not just slit the throat? Crack a skull?"

"Here," Alafin turned to the last page. "This is the African dialect. Ibo. A kind of epigraph. It says, in effect, that bloodsuckers are emblematic of western culture. Dracula, *nosferatu* were brought to Africa. Not the other way around."

"And this," asked Marie, her fingers tracing letters that had been written on the back binding. A rough scrawl, in blood.

"What does this say?"

"The unsayable. It's name. *Wazimamoto.* This is the only place in the book where the word is written out. The last page. Africans believed saying the name would call it."

"So they used a code," said DuLac.

"Parks," said Marie. "These are like the markings in Preservation Hall. Rudy, I mean the creature had been trying to name itself."

"What are you saying?" asked DuLac.

"There was blood above Rudy's body," said Parks. "But no blood left on or in his body."

"Amazing." Alafin nearly crowed with excitement. "There are origin myths. Tales about how such creatures are born. Knowing one's name, being able to say it, is powerful."

Marie stroked the pages tenderly. Starting from the beginning, she flipped the pages. Arrested.

"What do you see?" asked Parks.

"From the beginning you see fragments of the name. An angled line at first. Then another. Then the angles meeting."

"It's on every page with a death."

"Yes. After each draining."

The next to last page, the angles met, twice: VV. A young woman lying in the grass. Her neck arched back. Hair fanning across her breast. Her simple shift hitched high on her thighs. Her left arm thrown over her head, palm open to the sky, fingers gently bent. Puncture wounds. Deep, red.

"The first letter there. Completed," said Alafin. "Buried in the corner."

Parks's fingers traced the VV.

Marie turned to the last page. "It named itself. Tantamount to coming into being. Like a child learning to spell, to say its name."

"Relying on blood, on killing," said Alafin, "to create the first letter. Does it know what it is—or does the killing account for its knowing, its awareness of self? Maybe it isn't even aware of its self."

Marie thought of the markings on the wall in Preservation Hall. Agwé's sign. Rudy had tried to scratch his salvation. Like the book, the first letter of *waẓimamoto* had been scratched in blood. The evidence team had confirmed it.

"Rudy's blood," said Parks.

"What?" asked DuLac.

"This letter," said Marie, tracing, "was drawn with a victim's blood."

"Incredible," said Alafin. "Scribing its self into being."

"Yes and no." She spoke slowly, thinking, trying to articulate connections. "If it's a ghost—then *waẓimamoto* is what it *is*—its *genus*, vampire—but not its name. It would've had a life once—before becoming a vampire. A different name."

"Why didn't it write it?" asked Parks.

"Maybe it didn't know it," said DuLac. "Its name. This isn't a normal ghost. JT and Rudy are present day, presumably with present-day memories. This ghost—this *waẓimamoto*, has been where? For over a century. Do ghosts have memories?"

"Uncharted territory," said Marie.

"So little we know. Much we don't," said Alafin.

Marie's palms covered the name—*waẓimamoto*. *The page felt alive.*

"Written in blood. Draining blood. Again, why blood?" asked Parks. "Serial killers do it to demonstrate control. But a ghost?"

"All cultures revere blood," answered Alafin. "To lose blood is an offense that violates more than life, it violates human dignity. Implying the capturing of one's essence, the bloodlines. And who is to say the soul doesn't reside in the blood? Theologians talk about the heart—the engine of our blood—as our soul's resting place, our desires animated from the heart's blood."

"Anne Rice couldn't have written it better," said Parks, mumbling.

"Facts, not fiction," insisted DuLac. "Are you such a poor policeman that you abandon facts? What your eyes see? You saw what that thing did to the dancer. To Marie."

Parks studied his hands, clenching, then unclenching them. "Part of me still doesn't want to admit to what I saw. I don't understand anything you've all been saying. It's gibberish."

"Chaos," said Marie, nudging him toward acceptance. Understanding.

"I'm comfortable with chaos. But this is a mystery. Mystical."

"That's why you have me, Parks. The three of us," she said, her look embracing Alafin and DuLac.

"I feel I'm back at square one. Resisting. I'm being honest." He looked frankly at Marie. "Everything in me says I can't go down this path. I'm on it, been journeying. But part of me wants to turn around, keep trekking. Like I never met you. Any of you." He tapped his chest. "Look. If I can't smoke, give me another drink. I can't believe this," Parks said wiping his sweating brow, "drinking on the job."

DuLac poured. "Why'd you become a cop?"

"I hate seeing people victimized. No one should be hurt. Ever."

"You hate what it did to me?" asked Marie.

"Yes."

"Hold on to that, Parks," said DuLac.

"It isn't done with me," said Marie.

"Or with others," said Alafin.

"What do we know?" asked Marie. "Follow the evidence. Music calls it—as it calls the spirits. But, unlike a spirit, it can't possess. It inhabits, controls the body but not the self. This vampire—this *wazimamoto*—"

"This response to colonialism," said DuLac. "Racism—"

"We're living in the twenty-first century," said Parks.

"Exactly," said Marie. "The invisible dead. A ghost from some other time."

"It straddles both worlds," said Alafin.

"Multiple worlds," said Marie. "Past. Present. African. American. Old World. New World. Mythic. Real. Living. Dead."

"Why does it kill?"

"The policeman's question."

"Motive, Doc. Like your motivation for evil. Crimes don't happen without it."

"Don't they?" asked DuLac.

"Never," Parks said, adamant. "Even when it seems there isn't motiva-tion—a crazy man losing control—still, the cause is there, just buried. Maybe he was abused. Took mind-bending drugs. Thought his victim was an alien. Even when motives are unknown. Or seemingly not there. They're there. Motives move people. Cause them to act."

"But this isn't a person," said DuLac.

"Parks still has a point," said Marie. "It kills. Why? Why bother, after centuries, to kill? What's gained by the method of killing?"

"Food?" said DuLac. "A need for sustenance?"

"Control," said Alafin. "Claiming power."

"A taste for cruelty," said Parks.

"Vlad the Impaler," said Alafin.

"Stoker's Dracula," responded Parks. "Cruel, hungry."

He went to the window and pulled the cord, opening the blinds. "I've got to hit the streets. Sun's going down. Isn't that when vampires thrive? Besides, the French Quarter is jumping, half lit with booze. If music calls this thing—this *wazimamoto*—I can't think of any place better than Bourbon Street."

"I'll come with you."

"I don't think that's wise, Marie," said DuLac.

"Marie-Claire is with Louise. You'll go to her, DuLac? Take care of her until I'm home?"

"You needn't ask."

DuLac embraced her. "Take care. Parks, if you let any harm come to Marie, I'll hurt you myself."

Parks opened the office door; light rushed in from the hall.

"Professor." Marie wanted to ask one final question. "What does Agwé have to do with this?"

"He may be trying to control the creature."

"He's done a good job so far," quipped Parks.

"Or else," said Marie, "that's where it was born. Became reanimated. Inside Agwé. The Mississippi. Flowing out to the Gulf—"

"—out to sea," said Alafin.

"All the way to Africa," said DuLac.

"An ocean littered with bones," said Marie. "Souls."

"You remember that, Marie," said DuLac fiercely. "A lost soul. Not a god. And it feared you. Your name."

"You're not just a woman," said Alafin.

"I know. *Je suis* Marie Laveau." Then Marie smiled, brilliant and expansive. "Thank you, Professor."

Alafin bowed.

"DuLac. I promise to take good care." Marie paused. "Of Detective Parks."

DuLac chortled. "Touché."

"Let's go, Detective," said Marie.

"Women. Worse than vampires," said Parks.

"Don't get me started on detectives," said Marie. The two of them bickered down the hall.

Microstories

John Edgar Wideman

Rain

Never ending rain had seemed the truth forever until the day he'd been born, and rain stopped the very next day and no rain since. No one he'd spoken to had much to say about rain. Nothing good to say. They were glad it was finished. Envied his freedom from what rain had imposed on their lives. Why was he so curious about something people assured him had been no fun. Worse than no fun. Some people would shake their heads to suggest he harbored an unhealthy obsession. Why this worrying after rain. If he had known rain, they said, if he'd been there, he'd shut up about rain, they warned or advised or teased or just turned away to end a conversation they could not stomach. None of them, not a single soul yet, understood his need to recover what he'd missed, rain falling for the final time the day he'd been born, the rain other people had forgotten or had no desire to recall, and him with a million questions, a million dreams, tears once when he couldn't explain his yearning to the only person who had ever seemed really curious, but how could he describe to her something lost, and worse, lost irrevocably, before he had experienced it, how could he express his loss because what was rain, after all, what could he say except the next to nothing others had told him about rain that had never missed a day before he arrived and would start again, he was sure (and this might be the unbearable part), the instant he left.

Divorce

He is dressing for his grown-up daughter. How strange, he thinks, peering into his closet. To be picking this and discarding that as if he's going to a wedding or funeral. Since when (how long, how long) is meeting her an occasion. A date. The peacock dashiki to give her a laugh. The good suit to offend her. Bell-bottom jeans she'll smirk at or, worse, ignore. As if he can predict the consequences of his choices in her eyes. As if he knows what they'll talk about in the restaurant she's chosen. The waiter setting down a cup of coffee that rattles in its saucer, spotting the white blaze of tablecloth before they can even begin. Not the waiter's fault. Nobody's fault, really, that their table happens to be at the foot of a mountain range with jagged peaks looming above them, obdurate and unimpeachable as annular rings of a tree. The crack, the fissure begins under there, under the stony folds of mountains stacking up, stacking up. Too much weight, too many years. The earth shudders, dances the rug under the poor, pompadoured waiter's feet. *Sorry . . . sorry . . .* he faintly warbles, *. . . excuse me,* a canary dying of what's to come.

Thirteen

Now comes the thirteen story. Thirteen the day of my son's birth. Lucky. Unlucky. How could it happen. On the thirteenth, one fifteen-year-old kills another. The chance of that one particular thing happening small as a single breath in the universe. The universe the size of the chance against the possibility of that moment undoing itself, never happening, going away. With two Arizona lawyers, my son, his mother I'd stopped loving, and me in it, the car speeds south to north, Phoenix to Flagstaff. I'm driving, listening to one lawyer speak when the other, suffering unbeknownst to us from his own lonely addiction, interjects something about too bad it's not *Massachusetts,* which he pronounces *Massatwo-sits,* before he resumes staring out the window. Arizona wants to start executing juveniles, the other lawyer continues. The state's looking for the right kid to kill. A black kid would suit them perfectly. Plea bargaining our only chance to save your son's life.

Years before I'm able to sit through this ride again, before I can speak to anyone about Arizona's jails full of Mexicans and Indians, the zigzag mountain peaks stitching sky to earth, sumptuous oil spills of sunset, one sudden burst of rain battering dry plains like sheets of tears. On the last night of a Western tour, returning from the Grand Canyon, a group of fifteen-year-olds stay at an Arizona motel. Next morning my son's roommate found stabbed to death. My son missing. For days presumed dead, tortured, buried by some madman in the Arizona desert or mountains. Then my son calls home. We fly to Arizona to turn him in. Plead. Life the best we can hope for. After long silence Freddie Jackson's "You Are My Lady," my son's favorite song, on the car radio. One note breaks me down. Like one shooting-star mote of plaque can explode a brain. One instant of insanity explode two boys' lives. Sheets of tears. You only get one chance. That's all a father gets with a son. A child's life in your hands once. That's it. Once. He was born in New Jersey and I took classes to assist at his birth, but some clown passed out the day before, so on the thirteenth the delivery room off-limits for fathers and I missed the moment the earth cracked and she squeezed out his bloody head.

AT&T

They employ the same robot in prisons three thousand miles apart to inform you that you have a collect phone call from an inmate. Each time he wonders if part of the astronomical charge for a five-minute call from a prison includes a bill for forty or so seconds of the lady robot's time announcing, interrupting, signing off. Once he'd responded to her, imitating her recorded voice, the robot cadence and tone she'd taught him. Proposed marriage. Why not. Two could live as comfortably as one on the enormous profits she must reap participating how many goddamn times a day coast to coast and everywhere in between in the misery of conversations between the incarcerated and those not. If you can get away with it, why not charge a rate fifty, a hundred times more than what the unincarcerated pay to speak to one another. Are you still there, darling, he'd asked her after he said, I love you, and she didn't respond. Then he said, No . . . no, it's okay, you don't have to answer. You don't need to tell me your name and I won't tell you mine. After all, if we meet in the street, you, me, my brothers and sons and fathers when they're free, who'd want to remember all this.

Fat Liver

The campaign for attaining a higher level of enlightenment goes well. *Hurrah. Hurrah. No more foie gras.* A silly banner, she admits. And maybe a silly cause. Who gives a crap if it becomes a crime to force-feed ducks and geese, a crime to package and sell their agony, she asks herself. Imagines bloated black kids with tubes down their throats fed buckets of KFC, rivers of Orange Crush, tons of Big Macs. Imagines the iron maws of prisons pried open, dark bodies crammed in. Sees America's bare, fat ass upturned in the air, oil pumping in like an enema. Imagines her fellow citizens' fuzzy heads bobbing like baby birds in a nest, every beak propped open by a funnel, the grinning president stuffing them with lies, terror, disinformation, war. Maybe she'll skip the foie gras victory march and victory party this afternoon.

Ring. Ring. That must be Sarah calling. Or perhaps Samuel. Though a bit early for him. Either one, it will break her heart to answer. No, I'm staying home this afternoon. No, our chance for a life together is over. No. No. Please don't call me ever again. The disappointed faces of Sarah and Samuel blend. Separate tales for each one collapse into one long, sad story. *Ring. Ring.* She realizes she's crying and that her mouth's open. The phone with a million miles of AT&T cable spooled behind it pushing through her lips, filling her to bursting.

War Stories

I have a friend, a kind of friend anyway, I talked with only once, and that once we'd seemed simpatico. I learned a lot from a story he'd written about things men carried when they fought in Vietnam. Years have passed and I've lost track of him, so to speak. I need to talk with him now because I'm trying to understand the war here in America, the worst war, in spite of mounting casualties in wars abroad, this war filling prisons, filling pockets, emptying schools, minds, hearts, a war keeping people locked down at home, no foreign enemies to defeat, just ourselves defeated by fear of one another, a war incarcerating us all in killing fields, where the only rule is feed on the bodies of fellow inmates or surely they will feed on yours. What do combatants carry in this war, in this civil strife waged within stone walls, in glass cages, barbed-wire-enclosed ghettos of poverty and wealth, behind the lines, between the lines. Can friend be distinguished from foe by what they wear. By the way they walk, how they talk. Their words, their silence. A war different, though not entirely unlike others in Afghanistan, Iraq, and soon Iran or wherever else folly incites us to land our young men and women with whatever they will carry into battle this time and carry when they return like chickens Malcolm warned always come home to roost. Not separate wars, really. No more separate than different colors of skin that provide logic and cover for war. No more separate than the color of my skin from yours, my friend, if we could meet again and talk about carrying the things we carry, about what torments me, an old man ashamed of this country I assume you still live in, too.

Home from College

She counts her mother's missing fingers. Two more gone to the disease. Wonders if the rumor reaching her at school of toes rotting inside those ratty bedroom slippers is true. When she's away and scared, she counts the missing parts of her mother, and the count always equals one. One mother. She smiles and counts again. One. The magic answer calms her each time she figures out how many mothers she has left, just to be sure, just to make sure. One. One mother minus two fingers equals what. One. Take away ten toes. Still never equals less than one. Until a day no absent parts to count. No more lost fingers or toes. No sad little round potbelly looks like it's full to bursting, tiny as it is, because her mother, skinny as a string, keeps no food down. Nothing gone away to count. Just the pink, slinky robe that always reminds her of the silvery one she was never allowed to suck her thumb with the silky tail of sleeping on her mother's lap. No missing poke of knee or nipple under the pink robe draped flat over the couch arm next to the kitchen door, the couch end where her mother settles each morning. Nothing new to minus. Only a girl standing beside an empty couch who would, if she could, subtract one from herself, count a missing part that starts the count again.

Giblets

Clara's dog Giblets had four legs. One leg for each day of the week. Now, Clara Johnson understood as well as you understand that each week the Lord sends got seven days, but Clara's memories are not your memories. Once upon a time, every Friday and Saturday and Sunday of every week were holy days in her mama's house, and Clara'd get her ass kicked often and terribly, bloodied by any comb or switch or board or cord her mother could lay her hands on, because Clara never could satisfy her mama by being as good as she was s'posed to be from the hour they started till those three days of church and praying and singing and sitting still as stone were over. So as soon as Clara out on her own she amputated the merciless days. Her weeks four days long with no scars, no beatings, no screaming, no cringing in a dark corner. Go away, goddamn church, and she never missed one of the cruel three days she cut out of her week, not once, never, just like Giblets after one long howl just lay there quiet and didn't miss his leg she chopped off when Tyrone from over at Mason's lounge told her a church he'd heard about commenced its holy days on Thursdays.

Automatic

They stole my money, my father says. I know exactly what you mean, man, I could have responded, but don't want to get him started on the frozen poem of frustration and rage he can't help reciting, stanza by stanza, because the thieves won't send him the prizes their letters declare he's won. I've come to take away his car keys. Or rather do what our worried family has decided, Ask for his car keys. We'd tried before. No way, José, he let us know. Me and that old girl automatic. Drive this whole city blindfold. Today it's as if he knew before I knocked, someone would be coming by and there would be less of him left as soon as he opened his door, so he's reminding me, whatever my good intentions, that I'm also just like those others who'd lied, stripped, and stolen from him his entire life and aren't finished yet, vultures circling closer and closer, withholding his prizes, picking his bones clean because an old black man too tired to shoo them off anymore. His quick mind leaving him fast but thank goodness my father no pack rat. Until the end his apartment fairly neat. He keeps only the final letters in their boldly colored, big print envelopes guaranteeing a Corvette or condo in Acapulco or million in cash megaprize. Beside his bed and on the kitchen table large stacks of these lying motherfuckers that taunt and obsess him, his last chance, a glorious grand finale promised, though how and when not precisely spelled out in the fine print. He never quite figures out the voices on the other end of his daily 800 calls are robots. Curses the menus white women's voices chirp. His response to my request he surrender his keys gentler. A slightly puzzled glance, a smile breaking my heart, *No, Daddy, no. Don't do it,* I'm crying out helplessly, silently, as he passes me the keys.

Message

A message in red letters on the back of a jogger's T-shirt passed by too quickly for me to memorize exactly. Something about George Bush going too far in his search for terrorists and WMDs. A punch line sniggering that Bush could have stayed home and found the terrorist he was looking for in the mirror. I liked it. The message clever, I thought, and jacked the idea for my new line of black-lettered T-shirts: America went way too far looking for slaves. Plenty niggers in the mirror for sale.

Northstar

She said I find the idea of anal sex quite un-sexy, and he dropped the subject. A tube of lubricating cream that had appeared magically on the perforated seat of an antique, wire-legged stool that served as a bedside table disappeared. How come men think they can make up the rules to liberate women, she'd asked before the subject dropped. Two weeks later when it happens, on his knees hunched over her in the dark bedroom, he's alone. Alone as the last person alive on earth and wonders if that's how a fugitive slave might have felt the first night free, racing through black forests and swamps following the Northstar, and remembers a dinner party in her brother's garden, the moon and a solitary star shining high above the patio table where everybody's happy drinking and eating, then the two of them walking around a corner of the house, beyond the arc of light cast by a fat candle burning in a crystal globe on the tabletop, the sky full of stars, the quiet amazingly deep though they'd moved only a few steps from the others, and there he'd taken her hand and wanted to say, I'm sorry. I didn't mean to upset you. Just forget I ever brought up that business because it's not something that really matters, all that matters is how much we love each other, but he couldn't reassure her without bringing up the dropped subject, so didn't speak, and now on his knees, pressed against her in this even quieter darkness, gooey mess all over his hands, his presumptions melted, him too sloppy and droopy, alone, scared to move an inch forward or back, would she ever forgive him, would he ever forgive her.

Party

I go up to Aunt May's wheelchair. She gives me her crinkly hand and I take it. Why are you sprouting warts and whiskers, I want to ask her, looking down to find Aunt May's tiny green eyes twinkling in the folds of her moon face, the same pitted, pale flesh of the hand my pale hand squeezes, not too hard, not testing for bones I'm very curious about. Are they brittle or soupy-soft or sea-changed altogether to foam like is stuffed inside cloth animals to hold their shape. Draped by bead necklaces that dangle to her waist, her hips snug in a sequined flapper dress hemmed with fringe that starts at her knees and almost touches the silver buckles of her shoes, May smiles at me from a sepia-toned photo. No. That's not true. May smiles here, now, during this celebration of her eighty-third birthday, although unbeknownst to everybody at the party (and everyone at the party in the old photo) the surgeon forgot a metal clip in May's gut last week that's festering and will kill her next Christmas Eve. Not one party and then another and another. It's all one big party. Life ain't nothing but a party, May grins at me after I sugar her cheek, dance her hand, the fringe swish, swishing, brushing my trouser leg as she swirls out, spins, spools in, jitterbugging, camel walking, fox-trotting, buzzard lope. My, my, Miss May. Oh-blah-dee. Watch out, girl. You have only eighty-three years or eight months or eight seconds to live before the party's over and the flashbulb freezes you forever, the sepia photo's close-up portions the color of batter I used to lick from my finger after swiping it around the mixing bowl when my grandmother, your cousin, your fine running partner, light, bright, and almost white as you, May, finished pouring her cake in a pan, set the pan in the oven to bake, and turned me loose on that bowl. Don't miss none, she'd grin. Get it all, Mr. Doot.

Paris Morning

One, two, three, four birds flutter up and perch on top of a Paris apartment building. Birds the color of stains where the whitish, pillbox plain structure bleeds at its seams, corners, along the edge of its flat roof on which the birds stay just a few moments before dropping like stones past five or six upper stories, then treetops he can see from a window above the kitchen sink. The blank-walled, massive, squared unloveliness of the building squatting where it squats, the birds landing precisely when and where they land, staying precisely as long as they stay, tell time exactly as the church bells that morning when he'd awakened, and doesn't that mean all eternity has been waiting for those birds to rise up and putter, each on its appointed spot, each hopping about no more, no less than its allotted number of hops along the razor edge of rooftop, every second

accounted for, poised, primed to happen, must align itself ahead or behind the appearance of a flight of birds the dirt color of almost transpar-
ent shadows, four creatures gathering to touch down together on top of a
whitish building with its meager, barred terraces, deeply recessed windows, tiny heads and breasts all he could see of the birds until they swoop
off riding invisible ropes like mountain climbers rappelling, swiftly gone,
another eternity passing or the same one passing once again before the
birds, attuned to some simple fixed design, like seasons changing or clock
hands recycling, would alight again precisely as he'd glimpsed them
alighting just an instant ago, except meanwhile gears and pulleys, streaming particles of light and bundles of light tearing one another apart or
fumbling under one another's clothes inside dark rooms of the apartment
building across the way, have transformed in the twinkling of an eye, the
one, two, three, four birds and every other possible bird and each and
every concrete block stacked, cemented together to form the structure
atop which the birds jiggle a moment, all of that and the universes con-
taining it crumbled to dust then nothing then starting over and starting to
crumble again during an unfathomable interval between two iron links in
the chain of being, the stroke of one moment connected to the next
stroke, and if he misses the next one where would he be then.

Haiku

Toward the end of his life, a time he resided in France in self-imposed
exile from America, the negro novelist Richard Wright chose the Japan-
ese form haiku, an unrhymed poem of three lines, seventeen syllables, as
his principal means for speaking what burned inside him, the fire he
needed to express through some artistic medium or another each day till
he died. Thousands of haikus, and the thought of him working hour after
hour, a tired colored man from Mississippi, fifty-two years old, world famous once then nearly forgotten by his countrymen, trying again, one
more time, to squeeze himself into or out of a tiny, arbitrary allotment of
syllables dictated by a tradition conceived by dead strangers in a faraway
land, poor Richard Wright in Paris hunched over a sheet of paper mid-
wifing or executing himself within the walls of a prison built without ref-
erence to the dimensions required by anyone whose life arched
gigantically like Richard Wright's from slavery in the South almost to
men on the moon, the idea of this warrior and hero falling upon his own

sword on a battlefield chosen, rigged so Richard Wright's struggle doomed before it began, the still multiplying and heartbreaking ironies I perceive in the man's last, quiet, solitary efforts—counting one, two, three . . . five, six, seven, up and back like salsa dancers, or however, whatever you do, pacing, measuring your cage in order to do the thing he'd ended up doing, haiku, it makes me want to cry, but also sit back, shout in wonder.

Writing

All the years I never learned to write. Stop. Start. A man on a bicycle passes down Essex Street in the rain. Gray. Green. Don't go back. You won't write it any better. More. You can only write more or less. That's all. A man in a greenish gray slicker pedals down Essex in a slashing downpour. Leaves behind a pale brushstroke of color that pulsates, coming and going as you stare into empty slants of rain. A flash of color left behind. Where is the man. Where gone. What on his mind. The color not there really. Splashed and gone that quick. A bit of wishful thinking. A melancholy painting on air. Do not go back. It doesn't get better. Only more. Less. The years not written do not wait to be written. Wait nowhere. No. An unwritten story is one that never happens. A story is never until after the writing. Before is pipe dream. Something lost you wish you hadn't or wish you had. Gone before it got here. There is no world full of unwritten stories waiting to be written. Not even one. To hang people's hopes on, the hope that their story will be revealed one day, worth something, true, even if no one else can see it or touch it, a beautiful story like in that girl's sad eyes on the subway, her life story real as anyone's, as real as yours, her eyes say to me, a story no one has written, desperate to be written. Never will be. Rain blurs the image of a man steadfastly slashing down Essex Street on his bike through driving rain, rain whose force and weight any second will disintegrate the gray sheet of paper on which the figure's drawn, a man huddled under a gray-green slicker who doesn't know he's about to disappear and take his world with him. Except for a stroke of gray-green hovering in my eyes like it did the day we crossed the dunes and suddenly, for a moment, between steep hills of sand I saw framed in the distance what I thought might be a sliver of the sea we'd come so far to find.

Passing On

Why couldn't he choose. Blue suit or brown suit. Throughout a long life, he'd endeavored to make sense of life, and now, almost overnight it seemed, the small bit of sense he'd struggled to grasp had turned to non-sense. Even the toys his grandkids played with mocked him, beeping, ringing, squealing, flashing products of a new dispensation he'd never fathom. Only prickly pride remained, pride in how he dressed, how he spoke the language, pride he hoped would allow him a dignified passage through final disappointments and fickleness. Unbending pride a barely disguised admission he's been defeated by that world he no longer pretends to understand and refuses to acknowledge except as brutal intervention, as disorder and intimidation constructed to humiliate him personally, pride wearing so thin he's trying to recall skills his father had taught him. Not a list of the meager skills themselves—not shaving, not tying a tie—but evidence of intimate exchange. Traces of the manner in which, through which, his father might have said, Here are some things I know, some things I am, and I want you to know them and I hope they will serve you well. In other words he was attempting to remember any occasion when or if his father had granted him permission to enter that unknown world which intersected only rarely, unpredictably with a home his father shared with a wife and children. Who was his father. How was it possible to be the man his father was. Did anything that man ever say suggest a son would be welcome in the other spaces he occupied. Closure what he had learned from his father. The absolute abandonment of shutting down, disappearing. Cover-ups. Erasing all tracks. Eluding pursuit. Were those the skills. Teaching the shame of bearing an inexhaustible bag of useless tricks he knew better than to pass on.

Trouble

The man in the second place gives him a card and directions to a third place but the third place isn't the right one either, and he listens to a more complicated set of directions for reaching another place, which will be the fourth place if he's remembering correctly what's happened already this morning with car trouble in a strange town, and various strangers who seem quite willing to be helpful even to the extent of drawing maps on scratch paper or repeating numerous times their instructions, listening intently, patient with him as he explains his problem or the car's problem, and he requires their patience because for some reason this morning he feels like he's speaking a second language, one he's not very good at, one you might as well say he's forgotten how to speak, it's that bad, he's reduced to a kind of baby talk, pidgin, grunt, point translation of words he's unsure of in his original language, whatever it is, if he owns one, and wonders if he possesses the car's papers, his papers, the papers for whatever lumpy, large thing it is he has no word for but suddenly recalls stuffing last night hurriedly into the car's trunk, papers tucked away, locked somewhere safely inside the car, papers explaining everything he can't say so that if or when he ever reaches the fourth place or fifth or however many places it's going to take, someone will understand him, believe him, fix the problem.

Breath

Sometimes you feel so close it's like we're cheek to cheek sucking the breath of life from the same hole.

In a few hours the early flight to Pittsburgh because my mom's life hanging by a thread. Thunder and lightning you're sleeping through cracks the bedroom's dark ceiling like an egg. About 4:00 a.m. I need to get up. Drawing a deep breath, careful as always to avoid stress on the vulnerable base of my spine when I shift my weight in bed, I slide my butt toward the far edge, raise the covers, and pivot on one hipbone to a sitting position, letting my legs fold over the bed's side to find the floor, still holding my breath as I get both feet steady under me and slowly stand, hoping I didn't bounce the mattress, waiting to hear the steady pulse of your sleep before I exhale.

In the kitchen a yellowish cloud presses against the window. A cloud oddly lit and colored it seems by a source within itself. A kind of fog or dust or smoke that's opaque, unsettling, until I understand the color must come from security lights glaring below in the courtyard. It's snow. Big flakes not falling in orderly rows, a dervishing mob that swirls, lifts, goes limp, noiselessly spatters the glass. Snow obscuring the usual view greeting me when I'm up at crazy hours to relieve an old man's panicked kidneys or just up, up and wondering why, staring at blank, black windows of a hulking building that mirrors the twenty-story bulk of ours, up prowling instead of asleep in the peace I hope you're still enjoying, peace I wish upon the entire world, peace I should know better by now than to look for through a window, the peace I listen for beside you in the whispering of our tangled breaths.

The Gangsters

Colson Whitehead

First, you had to settle the question of out. *When did you get out?* Asking this was like showing off, even though anyone you could ask had already received the same gift: the same sun wrapped in shiny paper, the same soft benevolent sky, the same gravel road that sooner or later would skin you, pure joy in the town of Sag Harbor. Still, it was hard not to believe that it all belonged to you more than to anyone else, that it had been made for you, had been waiting for years for you to come along. We all felt that way. We were so grateful just to be there, in the heat, after a long bleak year in the city. *When did you get out?*

In the summer of 1985, I was fifteen years old. My brother, Reggie, was fourteen. That year, we got out the second Saturday in June, in an hour and a half flat from the Upper West Side, having beat the traffic. Over the course of the summer, you heard a lot of different strategies for how to beat the traffic, or at least slap it around a little. There were those who ditched the office early on Friday afternoon, casually letting their co-workers know the reason for their departure, in order to enjoy a little low-pressure envy. Others headed back to the city late on Sunday evening, choking every last pulse of joy from the weekend with cocoa-buttered hands. They stopped to grab a bite and watched the slow red surge outside the restaurant window while dragging clam strips through tartar sauce—soon, soon, not yet—until the coast was clear. My father's method was easy and brutal: hit the road at five in the morning, so that we were the only living souls on the Long Island Expressway, making a break for it in the haunted dark. Well, it wasn't really dark—June sunrises are up and at 'em—but I always remember the drives that way, perhaps because my eyes were closed most of the time. The trick of those early-morning jaunts was to wake up just enough to haul a bag of clothes down to the car, nestle in, and then retreat back into sleep. My brother and I did a zombie march, slow and mute, to the back seat, where we turned into our separate nooks, sniffing the upholstery, butt to butt, looking more or less like a Rorschach test. What do you see in this picture? Two brothers going off in different directions.

We had recently ceased to be twins. We were born ten months apart, and until I started high school we had come as a matched set, more Siamese than identical, defined by our uncanny inseparability. Joined not at the hip or the spleen or the nervous system but at that most important place—that spot on your self where you meet the world. There was something in the human DNA that had compelled people to say "Benji 'n' Reggie, Benji 'n' Reggie" in a singsong way, as if we were cartoon characters. On the rare occasions when we'd been caught alone, the first thing people had asked was "Where's Benji?" or "Where's Reggie?," whereupon we'd delivered a thorough account of our other's whereabouts, quickly including context, as if embarrassed to be caught out in the sunlight with only half a shadow: "He rode into town. He lost his CAT Diesel Power cap at the beach and went to get a new one at the five-and-ten."

Where is the surgeon gifted enough to undertake separating these hapless conjoined? Paging Doc Puberty, arms scrubbed, smocked to the hilt, smacking the nurses on the ass and well versed in the latest techniques. More suction! Javelin and shot put—that's about right. Hormones had sent me up and airborne, tall and skinny, a knock-kneed reed, while Reggie, always chubby in the cheeks and arms, had bulged out into something round and pinchable. Through junior high, we had disentangled week by week, one new hair at a time. There were no complications of the physical separation, but what about the mental one—severing the phantom connection whereby if Reggie stubbed his toe I cried out in pain, and vice versa? By the time we left for Sag Harbor in the summer of 1985, we'd reached the point where if someone asked, "Where's Reggie?" I didn't always know.

My mother said, "We're making good time." The L.I.E. had stopped slicing towns in half and now cut through untamed Nassau County greenery, always a good sign. I tried to claw my way back into sleep until we'd ditched Route 27 and cruise control and weaved down Scuttlehole Road, zipping past the white fencing and rusting wire that held back the bulging acres at the side of the road. I smelled the sweetly muddy fumes of the potato fields and pictured the cornstalks in their long regiments. My mother said, "That sweet Long Island corn," as she always did. She'd been coming out since she was a kid, her father part of the first wave of black folks from the city to start spending their summers in Sag Harbor. Which made my brother and me, and all our raggedy friends out there, the third generation. For what it was worth. Reggie had been farting for the last five minutes while pretending to be asleep. My feet scrabbled under the front seat in anticipation. Almost there. We slowed by the old red barn at the Turnpike and made the left. From there to our house was like falling down a chute: nothing left to do but prepare for landing. It was six-thirty in the morning. That was that. We were out for the summer.

※

All the ill shit went down on Thursdays.

Our parents went back to the city every Sunday night, leaving us alone in Sag for five days while they brought home the bacon. Mondays Reggie and I slept in, lulled by the silence in the rest of the house. The only racket was the sound of the carpenter ants gnawing the soft wood under the deck—not much of a racket at all. When we met up with the rest of our crew—most of our friends in Sag were similarly unsupervised during the week—we traded baroque schemes about what we'd get up to before all our parents came out again. The week was a vast continent for us to explore and conquer. Then suddenly we ran out of land. Wednesdays we woke up agitated, realizing that our idyll was half over. We got busy trying to cram it all in between minimum-wage shifts at the local fast-food spots. Sometimes we messed up on Wednesdays, but it was never a Thursday-size mess-up. No, Thursday we reserved for the thoroughly botched mishaps that called for shame and first aid and apologies. All the ill shit—the disasters we made with our own hands—went down on Thursdays, because on Fridays the parents returned and disasters were out of our control.

The first gun was Randy's. Which should have been a sign that we were heading toward a classic Thursday. This was Randy's first summer in our group of friends, the blame for which falls on his parents' love-making schedule. He was an in-betweener, living like a weed in the cracks between the micro-demographic groups of the Sag Harbor developments. Too old to hang out with us, really, and too young to be fully accepted by the older kids, he had wafted in a social netherworld for years. Now he had just finished his freshman year in college but, against usual custom, he still came out to Sag. He drove a moss-green Toyota hatchback that he claimed to have bought for a hundred bucks. Its fenders were dented and dimpled, rust mottled the frame in leprous clumps, and the inside smelled like hippie anarchists on the lam had made it their commune. But who was I to cast aspersions? Randy had a car, he was old enough to buy us beer, and for this we accepted him into our tribe and overlooked his shortcomings.

I usually didn't go to Randy's—he didn't have a hanging-out house. But everybody else was working that day. Nick at the Jonni Waffle ice-cream shop, where I worked, too, Clive bar-backing at the Long Wharf Restaurant, Reggie and Bobby flipping Whoppers at Burger King. I felt like I hadn't seen Reggie in weeks. We had contrary schedules, me working in town, him in Southampton. When we overlapped in the house we were usually too exhausted from work to even bicker properly. I had no other option but to call N.P., not my No. 1 choice, and his mother told me that he was at Randy's. Normally I would have said forget it, but there was a chance that they might be driving somewhere, an expedition to Karts-A-Go-Go or Hither Hills, and later I'd have to hear them exaggerate how much fun they had.

Randy lived in Sag Harbor Hills, on Hillside Drive, a dead-end street off our usual circuit. I knew it as the street where the Yellow House was, the one Mark Barrows used to stay in. Mark was a nerdy kid I got along with, who came out for a few summers to visit his grandmother. When I turned the corner to Hillside, I saw that the Yellow House's yard was overgrown and the blinds were drawn, as they had been for years now. I hadn't seen Mark in a long time, but a few weeks before I'd happened to ask my mother if she knew why he didn't come out anymore, and she'd said, "Oh, it turned out that Mr. Barrows had another family."

There was a lot of Other Family going around that summer. For a while it verged on an epidemic. I found it fascinating, wondering at the mechanics of it all. One family in New Jersey and one in Kansas—what kind of cover story hid those miles? These were lies to aspire to. And who was to say which was the Real Family and which was the Other Family? Was the Sag Harbor family of our acquaintance the shadowy antimatter family, or was it the other way around—that family living in a new Delaware subdivision, the one gobbling crumbs with a smile? I pictured the kids scrambling to the front door at the sound of Daddy's car in the driveway at last (the brief phone calls from the road only magnify his absence), and Daddy taking a moment after he turned off the ignition to orient himself and figure out who and where he was this time. *Yes, I recognize those people standing in the doorway—that's my family.* Everyone tucked in tight. The family ate together and communicated. And then Daddy lit out for this Zip Code, changed his face, and everything was reversed. One man, two houses. Two faces. Which house you lived in, kids, was the luck of the draw.

Randy and N.P. were in the street. They were bent over, looking at something on the ground. I yelled, "Yo!" They didn't respond. I walked up.

"Look at that," N.P. said.

"What happened to it?" I asked. A robin was lying on the asphalt, but it didn't have the familiar tread-mark tattoo of most roadkill. It was tiny and still.

"Randy shot it," N.P. said.

Randy grinned and held up his BB rifle proudly. The metal was sleek, inky black, the fake wood grain of the stock and forearm glossy in the sun. "I got it at Caldor," he said.

We looked down at the robin again.

"It landed on the power pole and I just took the shot," Randy said. "I've been practicing all day."

"Is it dead?" I asked.

"I don't see any blood," N.P. answered.

"Maybe it's just a concussion," I said.

"You should stuff it and mount it," N.P. said.

I thought, That's uncool, a judgment I'd picked up from the stoners at my "predominately white" private school, who had decided, toward the end of the spring semester, that I was O.K., and let me hang out in their vicinity, or at least linger unmolested, as a prelude to a provisional adoption by their clan next fall. I liked "uncool" because it meant that there was a code that everyone agreed on. The rules didn't change—everything in the universe was either cool or uncool, no confusion. "That's uncool," someone said, and "That is so uncool," another affirmed, the voice of justice itself, nasal and uncomplicated.

Randy let N.P. take the rifle and N.P. held it in his hands, testing its weight. It looked solid and formidable. He aimed at invisible knuckleheads loitering at the end of the street: "Stick 'em up!" He pumped the stock three times, *clack clack clack,* and pulled the trigger. And again.

"It's empty, dummy," Randy said.

To observe N.P. was to witness a haphazard choreography of joints and limbs. His invisible puppeteer had shaky hands, making it seem as if N.P. were always on the verge of busting out into some freaky dance move. Looking back, I think that his condition was more likely caused by him trying to keep his freaky dance moves in check—whatever convulsive thing he'd taken notes on at a party the week before and had just finished practicing in his room. That I wouldn't have heard of the dance was a given—the Phillie Bugaloo, the Reverse Cabbage Patch. To hang out with N.P. was to try to catch up on nine months of black slang and other sundry soulful artifacts I'd missed out on at school.

Not that I didn't learn anything at school, culturewise. The hallways between classes were a tutelage into the wide range of diversions that our country's white youth had come up with to occupy themselves. When I had free time between engineering my own humiliations, I was introduced to the hacky sack, a sort of miniature leather beanbag that compelled white kids to juggle with their feet. It was a wholesome communal activity, I saw, as they lobbed the object among each other, cheering themselves on. It appeared to foster teamwork and good will among its adherents. Bravo! There was also a kind of magical rod called a lacrosse stick. It directed the more outgoing and athletic specimens of my school to stalk the carpeted floors and obsessively wring their hands around it, as if to call forth popularity or a higher degree of social acceptance through diligent application of friction. You heard them muttering *"but but but"* in a masturbatory fervor as they approached. Good stuff, in an anthropological sense. But these things were not the Technotronic Bunny Hop, or the Go Go Bump-Stomp, the assorted field exercises of black boot camp.

We called him N.P., for "Nigger, please," because no matter what came out of his mouth, that was usually the most appropriate response. He was our best liar, a raconteur of baroque teen-age shenanigans. Everything in his field of vision reminded him of some escapade he needed to share, or directed him to some escapade about to begin, as soon as all the witnesses had departed. He was dependable for nonsense like "Yo, last night, after you left, I went back to that party and got with that Queens girl. She told me she was raised strict, but I was all up in those titties! She paid me fifty dollars!"

Nigger, please.

"Yo, yo, listen: I was walking by the Miller house and I went to take a look at their Rolls, and get this, I was, like, they left the keys in the ignition. You know I took that shit for a spin. I was like Thurston Howell III up in that bitch! With Gilligan!"

Nigger, please.

Like me and Reggie, N.P. had come out to Sag every summer of his life—and even before he was born, as his mother had waded out into the bay to cool her pregnant belly. We had beaten each other up, stolen each other's toys, fallen asleep in the back seats of station wagons together as we caravanned back from double features at the Bridgehampton Drive-In, the stars scrolling beyond the back window. We were copying our parents, who had been beating each other up, eating each other's barbecue, chasing each other down the hacked-out footpaths to the beach, thirty years earlier, under the same sky.

According to the world, we were the definition of paradox: black boys with beach houses. What kind of bourgie sellout Negroes were we, with BMWs (Black Man's Wagons, in case you didn't know) in our driveways and private schools to teach us how to use a knife and fork, and sort *that* from *dat*? What about keeping it real? What about the news, the statistics, the great narrative of black pathology? Just check out the newspapers, preferably in a movie-style montage sequence, the alarming headlines dropping in-frame with a thud, one after the other: "CRISIS IN THE INNER CITY!"; "WHITHER ALL THE BABY DADDIES"; "THE TRUTH ABOUT THE WELFARE STATE: THEY JUST DON'T WANT TO WORK"; "NOT LIKE IN THE GOOD OLD DAYS."

Black boys with beach houses. It could mess with your head sometimes, if you were the susceptible sort. And if it messed with your head, got under your brown skin, there were some typical and well-known remedies. You could embrace the beach part—revel in the luxury, the perception of status, wallow without care in what it meant to be born in America with money, or the appearance of money, as the case may be. No apologies. Or you could embrace the black part—take some idea you had about what real blackness was, and make theatre out of it, your own 24/7 one-man show. Street, ghetto. Act hard, act out, act in a way that would come to be called gangsterish, pulling petty crimes, a soft kind of tough, knowing that there'd always be someone to post bail if one of your grubby schemes fell apart. Or you could embrace the contradiction. You could say, What you call paradox, I call *myself*. At least, in theory: those inclined to this remedy didn't have a lot of obvious models.

We headed into Randy's house to get some more ammo. He opened the screen door and yelled, "Mom, I'm inside with my friends!" and the sound of a TV was silenced as a door closed with a thud. Randy got the BBs from his room, then led us out through the kitchen into the back-yard. Brown leaves drifted in dirty pools in the butts of chairs. Behind the house were woods, which allowed him to convert the patio into a firing range. He'd dragged the barbecue grill to the edge of the trees—I saw a trail of ashes—and around its three feet lay cans and cups riddled with tiny holes.

Steve Austin, the Six Million Dollar Man, who had been rebuilt at great expense with taxpayers' money, stood on the red dome of the barbecue, his bionic hands in eternal search of necks to throttle. Randy took aim. The action figure stared impassively, his extensive time on the operating table having granted him a stoic's quiet grace. It took five shots, Randy pumping and clacking the stock with increasing fury as we observed his shitty marksmanship. Then Steve Austin tumbled off the lid and lay on his side, his pose undisturbed in the dirt. Didn't even blink. They really knew how to make an action figure back then.

"I want to get the optional scope for greater accuracy," Randy ex-plained, "but that costs more money."

"Lemme try that shit now," N.P. said.

I left soon after. I threw out a "You guys want to head to East Hamp-ton to buy records?," but no one bit. I'd thought we were past playing with guns. I walked around the side of the house, and when I got to the street the bird was gone.

That was the first gun. The next was Bobby's. This one was a pistol, a replica of a 9mm.

Bobby was still in the early stages of his transformation into that weird creature the prep-school militant. The usual schedule for good middle-class black boys and girls called for them to get militant and fashionably Afrocentric in the first semester of freshman year of college: underlining key passages in *The Autobiography of Malcolm X* and that passed-around paperback of *Black Skin, White Masks;* organizing a march or two to protest the lack of tenure for that controversial professor in the Department of Black Studies; organizing a march or two to protest the lack of a Department of Black Studies. It passed the time until business school. But Bobby got an early start on all that, returning to Sag from his sophomore year of high school with a new, clipped pronunciation of the word "whitey," and a fondness for using the phrases "white-identified" and "false consciousness" while watching *The Cosby Show.* It caused problems as he fretted over his Zip Code ("Scarsdale ain't nothing but a high-class shantytown. It's a gilded lean-to") and how changing his name might affect his Ivy League prospects ("Your transcript says Bobby Emerson, but you said your name was Sadat X").

We used to make fun of him for being so light-skinned, and this probably contributed to some of his overcompensating. The joke was that, if the K.K.K. came pounding on Bobby's door and demanded, "Where the black people at?" (it's well known—the fondness of the K.K.K. for ending sentences with a preposition), he'd say, "They went thataway!" with a minstrel eye-roll and a vaudeville arm flourish. He rebelled against his genes, the Caucasian DNA in his veins square-dancing with strong African DNA. It's a tough battle, defending one flank against nature while nurture sneaks in from the east with whole battalions. He directed most of his hostile talk at his mother, who worked on Wall Street. "My mom wouldn't give me twenty dollars for the weekend. She's sucking the white man's dick all day, Morgan Stanley cracker, and can't give me twenty dollars!" His mother bore the brunt of his misguided rage, even though his father worked at Goldman Sachs and wasn't exactly a dashiki-clad community leader. But get a bunch of teen-age virgins together, and you're bound to rub up against some mother issues. Let he who is without sin cast the first plucked-out orb of Oedipal horror.

We were in Bobby's room. He had invited me over to play Lode Runner on his Apple II+, but when I got up there he dug under his mattress and pulled out a BB pistol.

I jerked my head toward the open door. "What about your grandpa?"

He pointed to his alarm clock. It was 7:35 p.m. Which meant that his grandparents had been asleep for five minutes. Bobby's parents were there only on weekends, like ours; unlike us, he was not completely unsupervised during the week. His grandparents were there to make sure that he got fed. But after seven-thirty he crawled over the wall.

"Me and N.P. went with Randy to Caldor and got one," Bobby said. "He got the silver one, but I wanted the black one. It's the joint, right?

Greg Tiller's cousin has a gun like this," he added, squinting down the pistol's sight. "I saw it once at his house. You know what he's into, right?"

"No, what?"

"You know, some hardcore shit. He was in jail." He held it out. "Do you want to hold it?"

"No, that's all right."

"What are you, a pussy?"

I shrugged.

"Me and Reggie were shooting stuff over at the creek today," Bobby said. "He has good aim. He should be a sniper in the Marine Corps."

I'd seen Reggie before he went off to Burger King, asked him what he'd been up to. "Nothing," he'd said.

"Let me see that," I said. It was heavier than it looked. I curled my finger around the trigger. O.K. Got the gist. I pretended to study it for a moment more, then gave it back to him.

"I'm going to bring this shit to school," Bobby said. He put his crazy face on. "Stick up some pink motherfuckers. *Bla-blam!*"

Which was bullshit. Hunting preppies—the Deadliest Game of All— would have cut into his daily vigil outside the college counsellor's office. This BB-gun shit was making people act like dummies.

To wit: he pointed it at me. "Hands in the air!"

I shielded my eyes with my hand. "Get that shit outta my face!"

He laughed. "Hot oil! Hot oil!" he said, rolling his eyes manically.

Reggie had started saying "Hot oil! Hot oil!" whenever I bossed him around or said something lame. After the twentieth time, I asked him why he kept saying that, and he said that there was a semi-retarded guy who worked at Burger King through a special program, and he always got agitated when he walked by the fryers, squealing "Hot oil! Hot oil!" to remind himself.

"Don't worry. I got the safety on," Bobby said, pulling the trigger. A BB shot out, hit the wall, ricocheted into his computer monitor, bounced against the window, and disappeared under his bed. "Sorry, man! Sorry, sorry!" he yelped. Downstairs, one might conjecture, Grandpa stirred in his sleep.

At least it was a plastic BB. Randy had copper BBs. The plastic ones didn't hurt that much. The copper ones could do some real damage, as I saw the following week when I found myself out on "target practice." We were on our way to Bridgehampton to walk around, Randy driving, Clive, N.P., and me. Then Randy pulled into the parking lot of Mashashimuet Park.

"I thought we were going to Bridgehampton," I said.

"After we go shooting," Randy said.

We walked onto the trails behind the park. N.P. carried a moldy cardboard box. When I asked him what was inside, he said, "That would be telling."

Randy had the spot all picked out. The abandoned Karmann Ghia. It made sense. We'd tried to make a plaything of it many a boredom-crazed afternoon, but it was too rusted to incorporate into high jinks beyond throwing rocks through its dwindling windows. (We were a tetanus-phobic group, lockjaw being the most sinister villain we could imagine.) But not anymore. The guns gave us the distance to hasten the car's ruin.

Randy's first attempts were unspectacular, his BBs zipping straight through the car's exterior, leaving a tiny, fingertip-size hole you had to get up close to see. But, as his aim improved and he figured out the key pressure points, a BB disintegrated a nice section of the car's weakened frame. "You see how I pump it?" he asked rhetorically. "The more you pump it, the faster the f.p.s." Feet per second, I guessed, and later confirmed when I sat on some ketchup-stained rifle literature in the back seat of Randy's car. "Low f.p.s. is good if you just want to scare a deer or another critter off your property. Higher f.p.s. is when you really want to send a message." *Yee-haw!*

N.P. and Clive took turns with N.P.'s pistol—Randy was clinging tight to his baby today—and although it was diverting for a while, I started to wonder if we'd have enough time to drive to Bridgehampton and back before my shift.

"We just got here, dag," N.P. said.

"I'm not ready to go," Randy said as he reloaded his rifle.

Clive had taken a few shots. He seemed to be enjoying himself. "Why don't you go ahead and try it?" he asked me.

Clive had always been the leader of our group. He was just cool, no joke. He was that rare thing among us: halfway normal, socialized, capable, and charismatic. Tall and muscular, he had the physical might to beat us up, but he broke up fights instead, separating combatants while dodging their whirling fists, and no one complained. Plus, he knew how to talk to girls, had girlfriends, plural. Good-looking girlfriends, too, by all accounts, with all their teeth and everything. Last summer he'd even dated an older woman—in her twenties! Who lived in Springs! Who had a kid! He had his problems, like the rest of us, but he hadn't let them deform his character. Not back then.

I took N.P.'s gun. Clive offered me the carton of BBs. In their small blue box, the copper BBs turned molten in the sun. N.P. said, "Let's break out the stuff," and opened the box he'd brought along. It was filled with items scavenged from his basement—a porcelain vase, a bunch of drinking glasses with groovy sixties designs, a Nerf football with tooth marks in it, a bottle of red nail polish, and other junk chosen for its breakable quality.

"Here, do the radio," N.P. said. He dug into the box and perched an old transistor radio on top of the Karmann Ghia. I took my time. I wiped the sweat off my forehead. I held my shooting arm with my left hand, gunslinger style. Drew a bead.

The radio made a sad *ting*, tottered in cheap suspense, and fell into the dirt. I'd hit it toward the top, knocking it off balance. The words "center of gravity" came to me, secondhand track-and-field lingo from my vain attempt to place out of P.E. that spring. I couldn't throw a ball worth shit with my girly arm, but somehow I'd hit the radio. N.P. whooped it up, slapping me on the back. Clive offered a terse "Good shooting," like a drill instructor trying not to be too affirming. I grinned.

We positioned the other relics from N.P.'s basement. The vase didn't explode, but each time it was hit another jagged section fell off, so that we could see more of its insides. It finally collapsed on its own while we were reloading. I aimed at an old lampshade of rainbow-colored glass, and, though I didn't re-create the swell marksmanship of my first attempt, I had to admit it was fun. Not the shooting itself, but the satisfaction of discovering a new way to kill a chunk of summer. It was like scraping out a little cave, making a new space in the hours to hide in for a time.

I placed the final victim on top of the car—the neon-green Nerf football. We'd saved it for last because nothing topped Nerf abuse. It was Randy's turn, but, as it was N.P.'s Nerf ball, he established dibs. It turned out that N.P. couldn't hit it. Time after time. We'd been out there in the sun for hours and we were dehydrated. The rush, the novelty, was gone, and we all felt it. Finally, N.P. gave up and handed his pistol to Clive. Randy said, "N.P. couldn't hit the broad side of a barn," that hoary marksman's slur.

N.P. exploded. He always had putdowns to spare, but now he grasped after his trademark finesse. "I could hit your fat fuckin' ass fine, you fuckin' Rerun-from-*What's Happ'ning*-looking motherfucker."

"What the fuck did you say?"

"You fuckin' biscuit-eatin' bitch!"

Randy's hours of picking off his old toys in the backyard finally found their true outlet. He stroked his rifle, *clack clack,* and started shooting the dirt at N.P.'s feet. "Dance, nigger, dance!" he shouted, in Old West saloon fashion, which was pretty fucked-up, and the copper BBs detonated in the ground in brief puffs. N.P. skipped from foot to foot, his bright-white sneakers flashing like surrender flags. "Dance!" I don't think Randy was aiming at N.P.'s feet, but I couldn't be sure. What if he missed? One of those BBs, depending on the f.p.s., would rip through the sneaker, definitely. How much deeper I didn't know.

Clive and I shouted for Randy to knock it off. Clive took a step toward Randy, hands out defensively. He was fast enough to rush him, but nevertheless. Randy glared at Clive—I swear he made a calculation—and then lowered the rifle, with an "I was just playing."

N.P. charged Randy, cursing like a motherfucker. Clive restrained him. "That's uncool," I said, but no one chimed in with the other-shoe "That's so uncool." The boys boiled off in their neutral corners, and we left soon after, scratching the Bridgehampton excursion without discussion.

That was on a Wednesday. The next Monday, we were back at the threshold of another empty week we needed to fill. We convened at our place that night: Reggie, Randy, Bobby, Clive, and Nick, who was living out there full time now. He'd been a summer kid, one of our gang through many adventures, but something had happened between his parents— we never asked about family processes, only accepted the results when informed—and now he and his mom were living in Sag Harbor Hills. He went to Pierson High School, was technically a townie, by definitions that he himself would have upheld, and was embarrassed by this. "This whole Sag thing is just temporary," he frequently told us, to reassure himself. I saw that he had a new gold chain. His old one had said "Nick," in two-inch letters. His new chain said "Big Nick," in two-inch letters, and was studded with tiny white rhinestones.

"Nice," I said.

"Got my man in Queens Plaza to do it," he said.

My father would've kicked me out of the house if I'd walked in with a gold chain around my neck. Not that it ever would've occurred to me to get a gold chain. But Nick! Circumstances had forced Nick to embrace the early-eighties fashions of urban black boys with verve and unashamed gusto. He loved two-tone jeans, gray in the front, black in the back, months out of fashion but authentic city artifacts out there in Sag. The laces on his Adidases were puffy and magnificent, and if he wasn't wearing his Jonni Waffle T-shirt with the sleeves rolled up, juvenile-delinquent style, he wore a Knicks jersey that showed off his muscles. Muscles that had been produced by lugging his enormous boom box around. His radio was the most ridiculous thing, the biggest radio any of us had ever seen or ever would see. It was a yard wide, half as much tall, a gleaming silver slab of stereophonic dynamism. It didn't do much. Played the terrible East End radio stations. Played cassettes. Made a dub at the touch of a button. For all I know it was mostly air inside, save for the bushel of double-D batteries it took to power the thing, and which Nick spent most of his wages on.

Randy had brought beer, which was a new feature of our lives that summer. The drinking age was nineteen then, which made Randy legal and Clive tall enough to buy take-out six-packs at the corner bar unchallenged. One beer and I was buzzed, two beers I was drunk. We asked one another, "Which one are you on?," to see who was ahead and who was falling behind. Pointing at the empties for proof.

"Why don't you open the screen door to let the air in here?" Randy said.

"It's a screen door. The air comes through," Reggie said. "Plus the mosquitoes will get us."

"Then leave the lights out. They won't come in," Randy said. "I'm hot."

Reggie opened the screen door, and we hunkered in the gloom. We had three days to fill. Clive suggested night blue-fishing off Montauk. But the rest of us agreed that it was too expensive to go more than once a season, given the realities of minimum wage, and we'd already been once. Reggie, who this summer had decided that he was no longer afraid of the water, disavowing a key tenet of the men in our family, said that we should borrow Nick's uncle's motorboat again. But Nick said that his uncle was having the hull refinished. Bobby busted out that old chestnut Ask Mrs. Upland if We Can Go in Her Pool, but Clive and Nick immediately said no dice. Mrs. Upland's son had died five years before. He'd grown up in Sag in a crew with Clive's father and Nick's father, and the last time they'd used her pool she'd kept calling them by their fathers' names and it had creeped them out.

Stumped, and it wasn't even August yet.

"Let's show dicks," Randy suggested.

Cricket, cricket.

"Why the hell would we do that?" Clive asked, finally.

"To see who has the biggest dick," Randy said.

"Next time we go to Karts-A-Go-Go, we should race for money and time ourselves to see who's the fastest," I said, steering the proceedings like a good host. I wasn't much of a go-cart driver, but I thought the novelty of the scheme might appeal.

Bobby turned on his m.c. voice: "One Two Three, in the place to be." And Reggie said, "All right!" They started their routine and I rolled my eyes in the darkness. Bobby and my brother had memorized the lyrics to Run-D.M.C.'s "Here We Go" and had to perform it at least ten times a day. Bobby was Run, Reggie was D.M.C. Bobby took the lead, Reggie sidekicking after each line like an exclamation point. Back and forth, a real fucking duo. Clive kept the beat with his hands.

"It's like that, y'all."

"That y'all!"

"It's like that, y'all."

"That y'all."

"It's like that-a-tha-that, a-like that, y'all."

"That y'all!"

"Cool chief rocker, I don't drink vodka, but keep a bag of cheeba inside my locker."

"HUH!"

"Go to school every day."

"HUH!"

"Always time to get paid."

"HA HUH!"

"'Cause I'm rockin' on the mic until the break of day!"

Run-D.M.C. boasting about staying in school—quaint days in the history of hip-hop. To my chagrin, I had never heard the song before Reggie and Bobby started singing it. I thought I knew all of Run-D.M.C.'s records, the self-titled début and *King of Rock*, but I was a square. The song was a limited-edition live recording made at a club called the Funhouse, taped "Funky fresh for 1983," according to the lyrics. Bobby had introduced the song to Reggie, who dubbed a copy on Nick's boom box.

Distracted, no one followed up on my Karts-A-Go-Go plan. In my jealousy, I pictured Bobby and Reggie performing their bit behind the counter at Burger King, their clubhouse where I was not allowed, in their paper Burger King caps and hairnets, while the retarded guy chimed in with "Hot oil! Hot oil!" like an amen.

We continued to brainstorm. No progress. Then someone said, "We should have a BB-gun fight," and it stuck. The only thing to silence the new hunger. That was that. Our house was full of mosquitoes for a week, and Reggie and I had to sleep with our heads under the sheets to keep them out of our ears.

The next day, Randy drove me and Clive to Caldor, the East End's one-stop emporium for action figures and beach towels, insect-repelling candles and beach chairs, lighter fluid and flip-flops. After consulting our savings, kept in battered envelopes in topnotch hiding places around the house to prevent each other from skimming some off the top, Reggie and I had decided that it would be best if we shared a BB pistol, with one of us borrowing Randy's spare for the fight itself. This arrangement would also allow me to keep track of Reggie's gun activity. I was sure he was going to hurt himself. Bobby would cook up some dumb idea and Reggie would go along with it and he'd get hurt. I had to look out for him; in fact, the night of the Mosquito Summit, I decided to try to get the BB-gun fight scheduled to overlap with one of his shifts at Burger King. We all missed key shenanigans because of work. There was no reason that this couldn't be one of Reggie's turns to listen to glorious tales and rue his absence until the end of time.

Reggie and I hadn't had toy guns, growing up, so we had to catch up. Green or orange water pistols had been O.K., but anything else had sent our father speechifying. "That's some whiteman shit," he'd say, confiscating the cap gun from a birthday-party goody bag. "Whitey loves his guns. Shoot somebody—he loves that shit. So let him. No kid of mine is going to get that mind-set." I practiced solo, deep in the recesses of the creek, out of sight of beachgoers and homeowners. Why startle the happy vacationers with the sight of a skinny, slouching teen-ager, the sun glinting off his braces and his handgun?

When it was Reggie's turn to practice, he'd disappear with Bobby for one of their secret confabs, probably a razzle-dazzle rapping/shooting extravaganza of great theatre. *It's like that, y'all.* Not that the rest of us were immune. N.P. tucked his piece into his belt like a swaggering cop on the take or the cracker sheriff of a Jim Crow Podunk. Clive was observed busting a Dirty Harry move when he thought we weren't looking, and Randy was often found cradling his rifle to his chest, a gruesome sneer on his face, as if he were about to take an East Hampton bistro hostage. I myself favored a two-handed promising-rookie pose, the kind used by *Starsky and Hutch* extras who got clipped before the first commercial and were avenged for the rest of the hour. "He woulda made a good cop, just like his old man."

It was only a matter of time before we started posing for album covers. Not one from innocent '85, but one from a few years later, after the music had changed from this:

> *Rhymes so def*
> *Rhymes rhymes galore*
> *Rhymes that you've never even heard before*
> *Now if you say you heard my rhyme*
> *We gonna have to fight*
> *'Cause I just made the motherfuckers up last night*

to this:

> *"Hey yo, Cube, there go that motherfucker right there."*
> *"No shit. Watch this . . . Hey, what's up, man?"*
> *"Not too much."*
> *"You know you won, G."*
> *"Won what?"*
> *"The wet T-shirt contest, motherfucker!"*
> [sounds of gunfire]

Lyrics from the aforementioned "Here We Go" and "Now I Gotta Wet 'Cha," copyright 1992, by Ice Cube, born the same year as me, who grew up on Run-D.M.C. just like we all did. "Wet 'cha," as in "wet your shirt with blood." Something happened in those nine years. Something happened that changed the terms, and we went from fighting (*I'll knock that grin off your face*) to annihilation (*I will wipe you from this earth*). How we got from here to there is a key passage in the history of young black men that no one cares to write.

✳

On Wednesday, we went over the rules at Clive's house. No shooting at the eyes or face—that was a no-brainer. No cheating—if you're hit, you're hit, don't be a bitch about it. Sag Harbor Hills was the boundary of the battlefield—no cutting through to other developments and sneaking back to emerge ambush-style. I said that we should all wear goggles, just in case, and to my surprise the others seemed to agree. There was talk of synchronizing watches, but no one wore a watch in the summer except me, because summer is its own time and I was the only one who didn't know this. When the scheduling question came up, I said, "Tomorrow night?," and everyone but Reggie was free then. The weekend was out—too many people around—and no one wanted to put it off till the following week. Reggie was benched and I was glad.

Not that it could have gone down any other way. Although we had hatched the plan for a BB-gun war on a Monday, there was no question that in the end it would go down on a Thursday.

There was just one matter left to discuss: the issue of Randy's rifle and the f.p.s. A metal BB from one of the pistols, at the range we were going to be shooting at one another, would hurt a little but not that much, according to hearsay. Pump the rifle enough times, however, and it was going to break the skin.

"But if I can't pump I'll be at a disadvantage," Randy moaned.

"We have to figure out how many rifle pumps is equal to the standard pistol shot," I offered.

"How do we figure that out?" Clive asked.

"We can test it out on Marcus," Randy said.

Marcus said, "O.K.," and we headed out into the yard.

Marcus was a key player in our group, in that he reassured us that there was someone more unfortunate than ourselves. He possessed three primary mutant powers. 1) He was able to attract to his person all the free-floating derision in the vicinity through a strange magnetism. 2) He bent light waves, rendering the rest of us invisible to bullies; when Marcus was present, the big kids were incapable of seeing us, picking on him exclusively, delivering noogies, knuckle punches, and Indian rope burns to his waiting flesh. 3) He had superior olfactory capability; he could smell barbecue from four miles away, attaining such mastery that he could ascertain, with the faintest nostril quivering, if the stuff on the grill had just been thrown on, or was about to come off, and acted accordingly. Like a knife and fork, he appeared around dinner time. Call him a mooch to hurt his feelings, and he'd just smile, wipe his mouth on his wrist, and snatch the last piece of chicken—probably a wing, damn him.

Marcus took off his shirt, and Randy loaded his rifle. "Let's start at one," he said.

I said, "Marcus, why don't you turn around so it doesn't go in your face or something?"

Marcus turned around and gritted his teeth. There was a routine he did when one of us got mad at him, pulling up his shirt and clowning, "Please, Massa, Massa, Massa, please," anticipating the whip, *Roots*-style. He had the same expression on his face now. Randy stood four yards away, aimed, and fired. The BB hit Marcus in the spine and bounced off.

"Shit, that didn't hurt," Marcus said. "Do I have a mark?"

We told him no. Randy said, "Then let's try three times," and stepped closer.

"Ow," Marcus cried. But it still didn't break the skin.

Clack clack clack clack clack. I noticed that Randy kept creeping closer between shots, but I didn't say anything. Neither did Clive.

Five times and Marcus screamed and a crescent of blood smiled on his skin. "So don't pump it more than four times," Clive said.

"Yo, that hurt," Marcus said.

"Let's make it no more than two, just to be safe," I said.

I couldn't sleep that night. I was thinking about Thursday and its tally over the years: the time N.P. broke his ankle sneaking into his bedroom window after hanging out late at the Rec Room with those townie girls; the time I didn't properly hose off the lounge chairs on the deck, and the next day I got confined to the property line for a week and obediently stuck around like a fool even when my parents were out of town and would never know; fight after fight, too many to count. When the chain fell off Marcus's bike and he smeared his bare feet all the way across the gravel of the Hill trying to stop—that was Thursday all over. Our weekly full moon.

I woke up late. I heard noises in the living room. It should have been quiet. "Why aren't you at work?" I asked my brother.

"I switched my shift so I can be in the war," he said.

I told him he couldn't go. He'd get hurt. "When Mom and Dad are away, I'm in charge," I reminded him.

"You're not in charge of me."

"Yes, I am."

"What are you going to do—tell on me?" he said, and he had me there. I couldn't rat him out or else I'd get it, too. He went off to get in some last-minute practice.

At fight time, I headed up Walker. I passed the stop sign at Meredith and noticed that it was freckled with silver, the red paint chipped away— target practice for one of our friends, probably Marcus, who lived two houses down. Nice cluster on the "T" and the "O." He had good aim, depending on how far away he'd been standing.

When I got to Clive's house, we were all there, except for Nick. He'd called, whispering about how his mom was home and he couldn't get out of the house with his BB gun. Marcus suggested that we start without him.

"But then we'd have uneven teams," Bobby said.

"One of us can sit out," I said. "Youngest first?"

"Four is better than three," Clive announced, and we caved. By the time Nick arrived, it was almost dark, so we got busy making teams. Everybody wanted to be on Clive's team because Clive's team always won, but Randy was a factor with his rifle expertise. Reggie said, "Me and Bobby are a mini-team because we've been practicing together," and I was appalled. Reggie and I had never not been a mini-team, what with the whole "Benji 'n' Reggie, Benji 'n' Reggie" singsong thing through the years. The only thing that had kept me calm that afternoon was knowing that I could protect him if he was on my team. Send him on some crazy mission out of the way. He didn't look at me.

The final teams were: me, Clive, Marcus, and Nick on the Vice (for *Miami Vice*) and Randy, Bobby, Reggie, and N.P. on the Cool Chief Rockers. When Nick finally got his ass over there, I pulled out the paint goggles I'd rescued from the cobwebs under our deck, and N.P. said, "Goggles?"

"No one said anything about goggles."

"I don't got goggles."

"I'm not wearing any pussy-ass goggles," Marcus said. Nor was Reggie—I didn't even bother to fight with him about it. I didn't wear them, either.

The sky was getting dark. We went over the rules again and then it was on. We started counting to two hundred, per the guidelines, as we ran away, scattering according to haywire teen-age logic toward the highway, toward the beach. I jogged around the corner, checking to see if I was in anyone's sights, and jumped into the undeveloped lot next to the Nichols House. I waded in deep enough that I couldn't be seen from the road, but shallow enough that I could see anyone coming. Fifty-two, fifty-three. Getting there. It was almost too dark to play at this point, but the poor visibility would help me. I was going to wait for one of the Cool Chief Rockers to recon my way and then ambush him, a favorite tactic of mine to this day. Wait for the right moment in an argument with a loved one, then ambush her with some hurt I've held on to for years, the list of in- dictments nurtured in the darkness of my hideout, and say, "Gotcha!" See how you ruined me. If I was lucky, Bobby and Reggie would stop right in front of where I was hiding, to regroup or break into song, and I'd take them both out. A firefly blinked into existence, drew half a word in the air. Then it was gone.

I moved closer to the street so that I could get a better view and some- one hit me in the face with a rock.

Hot oil! Hot oil!

A rock. That's what it felt like. My head snapped back and the top half of my face throbbed like I'd been slapped. I cursed and stumbled out into the street. Who throws rocks at a BB-gun fight? I yelled for a time-out.

Randy popped out of the woods on the other side of the street. "I hit you," he said, in surprise and pride.

"Why are you throwing rocks?"

"No, it was a BB."

I poked gingerly around my left eye. He'd hit me in the socket, in the hollow between the tear duct and the eyebrow. There may be a proper anatomical name for that part of the eye socket, but I don't know it. It felt like a rock. I couldn't see out of that eye. There was stuff in it. Randy reached forward and I batted his hand away. I heard N.P. say, "What's up?" I traced my fingertip along the lumpy hole in my face, the stinging flesh. It had broken the skin. He'd pumped it more than two times.

"What happened?" Clive asked.

"Benji's out. I hit him," Randy declared.

"I'm not out," I said. "He pumped it more than twice! I'm bleeding! He's disqualified!"

I touched the hole in my face and staggered into the cone of the street light. Fat June bugs crawled over each other on the ground in their wretched street-light ritual. I held up my finger. It was bloody.

Bobby and Reggie appeared, and then all the Cool Chief Rockers and

Vicers, guns dangling. Reggie grabbed my arm and wanted to know if I was all right. I hadn't heard him sound so concerned in a long time. I shook my head drunkenly. "What the hell did you do, Randy?" Reggie said.

"He pumped it more than twice," I said. Everybody murmured "dag," in their disparate dag registers. When they got a look at the wound, they re-dagged at how close it had come to my eye.

Then I realized the Horrible Thing. I probed around the wound. The skin was tough and swollen, but beneath that was something harder, like a pearl. "It's still in there," I said.

Randy didn't believe it. "Let me see," he said, his hands out.

"Get away from him," Reggie shouted. He stepped between us. "Benji," he started, squinting at the bloody hole in the poor light, "you have to go to the hospital."

"We can't do that," Marcus said. "We'll get in trouble."

"We'll all be in some serious trouble when our parents come out to-morrow."

I looked around. They had decided. Even Clive, who in his alpha-dogness could have grabbed Randy's car keys and taken me if he wanted, fuck everybody. He was looking down the street, as if he heard his parents pulling up, avoiding my gaze. Half-gaze.

Randy said, "How are you going to get there?"

"That's uncool," Reggie said. He was my brother. I loved him. The way he said it, I knew. He'd found the stoners, too. Maybe he was going to be all right after all.

"That's so uncool," I said. Justice according to brothers and stoners: If someone needs to go to the hospital and you've got the car, you have to take them.

Reggie said, "Bobby, your grandpa can drive us!"

Bobby got weaselly. "He's asleep—look, it's dark."

"I don't have to go to the hospital. I'm O.K.," I said. Reggie protested, but everyone else was so thoroughly relieved that it was someone else's Thursday that the point was moot. I'd take one for the team—I'd take the hit because that's what I did. The other guys turned on Randy for having put them in this position, bitching about the pumping and whether his aiming for my face was an accident or not. He didn't give an inch—"It just happened"—but he did offer me "automatic shotgun for two weeks" as compensation.

My plan was to go home and try to squeeze the BB out, pimple-style.

My brother and I walked away. I had one palm over my eye and my other hand on his shoulder.

In the bathroom mirror, my eye looked disgusting. Like I'd gone a few rounds with a real heavyweight. The socket was all swollen, and blood was trickling down over my nose and older, dried-up trickles of blood. I washed my face and got a better look. I could feel the BB in there. I couldn't move it. It was lodged in the flesh or something. Reggie hovered around, trying to be helpful, but he was freaking me out so I asked him to give me a minute. I tried to wiggle the BB again, applying the time-honored zit-popping principles of strategic leverage like a modern-day Archimedes. Nothing happened, and the inflamed flesh was so tender that I couldn't really have at it. Blood with dark little bits in it dribbled over my fingers. We'd thought it all out and decided that metal BBs were O.K. because, in theory, they weren't going to break the skin, but now I had a tetanus-covered time bomb in my head. I was going to wake up with lock-jaw and waste away in bone-popping misery. Should I have occasion to fly before my death day—to visit an international lockjaw specialist at his mountaintop clinic, for example—metal detectors would go off and I'd have to explain the whole dumb story.

We drank some of our father's seven-ounce Miller bottles. I put ice on my eye and we watched the last half of *The Paper Chase*. I decided to try again in the morning.

The next morning, the swelling had gone down a little and the hole was scabbed over. I tried squeezing it again. The BB wasn't stuck in the tough flesh anymore, but now the "entry wound" had closed over. Our parents were coming out that night and they were going to murder us. Playing with BB guns. Allowing Reggie to play with BB guns when I was in charge of the house. Each of us letting the other play with BB guns when we should have known better. Three capital offenses right there.

We didn't know what to do. It was like the good old days when we broke a lamp or put a hole in the couch and ran around each other like crazy cockroaches waiting for the Big Shoe. We prayed they'd decide at the last minute not to come out. We cleaned the house extra special; we even used Windex for the fingerprints on the fridge. Maybe that would distract them. We stuck the wad of bloody paper towels and a blood-soaked washcloth into a plastic King Kullen bag and shoved it way down in the garbage.

In the middle of the afternoon, Reggie went out to sell our gun to N.P., who bought it for fifty cents on the dollar. We rehearsed cover stories and settled on: We were running through the woods to Clive's house and I ran into a branch that was sticking out! I coulda poked my eye out! That way they could scold us for running in the woods, and leave it at that.

But they got home and never noticed. This big thing almost in my eye.

The BB guns didn't come out again that summer. The thrill was gone. Those were our first guns, a rehearsal. I'd like to say, all these years later, now that one of us is dead and another paralyzed from the waist down by actual bullets—drug-related, as the papers put it—that the game back then was innocent. But it's not true. We always fought for real. Only the nature of the fight changed. As time went on, we learned to arm ourselves in our different ways. Some of us with real guns, some of us with more ephemeral weapons—an improbable plan or some sort of formulation about how best to move through the world. An idea that would let us be. Protect us and keep us safe. But a weapon, nonetheless.

The BB is still there. Under the skin. It's good for a story, something to shock people with after I've known them for years and feel a need to surprise them with the boy I was. It's not a scar that people notice. I asked a doctor about it once, about blood poisoning over time. He shook his head. Then he shrugged. "It hasn't killed you yet," he said.

Where the Line Bleeds

Jesmyn Ward

Prologue

The river was young and small. At its start it seeped from the red clay earth in the piney woods of southern Mississippi, and then wound its way, brown and slow, over a bed of tiny gray and ochre pebbles through the pines, shallow as a hand, deep as three men standing, to the sandy, green lowlands of the gulf of Mexico. It slithered along, wide and narrow, crossed by small wood and concrete bridges, lined by thin slivers of white beach, in and out of the trees, before it divided itself into the bayou and emptied itself into the bay. Near the river's end, at one such bridge, two teenage boys, twins, stood at the apex. Legs over the side, they gripped the warm, sweaty steel at their backs. Underneath them, the water of the Wolf River lay dark and deep, feathered by the current. They were preparing to jump.

The sun had only risen a few hours ago, but it was hot even for late May. Christophe, thinner of the two, let his arms loosen and leaned out, testing the height. His muscles showed ropy and long over his shoulders and down his back. Christophe wondered how cold the water would be. Joshua, taller, and softer on account of the thin layer of fat across his stomach and chest and bigger in the arms, rested his rear lightly on the steel of the railing, shying from its heat. Christophe looked at his brother, and thought the air around him seemed to waver. Joshua kicked, spewing sand and gravel from the edge. He laughed. Christophe felt his hands slip and grabbed at the rail. He looked over at his brother and smiled, the side of his mouth curving into a fishhook. Christophe knew he was sweating more than normal in the heat, and it was making his hands slippery. He and his twin were still drunk from the night before. They were graduating from high school in three hours.

"What the hell y'all doing?"

Dunny, their cousin, stood below them on the sand at the edge of the water with a beer in his hand. He'd parked the car and walked to the bank while they'd taken off their shirts and shoes. His T-shirt hung long and loose on him except where it pulled tight over his beer belly, and his jean shorts sagged low. This was one of the tallest bridges on the coast. When they were younger, all the kids from Bois Sauvage would ride their bikes there and spend all day in a circuit: plummeting from the bridge, swimming to the shore, and then running on their toes over the scalding concrete to fall to the water again. Now, the twins were almost too old to jump. Christophe thought he and Joshua had jumped once the previous summer, but he was not sure. While Dunny had egged Christophe on when he thought of the bridge at 4:00 a.m. after he and Joshua finished off a case, Dunny had refused to jump. He was twenty-five, he had said, and while the twins could still balance on the iron railing like squirrels on a power line, he couldn't.

"Y'all niggas gonna jump or what?" Dunny asked.

Christophe squinted at Joshua, at the face that was his own, but not, full lips, a jutting round nose, and skin the color of the shallows of the water below that named them twins. If he leaned in closer, he could see that which was different: freckles over Joshua's cheeks and ears where Christophe's skin was clear, Joshua's eyes that turned hazel when the sun hit them while Christophe's eyes remained so dark brown they looked black, and Joshua's hair that was so fine at the neck, it was hard to braid. Christophe moved closer to his brother, and when his arm slid along the length of Joshua's forearm, for a second it was as if Christophe had touched himself, crossed his own forearms, toucher and touched. Christophe was ready to leap. His stomach roiled with a combination of beer and anxiety, but he'd wait. Christophe knew Joshua. Christophe knew that while he liked to do things quickly, Joshua was slower about some things. His brother was looking across the water, eyeing the river winding away into the distance, the houses like small toys along the shoreline that were half hidden by the oak, pine, and underbrush rustling at the water's edge.

"That one up there on the right—that white one. Looks like the one Ma-mee used to work at, huh?"

What Christophe could see of the house through the trees was large and white and glazed with windows. He nodded, feeling his balance.

"Yeah," Christophe said.

"I always wanted to have a house like that one day. Big like that. Nice."

Christophe loved to look at those houses, but hated it, too. They made him feel poor. They made him think of Ma-mee, his grandmother, back when she was healthy and could still see, scrubbing the dirt out of white people's floors for forty years. He knew she was waiting for them now at the house, regardless of her blindness and her diabetes, with their gowns laid out on the sofa, pressed. He swallowed, tasting warm beer. Those stupid houses were ruining the jump.

"Well, the house going to rot into the ground before we can buy it, Jay." Christophe laughed and spit a white glob out over the river. It arced and fell quickly. "Can we jump so we can graduate and make some money?"

Sweat stung Christophe's eyes. Joshua was staring at the water, blinking hard. Christophe saw Joshua swallow; his brother was nervous about the drop. His own throat was clenching with the idea of the fall. It was so early in the summer that Christophe knew the water would be cold.

"Come on then, Chris."

Joshua grabbed Christophe by the arm and pulled. He threw his other arm into the air, and leaned out into space. Christophe let go and leaped into Joshua, hugging him around his chest, and felt him burning and sweaty in his arms, squirming like a caught fish. They seemed to hang in the air for a moment, held in place by the heavy, humid blue sky, the surrounding green, the brown water below. In the distance, a car sounded as it approached on the road. Christophe heard Joshua exhale deeply, and he clenched his fingers around Joshua's arms. Then the moment passed, and they began to fall. They dropped and hit the water and an eruption of tepid water burned up their noses. Their mouths opening by instinct; the water was silty on their tongues and tasted like unsweetened tea. In the middle of the surging murky river, both brothers felt for the bottom with their feet even as they let go of each other and struggled to swim upward. They surfaced. The day exploded in color and light and sound around

them. They blew snot and water out their nostrils; Christophe tossed his
head and grinned while Joshua screwed a pinky finger into one ear.

On the bank, Dunny was rolling a blunt from his selling sack, laughing. He licked the cigar shut, blew on the paper, and lit it. White smoke
drifted from his mouth in tufts. He stood at the edge of the water, the
river lapping at the tips of his basketball shoes. Squinting, Christophe
could see the tips of the crimson leather turning dark red. Dunny hopped
away from the water and held the blunt towards them. Christophe's lungs
burned and his stomach fluttered with nausea.

"Y'all want to smoke?"

Joshua immediately shook his head no, and spit water in a sparkling
brown stream. Christophe thrust himself toward his brother and grabbed
him around his shoulders, trying to shove him below the surface. Joshua
squirmed and kicked, flipping them over. Christophe slid below the
water, the current gripping him, sure as his brother's fingers. He could
hear Joshua laughing above him, muted and deep beyond the bronze
wash of the river. Everything was dim and soft. Christophe exhaled crystal bubbles of air, grabbed his brother's soft, squirming sides, and pulled
him to the quiet below.

1

In the car, Joshua plucked a waterlogged twig, limp as a shoestring, from
Christophe's wet hair. Dunny drove slowly on the pebbled gray asphalt
back roads to Bois Sauvage, encountering a house, a trailer, another car
once every mile in the wilderness of woods, red dirt ditches, and stretches
of swampy undergrowth. Joshua watched Dunny blow smoke from his
mouth and attempt to pass the blunt he'd rolled on the river beach to
Christophe. Christophe shook his head no. Shrugging and sucking on the
blunt, Dunny turned the music up so Pastor Troy's voice rasped from the
speakers, calling God and the Devil, conjuring angels and demons, and
blasting them out. Christophe had taken off his shirt and lumped it into a
wet ball in his lap. His bare feet, like Joshua's, were caked with sand.

Joshua stretched across the backseat, shirtless also, and tossed the twig
on the carpet. He lay with his cheek on the upholstery of the door, his
head halfway out the window. Joshua loved the country; he loved the un-
dulating land they moved through, the trees that overhung the back roads
to create green tunnels that fractured sunlight. He and Christophe had

played basketball through junior high and high school, and after traveling on basketball trips to Jackson, to Hattiesburg, to Greenwood, and to New Orleans for tournaments, he knew that most of the south looked like this: pines and dirt interrupted by small towns. He knew that there shouldn't be anything special about Bois Sauvage, but there was: he knew every copse of trees, every stray dog, every bend of every half-paved road, every uneven plane of each warped, dilapidated house, every hidden swimming hole. While the other towns of the coast shared boundaries and melted into each other so that he could only tell he was leaving one and arriving in the other by some landmark, like a Circle K or a Catholic church, Bois Sauvage dug in small on the back of the Bay, isolated. Natural boundaries surrounded it on three sides. To the south, east, and west, a bayou bordered it, the same bayou that the Wolf River emptied into before it pooled into the Bay of Angels and then out to the Gulf of Mexico. There were only two roads that crossed the bayou and led out of Bois Sauvage to St. Catherine, the next town over. To the north, the interstate capped the small town like a ruler, beyond which a thick bristle of pine forest stretched off and away into the horizon. It was beautiful.

Joshua could understand why Ma-mee's and Papa's families had migrated here from New Orleans, had struggled to domesticate the low-lying, sandy earth that reeked of rotten eggs in a dry summer and washed away easily in a wet one. Land had been cheaper along the Mississippi gulf, and black Creoles had spread along the coastline. They'd bargained in broken English and French to buy tens of acres of land. Still, they and their poor white neighbors were dependent on the rich for their livelihood, just as they had been in New Orleans: they built weekend mansions along the beach for wealthy New Orleans expatriates, cleaned them, did their yardwork, and fished, shrimped, and harvested oysters. Yet here, they had space and earth.

They developed their own small, self-contained communities: they intermarried with others like themselves, raised small, uneven houses from the red mud. They planted and harvested small crops. They kept horses and chickens and pigs. They built tiny stills in the wood behind their houses that were renowned for the clarity of the liquor, the strong oily consistency of it, the way it bore a hole down the throat raw. They parceled out their acres to their children, to their passels of seven and twelve. They taught their children to shoot and to drive young, and sent them to one-room schoolhouses that only advanced to the seventh grade.

Their children built small, uneven houses, married at seventeen and fourteen, and started families. They called Bois Sauvage God's country.

Their children's children grew, the government desegregated the schools, and they sent them to the public schools in St. Catherine to sit for the first time next to white people. Their children's children could walk along the beaches, could walk through the park in St. Catherine without the caretakers chasing them away, hollering nigger. Their children's children graduated from high school and got jobs at the docks, at convenience stores, at restaurants, as maids and carpenters and landscapers like their mothers and fathers, and they stayed. Like the oyster shell foundation upon which the county workers packed sand to pave the roads, the communities of Bois Sauvage, both black and white, embedded themselves in the red clay and remained. Every time Joshua returned from a school trip and the bus crossed the bayou or took the exit for Bois Sauvage from the highway, he felt that he could breathe again. Even seeing the small, green metal exit sign made something ease in his chest. Joshua rubbed his feet together and the sand slid away from his skin in small, wet clumps that reminded him of lukewarm grits.

When Joshua and Christophe talked about what they wanted to do with their lives, it never included leaving Bois Sauvage, even though they could have joined their mother, Cille, who lived in Atlanta. She sent Mamee money by Western Union once a month to help with groceries and clothing. Cille had still been living with Ma-mee when she had the twins, and when she decided to go to Atlanta to make something of herself when the boys were five, she left them. She told Ma-mee she was tired of accompanying her on jobs, of cleaning messes she didn't make, of dusting the underside of tabletops, of mopping wooden living room floors that stretched the entire length of Ma-mee's house, of feeling invisible when she was in the same room with women who always smelled of refined roses. She told Ma-mee she'd send for the twins once she found an apartment and a job, but she didn't. Ma-mee said that one day after Cille had been gone for eleven months, she stood in the doorway of their room and watched them sleep in their twin beds. She gazed at their curly, rough red-brown hair, their small bunched limbs, their skin the color of amber, and she decided to never ask Cille if she was ready to take them again. That was the summer their hair had turned deep red, the same color as Cille's, before it turned to brown, like a flame fading to ash, Ma-mee said.

Three weeks after that morning, Cille visited. She didn't broach the subject of them coming back to Atlanta with her. She and Ma-mee had sat on the porch, and Ma-mee told her to send $200 a month: the boys would remain in Bois Sauvage, with her. Cille had assented as the sound of the twins chasing Ma-mee's chickens, whooping and squealing, drifted onto the screened porch from the yard. Ma-mee said it was common to apportion the raising of children to different family members in Bois Sauvage. It was the rule when she was a little girl; in the 1940s, medicine and food had been scarce, and it was normal for those with eleven or twelve children to give one or two away to childless couples, and even more normal for children to be shuffled around within the family, she said. Joshua knew plenty of people at school that had been raised by grandparents or an aunt or a cousin. Even so, he wished he hadn't been torturing the chickens; he wished that he'd been able to see them talking, to see Cille's face, to see if it hurt her to leave them.

Now Cille was working as a manager at a beauty supply store. She had green eyes she'd inherited from Papa and long, kinky hair, and Joshua didn't know how he felt about her. He thought he had the kind of feelings for her that he had for her sisters, his aunts, but sometimes he thought he loved her most, and other times not at all. When she visited them twice a year, she went out to nightclubs and restaurants, and shopped with her friends. Joshua and Christophe talked about it, and Joshua thought they shared a distanced affection for her, but he wasn't sure. Christophe never stayed on the phone with Cille longer than five minutes, while Joshua would drag the conversation out, ask her questions until she would beg off the phone.

But once when she'd come home during the summer of their sophomore year, a kid named Rook from St. Catherine's had said something dirty about her at the basketball court down at the park while they were playing a game, something about how fine her ass was. Christophe had told Joshua later the particulars of what Rook had said, how the words had come out of Rook's mouth all breathy and hot because he was panting, and to Christophe, it had sounded so dirty. Joshua hadn't heard it because he was under the net, digging his elbow into Dunny's ribs, because he was the bigger man of the two. Christophe was at the edge of the court with the ball, trying to shake Rook, because he was smaller and faster, when Rook said it. Christophe had turned red in the face, pushed Rook away, brought the ball up, and with the sudden violence of a piston had fired the ball straight at Rook's face. It hit him squarely in the nose. There was blood everywhere and Christophe was yelling and calling Rook a bitch and Rook had his hand under his eyes and there was blood seeping through the cracks of his fingers, and Dunny was running to stand between them and laughing, telling Rook if he wouldn't have said shit about his aunt Cille, then maybe he wouldn't have gotten fucked up. Joshua was surprised because he felt his face burn and his hands twitch into fists and he realized he wanted to whip the shit out of dark little Rook, Rook with the nose that all the girls liked because it was fine and sharp as a crow's beak but that now was swollen fat and gorged with blood. Even now Joshua swallowed at the thought, and realized he was digging his fingers into his sides. Rook, little bitch.

Joshua felt the wind flatten his eyelids and wondered if Cille would be at the school. He knew she knew they were graduating: he'd addressed the graduation invitations himself, and hers was the first he'd done. He thought of her last visit. She'd come down for a week at Christmas, had given him and Christophe money and two gold rope chains. He and Christophe had drunk moonshine and ate fried turkey with the uncles on Christmas night in Uncle Paul's yard, and he'd listened as his uncles talked about Cille as she left the house after midnight. She'd sparkled in the dark when the light caught her jewelry and lit it like a cool, clean metal chain.

"Where you going, girl?" Uncle Paul had yelled at her outline.

"None of your damn business!" she'd yelled back.

"That's Cille," Paul had said. "Never could stay still."

"That's cause she spoiled." Uncle Julian, short and dark with baby-fine black hair, had said over the mouth of his bottle. "She the baby girl: Papa's favorite. Plus, she look just like Mama."

"Stop hogging the bottle, Jule," Uncle Paul had said.

Joshua and Christophe had come in later that night to find Cille back in the house. She was asleep at the kitchen table with her head on her arms, breathing softly into the tablecloth. When they carried her to bed, she smelled sweetly, of alcohol and perfume. The last Joshua remembered seeing of her was on New Year's morning; she'd been bleary and puffy eyed from driving an hour and a half to New Orleans the night before and partying on Bourbon Street in the French Quarter. He and Christophe had walked into the kitchen in the same clothes from the previous day, fresh from the party up on the Hill at Remy's house that had ended when the sun rose, to see Cille eating greens and cornbread and black-eyed peas with Ma-mee. Ma-mee had wished them a Happy New Year and told them they stank and needed to take a bath. They had stopped to kiss and hug her, and after he embraced Ma-mee, Joshua had moved to hug Cille. She stopped him with a raised arm, and spoke words he could still hear.

"What a way to start off the New Year."

He had known she was talking about his smell, his hangover, his dirt. He had given her a small, thin smile and backed away. Christophe left the room without trying to hug her, and Joshua followed. After they both took showers, Cille came to their room and embraced them both. Joshua had followed her back to the kitchen, wistfully, and saw her hand a small bank envelope filled with money to Ma-mee. She left. Joshua thought that on average now, she talked to them less and gave them more.

He couldn't help it, but a small part of him wished she would be there when they got home, that she had come in late last night while he and Christophe were out celebrating with Dunny at a pre-graduation party in the middle of a field up further in the country in a smattering of cars and music under the full stars. Wrapped in the somnolent thump of the bass, Joshua closed his eyes, the sun through the leaves of the trees hot on his face, and fell asleep. When he woke up, they were pulling into the yard, Dunny was turning down the music, and there was no rental car in the dirt driveway of the small gray house surrounded by azalea bushes and old reaching oaks. Something dropped in his chest, and he decided not to think about it.

Ma-mee heard the car pull into the yard: a loud, rough motor and the whine of an old steel body. Rap music: muffled men yelling and thumping bass. That was Dunny's car. The twins were home, and judging by the warmth of the air on her skin that made her housedress stick, the rising drone of the crickets, and the absence of what little traffic there was along the road in front of her house, they were late. She'd pressed their gowns and hung them with wire hangers over the front door. She thought to fuss, but didn't. They were boys, and they were grown; they took her to her doctor's appointments, cooked for her, spoke to her with respect. They kept her company sometimes in the evenings, and over the wooing of the cicadas coming through the open windows in the summer or the buzzing of the electric space heater in the winter in the living room, described the action on TV shows for her: *Oprah* and reruns of *The Cosby Show* and nature shows about crocodiles and snakes, which she loved. They called her ma'am, like they were children still, and never talked back. They were good boys.

The front screen door squealed open and she heard them walk across the porch. She heard Dunny step heavily behind them and the sound of wet jeans pant legs rubbing together. The twins' light tread advanced from the front porch and through the door. The smell of outside: sun-baked skin and sweat and freshwater and the juice of green growing things bloomed in her nose. From her recliner seat, she saw their shadows dimly against the walls she'd had them paint blue, after she found out she was blind: the old whitewash that had coated the walls and the low, white ceiling had made her feel like she was lost in an indefinite space. She liked the idea of the blue mirroring the air outside, and the white ceiling like the clouds. When she walked down the narrow, dim hallway, she'd run her fingers over the pine paneling there and imagined she was in her own private grove of young pines, as most of Bois Sauvage had been when she was younger. She'd breathe in the hot piney smell and imagine herself slim-hipped and fierce, before she'd married and born her children, before she started cleaning for rich white folks, when she filled as many sacks as her brothers did with sweet potatoes, melons, and corn. She spoke over the tinny sound of the old radio in the window of the kitchen that was playing midday blues: Clarence Carter.

"Y'all been swimming, huh?"

Christophe bent to kiss her.

"And drinking, huh? You smell like a still."

Joshua laughed and brushed her other cheek.

"You, too!" She swatted him with her hand. "Y'all stink like all out-side! We going to be late. Go take a shower. Laila came over here to braid y'all's hair, but left cause y'all wasn't here, your Uncle Paul coming in an hour to take us to the ceremony, and y'all know y'all worse than women—take forever to take a bath. Go on!" Under the smell of the worn sofa upholstery, mothballs, Pine Sol, and potpourri, she smelled something harsh and heavy. Something that caressed the back of her throat. "That Dunny on the porch smoking?"

"Hey, Grandma Ma-mee," Dunny said.

"Don't 'hey Grandma Ma-mee' me. You dressed for the service?"

"I ain't going." His voice echoed from the porch. The sweet, warm smell of his cigarillo grew stronger.

"Yeah, right, you ain't going. You better get off my porch smok-ing . . ."

"Aaaw, Ma-mee."

"And take your ass down the street and get cleaned up. You going to watch my boys graduate. And tell your Mama that I told Marianne and Lilly and them to be over at her house at around six for the cookout, so I hope she got everything ready." His feet hit the grass with a wet crunch. "And don't you throw that butt in my yard. Them boys'll have to clean it up."

"Yes, Ma-mee."

"Hurry up, Dunny."

"Yes, Ma-mee."

From a bedroom deep in the house, she heard Joshua laughing, high and full, more soprano for a boy than she expected, and as usual, it reminded her vaguely of the cartoon with the singing chipmunks in it. It made her smile.

"I don't know what you laughing for," she yelled.

Joshua's laugh was joined by his brother's muffled guffawing from the shower. One couldn't laugh without the other. She pulled her dress away from her front so as to cool some of the sweat there: she wanted to be fresh and cool for the service. She'd bought a dress from Sears for Cille's graduation; where this one was shapeless, the other had fit tighter, and had itched. It was polyester. Ma-mee had given Cille a bougainvillea flower to wear. She closed her eyes and leaned her head back into the sofa cushion, and she could see Cille at eighteen, her skin lovely and glowing as a ripe scopanine as she walked to collect her diploma. She had just fallen in love with the twins' father then, and it showed. Cille bore the twins two years later, and by then her face had changed; it looked as if it had been glazed with a hard candy.

Joshua replied; it sounded as if he was speaking through clothing. Probably pulling a shirt over his head, she thought.

"Yes, Ma-mee."

In the shower, Christophe soaped the rag, stood with the slimy, shimmering cloth in his hand and let the water, so cold it made his nipples pebble, hit him across the face. In the bottom of the tub, he saw sand, tiny brown grains, traced in thin rivulets on the porcelain. He washed his stomach first, as he had done since he was small: it was the way Ma-mee had taught him when they'd first started bathing themselves when they were seven. That was when she had first learned that she had diabetes.

It wasn't until Christophe was fifteen that her vision really started going: that he noticed that she was reaching for pots and pillows and papers without turning her face to look for them, and that sometimes when he was talking to her and she looked at him, she wouldn't focus on his face. She scaled back on the housekeeping jobs she'd been doing. She said that some of her clients had started complaining that she was missing spots, which she'd denied: she said the richer they got, the lazier and pickier they became. She hated going to the doctor, and so she had hidden it from them until he'd noticed these things. Late one night after they'd come back from riding with Dunny, he lay in the twin bed across the room from Joshua, and told him what he suspected. He'd heard of people with diabetes going blind, but he never thought it would happen to Mamee.

After Joshua had fallen asleep, Christophe had turned to the wall and cried: breathing through his mouth, swallowing the mucus brought up by the tears, his heart burned bitter and pulled small at the thought of her not being able to see them ever again, at the thought of her stumbling around the house. He'd talked to his Aunt Rita, Dunny's mother, and she'd forced Ma-mee to go to the doctor. He'd confirmed she was legally blind. While Rita sat in a chair next to Ma-mee holding her hand, Christophe and Joshua stood behind them, half leaning against the wall, their heads empty with air and disbelief, as the doctor told them that if they had caught it earlier, they could have done laser surgery on her eyes to stop the blindness from progressing. So then, too late, she'd had the operation. Afterwards, she sat pale and quiet in the living room that she'd had them empty of most of the porcelain knick-knacks and small, cheap plastic vases and shelves so she'd have less to clean and worry about breaking or banging into. The bandages were a blankness on her face. When the doctor took them off and proclaimed her healed, she said she could see blobs of color, nothing else, but Christophe felt a little better in knowing that at least she wouldn't be closed in total darkness, that at least she could still see the color of his skin, the circle of his head.

He dried himself off, wiped the mirror clear, and tried not to, but thought of his father. Their father: the one that gave them these noses and these bodies quick to muscle. Before their mother left them, he was someone the twins saw twice or three times a month. They were happiest when he would stay over for days at Ma-mee's house: the twins would stay awake and listen to him and Cille talk in the kitchen, and later the muffled laughter that came from Cille's room. Inevitably, he and Cille would fight, and he would leave, only to come back a week or two later. Ma-mee had told them that their father refused to go to Atlanta with Cille, and that he liked living in Bois Sauvage just fine; that had caused the final break between them.

After Cille went to Atlanta, he became scarce. His visits tapered off until a day came when Christophe saw him from the school bus on the way home and realized his father hadn't visited them in months. His father was filling the tank of his car with gas at a corner store, and Christophe jumped. Christophe had nudged his brother, and Joshua had joined him in looking out the window, in watching their father shrink until he was small and unreal-looking as a plastic toy soldier stuck in one position: right hand on the roof of the car, the left on the hose, his head down. Suddenly trees obscured their view, and Christophe had turned around in his seat to face the front of the bus, and Joshua, who had been leaning over him in his seat, straightened up and faced forward. Both of them stared at the sweating green plastic upholstery of the seat before them: they were so short they could not see over it.

Christophe wiped a rag over his face and bore down on his nose. Over the years, Christophe and Joshua would see their father around Bois Sauvage when they were riding their bikes and doing wheelies in and out of the ditches, or when they were stealing pears from Mudda Ma'am's pear tree and carting them down the road in their red wagon, and later when they were older, walking with their friends and sneaking blunts. His name was Samuel, and while the boys grew up calling Cille by her name instead of calling her mother, they didn't call Samuel by his name because he didn't talk to them, and because they felt more abandoned by him than by their mother, who at least had the excuse of being "far away." Whenever they saw Samuel, he was always with his friends, and had a red and white Budweiser can in his hands. When they talked about him, they called him "Him" and "He," and any questions or comments about him from others they ignored, or stared hard at the asker, silently, until the question evaporated in the air. As they grew older, when he came up in conversation with others, they called him what everyone in the neighborhood called him: Sandman. When they were thirteen, they began to hear rumors filtered from the neighborhood drug dealers, who had just discovered crack cocaine, and were learning how to cook it from cousins who were visiting from New Orleans, from Chicago, from Florida: these rumors explained why he seemed to be skinnier each time they saw him, why he never drove a better car than his old beat-up, rust-laced Ford pickup, and why he hung out in his friends' yards so much.

Sandman was an addict. Fresh told it to Christophe one day down at the park. While Christophe sat on the picnic table bench and watched Fresh count his money into neat piles of hundreds and twenties and rebag his crumbs of crack and stash them according to size and price in different pockets on his carpenter's pants, Fresh had said to him, "Boy, except for your nose, you look just like your mama." He'd paused while he folded his wad of bills, had looked up and stared at Christophe, weighing him like a pit he was thinking about buying, and then said, "You know he on this shit, right?" And in that moment, Christophe knew by Fresh's look who he was talking about. Everything had clicked into order in his head like a stack of dominoes falling in a line. "All of them older ones that used to snort powder when they was young for fun, all of them doing it now. This take them to that other level." Fresh had glared at Christophe. "Don't never do that shit. I keep my shit clean, still got all the hair in my nose." Christophe had looked away from Fresh's diamond-studded gold tooth gleaming in his mouth and had shrugged his small thirteen-year-old shoulders, bony and broad under his too big jersey top, and looked away across the park to the basketball court, the baseball diamond, the trees bristling green and rising on all sides. Christophe watched a crow circle and land at the top of a pine and join about a dozen more so that they looked like dark flowers blooming in the blowsy needles, and thought of the last time he'd seen him. He hadn't even so much as nodded at Christophe: Sandman was sitting on the tail of his pickup in Mr. Joe's yard and was so drunk he hadn't even known Christophe was the pre-teen walking past him.

Now, Christophe swiped his hand through his hair and curled it backwards. According to what Fresh had told him about six months ago, Sandman was in Alabama, where he'd gone to stay with his brother and enter rehab. Christophe put on lotion, and walked in a towel to the bedroom. He passed Joshua and punched him in his shoulder as Joshua brushed against him in the narrow hall on the way to the bathroom.

"Hope you left some cold water for me."

"Ha."

Christophe shut the door and began to dress, pulling on jeans, a Polo shirt, his new Reeboks, and greased his hair with Pink Oil Moisturizer so that it curled close to his scalp. He'd be clean, look nice for his aunt and uncles so they could watch him cross the stage, grab his diploma, and throw his tassel across the cap. He wanted to hug Ma-mee with his diploma in his hand and smell good for her, smell clean with soap and cologne. He sprayed a little on himself from the bottle he shared with Joshua, and then went out to the living room to sit next to Ma-mee on the sofa, to move as little as possible to guard himself from sweating unduly, to talk to her about the day, about the cookout at his Aunt Rita's, about whether she cared if he had a beer once they were there even though he knew he'd probably drink regardless of what she said: he'd just hide it. Christophe fleetingly thought that Sandman might show up, but then he told himself that he didn't give a damn if he showed up or not. Crackheads were known for taking credit where none was due. Most of them were a little crazy. Christophe would rather that he didn't show up. Christophe decided that if he did appear out of some misplaced sense of pride or because he was trying to fulfill some stupid rehab self-help shit, Joshua would have to stop him from punching Sandman in his face.

On the way to the graduation, Ma-mee sat in the front seat with one arm out the window. While her fingers felt at the seam of the glass, her unseeing eyes turned to blink watery and half-closed at the bayou as the wind pushed thick and heavy as a hand at her throat. Paul drove, his blue short-sleeved button-down shirt fastened to his neck, his hands careful on the steering wheel as he slowly followed the curves; his fists were positioned at ten and two. Already, he was sweating dark rings under his arms. Christophe and Joshua sat awkwardly in the backseat of the Oldsmobile with their legs open at the same angles as their uncle's forearms and their arms akimbo at their sides. They leaned away from each other and watched the bright green marsh grass lining the side of the road, the water, interrupted by islands thick with pelicans and white cranes and brush, slide by. The bayou splayed out away from the gray asphalt on both sides, eclipsed the horizon, and sizzled with cicadas and crickets. The twins' windows were rolled down as well.

Ma-mee hated air-conditioning. She never wanted it on in the car, and she refused to install an air-conditioning unit in the house. She said the cold air made her feel like she couldn't breathe, and that it made her short of breath. So in the summer months, they sweated. The boys grew up accustomed to the wet heat, the droning indoor fans, the doors that swelled and stuck with the rise in temperature. In their shared room, they slept on top of their twin beds' coverlets with their mouths open, their spindly limbs and knobby knees and elbows exposed, and wore only white briefs. As they grew older, they stripped their beds to the fitted and flat sheets, and took to sleeping in old gym shorts, or boxers.

Joshua propped one arm on the door, and rested his hand on his chin. He didn't lean back because he didn't want to crush his curls flat against the headrest. Outside, the edge of the road shimmered, and ahead the road wavered so that it looked as if snakes, tens of them, were crossing the road in the distance. When he was little he'd always been amazed when they disappeared the closer he got: but then again, back then he'd twisted around in his seat facing the rear window because he'd thought the moon and the sun followed the car, and he liked to watch them sail through the sky and chase him. He looked over to Christophe, who had arranged his head and arm similarly, and was looking intently out the other window. As they were walking to the car, Christophe whispered his warning about the possibility of seeing Sandman there. Joshua had started to laugh at the impossibility of it. Then Joshua had looked at Christophe's mouth, and he'd stopped laughing and nodded: yes, he'd watch out for Sandman. The set of Christophe's shoulders as they got in the car made him think of Cille: he wondered if Christophe was wondering if she was coming, if perhaps Ma-mee knew she was coming and was trying to keep it a secret so it would be a surprise. He let his hand fall out the window and drag in the current of the wind: she would wear red, her favorite color, he knew.

They arrived at the school ten minutes before the start of the program. With their gowns held gingerly in their hands, they climbed out of the car and walked across the small parking lot, past the sprawling red-brick buildings couched among the moss-strewn oaks and the football field stretching away to the left, to the gym directly behind the cluster of classrooms. The family entered the gym together and stood still for a moment; they were a small group in a milling confusion of parents and students and relatives.

Every other person led neon balloons that read "Congratulations Class of 2005" in yellow and sported tails of sparkling, curly streamers, and carried cards stuffed fat with money. The smell of perfume and cologne was thick in the air. The basketball court had been remade into an auditorium: folding metal chairs were lined in precise rows down the length of the floor. The more punctual family members claimed choice seats in the metal rows while the less punctual consigned themselves to the bleachers. While Uncle Paul led Ma-mee by the elbow to her seat next to Aunt Rita and the rest of the extended family at the front of the gym near the long dais that served as the stage, Joshua and Christophe skirted the crowd and found their way to the rows of graduating students. The graduating class had nearly two hundred students, but still, they filled only around ten rows: St. Catherine High was a small high school, even with all the students from the town of St. Catherine and its country neighbor, Bois Sauvage. About half the students were white, half were black, and there was a smattering of Vietnamese. While most of the Vietnamese kids' parents had immigrated to the area after the Vietnam War to work in the shrimping and fishing industries, most of the black and white families had been living in the two towns since their foundings, and some of them even shared last names with each other, which was the result of little-acknowledged intermarriage. Their seating in the gym belied their social interactions: the two groups lived mostly segregated lives.

Joshua peered into the crowd and saw Laila; he waved. She had eyes that turned to slits when she laughed, a curvy waist, and lips he thought about kissing every time he saw her, but he'd never told her that. He and Christophe had lost their virginity to two sisters from St. Catherine when they were fifteen. Dunny had taken them along when he'd gone to their house to visit the oldest sister. While Dunny disappeared in the bedroom with his girl, Christophe and Joshua had sat sweating on the sofa. Lisa, the middle sister, had just walked over and sat on Christophe's lap and flirted with him. She laughed at his jokes. Within minutes, they'd disappeared down the hallway. Nina, the youngest, had sat next to Joshua and told him she had seen him around school—and did he think she was cute for a ninth grader? When he'd told her yes, she'd kissed him. The next thing he knew, she was partly naked and on top of him and the remote control was digging into his back and the TV went black and he didn't care.

Afterwards, Christophe had laughed when Dunny asked him about it, but Joshua had been quiet in the backseat. Since then, every time he had sex seemed a lucky accident, while Christophe grew more and more confident. He had just broken up with his latest girlfriend, he said, for being too clingy. Christophe tugged him toward their seats. Joshua and Christophe found their assigned chairs in the "D" row; Christy Desiree sat on their right, and Fabian Daniels on their left. Christy was busy pulling at her blond hair and reapplying lip-gloss. Fabian curved into his seat with his arms crossed over his chest: he looked as if he were sinking. Joshua ignored Christy and perched at the edge of his chair, scanning the program.

"So what y'all going to be doing after this?"

Christophe turned to Fabian and adjusted his robe where it had bunched beneath his legs. He could hardly move. He knew it was going to be wrinkled when he walked across the stage, but he didn't want it to be too wrinkled. He knew Aunt Rita would talk.

"Look for a job, I guess. You don't know anybody trying to get rid of a old car for cheap, do you?"

"Naw." Fabian pushed his cap up and back on his head since it had begun to slip down over his dark, broad forehead. "If I hear something, I'll let you know. I probably won't hear nothing before I leave—I'm going offshore. My uncle already got my application in. I start in two weeks."

"I couldn't be out there on that water all the time, cooped up. I'd go crazy." Christophe shifted his robe again, resettling it flatly beneath him. "Who knows, though. They make good money. Maybe when I get older, I'd go offshore for that kind of money." The only way he could ever consider leaving Bois Sauvage to work was if he was older, and only if Mamee was gone. She'd spent her entire life working for one rich white household or another to earn money to feed them, dressing them when they were younger in clothes her employers had given her to take to the Salvation Army, providing for them the best she could. Now it was their turn.

The hum of conversation in the gym was almost deafening, and already Christophe was growing tired of the rustling of programs, the shrieking of small children, the loud boasting of men, and the sense of interminable wait. He hated official shit like this. He just wanted to get his diploma and hear his name over the loudspeaker, the light patter of applause, and then get to the cookout, to the rest of the summer, to the rest of his life. He was ready to be done with school; he was tired of watching his principal, sweating at the neck, now barking orders at the first five rows, his teachers, dressed in long, loose dresses replete with maiden collars, darting around nervously, the secretaries, bored and severe, picking at the microphone and the fake flowers next to the podium. The gym was cold, and he felt the sweat dry on him and goose pimples rise on his arms under his gown as the satin, now cool like water, slid over them. The principal, Mr. Farbege, leaned into the row and barked, "Remember your cues!" and Christophe barely resisted the urge to flip him off. Joshua leaned over to Christophe, the program in his hand.

"Look at this," he said.

Joshua thought she might do something like this. The only reason he was looking at the program was to look at the family advertisements in the back: he knew that he'd find at least a couple of choice photographs of his classmates in embarrassing ads that said things like, "You're a star! Follow your dreams" and "From Maw-maw and Paw-paw. We love you." There, on the last page, was a small ad, measuring around three by five inches. In it was a small picture of him and Christophe; it had been taken when they were five. Cille had asked Aunt Rita to take it, a picture of all three of them, on the day she left for Atlanta. She was kneeling on the ground between them with her arms over both of their shoulders: her smile was wide, and she had sunglasses on, large dark ovals, because as Christophe remembered it, she had been crying. At her sides, the twins looked like small, young-faced old men: their T-shirts hung on them, their heads were cocked to the side, and neither of them was looking toward the camera. Joshua was looking off into the distance, his fists clutching the bottom of his shirt as he pulled it away from his small round stomach. Christophe's eyes were squinted nearly shut, and the set of his mouth was curved downward and puckered: he looked as if he had just eaten something bitter, like he looked on the day they snuck the small, bitter grapes from Papa's old grapevine that grew curled on crude posts behind the house and ate them.

Under the picture was printed in small, bold-faced print: *Congratulations to Joshua and Christophe. Love, Cille.* That was it. Joshua knew as soon as he saw the small picture, the minuscule line, that she wasn't coming. He knew that she wasn't already sitting in the audience with Aunt Rita, that she wasn't just running late, that she wouldn't appear at their cook-out with the rest of the family, that she wasn't just going to walk casually out of the kitchen with a pot in her arms to set on the long wax-covered table beneath the trees while the outdoor fans buzzed in the background and blew her dress away from her legs. Joshua let Christophe take the paper as he leaned further back and down in his chair. He purposefully spread his legs to take up more space so that Christy squeaked as she had to smash her knees together to make room for him; he hated her lip-gloss and her prissiness and for a second he felt a strong urge to press his hand across her face, to smudge her makeup. He didn't turn and say he was sorry.

Christophe read the program and folded it in fourths and placed it in his back pocket along with his own program. Who knows, he thought, one day Joshua might actually want it. He heard Mr. Farbege giving the opening remarks, and he tuned out as he began to make a list in his head of where he and Joshua could go to look for jobs: Wal-Mart, the grocery store in St. Catherine, the McDonald's.

Joshua ignored the valedictorian and salutatorian's speeches, the cheesy slide show (he and Christophe were in one picture: their hands in their pockets, they stood outside on the benches used for break—he thought that Christophe looked like he was high). When the principal began calling graduates' names, Joshua waited patiently as he watched the other students cross the dais: some of them danced and played the crowd for laughs when they got their diplomas, some pumped their fists in the air, while others walked across quickly, heads down, nervous, and seemed to shy away from the applause that clattered from the stands.

"Christophe DeLisle."

Christophe rose, walked to the podium, and smoothed his gown. Once there, he shook Mr. Farbege's hand with his left and grabbed his diploma with his right. The leather casing was cool in his hand, and it slipped slightly, and he realized he was sweating. The lights were so bright and hot that he didn't attempt to look out into the crowd or find Ma-mee: instead, he turned and put on his cockiest smile, hoping Aunt Rita was relating everything to her, and walked off the stage.

Joshua stood when he saw his brother exit.

"Joshua DeLisle."

Joshua ascended to greet the principal. He couldn't focus on Mr. Farbege's sweating, red face or the secretary fumbling with the diplomas. He turned to the audience, the lights blaring, squinted, and tried to smile. He knew he wouldn't be able to make them out against the glare of the spotlight, but he looked in the direction Ma-mee and Uncle Paul had gone anyway, and tried to see if he could see her. He saw nothing but a mess of faces and bright, bold outfits, so he raised his hand and waved a little in their direction in time to the applause, and hoped that they knew he was waving for them. He walked to his seat, shuffled past the rows of the students, sat, and realized that he'd been nervous, that the tiny, golden hairs at the back of his neck and on his arms and legs were standing on end. He shivered, feeling as he had when he was little and he'd run into the river just after the sun rose. They'd camped with Aunt Rita and Uncle Paul and the rest of the family on a Friday night, and he'd awoken the next day before everyone else, jarred awake by the sand pressing into his stomach through the sleeping bag where he'd slept on the floor of the tent. He'd run out to the water, wanting to be the first one in, expecting it to be languid and warm, but instead was shocked by the cold of it, the bite of it on his legs up to his knees, how his skin seemed to tighten and retreat across his muscles from the chill. He grimaced and gripped his diploma. He couldn't believe that he and Christophe had graduated. He leaned closer to his brother, sideways, in his chair, until he could feel their shoulders touching. The litany of names was a buzzing drone in his head, and he waited for it to end.

The sun was turning the tops of the trees red, and from the woods surrounding Aunt Rita's trailer, the night insects began calling to one another, heralding the approach of the cooler night. Under the young, spindly oaks dotting the yard, Christophe, Joshua, and Dunny sat at one of several folding wooden tables in creaking metal and plastic chairs, plates of food before them. Ma-mee ate slowly, feeling her way around the food on her plate: tiny barbecued drumsticks, meatballs, and potato salad. Children darted back and forth across the yard like small animals, chasing and teasing each other in packs. Most of the twins' uncles, Cille's brothers, sat in a circle away from the steel drum barbecue grill, passing what Joshua suspected to be a bottle of homemade wine around and smoking.

There were four of them: Paul, Julian, Maxwell, and David. Aunt Rita, Cille's only sister, was sweating over the grill: her hair was pulled back in a loose ponytail, frizzed and messed by the humidity, and she cooked with one hand on her hip while the other basted the chicken and ribs with sauce. Myriad gold earrings shone at her ears. She swatted a mosquito away from her head, and lifting one foot to scratch her leg, continued the cooking, mumbling to herself. She was a shorter, rounder version of her sister: Joshua thought there was something different about her movements, something more settled than Cille, as if her lower center of gravity made her more solid, more dependable, less susceptible to disappear from a place. Friends and neighbors filled the chairs around the twins, drinking and smoking, talking and laughing. Joshua waved a fly away from his food and took a sip of his Budweiser; the can was pleasantly cool in the palm of his hand. Christophe was busy fielding questions from Uncle Eze, Rita's husband. Eze had moved his chair close and ate with both elbows on the table; his arms dark and thick with muscle as he licked his fingers. Once every few minutes, he'd pause to reach over and snake his hand around Aunt Rita's waist. Then he'd grab his napkin and dab at his face where beads of sweat bloomed large as pearls.

"So, what y'all going to do now? Y'all thought about going to school?"

Joshua snorted and half-smiled, then picked up a boiled shrimp from his plate and began to peel it.

"You better be glad we graduated!" Christophe laughed.

They'd barely passed senior English, and the only reason they hadn't been in more detention was because they were a team. After smoking blunts with Dunny a few mornings when he gave them rides to school or when they checked themselves out early and skipped class, they watched out for each other: they juggled each other's excuses, finished one another's lies, and generally kept one another out of trouble. Joshua placed the naked, pink shrimp on Ma-mee's plate, and she smiled and reached for his hand before he could remove it and squeezed; the pads of her fingers, even after all those years of scrubbing and washing, were still soft and full on his wrist. He squeezed in return and then began peeling another shrimp.

"Well, then, what y'all going to do?"

Christophe scooped potato salad onto a piece of white bread in spoonfuls so big they threatened to break the plastic spoon in half. He folded the bread and then took a large bite of his potato salad sandwich before chasing it with a swallow of his own beer: the rim of the can was flecked with bits of barbecue sauce and meat, and smeared with grease.

"We going to get a job. We got a whole bunch of places we can go put applications in at. We going to make some money."

Eze paused to wipe his hands on his napkin, and leaned back in his own chair. He'd sucked the bones on his plate clean. His voice was lower when he spoke.

"Y'all thought about what y'all going to do about a car?"

Christophe took another bite of his sandwich and frowned.

"We was gonna borrow Dunny's car while he was at work to fill out applications until we could save up enough money to buy one. Somebody got to be selling one for cheap sometime soon. People always trying to get rid of old Cutlasses; it shouldn't take too much money to buy one and get it running good."

Joshua noticed Aunt Rita had closed the top of the grill and was standing behind Eze. Her arms were folded across her chest, and her head was cocked to the side. He realized she was looking at him, that she was blinking at him solemnly. Her eyes were large and dark in her face and the liquid eyeliner she'd worn at the graduation was smudged below her eyes; it made them appear bruised. Dunny picked up a beer and paused with the rim of the can to his mouth and found Joshua watching him. Dunny winked, grinned around the can, and tipped the beer back so that it hid his face.

Eze tapped his finger on the table once, twice, and then stood. He dropped his napkin so that it fell as slowly as snow to the paper tablecloth. Christophe looked at Ma-mee. She was chewing thoughtfully on the shrimp and had a small grin on her face. Shrimp were her favorite food. Away from the citronella candles and electric bulbs illuminating the trees into the surrounding darkness, Eze walked into the ascending crescendo of the raucous night, calling back over his shoulder, "Well, come on, I got something to show you."

Christophe glanced at Joshua and widened his eyes. Joshua shrugged and stood to follow Eze. Christophe stabbed a hot link with a fork and took it with him when he pushed away from the table. Joshua waited for him to catch up. Eze disappeared around the side of the trailer where he and Aunt Rita parked their cars. Once Christophe rounded the corner, he stopped alongside his brother, who stood at the tailgate of Eze's Ford pickup. Joshua was still. He stared past Eze's trunk and Aunt Rita's small red Toyota and noticed that there was another car in the hard-packed dirt driveway, a four-door, gray-blue Caprice. Eze was leaning against the hood. Joshua heard Dunny's dog, chained to a post in the woods at the side of the house, growl and bark once, high and sharp.

"What do y'all think?" Eze placed one hand on the body and patted it twice, softly. "Your mama Cille sent me the money for it, told me to find something for y'all so that y'all could have something to drive once y'all got out of school. Bookie from over in St. Cats was selling the body for five hundred: I got a motor for six hundred, and then parts came to a little less than four. Used up all the money she sent. She said she'd been saving up for a little bit and she wanted y'all to have something dependable. I got it running pretty good, and it should get y'all to work and back." He smiled, a glimpse of his teeth in the dark, then walked towards them and held out a key ring with four bright metal keys on it before them. "It's a good car."

Joshua stared at the ring that gleamed from the faint reach of the porch light. Christophe was the first to react: he plucked the key ring from Eze's hand. Neither twin spoke until Eze cleared his throat, nodded to them almost awkwardly, and then walked away and around the trailer.

"Well," Christophe said low, out of the side of his mouth, "I guess we know why she didn't come." He tossed the keys in the air; they glittered in the dim light and fell with a dull metal crush into Christophe's palm.

"Why show up when you give us a car? Guess she's really done, now."

"Yeah, I guess she is."

Joshua blinked, felt his eyelids slide heavily down, then open. He let the feeling of her absence sink to his throat, skirt his collarbone to settle in his chest, to throb stronger than it had when he had seen her dedication to them in the program. He looked away from the car. He was glad that Christophe had grabbed the keys; he would let his brother do all the driving. He knew that if he reached out to touch the metal of the hood, it would be warm as the night, insect-ridden air, warm as skin, but not so soft. Joshua spoke in a voice lower than his brother's.

Christophe slid the key ring into his pocket. He moved to nudge Joshua with his other hand, but then seemed to remember the sausage on the fork.

"Shit." He plucked the sausage away from the metal and then wound his arm back and threw it in the direction of the dog in the woods. It flew through the air, a dark blur, and hit the leaves of the trees with a falling rustle. The dog barked again, sharply, once. Christophe sucked the sauce from his thumb and forefinger and bumped his brother with his shoulder. He was still hungry, and while there was nothing but them and the silence and this car here, there was more potato salad and hot, spicy meat in the front, and Ma-mee was waiting for them. So, Cille hadn't shown up, and she'd gotten them this car instead. It felt like a bribe. From the front, Christophe heard Dunny shout at one of the little kids, and an answering giggle. Christophe gnawed at a piece of jagged skin on his thumb, and thought of Ma-mee, smiling and expectant in her pressed dress waiting for them out front. This would make it easier for them. He would be grateful. "Well, we did need a car. Come on."

Christophe turned, and Joshua followed him into the dark brush at the side of the trailer. Joshua was an inverse shadow: full where Christophe was thin. Christophe seemed more of the darkness. The dog was quiet, and Christophe hoped he had been able to find and reach the food. Under the night sounds, Christophe heard the links of its chain clink.

Arrivederci, Aldo

Kim Sykes

I love my job. How many people can say that?

I could be working security in a department store over in Manhattan, where they make you follow old ladies with large purses and mothers with baby strollers. Or in an office tower doing Homeland Security detail, looking at photo IDs all day and pretending I care whether you belong in a building full of uninteresting lawyers and accountants, most of whom come to work hoping I'd find a reason to stop them from going in. Or guarding a bank where you're so bored that you consider robbing it yourself or kicking one of those lousy machines that charge two dollars to do what a bank is supposed to do for free.

My friends tell me I got it pretty good because I work security at Silvercup Studios where they shoot television shows, movies, and commercials. Not to mention the fact that it's not far from my walkup in Long Island City. My neighbors treat me like I'm a celebrity. Which is pretty funny since my mother worked at Silvercup in the '50s baking bread and nobody ever treated her like she was somebody, except me and my father.

Yeah, okay, I see lots of good-looking men and pretty girls, famous singers and movie stars. No big deal. They're just like you and me. Especially without the makeup and the fancy clothes. They all come in with uncombed hair, comfortable shoes, and sunglasses. Some of them got egos to match the size of the cars they drive up in. They arrive with their assistants and their entourages carrying everything from little dogs to adopted babies. Some of them pride themselves as just folks and come in on the subway. The one thing they all got in common is that I make them sign in. It's my job. They might be celebrities, but I treat them all the same.

There *are* exceptions, like the directors and the producers. They don't bother to sign in. Every day they walk past my security desk and one of their "people" will whisper to me who they are. You'd think they were royalty or something. I check their names off a special list the office gives me. The boss says that they pay the bills and we should make them happy no matter what. I guess when you're in charge of making multimillion-dollar movies, it's the little things that matter, like not having to write down your own name.

Then there's everybody in between, the ones who are not movie stars—the supporting and background actors, backup singers, and the hoochie girls in the music videos. When they come in, all eager and excited, they usually put their names in the wrong places and walk through the wrong doors. Especially the first-timers. They don't pay much attention to anything except the hopes and dreams in their heads.

Last, but not least, there's the crew. Most of these guys I know by sight. They come in when it's still dark outside and that's usually when they leave too. They walk past me half asleep. It's hard work getting up before dawn every day, unloading, setting up and breaking down and loading up again—not to mention looking after all those people. So sometimes I try to make their days a little easier. If I've never seen them before, they sign in. If I know them, I let them go through, but you didn't hear that from me. You see, we got thirteen studios and they're in a constant state of shooting something. So sometimes I have to bend the rules.

The phone at my security desk rings and I almost fall backwards in my chair. It's probably the boss's office telling me about an unexpected delivery or adding a name to the list. You see, they got it under control up there. The next day's schedule and sign-in sheets are usually done at midnight and placed on my desk for the following morning. We run a tight ship around here, so when the phone rings it's pretty important. I answer it on the second ring.

"Yes, sir?" I straighten up in my seat. It's the boss himself.

"Listen, Josephine, we got an intruder walking around the premises."

I can hardly believe my ears. The news makes me stand up and grab hold of my nightstick, my only weapon.

"I'm sorry, sir," comes tumbling out of my mouth. I feel as if I've let him down. Being the only woman in security here at Silvercup, I know I have to work harder than everybody else.

"He's walking in on sets, Jo. He's ruined a shot in Studio Seven, for Christ's sake. See who the hell this guy is, will you? Probably some damn background actor looking to be discovered."

It happens occasionally that extra players, bored with waiting around, go exploring the place in hopes of finding the next job. Sooner or later a production assistant spots them and sends the poor thing back to where he or she belongs. The fact is, Silvercup is the last place you'll be discovered. By the time actors get here, they're just numbers in a producer's budget. If you're not in the budget, you're not in the shot. Of course, there are exceptions to every rule, but I can count them on one hand.

"Anybody say what he looks like?" I ask my boss.

"White, around thirty. Wearing clogs."

"*Clogs?*"

"That's what they tell me. Just take care of it, Jo."

"Yes, sir."

※

There are thirteen studios here at Silvercup, and at least two sign-in sheets for each one. We're talking hundreds of people. It's barely ten o'clock and the place is packed. This is not going to be easy. On one of the sheets, a couple of wise-asses signed in as Mick Jagger and Flavor Flav. They came in early. I can tell by the names before and after them. That means these comedians are with the crew. I take a moment to remember who came by my desk just before dawn. There was nobody I didn't know. And I would have remembered a guy wearing clogs.

The new guard, Kenneth, is checking out the *Daily News* and eating his second meal of the morning. His plate is piled high. He is reading his horoscope and is oblivious to my panic. I watch him dunk a powdered donut into milky coffee and drip the muddy mess on his blue vest. I hand him a paper napkin and look past him at the tiny security screens mounted on the wall. Like I said, there are thirteen studios here, with at least three times that many bathrooms, not to mention dressing rooms, storage rooms, production offices. These little screens are useless to me. You'd think we'd have better video equipment here, but we don't.

Still, nobody-but-nobody gets past me. I pride myself on that. I'm famous, if you will, for keeping the place tight and secure. Okay, I'm not going to make it seem like I'm guarding the U.S. Mint, but we get a lot of people trying to come in here, like rag reporters or crazed fans or desperate actors. They don't have weapons but they have things that are far more lethal to us like pens, cameras, and unrealistic expectations. It's my job to protect Silvercup and everybody inside from all that. My job and reputation are at stake, and I'm not going to let some clog-wearing twerp or donut-eating knuckle-head ruin it.

Just my luck, my other two colleagues are at lunch. That leaves me and the munching machine, who since he got here has been visiting the different sets and mooching free meals. I watch him fold the *News* and start the *Post*. He reminds me of myself when I started on the job years ago. After the rush of the morning, it slows down to a crawl. Keeping yourself awake is a chore. Thanks to plenty of coffee, newspapers and magazines, and hopefully some good conversation, you can remain alert most of your shift.

Then there's the food. Each production has it's own catered breakfast, lunch, and if they're here long enough, dinner. My first six months I gained twenty pounds and it's been with me ever since. One day it's fresh lobsters from a restaurant chain shooting commercials, then it's a week of birthday cakes from a television show. Here, at any given time, someone somewhere is eating something. Makes you wonder where the term "starving actor" came from.

I'm not too confident in this boy's abilities, especially after I see him bite into his breakfast burrito and squirt half of it on his lap. But he's the only guy I got on the desk right now, since the other two have gone off on a break. So I tell him to keep an eye out for a white guy wearing clogs and to call me on the walkie if he sees anything suspicious. He doesn't bother to ask me what's going on or about the clogs even, and I don't bother to fill him in. I give him two weeks, if that.

I take today's schedule with me. I have to be careful not to excite or disturb the productions going on. Today we've got four commercials, two cop shows, three sitcoms, one movie, and two music videos shooting, not to mention the Home Shopping Network, which has it's permanent home here. That means hundreds of actors and crew roaming the place. I decide to go up and work my way down. I don't bother with the top floor where the boss's office is. I figure a guy in clogs is not interested in that. A guy in clogs wants attention. He wants to be discovered. And that means I got to go where the directors and the actors are. I take the freight elevator to the second floor.

When the doors open, I see a herd of suits, some eating bagels, others reading or having intense conversations. It's like I just walked in on a business conference at some firm on Wall Street, only the men are wearing makeup and the women have rollers in their hair. I move past them to Frank, a production assistant I know pretty well. He's worked here at Silvercup almost as long as I have.

"Yo, Frank, all your people accounted for?" I ask him.

Frank silently counts the actors.

"Yeah. Why?"

"We got somebody walking around the place. He screwed up a shot in seven."

"Moron."

"Yeah. You see anyone who doesn't belong, call me."

"You got it, Jo.

"Oh, and he's wearing clogs."

Frank raises an eyebrow.

"Don't ask," I tell him.

I walk to the other side of the building. Past storage rooms that have complicated lock systems installed. You have to have a combination or a special key. On some of them you need both. I try the doors anyway. Better to be sure.

My schedule says they're setting up a music video in the next studio. Whether they want to or not, they usually start shooting later in the day. Pop and rap singers don't like to get up in the morning. They can afford not to. The crew was there, however, installing stripper poles for a rap video.

"What's shaking, Jo?" says Dimples, a pot-bellied Irishman carrying heavy cables. I cross the studio floor toward him.

"You won't believe it," I say as I approach. "I've got some guy walking around the place messing up shots."

His cheeks flushed, betraying his nickname. "Was he wearing clogs?"

I nearly choke on the chocolate-covered peanuts I just snatched from the Kraft table. "Yeah, you seen him?"

"About ten minutes ago. He walked in here asking for Tony Soprano. I thought he was joking." Dimples takes off one of his thick gloves and scratches his bulbous nose. "He had an accent. Italian, or maybe Spanish. It's hard to tell. Tiny guy, though. No bigger than my leg. Kept stuffing bagels into his pants, like he was saving them for later. He creeped me, so I chased him out of here."

"Which way did he go?" I ask, licking chocolate from my fingers.

"I followed him out to the hall and watched him take the stairs down. That's the last I saw of him."

"Thanks."

I run toward the exit and take the steps two at a time. I figure if I move quickly enough, I can catch up with him. Besides, how fast can a guy in clogs go? But when I get to the bottom landing, I have to sit down. They say, if you don't use it you lose it. And after all these years, I have definitely lost it. When I was younger, if somebody had said to me I would be tired after running down a flight of stairs, I would have kicked his ass. Now the very thought of lifting my foot to carry out my threat exhausts me. Not counting vacations and holidays, I have mostly spent my time sitting behind the security desk watching others come and go. The last time I chased anyone was awhile back when a mother-daughter team tried to get an autographed picture of Sarah Jessica Parker. They would have succeeded if they hadn't been as out of shape as I was.

I look down at my ankles. They're swollen. It makes me think of my mother, who would come home from work, worn out, same swollen feet as mine, in the days when this place supplied bread for schools in Queens and the Bronx and parts of Manhattan. Now, instead of filling their stomachs with dough, we fill their heads with it.

The mayor keeps telling us that New York City has grown safer now that violent crimes are at the lowest rates they've been in a decade. That's true everywhere except on television and in the movies. It's as if Hollywood didn't get the memo. Production companies spit out cop show after cop show, movies full of mobsters and gangbangers who kill and rape, rob and shoot one another—in the name of entertainment. It's not Silvercup's fault. We don't write the scripts. We just provide the space to film them in.

I push myself up from the steps and enter the first floor. First thing, down the hall, I see two guys about to come to blows. Any moment the fists are going to fly. I stand quietly off to the side and watch. I know that when the time comes for one of them to throw the first punch, they'll calm down and probably laugh or pat each other on the back. This time they do both.

"Hey, Jo, what's up?" Edward, the one with the perfect teeth, calls me over. I shake his manicured hand. He plays a serial killer on one of the cop shows. He's on for the whole season. Nice guy, great family man, good kids.

"Same ole, same ole," I answer. "You seen a guy running around here in clogs?"

The actors laugh, thinking I am about to tell a joke.

"I'm not kidding." I say this with my best poker face.

Ed drops his grin. "No, just us up here running lines before our scene. Why?"

"Nothing serious. Sorry I interrupted you."

"Don't worry about it," the new guy chirps. He has a shaved head, which from a distance made him look thuggish, but now that I'm closer to him, I can see that he's a kid barely out of school. Must be his first big part. This morning when he signed in he was a little anxious around the eyes; polite though. Probably right out of college and here he is playing a street thug, the kind his mother and father sent him to university so as not to become. If this script is like all the others, his character's going to be shot or killed and sent off to prison by the afternoon. That's show business.

I stick my hands in my pockets. It's cold in here, I want to get back to my desk where I keep a space heater tucked down below. The boss has the thermostat in the low sixties, even in winter. He says it keeps everybody on their toes.

The next studio is dark except for the set, which looks like a doctor's office. They're rehearsing a scene for a pharmaceutical commercial. A very nervous actor in a doctor's coat is having trouble with his lines. When he gets to the part about the side effects, he starts to laugh. But no one else thinks it's funny. Time is money and everyone is frustrated, including the director, who makes the actor even more uncomfortable by sighing loudly and storming off between takes.

After my eyes have adjusted to the dark, I glance around the room. The crew, producers, and other actors are standing around, quietly waiting for the next take, hoping this day will come to an end so they can all go home. Everyone except what I will later describe to the press as a deranged imp—no more than five feet tall. He's standing off to the side, eating a bagel that he has just pulled out of his tights.

He has on a billowy white shirt that looks like it's from one of those Shakespearean movies—it's hanging over his wiry shoulders and flared out past his nonexistent hips. On his small feet are a pair of genuine wooden clogs.

We make eye contact and he quickly figures out why I'm here. The actor and the director head back to the set. I search around for a couple of guys who I can recruit to help me. When I turn back, the little guy is standing right next to me.

"Have you seen Tony Soprano?" he whispers in an Italian accent. His eyes are bright, even in the dark, and his breath smells of cheese.

"Quiet on the set!" The alarm bell rings, signaling that the camera's about to roll. I grab his skinny arm but he twists around and frees himself from my grip.

"Action!" The director cues the actor, who begins his lines.

"I'm a doctor, so people are surprised when I tell them that I suffer from irritable bowel syndrome."

No one is watching me or the imp as he makes his way behind several clients from the pharmaceutical industry who are engrossed in the actor's performance. Imagine spending a good part of your career having meetings and conference calls about irritable bowels. I squeeze past them and follow my quarry who is creeping closer to the set.

"If you suffer from irritable bowel syndrome, do like I did. Call your doctor. Side effects include stomachache, fever, bloody stool, and on rare occasions, death."

This time the actor does not laugh, but the imp does, as he dashes right in front of the camera.

"Cut!" What the . . . ?" The director is about to have a nervous breakdown.

I know better than to follow the imp in front of the camera. I figure there will be enough people waiting to kill him for messing up this shot. Someone switches on the overhead lights just in time to see him open the door and scurry out.

The first year *The Sopranos* shot here were my hardest as a security guard. We had the press, fans, everybody coming by asking to speak to the fictional mob boss, Tony Soprano. We even had real gangsters come around. It wasn't easy turning these kinds of fans away. We had to hire two extra security guards to handle the crush. But now the show is winding down. The actors are bored. The reporters have moved on. Things were getting back to normal until this clog-footed fruitcake came along.

I go out into the hall but there is no sign of him. I call Kenneth on the walkie but he doesn't answer. He's probably in the john, making room for another meal. Did I say he'd last two weeks? Make that one.

As I struggle to put my walkie back in its cradle, the imp exits a john and sprints into the stairwell. By this time I'm joined by the actor/doctor, the director, and several guys from the crew.

We follow him up one flight. My heart is thumping. He better hope I catch him before the director does. I can see the tabloid headline: *IMP MAIMED AT SILVERCUP*. We chase him down the narrow hall toward the Wall Street herd waiting to go on set. Because he's limber and small, the imp cuts through the crowd barely touching anybody.

"Stop him!" I yell out.

A few of the actors look at me like I'm a 300-pound woman who just walked into a gym. Let's face it. In a place where there are actors and little guys in clogs, I'm the odd one. Thankfully, a banker type catches on and grabs the imp from behind, lifting him off the ground. An actress who looks like an H&R Block agent screams. Everyone panics.

Coffee and bagels splatter and fly into the air. This is the imp's second big mistake. You don't mess up a director's shot and you don't spill coffee on an actor's wardrobe before he goes on. I start to feel sorry for the little guy, until he reaches back and grabs his captor by his private parts and gives them a yank.

"Aaaah, Christ!" groans the actor, who lets go. The imp lands on his feet and darts toward the east end of the building.

Now this is where it gets interesting. I couldn't make this up if I wanted to. It's the kind of stuff that Hollywood pays big bucks for. I got to remember to put that in the screenplay I'm writing. Did I mention that I'm writing a screenplay?

The light outside of the Home Shopping Network set is flashing red. This means only one thing: No one can enter. They're shooting. I've seen movie stars stop in their tracks when they see it. Directors, producers, even the boss. But the imp ignores it and, once again, goes in without hesitation.

I move to stop the others from following him, but then I realize I don't have to. The consequences of entering a set when the red light is flashing differs from set to set. It can be anything from a stern talking-to, to getting punched out by a Teamster, to having the cops called in to haul you away. Home Shopping has a full-time bodyguard and ex-cop named Zack, who carries a .38. Whatever happens, it's going to be the last set the imp crashes.

I wonder how long it will take for Zack to spot him. As soon as I finish the thought, the doors burst open and Zack emerges with the imp tightly pinned under his arm and a meaty hand clamped over his mouth. None of us say anything.

Ready for revenge, we all silently followed Zack down the hall to the bathroom. It's like watching David and Goliath. Man, the little guy is *strong*. His arms bulge like small cantaloupes and his legs are like iron rods. Every time Zack tries to go through the door, the imp's arms and legs stop him. This goes on for a while until the imp bites down on Zack's hand. The ex-cop screams like a eunuch and drops him to the ground.

We don't waste time. We all dive on top of him, arms and legs grabbing and pulling at other arms and legs. I swear I have him until I find myself pinned to the ground by a sweaty stockbroker. A Teamster has to be stopped from strangling the director. By the time we realize what's going on, the imp has wiggled out from under us.

"*Ciao!*" he calls over to us before entering the stairwell a couple of feet away.

I watch Zack and the others follow him up. The next floor is administrative and is rigged with an alarm. His only option is the rooftop, and from there he'll be trapped. So I save myself the climb and take the freight elevator to the roof.

A couple of years ago, the boss had a series of solar panels and plants installed to help generate electricity for the building. I thought it was a crock myself, but apparently it works. At least it's gotten the boss off our backs about portable heaters and keeping the doors open for too long, and in August I can take home all the tomatoes I can eat.

On three sides of the building, Silvercup Studios is encircled by two exit ramps to the Queensboro Bridge and the elevated subway tracks of the seven train. Four flights down is the street. Unless the imp can do like Spiderman and climb brick, he's mine.

Row after row of raised square planting beds lie next to solar panels angled to the east. Large generators, the size of trucks, stand off to the west side harvesting the energy. Above me is the towering *S* of the famous *SILVERCUP* sign that lights up the entrance to Queens from the bridge at night. The sign stretches from one end of the building to the other, above the elevated tracks of the subway.

I walk to the west to get a better view of the roof and spot the imp standing under the *P*, waving at me like I'm his long-lost sister.

I don't like coming up here when it's not warm, especially on days like today when there's nothing but gray clouds and a damp wind that cuts through my thin uniform right to my bones. I can't wait to get my frozen hands on this little creep. But before I start after him, Zack and the others come bursting out of the rooftop door like the Canadian Mounties, only without the horses.

We spread out and begin walking slowly toward him, just like in the movies, but the closer we get, the further he backs away, until finally he reaches the far edge of the building. Listen, I don't want the imp to jump. His death is the last thing I need on my conscience, so I motion for everyone else to hold back while I try and talk to him, even though the traffic from the bridge and the trucks unloading below make that impossible.

I wish I could tell you that I get him to move from the edge or that he drops that stupid grin and runs sobbing into my arms, but things like that only happen on television. Real life is much more complicated. Instead, he rubs his hands along his thighs and then, with an operatic flourish, he calls out to us, "*Arrivederci!*" Then he turns around and jumps.

I must've looked like the wide-mouth bass in the window of the fish store on Queens Plaza South. At least that's what I felt like: a cold dead fish. I ran with the others to the edge, expecting to see Italian sauce splattered all over the pavement below. Just one story down, however, there's the imp, rubbing his hands on his thighs again and grabbing hold of a rope hanging from the 25A exit ramp of the Queensboro Bridge.

I forgot that this end of the building has an extension to it: a freight garage that's only three stories high, connected to the main Silvercup building. It looks like he got into the building by lowering himself from the exit ramp to the garage and then climbed up the emergency fire ladder to the main building. When I tell the boss about this, he's going to lose it.

I decide not to follow him, especially since he's scurrying up that rope faster than an Olympic gymnast. Besides, now that this jerk's off the premises, he's no longer my problem. If this were a television show, it would be a good time to cut to commercial. I could use a donut and a hot cup of coffee, only my curiosity is getting the better of me.

We all stand there and watch as he scurries up the rope jammed between the crack of the concrete barrier and onto the exit ramp to 25A. He loses one of his clogs but it doesn't faze him. Like a tight-rope walker, he steps along the ledge, against traffic, to exit 25, which runs parallel to

25A, but then veers off and under the elevated subway tracks of the seven train. Once he's on exit 25, he crosses the lane and hops up on the ledge again and reaches for another rope. This one is tied to the iron gridwork that holds up the track, and instead of going up, he goes down. We lose sight of him behind the Silvercup parking lot, so we all rush to the west end of the roof just in time to see him running, with one clog, up Queens Plaza South toward the subway entrance a block away.

The End.

Or so I think.

A week later, I'm sitting with Kenneth at the desk (yes, he's still here and he's five pounds heavier) and we're reading the *News*. A headline screams, *ALIEN ACTOR NABBED BY HOMELAND SECURITY,* and there's a picture of the imp, smiling for his close-up.

His name is Aldo Phillippe and he's a street performer from Naples who overstayed his visa. He came to the United States to do three things: meet Tony Soprano, get discovered for the movies, find a wife.

According to the paper, Aldo decided that a good way to get publicity was to climb to the top of the Statue of Liberty, crawl through the window of her crown, and sit on her head. You probably think they caught him because they have better security over at the Liberty, but it wasn't that. According to the article, they had to close the visitors' center and chase him around for over an hour. The only way they caught him was by cornering him at the tip of the island, and evidently Aldo can't swim. If he's lucky, they won't send him to Guantánamo Bay.

I keep Aldo's clog on my desk filled with pens for people to use when they sign in. No one notices it except when the director and actors who were with me that day come back to work. Everybody else is too busy making entertainment.

Young
Adult
Literature

———————————— ✳ ————————————

Chains

Laurie Halse Anderson

Chapter I

Monday, May 27, 1776

> *Youth is the seed time of good habits, as well in nations as in individuals.*
>
> —THOMAS PAINE, *COMMON SENSE*

The best time to talk to ghosts is just before the sun comes up. That's when they can hear us true, Momma said. That's when ghosts can answer us.

The eastern sky was peach colored, but a handful of lazy stars still blinked in the west. It was almost time.

"May I run ahead, sir?" I asked.

Pastor Weeks sat at the front of his squeaky wagon with Old Ben next to him, the mules' reins loose in his hands. The pine coffin that held Miss Mary Finch—wearing her best dress, with her hair washed clean and combed—bounced in the back when the wagon wheels hit a rut. My sister, Ruth, sat next to the coffin. Ruth was too big to carry, plus the pastor knew about her peculiar manner of being, so it was the wagon for her and the road for me.

Old Ben looked to the east and gave me a little nod. He knew a few things about ghosts, too.

Pastor Weeks turned around to talk to Mr. Robert Finch, who rode his horse a few lengths behind the wagon.

"The child wants to run ahead," Pastor explained to him. "She has kin buried there. Do you give leave for a quick visit?"

Mr. Robert's mouth tightened like a rope pulled taut. He had showed up a few weeks earlier to visit Miss Mary Finch, his aunt and only living relation. He looked around her tidy farm, listened to her ragged, wet cough, and moved in. Miss Mary wasn't even cold on her deathbed when he helped himself to the coins in her strongbox. He hurried along her burying, too, most improper. He didn't care that the neighbors would want to come around with cakes and platters of cold meat, and drink ale to the rememory of Miss Mary Finch of Tew, Rhode Island. He had to get on with things, he said.

I stole a look backward. Mr. Robert Finch was filled up with trouble from his dirty boots to the brim of his scraggly hat.

"Please, sir," I said.

"Go then," he said. "But don't tarry. I've much business today."

I ran as fast as I could.

✳

I hurried past the stone fence that surrounded the white graveyard, to the split-rail fence that marked our ground, and stopped outside the gate to pick a handful of chilly violets, wet with dew. The morning mist twisted and hung low over the field. No ghosts yet, just ash trees and maples lined up in a mournful row.

I entered.

Momma was buried in the back, her feet to the east, her head to the west. Someday I would pay the stone carver for a proper marker with her name on it: *Dinah, wife of Cuffe, mother of Isabel and Ruth*. For now, there was a wooden cross and a gray rock the size of a dinner plate lying flat on the ground in front of it.

We had buried her the year before, when the first roses bloomed.

"Smallpox is tricky," Miss Mary Finch said to me when Momma died. "There's no telling who it'll take." The pox had left Ruth and me with scars like tiny stars scattered on our skin. It took Momma home to Our Maker.

I looked back at the road. Old Ben had slowed the mules to give me time. I knelt down and set the violets on the grave. "It's here, Momma," I whispered. "The day you promised. But I need your help. Can you please cross back over for just a little bit?"

I stared without blinking at the mist, looking for the curve of her back or the silhouette of her head wrapped in a pretty kerchief. A small flock of robins swooped out of the maple trees.

"I don't have much time," I told the grass-covered grave. "Where do you want us to go? What should we do?"

The mist swirled between the tall grass and the low-hanging branches. Two black butterflies danced through a cloud of bugs and disappeared. Chickadees and barn swallows called overhead.

"Whoa." Old Ben stopped the wagon next to the open hole near the iron fence, then climbed down and walked to where Nehemiah the gravedigger was waiting. The two men reached for the coffin.

"Please, Momma," I whispered urgently. "I need your help." I squinted into the ash grove, where the mist was heaviest.

No ghosts. Nothing.

I'd been making like this for near a year. No matter what I said, or where the sun and the moon and the stars hung, Momma never answered. Maybe she was angry because I'd buried her wrong. I'd heard stories of old country burials with singers and dancers, but I wasn't sure what to do, so we just dug a hole and said a passel of prayers. Maybe Momma's ghost was lost and wandering because I didn't send her home the right way.

The men set Miss Mary's coffin on the ground. Mr. Robert got off his horse and said something I couldn't hear. Ruth stayed in the wagon, her bare feet curled up under her skirt and her thumb in her mouth.

I reached in the pocket under my apron and took out the oatcake. It was in two pieces, with honey smeared between them. The smell made my stomach rumble, but I didn't dare nibble. I picked up the flat rock in front of the cross and set the offering in the hollow under it. Then I put the rock back and sat still, my eyes closed tight to keep the tears inside my head where they belonged.

I could smell the honey that had dripped on my hands, the damp ground under me, and the salt of the ocean. I could hear cows mooing in a far pasture and bees buzzing in a nearby clover patch.

If she would just say my name, just once . . .

"Girl!" Mr. Robert shouted. "You there, girl!"

I sniffed, opened my eyes, and wiped my face on my sleeve. The sun had popped up in the east like a cork and was burning through the morning mist. The ghosts had all gone to ground. I wouldn't see her today, either.

He grabbed my arm and pulled me roughly to my feet. "I told you to move," Mr. Robert snarled at me.

"Apologies, sir," I said, wincing with pain.

He released me with a shove and pointed to the cemetery where they buried white people. "Go pray for her that owned you, girl."

Chapter II

Monday, May 27, 1776

> *I, young in life, by seeming cruel fate*
> *Was snatch'd from Afric's fancyied happy seat: . . .*
> *. . . That from a father seiz'd his babe belov'd:*
> *Such, such my case. And can I then but pray*
> *Others may never feel tyrannic sway?*
> —PHILLIS WHEATLEY, "TO THE RIGHT HONOURABLE
> WILLIAM, EARL OF DARTMOUTH"

"Amen," we said together.

Pastor Weeks closed his Bible, and the funeral was over.

Nehemiah drove his shovel into the mound of dirt and pitched some into the open grave. The earth rattled and bounced on the coffin lid. Old Ben put on his hat and walked toward the mule team. Mr. Robert reached for coins to pay the pastor. Ruth drew a line in the dust with her toe.

My belly flipped with worry. I was breathing hard as if I'd run all the way to the village and back. This was the moment we'd been waiting for, the one that Momma promised would come. It was up to me to take care of things, to find a place for us. I had to be bold.

I stood up proper, the way I had been taught—chin up, eyes down—took Ruth by the hand, and walked over to the men.

"Pardon me, Pastor Weeks, sir," I said. "May I ask you something?"

He set his hat on his head. "Certainly, Isabel."

I held Ruth's hand tighter. "Where do you think we should go?"

"What do you mean, child?"

"I know I'll find work, but I can't figure where to sleep, me and Ruth. I thought you might know a place."

Pastor Weeks frowned. "I don't understand what you're saying, Isabel. You're to return with Mr. Robert here. You and your sister belong to him now."

I spoke slowly, saying the words I had practiced in my head since Miss Mary Finch took her last breath, the words that would change everything. "Ruth and me are free, Pastor. Miss Finch freed us in her will. Momma, too, if she had lived. It was done up legal, on paper with wax seals."

Mr. Robert snorted. "That's enough out of you, girl. Time for us to be on the road to Newport."

"Was there a will?" Pastor Weeks asked him.

"She didn't need one," Mr. Robert replied. "I was Aunt Mary's only relative."

I planted my feet firmly in the dirt and fought to keep my voice polite and proper. "I saw the will, sir. After the lawyer wrote it, Miss Mary had me read it out loud on account of her eyes being bad."

"Slaves don't read," Mr. Robert said. "I should beat you for lying, girl."

Pastor Weeks held up his hand. "It's true. Your aunt had some odd notions. She taught the child herself. I disapproved, of course. Only leads to trouble."

I spoke up again. "We're to be freed, sir. The lawyer, Mr. Cornell, he'll tell you. Ruth and me, we're going to get work and a place of our own to sleep."

"That's enough." Mr. Robert narrowed his eyes at me.

"But Mr. Cornell—" I started.

"Shut your mouth!" he snapped.

The pastor cleared his throat. "Perhaps we should inquire . . ."

"Where is this Cornell?" Mr. Robert demanded. "Newport?"

"He left for Boston before the blockade," the pastor said. "Took his papers with him."

"The girl is lying, then," Mr. Robert said. "She knows the lawyer is absent and her cause cannot be proved. The sooner I'm rid of her, the better."

"It's the truth," I blurted out. Ruth looked up at me anxiously and gripped my hand tighter.

"I said, silence!" Mr. Robert yelled.

"Isabel, remember your place." Pastor Weeks fumbled with the latch on his Bible. "You and your sister belong to Mr. Robert now. He'll be a good master to you."

My insides went cold, like I'd swallowed water straight from a deep, dark well. This couldn't be happening. "Couldn't you send a message to Boston, seeking Mr. Cornell?"

"The matter is settled." Mr. Robert pulled on his gloves. "If I might borrow your wagon and man for the drive to Newport, Pastor, I'd be grateful. These girls should bring a decent price at auction."

"You're selling us?" The words flew out of my mouth before I could weigh them.

"Hush, Isabel," Pastor Weeks cautioned.

The cold inside me snaked down to my feet and up around my neck. I shivered in the warm spring sunshine. Ruth bent down and picked up a shiny pebble. What if we were split up? Who would take care of her?

I fought back the tears. "Pastor Weeks, please, sir."

Mr. Robert knocked the dust from his hat. "They should go quick. Your wagon will be back by nightfall."

The minister placed the Bible in his leather satchel and pulled it up over his shoulder. He studied the ground, his hands, Mr. Robert's horse, and the clouds. He did not look at me. "You'll be wanting to bring their shoes and blankets," he finally said. "They'll fetch a better price that way."

"True enough."

"I'll have a word with Ben. Explain matters."

Pastor Weeks walked toward his own slave, keeping a hand on the satchel so it didn't bump against his side.

My heart wanted to force my feet to run, but I couldn't feel them, couldn't feel my hands, nor my arms, nor any part of myself. I had froze solid, sticking to the dirt. We were sold once before, back when Ruth was a tiny baby, not even baptized yet. They sold all of us from the plantation when old Mister Malbone run up his debts too high. His bankers wanted their pounds of flesh. Our flesh.

One by one they dragged us forward, and a man shouted out prices to the crowd of likely buyers and baby Ruth cried, and Momma shook like the last leaf on a tree, and Poppa . . . and Poppa, he didn't want them to bust up our family like we were sheep or hogs. "I am a man," he shouted, and he was Momma's husband and our father, and baby Ruth, she cried and cried, and I thought Momma would shatter like a bowl when it falls off a table. Poppa fought like a lion when they came for him, the strongest lion, roaring; it took five of them with hickory clubs, and then Momma fainted, and I caught baby Ruth just in time and there was lion's blood on the ground mixed with the dust like the very earth was bleeding, and we left there, we three in Miss Mary Finch's wagon, and everything in the whole world was froze in ice for near two years after that.

I opened my mouth to roar, but not a sound escaped. I could not even mewl like a kitten.

Chapter III

Monday, May 27, 1776

> *RUN-AWAY from the Subscriber, living at No. 110, Water-street, near the new Slip. A Negro girl named POLL, about 13 years of age, very black, marked with the Small-Pox, and had on when she went away a red cloth petticoat, and a light blue short gown, home made. Whoever will take up and secure the said Girl so that the owner may get her, shall be handsomely rewarded.*

—Newspaper advertisement
in the *Royal Gazette* (New York)

The snake took us to Miss Mary's house to collect our blankets and too-small shoes but nothing else. We couldn't take Momma's shells, nor Ruth's baby doll made of flannel bits and calico, nor the wooden bowl Poppa made for me. Nothing belonged to us.

As I folded the blankets, Mr. Robert went out to the privy. There was no point in grabbing Ruth and running. He had a horse and a gun, and we were known to all. I looked around our small room, searching for a tiny piece of home I could hide in my pocket.

What to take?

Seeds.

On the hearth stood the jar of flower seeds that Momma had collected, seeds she never had a chance to put into the ground. I didn't know what they'd grow into. I didn't know if they'd grow at all. It was fanciful notion, but I uncorked the jar, snatched a handful, and buried it deep in my pocket just as the privy door creaked open.

As the wagon drove us away, Ruth turned to see the little house disappear. I pulled her into my lap and stared straight ahead, afraid that if I looked back, I might break.

✳

By midday we were in Newport, following Mr. Robert up the steps of Sullivan's Tavern. I had never been inside a tavern before. It was a large room, twice as big as Miss Mary's house, with two wide fireplaces, one on each of the far walls. The room was crowded with tables and chairs and as many people as church on Easter Sunday, except church was never cloudy with tobacco smoke nor the smell of roast beef.

Most of the customers were men, and a few had their wives with them. Some seemed like regular country folk, but others wore rich clothes not useful for muck shoveling. They made haste tucking into their dinners, playing cards, paging newspapers, and arguing loud about the British soldiers and their navy and taxes and a war.

Ruth didn't like the noise and covered her ears with her hands. I pulled her toward me and patted her on the back. Ruth was simpleminded and prone to fits, which spooked ignorant folk. Noise could bring them on, as well as a state of nervous excitement. She was in the middle of both.

As I patted, her eyes grew wide at the sight of a thick slice of buttered bread perched near the edge of a table. We hadn't eaten all day, and there had been little food the day before, what with Miss Mary dying. I snatched her hand away as she reached for it.

"Soon," I whispered.

Mr. Robert pointed to a spot in the corner. "Stand there," he ordered.

A woman burst through the kitchen door carrying a tray heavy with food. She was a big woman, twice the size of my mother, with milky skin and freckles. She looked familiar and caused me to search my remembery.

"We'll have Jenny fatten up the British navy and make their ships sink to the bottom of the sea!" yelled a red-faced man.

The big woman, Jenny, laughed as she set a bowl in front of the man. The proprietor called her over to join us. She frowned as she approached, giving Ruth and me a quick once-over while tucking a stray curl under her cap.

"These are the girls," Mr. Robert explained.

"It don't matter," the proprietor said as he put his hand on Jenny's back. "We don't hold with slaves being auctioned on our front steps. Won't stand for it, in fact."

"I thought this was a business establishment," Mr. Robert said. "Are you opposed to earning your percentage?"

"You want to listen to my Bill, mister," Jenny said. "Advertise in the paper, that's what we do around here."

"I don't have time for that. These are fine girls, they'll go quickly.

Give me half an hour's time on your front steps, and we both walk away with heavier pockets."

Jenny's husband pulled out a rag and wiped his hands on it. "Auctions of people ain't seemly. Why don't you just talk quiet-like to folks? Or leave a notice tacked up, that's proper."

"I recall an auction not twenty yards from here," Mr. Robert said. "One of Brown's ships brought up a load of rum and slaves from the islands. They must have sold thirty-five, forty people in two hours' time."

"Rhode Island don't import slaves, not for two years now," Jenny said.

"All the more reason why folks want to buy what I have to sell. I want this done quickly. I have other business to tend to."

"Is that our problem, Bill?" Jenny asked her husband. "He says that like it's our problem."

"Ease off, Jenny," Bill said. "The girls look hungry. Why don't you take them to the kitchen?"

Jenny looked like she had plenty more to say to Mr. Robert, but she gave Ruth and me a quick glance and said, "Follow me."

Mr. Robert grabbed my shoulder. "They've already eaten."

"No charge," Jenny said evenly. "I like feeding children."

"Oh." Mr. Robert released me. "Well then, that's different."

Jenny closed the kitchen door behind her and motioned for Ruth and me to sit at the table in the middle of the room. A cauldron of stew hung above the fire in the hearth, and two fresh pies were cooling by the window.

"Eat first," she said. "Then talk."

She cut us slices of brown bread and ham and poured us both big mugs of cider. Ruth gulped hers down quick and held out her mug for more. Jenny smiled and refilled it. I made short work of the food, keeping one eye on the door in case Mr. Robert walked in. The back door to the kitchen was wide open to let in the breeze. Should I grab Ruth's hand and try to escape?

Jenny read my mind. "No sense in running." She shook her head from side to side. "He'd find you right away."

I scowled at my bread and took another bite.

"I'd help you if I could," she said. "It'd be the least I could do for Dinah."

I wasn't sure I had heard her right. "Pardon me, ma'am?"

"You're Dinah's girl. Knew you when you walked in the door."

"You knew my mother?"

Jenny stirred the cauldron of stew. "Your mother and your father both. I held you when you were just a day old. I heard she passed away last year. My condolences."

She cut two pieces from the apple pie and gave them to Ruth and me. "I was indentured when I was your age. Old Mister Malbone had five of us from Ireland, along with near thirty slaves. Worked us all just as hard, but after seven years, I could walk away, thank the Lord. Dinah was real friendly to me when I first got there, helped me get used to a new place, and people ordering me around."

"I thought I knew you," I said.

She smiled warmly and snatched a piece of apple from the pie plate. "You always were the best rememberer I ever saw. We used to make a game of it. Tell you a line to memorize, or a song. Didn't matter how much time passed, you'd have the whole thing in your mouth. Made your parents proud."

A serving girl came through the door and the talk stopped. Once Jenny had loaded up her tray and sent her back out, she sat down next to me. "How did you come to be with that man?" she asked. "I thought you were at Miss Finch's place."

I quickly explained the dizzy events of the last two days.

"There's no telling what happened to the lawyer," Jenny said when I was finished. "Boston is a terrible confusion—first the King's army, and now Washington's."

"What should I do?" I asked. The words came out louder than they should have.

Jenny gently covered my mouth with her hand. "Shhh," she warned. "You got to use your head."

I grabbed her hand. "Could you take us? Please? You knew Momma . . ."

She slowly pulled her hand from mine, shaking her head. "I'm sorry, Isabel. I dare not."

"But—"

Bill opened the door and poked his head in. "He wants the girls. Best to hurry."

✳

A thin woman stood next to Mr. Robert. Her plum-colored gown was crisp and well sewn, and expensive lace trailed from the small cap on her head. She was perhaps five and forty years, with pale eyebrows and small eyes like apple seeds. A fading yellow bruise circled her right wrist like a bracelet.

She looked us over quickly. "Sisters?"

"Two for the price of one," Mr. Robert said. "Hardest-working girls you'll ever own."

"What's wrong with them?" the woman asked bluntly. "Why such a cheap price?"

Mr. Robert's snake smile widened. "My haste is your good fortune, madam. These girls were the servants of my late aunt, whose passing I mourn deeply. I must quickly conclude the matters of her estate. The recent unrest, you know."

A man joined the woman, his eyes suspicious and flinty. He wore a red silk waistcoat under a snuff-colored coat with silver buttons, a starched linen shirt, and black breeches. The buckles on his boots were as big as my fists. "And what side do you take in the current situation, sir?" he asked. "Are you for the King or do you support rebellion?"

Conversation at nearby tables stopped as people listened in.

"I pledge myself to our rightful sovereign, the King, sir," Mr. Robert said. "Washington and his rabble may have taken Boston, but that's the last thing they'll take."

The stranger gave a little bow and introduced himself. "Elihu Lockton, at your service, sir. This is my wife, Anne."

Mr. Robert bowed politely in return, ignoring the muttering at the table behind him. "May I offer you both some sup and drink that we might be better acquainted?"

They all sat, and Jenny swooped over to take their orders. Ruth and I stood with our backs against the wall as Mr. Robert and the Locktons ate and drank. I watched them close. The husband was a head taller and twice the girth of most men. His shoulders rounded forward and his neck seemed to pain him, for he often reached up to rub it. He said he was a merchant with business in Boston, New York, and Charleston, and complained about how much the Boston uprising cost him.

His missus sipped Jenny's chowder, shuddered at the taste, and reached for her mug of small beer. She stole glances at us from time to time. I could not figure what kind of mistress she would be. In truth, I was struggling to think straight. The air in the tavern had grown heavy, and the weight of the day pressed against my head.

When the men took out their pipes and lit their tobacco, Ruth sneezed, and the company all turned and considered us.

"Well, then," Lockton said, pushing back from the table to give his belly some room. "The wife is looking for a serving wench."

Missus Lockton crooked a finger at us. "Come here, girls."

I took Ruth by the hand and stepped within reach. Missus Lockton studied our hands and arms, looked at our feet, and made us take off our kerchiefs to look in our hair for nits.

"Can you cook?" she finally asked me.

"Not much, ma'am," I admitted.

"Just as well," she said. "I don't need another cook. What do you do?"

I put my arm around Ruth. "We can scrub your house clean, care for cows and pigs, work your garden, and carry just about anything."

"My aunt trained them up herself," Mr. Robert added. "And they come with blankets and shoes."

Lockton sighed. "Why not wait, Anne, and procure another indentured girl in New York?"

His wife sat back as Jenny arrived with coffee. "Indentured servants complain all the time and steal us blind at the first opportunity. I'll never hire another."

Jenny set the tray on the table so hard the cups rattled in their saucers.

Lockton reached for a plate of apple pie. "Are you sure we need two? These are uncertain times, dear."

Missus regarded Ruth. "This one looks simple. Is she addlepated?"

Ruth gave a shy smile.

I spoke before Mr. Robert could open his mouth. "She's a good simple, ma'am. Does what she's told. In truth, she's a harder worker than me. Give her a broom and tell her to sweep, and you'll be able to eat off your floor."

Jenny poured a cup of coffee and set it in front of the missus, spilling a little on the table.

"She's prettier than you," Missus said. "And she knows how to hold her tongue." She turned to her husband. "The little one might be an amusement in the parlor. The big one could help Becky with the firewood and housekeeping."

Jenny pressed her lips tight together and poured coffee for Lockton and for Mr. Robert.

Missus bent close to Ruth's face. "I do not brook foolishness," she said.

Ruth shook her head from side to side. "No foolin'," she said.

The missus cocked her head to one side and stared at me. "And you. You are to address me as Madam. I expect obedience at all times. Insolence will not be tolerated, not one bit. And you will curb your tendency to talk."

"Yes, ma'am, M-Madam," I stuttered.

"What say you, Anne?" Lockton said. "We sail with the tide."

"I want these girls, husband," Madam said. "It is Providence that put them in our path."

"How much do you want for them?" Lockton asked.

Mr. Robert named his price. Our price. Two for one, us being sold like bolts of faded cloth or chipped porridge bowls.

"Wait," Jenny announced loudly. "I'll . . . I'll take them."

The table froze. A person like Jenny did not speak to folks like the Locktons or Mr. Robert, not in that manner. Lockton stared at her as if she had grown a second head. "I beg your pardon."

Jenny set the kettle on the table, stood straight, and wiped her palms on her skirt. "I want them two girls. I need the help. We'll pay cash."

"Keep to your kitchen, woman." Madam Lockton's words came out sharp and loud.

Did she change her mind? Will she really take us?

Work in the tavern wouldn't be bad, maybe, and Jenny would be kind to Ruth. I could ask around about Lawyer Cornell's papers. When we found Miss Mary's will, I'd work extra to pay Jenny back for the money we cost her, fair and square. Ruth and me would stay together, and we'd stay here, close to Momma.

Please, God, please, God.

"Leave us," Lockton said to Jenny. "And send your husband over."

Jenny ignored him. "It'll take us a couple of days to get your money together," she said to Mr. Robert. "We'll give you free lodging in the meantime."

Mr. Robert's eyes darted between the two bidders. Ruth yawned. I crossed my fingers behind my back. *Please, God, please, God, please, God, please.*

Madam Lockton flicked crumbs to the floor with her handkerchief. "Dear husband," she said. "These girls are a bargain at double the price. With your permission, might we increase our offer twofold?"

Lockton picked at his teeth. "As long as we can conclude this business quickly."

Madam stared at Jenny. "Can you top the offer?"

Jenny wiped her hands on her apron, silent.

"Well?" Madam Lockton demanded.

Jenny shook her head. "I cannot pay more." She bobbed a little curtsy. "My husband will tally your account." She hurried for the kitchen door.

Mr. Robert chuckled and reached for his pie. "Well, then. We had a little auction here, after all."

"Such impudence is disturbing," Lockton said. "This is why we need the King's soldiers to return." He pulled out a small sack and counted out the coins to pay for us. "I thank you, sir, for the meal and the transaction. You may deliver the girls to the *Hartsborn*, if you please. Come now, Anne."

Madam Lockton stood and the men stood with her. "Good day to you, sir."

"Safe voyage, ma'am," Mr. Robert replied.

As the Locktons made their way through the crowded room, Mr. Robert dropped the heavy coins into a worn velvet bag. The thudding sound they made as they fell to the bottom reminded me of clods of dirt raining down on a fresh coffin.

Ruth put her arm around my waist and leaned against me.

Up for It: A Tale of
the Underground

Written and Annotated by L. F. Haines

4.

Holy Week, April 7, 1993, Wednesday Afternoon

What is jazz? The rhythm . . .
—TENOR SAXOPHONIST COLEMAN HAWKINS

Jazz is America musically.
—JAZZ PIANIST THELONIOUS MONK

Don't blame me. That's right. That's what I told L. F. Haines, who kept bugging me for the story, the guy, I mean girl, whatever he or she is now, who wrote the books about my Dad, Justin Arion. I kept telling him that, her that, whatever. Don't blame me if this isn't altogether accurate. It mostly is, I guess. And I tried to tell it, everything just right, just as it happened. But if it still gets messed up and nobody has it straight, it's not my fault. I tried, believe me, I tried. Putting this down straight and true and honest and still believable is not easy. And I don't even know everything myself and the crap happened to me, for Christ sakes! I mean, mostly to me and to some other people, too. Geez, how can you not totally know your own life!

It started out like this: I had this funny feeling all during the time I was taking my World History midterm that something about this whole day wasn't right, that something about time itself wasn't right. Nothing was real. Everything felt all Twilight Zone–ish and all, all wigged out on muggles, like your life is in some kind of movie and you aren't living it anymore but watching somebody living your life. Like, you ever have that feeling? You know, it's messed up. I don't mean the fact that I was, like, royally screwing up this exam. Like, it occurred to me that I didn't know anything about World History much and that I didn't care that I didn't know. It was the last exam of the day. I was tired. And, like, I'm suddenly thinking, who gives a rat's ass about any of this, anyway. I had been thinking a lot like that lately, like, who gives a rat's ass about any of this, anyway?

No, I don't mean the fact that Mr. Ellison was so concerned about my playing that he had Wilbur Johnson take over all my parts. That wasn't it either. Maybe at the time I was thinking that it was but it really wasn't, if you know what I mean. It was something I couldn't quite put my finger on. I could feel something strange. Although I must admit that what Old JAS Ellison did in dumping me for Wilbur didn't exactly make the day normal for me. But I was, in a way, kind of expecting that.

But it all stayed with me and I kept feeling the whole day that emergency feeling, like blood rushing in my nose, a shock that's like a quivering in your stomach, that made me think something else was coming down the pike before the day was over, something a lot worse. I heard earlier in the day that Mr. Mingus got real sick yesterday and had to be rushed to the hospital. He is the school custodian. Not everybody liked him, especially not my brother, Monk, but I did. That just depressed me like anything. And I was already pretty damn depressed to begin with. I mean, I was so depressed that I was seeing a doctor or therapist or whatever they call her about being depressed. You know, what they call a grief counselor or whatever. But being treated for depression only made me more depressed. I mean, being depressed wasn't what I thought I was. It was what they told me I was. But what I was feeling was something that was really not connected with that, depression and all that. Actually, everything seemed like it was reaching some kind of head or something, like a swollen pimple. I felt badly about Mr. Mingus but it wasn't what was making the day so damn strange.

Plus, I forgot to mention that I was so hungry, I was light-headed. My head fell on my desk with a thump during the middle of the exam and I could see everybody looking at me, like, oh yeah, it's that weird Kid Ryder, maybe she, like, died or something. People wouldn't say that now because I'm just a big object of sympathy and empathy and pity and all that kind of stuff. Poor old Menken Arion, they would say now. They would have said what an ass, what a total ass I was back in September or something. She just goes around acting weird and looking weird and having that weird name 'cause she wants to be so different! You know, like everybody thought I was weird even before my Dad died. So, now they think I'm weirder but people want to cut me some slack because they don't think it's nice to think someone's whose Dad just got killed is a jerk or a total loser or a complete, unmitigated ass or something, you know. But I wasn't collapsing because of my Dad.

It was because I gave up snack foods for Lent and I thought, at that moment when I was taking this test, that that was about the dumbest thing I ever did. I could have just given up one snack food, like pretzels or snickerdoodles or Pop Tarts or Mike and Ikes or something else I don't like or even some stuff I do like but not that much. But no, good old God-fearing me has to go the whole nine yards and give up snacking, show discipline and all that, sacrifice to know how our Lord sacrificed for us, for Christ sakes. I really fell for Father Benson's palaver this year. Maybe my Dad's death made me a little more susceptible to all that. What the heck is the Church good for if you can't hide out in it when you're feeling bad? Keeping a strict Lent gave me something to do or think about or something. Heck, it was good to be hungry. At least I knew I was alive. Sometimes in the last few months, I couldn't really be sure.

But that was it. You know, hunger. That's why my head fell on the desk, like I was some kind of drug addict or something. I felt like I hadn't eaten anything in nine years. At least, that seemed about how long ago lunch was. And I had a lot of lunch. Let's get this straight from the jump: I have no eating disorder. I'm just lenting too much. It's funny that the one thing my Dad's death didn't do to me was reduce my appetite. I like to eat, really.

Mrs. Petrovsky asked me if anything was wrong. I raised my head and told her I was fine and could I go back now and hallucinate in peace. "Your test inspires delusions," I said. *What the heck am I saying,* I thought. She didn't bother me anymore after that. She's not one of my favorite teachers, I can assure you. And Ms. Arion, as she calls me, is not one of her favorite students. I overheard her say to another teacher, "That Menken Arion is one smart-ass kid." And I was, like, "And I love you, too, Mrs. Petrovsky." The next time I saw her in the hall, I winked and blew her a kiss and, boy, she was, like, what's up with that. She's trying to be nice to me these days because of Dad and so she comes over to my desk and whispers if I'm not feeling up for it that I can just take the test another day. And I'm just looking at her, like, lady, go leave me alone or something and why the heck would I want to take this dumb test another day? I'm not going to know anything more next week or next month. But I'm like:

"Everything's fine, Mrs. Petrovsky. Everything's cool. The test is cool. It's a lovely test," I said, like some kind of bipolar maniac. Mrs. Petrovsky walked away. They let me get away with anything these days. I could have walked out without saying a word, turned in a blank test, and she would have let me take the test anytime I wanted. She probably would have let me take the test home and do it there. Maybe I should take more advantage of this as it sure won't last forever. But I'm like totally sick of people being understanding and all like that. I don't want to be understood, for Christ sake! How the heck can anyone understand how I'm feeling! How many people have a famous dad like me and have his brains blown out somewhere?

I mumbled a prayer to my favorite saint, Maria Goretti, but I doubt she was listening. Saint Maria was probably thinking, dumb girl. Maria, I like to eat, to be honest, and I don't much mind periods except when I get that crampy feeling sometimes that makes you feel bad and all like you need to fart but can't and your kootchy feels like somebody just hit it with a rock thrown at about ninety miles an hour. So, what am I doing to myself? Giving myself an eating disorder? Go eat, girl, Maria Goretti would say, your father would want you to eat. Don't go lenting too much!

II.

Okay, so everything really began with my Dad being killed in some sketch bar in the worst section of Westmoreland, my hometown, down in S4. That wasn't so weird my Dad being in such a place because a lot of musicians hang out in places like that, a lot of people in the low-rent district of the music business, I guess. Besides, since Shere Khan made that movie about hip-hop down there, S4 had become like some kind of almost tourist attraction. Busloads of people want to go to S4 'cause they want to see up close the crazy darkies and their rhythm-a-ning and rhyming. So, my Dad went down there, not a lot, but it wasn't a strange land to him. He knew all about the hip-hop scene there. People whispered that my Dad was having an affair but why would my Dad meet some woman in some hole down in S4? Heck, my Dad could rent suites at the Ritz and at least upgrade that ghetto floozy, if he had jungle-bunny fever, which I doubt. Shucks, he could have screwed her in the back of his limo, in his office, told her to take a cab to the better part of town, find out how the other half lives and all like that. Besides, my Dad wasn't that type of guy. Then, people said that maybe there were drugs or some kind of bad stuff my Dad was in. As much as my Dad has done for this friggin' town, giving money away left and right to a lot of whiners and beggars with some dumb charity, and people started saying stuff like because of the way he was killed. It's like pathetic, really, but people can't stand it unless they can say something bad about somebody. The police figured my Dad was there to meet somebody but couldn't figure out who. Whoever it was never showed up, I guess, unless it was the person who killed my Dad. It wasn't some musician or anybody that anybody knew about because it wasn't in Dad's appointment book or anything and he usually wrote down everything, including after-hours stuff, like meeting Gentleman Brown in some restaurant back just before he got killed, or listening to some jazz trio in some hotel ballroom doing a late set for some local losers like the Rotary Club or some bunch like that, or some gospel choir at Somebody or the other's Pentecostal church. You read my Dad's date book and you could reconstruct his life minute by minute. This was strange that my Dad didn't write this down. It was even stranger that he didn't have his driver with him. He drove himself and my Dad hated to drive.

So, there was this lull of learning to live with that bit of total unreality which I don't even want to talk about, to be honest. It hurts like anything, even now, five months later. The damn thing hurts like it happened yesterday. But it happened a couple of weeks before Thanksgiving. No one enjoys the so-called "holiday season" in the Arion household now. Easter might be better. Christmas and Thanksgiving, I can't take anymore.

Then, this past Christmastime when Prince Timmons got into trouble, the weirdness got even weirder. It was the strangest thing, the warmest

Christmas ever, maybe 85 degrees, sun shining like Florida or something, then on New Year's Eve, even then, it was so warm that we had a big thunderstorm that night. Whoever heard of a thunderstorm in December in this part of the country? It was supposed to be snowing. But it was a thunderstorm just like the middle of summer. A bunch of wild thunderstorms, really.

So, after the thunderstorms on New Year's Eve night, things started getting weirder on January 2, when I came back to school from Christmas vacation. I go to open my locker and what do you think I find in there? I mean, like, at first I don't even notice them, then, I'm kind of looking at them but it's not registering, the reality of it all just isn't, like, registering. There, in my locker, which I admit is not the neatest thing you ever saw, were three dirty brown eggs. I knew right off that they weren't hen eggs because they were bigger, like ostrich eggs. And I'm thinking, is this some kind of freshman hazing thing or is somebody trying to give me some sort of secret message or what? Was this some kind of oddball sign of sympathy for me? There are some real creep kids who go to N_____ Latin High School for the Academically Gifted, and it wouldn't surprise me somebody doing something like this like some kind of bad joke, although I must admit it seemed a bit too subtle and bizarre for most of those petty minds. It was almost creative. Then, I was thinking, maybe, they aren't even real eggs. But then I pick them up and look at 'em closely and I can tell they are real eggs. They smelled like real eggs! And like somebody washed them in soap or something! And I'm thinking what are they doing in my locker? I mean, I'm not mystified that somebody got into my locker. Half the time I forget to lock it and the lock doesn't work that well and I tell the combination to just about anyone who asks. I only leave textbooks in my locker and nobody's going to steal those. You couldn't even pay people to take 'em! Why lock the thing and make thieves think you got something in there worth stealing? I know this is a real ritzy school but there are thieves even among the tony, just stealing for kicks. I'm just mystified that the eggs are there at all, because I figured right away that they were something like heron eggs or crane eggs or something like that. And the birds being killed at the zoo was all in the newspapers. At the time I had no idea who might have put them in my locker because Prince hadn't been connected with all that nonsense. I looked suspiciously at half the kids in school.

I gave the eggs to my Mom, who, incidentally, is a veterinarian and a damn good one, if you've got to know, and after she reported it to the police, knowing them to be crane eggs and knowing that all the eggs hadn't been accounted for in the zoo incident, you know the one where a bunch of birds got killed by some gang kids, she took 'em to a hatchery where finally in, like, two weeks, two of the three produced live and healthy chick cranes. So, that was when the weirdness reached, like, say, a certain pitch and hum for me personally was getting those eggs. I figured I had enough trouble being in high school and in the advanced concert band without this. I figured I had enough trouble with my Dad's death and that not too long before that my Aunt Agnes got killed in Liberia and it was all sort of like the whole world, the whole damn cosmos or something, like, decided to gang up on anyone named Arion. It was as bad as being a Kennedy in the 1960s. It was enough to make you depressed and pretty doggone paranoid. Nuts to you, universe, was pretty much my response on days when I just didn't cry or simply go catatonic. After I found those eggs in my locker, I, like, fell into this total funk, like I became totally dysfunctional. I missed a week of school. I spent nearly all that time in bed. I couldn't face the world at all and they had to give me some meds and stuff and a lot of talking to get me together enough to get back to school. That was more or less how, like, the New Year started for me. How was yours?

Once the cat got out of the bag that Prince was suspected in the zoo animal killings, then I started thinking, well, maybe that jerk was trying to get me blamed for what happened by planting those eggs on me. Then, I thought about it, like, some more and thought even he wouldn't be that stupid. Why the heck would anybody think I would be out in the zoo trying to kill birds on New Year's Eve night? But then why did he leave the eggs in my locker? I mean, like the boy was, like, a total and complete egotistical ass, but he wasn't a fool. A boy got killed at the zoo, too, when these animals got killed there. I'll get to that, eventually. That really jacked Prince up, the dead boy, I mean. But killing the birds was bad serious stuff without that.

Of course, I never did get into any trouble for the eggs and all. I just said I found them in my locker and people like the principal and everybody accepted that. I was, after all, a poor girl who had lost her father, and verging on a nervous breakdown, so everybody was being extra cool with me. I probably could have been at the zoo and snatched the eggs and killed a bunch of animals, and people still would have been, like, cool about it. I should be taking advantage of this more and really go crazy.

But folks figured out it was Prince, like, right away, and then his troubles started. It was funny that Shere Khan was supposed to be real interested in helping Prince and all, at least, that is what my Dad said and I figured he believed it. Who in his right damn mind would want to be buddy-buddy with Shere Khan—I mean he is one of the reasons S4 is so frigging messed up—the guy has killed people, for Christ sakes—some people think he might have killed my Dad—and so I figured that proved what a numskull Prince was. I thought maybe Gentleman Brown might be able to help him out because, after all, he was, a long time ago, my Dad's friend and my Aunt Agnes really like The Gentleman, as he was called. I mean, really, really, really liked him, which I understood because she was such a cool lady, otherwise. Dumb me! What an idea that was! Gentleman Brown help-ing somebody! When I told Brown how Prince was in trouble with, you know, the egg business because everybody figured if he had the eggs he must have been to the zoo, and him getting arrested right there in school and everything like that, Gentleman Brown just laughed and said that Easter had come early for me this year and that blacks weren't Jungle Bunnies but Easter Bunnies. He was just high and crazy, with his one-eyed self. He just dismissed it! That's why I call Brown, like, a total cocaine, wacked-out, rude, untrustworthy, sneaking, jealous (of my Dad, like totally) horse's ass (not exactly to his face, naturally, sort of under my breath). I thought that was an insult to horse's asses, personally, which have never done anything to anybody. But like, what can you expect from somebody producing records for Death House, Inc. and a buddy of Shere Khan. I shouldn't, nat-urally, be calling people things like that. It's mean and I confess it every week to Father Benson. But some asses in the world really deserve to be called by their right name as, like, a kind of public service. It's what I do to make the world a better place for democracy.

III.

Good old N_____ Latin High School for the Academically Gifted, one of the five best private high schools in America, according to *US News and World Report*, had one of the best music programs this side of Juilliard, I guess. We are not only super-smart, we could play musical instruments with the best of 'em. And this band has some good players, very good, who practice very hard, even though some of them are king-sized morons, shallow kids, who want to lord it over other kids. Like "I'm so special because I play in the band" and all that and wearing the band jacket with your letter and all that show-off crap. Although I must admit that when I finished band camp the summer before ninth grade and got my band jacket I was wearing that thing everywhere, even when it was ninety degrees outside. The thing is made of wool, too. But band kids always thought they were something special because our school is like really known for its bands and orchestras. Several of our graduates went on to careers in music, big careers, famous musicians and all that, big, not like my Dad, who was bigger than anyone, except maybe the Beatles and Elvis, some people like that, but still pretty big. Maybe they're former morons now, you know. But I kind of doubt it. My Mom's a bigtime band Mom and is always out with us on trips and band camp and stuff like that. Funny, but my Dad wasn't so much into it. And he was the musician. My Mom, like, she can't play a note on a kazoo.

IV.

This particular morning, you know, Mr. Ellison decided that I had to take a back seat and not play lead percussion in the band because I wasn't executing my parts real well, as someone might say. I mean, I really pretty much stunk up the joint this morning at practice and Mr. Ellison was thinking that I'm like so screwed up in the head because of my Dad and all that my mind isn't on the music, it's never really been on the music, and so he just eased me out and by the end of practice Old Wilbur, that no-playing fool, was trying to drive a band behind a drum kit which was like asking a mouse to pull a train with its teeth, if you asked me. His technique is passable but he has no passion, no presence. You might as well have a metronome driving the band. And that jerk even reassembled the kit! Can you believe it?! Yeah, I know I did it too after Prince Timmons left, but like Wilbur doing that was borderline disgusting. I should have told him where to get off doing that. Even kinda bad, I figure I'm pretty much better than that boy. But maybe not. I played so listlessly that morning that I was, like, completely off. I would forget where I was in the music. I wasn't even tuning the drums right. It was like I had lost my frigging ear. I must admit that I hadn't been practicing much and my technique had gotten a little ragged. Half the time when I was in school, all I ever thought about was going home to bed and never coming back out. But today was the worst, the absolutely worst I've ever played. It was scary. I couldn't like hear anything. It was worse than Beethoven. I couldn't hear the music, I mean in the way a musician hears music. I needed a teacher something bad. I mean, I had one and all but I hadn't gone to a lesson in months.

Mr. Ellison had taken to calling me Menken, and I wasn't Kid Ryder anymore for him, since my Dad died and I knew that somehow or other nothing was going to go right for me anymore with him. I was not a struggling but promising musician anymore, which he could deal with, but a messed-up kid on Paxil, which he couldn't. In the beginning, I liked my job drumming for the band, too, on most days.

It was something to drive a band, more than a notion, let me tell you. And understand this, pilgrims: Drummers are damn important to a band. I don't care what you've heard otherwise. If they don't get the rhythm right, they throw the whole band off and nobody can play right. Being a little bit slow on the beat or rushing the tempo can mess up things real bad because a band is a delicate thing, like a clock or a race car or something, and you've got to have good coordination. We drummers do more than just keep time but keeping time well is very important. And we get tired of hearing people say we play too loud. If the other retards in any given band would learn something about harmony and dynamics, then we wouldn't need to play so damn loud. We're not trying to overshadow the band; we're trying to make sure the damn band can hear us and know what the damn beat is. But don't get me started. Drummers get no respect!

But with Mr. Ellison all full of the syrup for me and thinking I might be sort of psycho or something, it was hard to know which way the cat jumped at any given moment. It was hard to know that with anyone because no one got pissed at you anymore for anything. Everyone was walking around you like they were walking on eggs or something and trying to be real nice and treating you like you were sort of nuts and they didn't want to do anything to make you all-the-way nuts. It was real phony and irritated me like heck because it was, like, patronizing, like, I'm sane and you're not and I'm so sorry for your little depressed, screwed up butt. I knew Old JAS was thinking maybe if I demote her she might get herself together but he was scared too of maybe I'd go off the deep-end. Maybe weird old Menken is suicidal or something. Believe me, I didn't want to die. I wanted some other people to die, like the people who killed my Dad. I wanted a little cowboy justice. But I wasn't going to do myself in, at least, not for playing bad in a band and not before the people who killed my Dad got caught and punished.

Actually, I had been playing so bad for so long that he might have put me out of the band, except he couldn't. I mean, he put up with it for a while, missing school because I couldn't get out of bed, and not practicing and all like that. If it had been me, I would have put my little deranged hiney out of the band a long time ago. But he didn't because he would have felt bad, for one thing. My Dad played in his band when he was still touring as a professional musician and all like that and my Dad was big in the music business, so I think he was really cutting me a huge break. Then, he needed me to back up, even if I wasn't the main drummer anymore. I mean, nobody besides me could back up Wilbur, really, as piss-poor as I was, at least I knew the parts and could play them, sort of. And I was kind of thinking he wanted my brother, Monk, because he's as good as it gets, when it comes to music. I figured Old JAS Ellison would put up with a lot of grief-type horse manure in order to keep my brother. I couldn't tell how it would affect Monk if I left the band. And Old JAS couldn't, either. Besides, actually, before my Dad died, I was really pretty good, if I do say so myself. I'm a respectable musician when I'm not screwed up in the head. I know some of you are thinking, how can you be a good musician and not be screwed up in the head.

Monk had sort of flipped out since our Dad died. I mean, flipped out more than me, and I flipped out a lot because my playing sure did get worse, a lot worse. Monk really wasn't right. He started practicing like a maniac, all the time. I didn't practice and he couldn't stop. All he did was play his horns and not talk to anybody. I missed rehearsals. He made them all. But something had happened to his playing after Dad died. Before his playing was warm and full and fun, so brimming with everything, and all gorgeous like poetry by some real good poet. Afterward, his playing became very clean, neat, precise, functional. Everything was very minimal and very detached like he was watching himself play. He played like someone making very pretty picture postcards. Before he played like somebody exploding gallons of paint on the world's biggest canvas with all the imagination of his soul. He had a lot of that, Monk did, a lot of soul. Now, he just had technique. He was playing, I hate to say it, a lot of thin drivel. When Prince got arrested at school, Monk got even crazier, if that's possible. He started to hate N_____ Latin School and Mr. Ellison quite a lot. Quite a lot, to be honest.

V.

Old Bandmaster Ellison, the Grand JAS, was really hard on the advanced concert band, which I was in and Monk was in. The best kids, the most talented kids were in that band. And Mr. Ellison took the band showcases seriously. You are being prepared to do the Great Work, he would always tell us, like we knew what that meant. I always kind of meant to ask him, what's the Great Work? But I never did get around to it. He handed out a lot of palaver to those blockhead teachers and the parents and that crowd; but with the kids, he was straight up and hardcore and true. I guess he thought giving us a lot of praise was like carrying coals to Newcastle; after all, we were *supposed* to be very good. It wasn't supposed to be some kind of news bulletin. Being in that band was tough. The boards, as they say, sat pretty rough on everybody's butts, except if you were some kind of damn genius or something like Monk, and even they were sweating some. Even in my better days, I was always, like, some funky salmon swimming upstream. On the bad days, I was just one lost drowning little waterbaby.

"I feel dreadful about your plight," said Mr. Ellison with a kind of heaviness, like this was a real effort for him. I guess Mr. Mingus was on his mind, too. "But your playing has regressed to the point where it threatens the stability and viability of the band itself. So, I regret very much that I must have Wilbur take your place as the lead percussionist." I sense a little bit that Old JAS was a little frustrated and a little depressed about me. Maybe he was kind of depressed about everything, Prince, too. He was never the type to pitch a boogie-woogie. He was almost always righteous because he was so, you know, like, cool and everything. In a way, I would have been kind of glad if he had been a little mad because, like, I didn't want people feeling sorry for me because my Dad got killed and cutting me slack I really didn't deserve. After all, if I'm that messed up because of my Dad I should have done the right thing and resigned from the band back in January and maybe Prince might still be at N_____ Latin and Mr. Ellison wouldn't be faced with this, you know, like being on the verge of needing to rent a drum machine. Maybe Prince wouldn't have transferred but then again maybe I'm ego-tripping and I didn't affect his leaving one way or another. In fact, I know I didn't and I know I'm on an ego trip. Alas, poor Kid Ryder, I knew her well.

Mr. Ellison was worried about the high school band showcases that started right after Easter, Easter Monday, in fact. They weren't as important as the state competitions in May, but they were kind of, if you get my drift. The finalists for State were chosen based on performances at the band showcases. Our band was going to give a performance at Du Bois High next week. Du Bois is what they call an inner-city school, you know, a public school in the heart of darkness down in S4 and all like that, and it was good at three things, very good: concert band, varsity football, and varsity basketball. Their concert band was better than good.

I once heard them play when I was in the eighth grade. They came to my school and just about blew the roof off the sucker, if you'll pardon the expression. I remember particularly a tune by John Coltrane called "Giant Steps," with those crazy, hard-ass intervals, and I mean they'd handle those chord changes like they were born to the manor, so to speak. "How the heck can they play that?" I was thinking. I can barely even read that chart, let alone play that stupid crap worth anything. The tune was nothing I could appreciate in those days, but the way they played it, well, there you are: play your heart out and your ass off. Now, that's a motto I can deal with. It wasn't just technique, although they had a bunch of that, it was the passion and the feeling. Those kids played like they were announcing, we're in the ass-kicking business, so don't come with any damn pacifism around us. And they took names, too. Lots of 'em. Kicking ass and taking names. As far as I'm concerned, that's how you had to be on the bandstand with that band. You had to be up for it if you were going to play against that band. Sweet Maria Goretti, I was scared like anything to be playing at Du Bois on the stage against their band. I think it was worse than the idea of playing at Carnegie Hall. And it meant the world to Mr. Ellison to play there, to do well at that school. It was the first band showcase N_____ Latin was having there in ten years. It was our turn to play there again. And believe me, none of us would be going to that school or that neighborhood if Du Bois did not have one, like, totally frightening band that scared the living crap out of most of the school musicians in Westmoreland and across most of the state. I wondered how they were able to be so good, those kids at Du Bois, without our advantages. Plus those kids liked jazz less than we did. Go figure.

"I'm, I'm just p-p-prostrate with r-remorse, Mr. Ellison," I went, about screwing up, about being demoted to backup. I couldn't believe it was me talking like that. It sounded ridiculous to say something like that. I had to be crazy to say that, to stutter like that. Who would say a thing like "I'm just prostrate with remorse"? Like, only a total loser. Like, he's only going to think, she's so upset about her Dad that she's talking like a complete fool, an utter moron, a total retard.

Du Bois had one hell of a drummer in their band. We had one, too, when Prince Timmons was in the band. In fact, we had the best jazz drummer in the state. But we didn't anymore. Now he was a student at

Du Bois. I guess now they had a very good drummer and the best drummer, too. How lucky can you get!

VI.

Prince Michael Timmons was a sophomore, and whatever else can be said about the jerk (even now I still think he's something of a semi-jerk and the guy pretty much sort of saved my life), he can really play, when he wasn't showing off. He could play everything, traps, congas, timbales, bongos, vibraharp, the whole nine yards. Like the guy was totally into percussion. If you had to hit something, mid-beat, in rhythm, he could do it. If you came up with something like 11:4 time or 12:8 or 7:6 time and you needed someone to play it or clap it, he could do it, no sweat.

Once, when the percussionist for the classical orchestra got sick and couldn't play, Mr. Ellison recommended Prince to replace him and those classical teachers were pretty much like skeptical about that. At first, they didn't think he could read the score and all, but Prince could read music pretty well, real well, actually. I have to give him that. Mr. Ellison didn't tolerate anybody who couldn't read. Everybody in the jazz band could read their asses off, actually, excluding me. I'm an OK reader. But the classical people always wanted to think we were some kind of primitives or something. They wouldn't let jazz kids in the classical band, something about the seasons overlapping, but I think they didn't like our technique, all this crap about we didn't know how to tune our instruments; no jazz musicians did.

Then, they thought Prince Timmons couldn't get it together in time because this was all a last-minute kind of thing, but he learned the parts like in a day or something. They were doing Grieg's Piano Concerto in A-minor, you know, the one with the big drum roll and flourish at the beginning. Prince was terrific when they played but they kicked him out of the classical orchestra right after that little emergency was over. I heard it was because when one of the classical teachers asked him if he found classical music difficult, he said, "Yeah, it's difficult stayin' awake. The rest is just notes and beats like any other music." He was just messing around with them. He liked classical music, sometimes.

Last year, when he was a freshman, he broke his arm and showed up for a jazz concert band performance, fedora and sunglasses and all that, and played his parts with one hand better than anyone with two hands could have played them. He got a standing ovation. He became something of a legend after that, what with his playing with a drumstick in each hand and one behind each ear and breaking a stick on purpose to take one from behind his ear, real cool-like, with a lot of bravado. Nothing could have been worse because he was a conceited moron, and they're the worst kind of morons. But that's the way it is.

Nobody had to tell him. The guy just figured out, all by his lonesome, that he was a star and that everybody should, you know, like, kiss his ass or something. I had to give it to him, though, that he had a real air of command. He made it clear that he didn't play drums, but that he led the band. "Mr. Ellison is the biggest dog. And I'm the next big dog. I make the sound of this band possible and don't forget it. I'm the soul driver; y'all jump to the crack of the whip," he told everybody at band camp and nobody contradicted him. I couldn't stand him. He was one of those black kids from a poor neighborhood with a chip on his shoulder. Like, I'm out here with these white kids, I've got to prove something. My brother got along with him much better. In fact, I think Monk was probably Prince Timmons's best friend. That's the way it ended up, anyhow. But even I thought they did Prince Timmons wrong when they arrested him and all and I was thinking, man, that's a cold thing to do and hard, too. Like, even a total jerk like him didn't deserve that. No wonder he never came back to N_____ Latin School.

VII.

Well, anyway, like I was saying, I got into the advanced bands, I mean I became the lead percussionist (I like that word; that's Mr. Ellison's word) because the kid who was lead percussionist, Prince Michael Timmons, got arrested at school, they got him out on bail, like Shere Khan did, is what I heard. And he was supposed to be coming back to N_____ Latin School. But he didn't. He transferred. I was playing lead parts even when Prince was there because Mr. Ellison liked me and thought I could use the experience. Besides, I was good, then. Even Prince Timmons knew I was good, although he would never admit it, never admit that I actually showed him something about music. Then, suddenly I was the lead drummer. After the first two weeks, when Mr. Ellison thought I was making pretty good progress, I missed several days of school because I had stopped taking the meds and I got a little whacked out again. The whole thing with Prince was actually bothering me, sort of, but I didn't know it at the time. This kind of thing drove Mr. Ellison crazy but he took it in stride. He actually thought my staying in the band would be good for me, mental-wise. I think it might have been, for a while, some, a little, maybe, you know.

VIII.

It was at band camp the summer before ninth grade that Mr. Ellison saw me sitting behind a drum kit one afternoon, playing some stuff with my brother, Monk, just messing around, really, without a bass player. Monk and I have done that a lot since we were little kids. I love to play with Monk because he is so good and he can make you sound good, even if you aren't playing that well. And when The Monk is in the mood, it can be the funnest thing on earth, a total adventure, like, totally. So we were just playing something and Monk's sense of rhythm just lifted me right up, higher and higher, like holiness or something. It was better than church. We were playing a tune called "Dearly Beloved" by Jerome Kern, because Monk knows a lot of tunes like that and he just sings 'em to me and snaps out a rhythm and tempo and we just play. Now, don't get me wrong; me and The Monk never thought we were playing jazz or anything. I left that to my Dad. Besides, to be honest, I didn't even like jazz that much. It was cool because my Dad played it but it wasn't cool, like, just in and of itself, if you know what I mean. I couldn't decide whether playing jazz was like playing tennis without a net or walking a tightrope without a net. I never sat down and listened to jazz records, except, of course, my Dad's. His are cool. Monk listened to a lot more jazz records. And he knew he was named after that crazy pianist Thelonious Monk, which, like, kind of irritated him and maybe Dad had put a weight on him he didn't want. All that jazz stuff was a little too much for me. Like, I didn't get the point. The last thing I wanted to hear was a jazz record, to be honest. Anyway, I always thought we were playing stuff pretty straight with just the Arion twist on it. Mr. JAS watched for I don't know how long because I didn't know he was even there at first.

In fact, if I am not mistaken, I think that day was the first time I saw Mr. Ellison, really. And there he was, in all that heat, in the middle of the summer on this God-forsaken college campus where the band teachers were marching our butts off all morning and all afternoon and the concert band occupied the whole evening—and I wasn't even in the marching band and I was still marching around like a moron. Old Sturdy Ellison in all his glory, dressed in a white silk suit. He didn't have a drop of perspiration on him. His hair was all slicked back. He was smelling all cologney and everything, like, you know, everything was cool and nothing could touch him. I like Mr. Ellison a lot most of the time. He is a real cool guy. He dressed in these expensive suits all the time, wafer-thin shoes, and his nails were all polished and manicured and he was always all powdered-up like a bronze baby. He had style, you know. And that was, like, something.

He isn't human, I thought. He came up to me afterward and said, "I think I'll use you for backup percussion. You've got possibilities." He gave me this book called *Modern Rudimental Swing Solos* by some joker named Charles Wilcoxin. It's become sort of my Bible. It taught me pretty damn quick that I had, like, miles to go if I really wanted to play the drums, like, miles and miles. But the book also made me realize that I knew something, too. Like, I wasn't totally helpless in back of a drum kit.

Well, to be honest, Wilbur Johnson wanted to take Prince's place all along when Prince left, and I think a couple of those other dopey boys in the band were thinking they were going to play drums and I kind of half-hoped they would (*half*-hoped), but Mr. Ellison was determined not to use Wilbur, even though he was a junior and had played with the band since last year. My being promoted over him didn't sit too well with him or make me real popular in his circles, such as they were. And he had his supporters in the band, particularly with some of the black kids, who thought I got promoted because I am white, and because of my brother, Monk, and because of my Dad who was famous.

Like, in the early fall, when I was, like, myself, totally, Wilbur wanted to show me some stuff once for the big swing number we were doing called "Sing, Sing, Sing." I looked at him like, "Boy, since when you became Gene Krupa and somebody is going to pay attention to you about playing drums! You had better go somewhere and leave me alone!" Then, at that moment, I did one of my crispest, sharpest open press rolls, I mean, real even and feathery and almost made that boy pee in his pants with that little demonstration. Then, I did a real nice closed press roll, just for good measure. Didn't bounce my sticks once on the drumhead (although I darn near destroyed the ligaments in my wrists doing that). Go home and practice your paradiddles and ratamacues, little man, I was telling him. I ain't Prince Timmons but I'm better than you. I was kind of glad, in the end, that Mr. Ellison had more confidence in me than in that loser. But I was sure hoping I wasn't going to wind up being a loser, too. I used to be confident back in those days and actually thought I could be a player, you know. A player, a killer player in a band.

X.

I tore out of Mrs. Petrovsky's exam as soon as she called time, went to the bathroom and ran water over my wrists. Then, I went to the nasty school water fountain and drank water until my stomach felt bloated. That really made me feel like throwing up for a minute. But I kind of steadied and didn't feel hungry anymore. I had to stay true to my Lent, you know. I couldn't eat until dinnertime.

I walked over to the band room. I don't why I did, exactly. I was sort of thinking about the last thing Mr. Ellison said to me that day.

"Do you really want Wilbur to be the lead percussionist for the band? He doesn't have to be if you reassure me that you still *want* to play. I am sure you can accept that situation, as he is, frankly, an inferior though hopeful player, if you are not, for whatever reason, as it is colloquially put, up for it," he went on, smiling in a kind of sad way. "You might need more time than you think to get back to where you were. Take the time you require." And he turned on his heels and walked away from me. I was sort of thinking that he was wanting me not to be in the band, messing up, and thinking I was having a nervous breakdown and all like that but then something in what he said was sort of saying, like, he wanted me to stay, if I could. Heck, Wilbur shouldn't be lead percussionist, the lead drummer, not with a *good* band, not with a band that had something at stake, not with the band playing at Du Bois. But I guess I shouldn't be, either. And, funny thing it was, that right now Wilbur was probably playing better than me, if I was going to be honest with myself. I mean, at the last couple of rehearsals, I had to admit he was better, only because I was such total, complete, absolute, and utter crud, for Christ sakes. That's the level of incompetence I have to sink to for him to be good, so I guess you know what that meant for the band, to have that little timid half-ass technician back there. He knew how to keep time and that was it. He didn't have a creative bone in his body, no feel for how to play behind the soloist and help them along, no sense of when to goose the band a little and when to ease up. O, what a mess this is!

I don't know, the more I thought about it, the dumber it seemed. I mean, being in the band room and feeling bad and hungry. I sat down on the piano bench, took off my pilot helmet, and just let my head drop gently on the wood. It was cool and felt good. My head felt hot. I knew Mr. Ellison had gone to the hospital to see about Mr. Mingus, probably the other concert band teachers had gone, too. I was trying to think the thing through. Like, did I owe something to the band? And did I really want to be in the band now? Maybe, I never really wanted to be in the band. Maybe, it was always somebody else's idea, like Monk's or maybe it was because of my Dad encouraging me to play music. Not making me but encouraging me. And I thought it was me, all the time. But, you know, maybe, I was just doing it for them. I lifted my head up, put my helmet back on, and got up from the piano. I clodhopped around the room in my combat boots, then I just stopped.

I stood in the band room, and thought it over for about a minute, maybe two. I stuck a wad of bubble gum in my mouth because I always seem to think better chewing and blowing bubbles, the bovine brown study, as my Mom says, like a cow chewing its cud. I always yell at my Mom when she says that and go, "That's gross. Cud is vomit, for heaven's sake." I worked that gum into pretty passable shape, then started blowing away, talking to myself between bubbles. It also cuts bad breath, gum does, and my breath was pretty bad, not having eaten in, like, twenty years or something.

I looked around the band room slowly. The room was very neat. Mr. Ellison didn't like it when people threw sheet music around or didn't take care of their instruments. I was standing there imagining what it was like when the room was full of people: Instruments were on seats, on the floor, tambourines, bongos, snare drums, chimes, all the percussion and stuff like that, all the instruments the school owned and the kids owned. A trombone slide, some used reeds, a trumpet mouthpiece, a cheap folk guitar, cork grease. An electric bass, which Mr. Ellison didn't like much but used anyway, would be in the corner. The only instruments in the room now were pianos: a grand piano, a Steinway, at one end of the room and a battered upright piano, a Baldwin, at the other. And, in one corner, an instrument that never moved, that totally mystified me. Mr. Ellison told the kids once that only twenty or so of them existed in the world. I was starting to feel even more depressed than I had been. And what am I doing here anyway, looking at this monstrosity. It was awful to be in this room when it was empty. I thought maybe ghosts came out of that instrument in the corner, old jazz heads jumping out screaming at us young kids about how we weren't worthy of their tradition. That's all old people ever tell you, anyway. The Gentleman told me once that old heads weren't worthy of a damn thing, either! "What the hell did those egotistical, doped-up, pussy-hunting, white-controlled, half-illiterate, narrow-minded fools, those footnotes of music, ever do but try to wreck what little tradition they had by not passing it on to anybody," he said. Pussy-hunting! Brown said that to me! What a mouth! Besides, what about the women who played? I got his drift and didn't like it. He was talking about guys like Mr. Mingus, and I liked him.

The whole thing was pretty, I don't know, off-kilter. A couple of weeks ago, someone had painted on the bell of this thing an obscene picture of a boy and a girl. Underneath was written: "The second biggest blow job in the world." I was pretty embarrassed by that drawing, I guess. "That's fellatio," Enid Springer giggled, when she saw it and I said, "What? What the heck is fellatio?" (*That* won't be on the SAT.) I guess I've led a pretty sheltered life. Enid Springer sure hasn't or acts like she hasn't. But what do you expect from a girl who wears a sweatshirt to school that says "Porn Star: Pam Posterior and Puffy Pussy." Her parents had to come to school about that one. I thought the drawing was disgusting, just the kind of stupid thing that stupid shallow kids do, real morons. You know, kids are always making obscene drawings in their textbooks, on their desktops, in the bathroom stalls, bringing *Tijuana Bibles*, and *Hustler*, and *Penthouse*, and bunches of crap that were a lot worse to school and showing it around like silicone babes doing a lot of stuff nobody short of being a psychotic, self-hating slut would do, and downright bad drawings of cartoon characters having sex are supposed to be interesting, when it's just depressing as all get out and seems like a big waste. Don't get me wrong. I'm no prude or anything or some self-righteous ass. When Enid Springer started nosing around me to sound me to play in her all-girl rock band, because I was the only girl drummer worth anything for miles, probably in the entire city of Westmoreland, and she said she wanted to call it Porn Star, you know, the band. I was like, well, let's call it Fire in the Hole. And that thick moron never got it. Damn, I thought it was pretty risqué and all like that and kind of funny. Monk laughed his fool head off when he heard it. I never joined her band anyway, everything being so predictable, including her chord changes.

It was a kind of gloomy day anyway and it was sad, everything was. And I started, for some reason, thinking about Mom and how she tried to save those dead cranes at the zoo that New Year's Day when it had, after all that wild rain and those thunderstorms, turned so cold, and I was just watching my Mom there, her skirt all stained with crane blood and bloody feathers and bird poop and mud from all the rain the previous night, the wind blowing real chilly and my Mom without her coat on, so cold that her nose was turning red and running, all surrounded by dead and bloody birds, moaning, whooping wounded birds, sounding like low-pitched trumpets and that was what the air was like, like it was full of trumpets from those wounded birds, bloody and broken like from a war or something that somebody fought and nobody told the birds what was being fought and me sort of half-wishing I could bawl and watching my Mom looking grim, on her knees, wearing bloody gloves, trying to save one bird, in particular, and saying over and over again, under her breath, "Who would do something like this? Who would do something like this?" It was the same thing my Mom said when the police officer came to our home that night and told us that our Dad had been killed. "Who would do something like that?" She said it real soft, almost to herself. And she just kind of fell to her knees, almost like she was praying or something, and stared into space as if someone had just knocked her senseless with a baseball bat but she didn't know she was unconscious and was still going around acting like she was conscious but she really wasn't. She never did cry that night, as I remember. She just held me and Monk and told us everything would be all right. It wasn't, but that wasn't her fault.

Everybody was, like, shocked when a couple of weeks after the New Year, when I just got back again to the band that Prince got arrested in the band room, right during rehearsal. We had just finished playing when three cops came busting into the room and just like that grabbed Prince and pushed him to the floor to handcuff him. I was, like, boy, this can't be happening and the principal was there and all, and Mr. Ellison was all upset because he didn't know, you could tell, that this was going to happen. The principal, Mr. Scott, seemed pretty surprised, too, and kept saying to the cops, "Is this necessary? Do you have to handcuff him?" Rumors started flying afterward that one of the cops pulled a gun on Prince, that he got smacked around with a nightstick, but none of that was true. Nobody pulled a gun or hit Prince. I should know. I was there. What happened, even without the gun-pulling or the head-whipping, was bad enough, I figured. Geez, who wants to get arrested at school? And when they stood Prince up he was, like, really upset and nearly bawling and yelling:

"Mr. Ellison, why you lettin' them do this to me? Man, why y'all got to do me like this? Y'all got to come and arrest me in school and embarrass me like this? In front of everybody like I'm some kind of criminal or something? Man, this ain't right."

Even I was feeling bad about it and, like, I can't stand the guy. They could have done this in the principal's office and not here in the band room in front of the jerk kids in the band. But I looked at Monk and he was, oh, I can't describe it. He was red at first, then, he went so white. I didn't believe that Monk could get that pale. I thought he was going to pass out. His horn slipped from his hand and fell to the floor.

"Please, Mr. Ellison, don't have them take me out like this," Prince went and Mr. Ellison was talking to the principal, asking him what it was all about, what had Prince done, what was he being accused of, why was he being arrested like this. The cops said they thought he might have a gun on him or hidden somewhere. They came to school because they were sure to find him here. Prince was considered potentially dangerous, they said.

"Does it look like I have a gun?" Prince shouted. The cops had to drag him from the room. Mr. Ellison went with the cops, yelling at the principal and at the cops. It was bedlam. Prince was shrieking: "What you think? I play the drums with two guns instead of sticks? I ain't never held a god-dam gun in my whole life." Naturally, there was no more rehearsal and we all sort of looked at each other for a moment, like maybe what had just happened hadn't really happened. Then, somebody, I don't know who, giggled. It was one of those nervous things, you know, when you can't think of anything else to do. You just kind of laugh but you know there's nothing funny. Then, somebody said, trying to break the tension, "Man, they're sure getting tough around here if you screw up at practice." That was actually kind of funny and I almost wanted to laugh myself because the whole thing was so lunatic. Somebody farted out of nervousness. It was a stinker, too. Monk just bolted from the room and I took off after him. He went into the boys' room. I waited like one minute, maybe two, and then I just busted in there. I figured if there were other boys in there, well, so what? Everybody's got to piss and crap. I could hear this coughing sound coming from one of the stalls and I knew that Monk was retching. I go over to the stall and he just upchucks some more. He's sweating and everything, like people do when they're upchucking. He gives me a look like I don't know what. I ran out of there double quick.

A couple of days later, at the end of rehearsal, as I was putting up some tambourines on a shelf, Monk asked Mr. Ellison if he was going to resign from the band because of what happened to Prince, I guess in protest or something.

"Why would I do that?" Mr. Ellison asked, "I have a responsibility. I know you are upset about what happened to Prince. But that matter is being attended to properly and forthrightly. The principal was not aware that the police were going to handle the situation in that way. He's extremely upset about it. Prince has many friends here. Prince will be out on bond today or tomorrow. That is good news, indeed. And he should be back in school next week. Despite what happened, Prince needs this school."

"If he doesn't come back, I'm quitting the band as soon as the year's over," Monk said.

"I am aware that Prince is your friend, Monk, and I believe that I know how you feel—"

"No, Mr. Ellison, you don't," Monk said angrily. "You don't know how I feel, how ashamed I am of you and this school to let Prince get treated like that. Who cares who was upset about it? Nobody did anything about it. How could you let them treat our best player like that, like he was a thug or something? You didn't fight for him, Mr. Ellison." Monk was nearly choking. Mr. Ellison just shook his head.

Monk said nothing else and neither did Mr. Ellison. He simply left, although I knew that Mr. Ellison knew that his answer was lame. That there was nothing he could say that would have made a difference. Maybe he was doing stuff behind the scene for Prince but who knows about that kind of stuff.

"If I run away in anger every time something untoward happens here, how can I be of assistance to anyone?" Mr. Ellison asked me kind of helpless-like. It was the most perturbed, the most uncool I ever heard him. And Prince wasn't back in school next week, either. At least not at N_____ Latin School. As Monk left the room, he did a funny thing. When he passed the big bass saxophone, he spat in the bell. And when Prince didn't come back, he made sure to remind Mr. Ellison about what he was going to do.

There's a moment when I can look at the ugly bass saxophone, like, kind of from the top, and look down at the bell, like I'm looking down a well, a deep, deep well, and maybe out of it were coming voices of long ago, so long ago and so far, that kept crying out for those of us looking in, to remember them. And looking at it from the top like that kind of makes the bell seem one-dimensional and it looks, for all the world, to me, like a ring of gold. But I can only see that sometimes. And I didn't see it today. All I saw today was a god-ugly instrument scrawled with a dumb obscenity. And me, some gawky, dorky girl with a pilot's helmet and wearing combat boots, some knit plaid skirt that showed my knobby knees, one of them covered by a big bandage because I bammed it riding my bike the other day. Geez! Looking at this freak saxophone can really do things to you.

Mr. Ellison wanted the guilty person to wipe off the drawing from the bell of the instrument. But it wasn't so easy to remove because someone had drawn it in paint. A special solution was required. So far, up to that day, no one had done anything. Mr. Ellison ignored it, saying that he expected it to be removed soon. It wasn't so bad, though. It couldn't be made out from a distance. A person had to be close to the contrabasso saxophone to tell what the drawing was. No one knew what it was from the front of the room.

I started thinking why didn't Mr. Ellison just get rid of this thing. No one can play it. No one would ever want to.

We were on school holiday for the rest of the week; tomorrow was Maundy Thursday. Band kids had to come to school for a rehearsal in the morning. No rehearsal on Good Friday. But there would be another rehearsal on Saturday. Nothing on Easter Sunday. Then, Easter Monday we go to Du Bois and either do it or die. I didn't have a lot of time. I walked up and down the room. After about five minutes, I rushed to the door, looked up and down the hall to make sure that no one from the band was around. I rushed back to Mr. Ellison's desk, pulled a sheet a paper from one of my notebooks and wrote a message. I had made up my mind and I wanted to tell Mr. Ellison before I changed it and would just be sitting there doing nothing but thinking about what I ought to do.

> *To Mr. Ellison:*
> *I have thought it over and I think Wilbur should be the lead drummer for the band. I am quitting the band because I cannot play well anymore because my mind is not on the music. I do not want to be a hindarance to the band and so I am leaving because Wilbur can probably do a better job than me right now.*
>
> *(Signed),*
> *Menken Arion*

I didn't quite like it as I looked it over, so I added:

(Signed),
Menken Arion
AKA The Kid Ryder, your ex-percussionist and accordionist. Thank
you for giving me the job and having a lot of faith in me. I'm real sorry
I let you down.

(I forgot to mention I play the accordion, too. But that's not important.)

That was better. I didn't know if I was doing the right thing but it was the only thing I could do. I looked at the sign on the band room door. I don't know why, I just sort of did at that moment, like, I was still thinking if this was something I wanted to do. The sign kind of made me grin a little. It read:

A minor must always
Be natural and
See Sharp to not
D Flat (e).

—*The Musician's Code of Behavior* by Roman T. Sizes

I think Mr. Ellison made that up, because he was always signing things Roman T. Sizes, like a kind of joke. It made me feel a little better, but not much. But I felt I had to get out of the band. I wasn't all there anymore and I wasn't playing well and I didn't think I was going to get better in three or four days. It was nice to know that despite him thinking I needed to take a leave from the band, Mr. Ellison still wanted me to stay. I was kind of surprised that I decided to drop out. I'm not the quitting kind, to be honest. At least, I don't think I am. I haven't had the opportunity to quit much, though, I guess. I looked at the band jacket I was wearing and I was really pretty damn, like, proud of it, and everything like that. And I was figuring, well, if I'm quitting the band I need to give up the jacket. I mean, I know my parents paid for it and everything, but still it wasn't right to keep it if I wasn't in the band. It would be kind of like a lie to keep it now or maybe I just thought it would remind me of my failure. Who needs to be reminded of that? I took it off, draped it on a chair, then looked at it there. It looked like an athletic jacket, the kind of thing that a school would give the football team or something. Monk never wore his but I always wore mine. Don't know why he didn't like the jacket, but I'm glad he didn't, so that way we didn't have go around looking like some dorky twins or something like that. Then, I picked it up and put it back on. I couldn't give it up just then. I was thinking, like, maybe I better hang on to it till tomorrow, like, anything might happen from now till then, and maybe I won't be out of the band. Besides, it was cold outside and I didn't have anything else to wear.

I placed the note on Mr. Ellison's desk, put my notebook back in my satchel and was about to fly out of that room like a truck was bearing down on somebody at ninety miles per hour with bad intentions. I had to catch up with The Monk and figure out what he was doing and where he was going and what was all this going on with Prince Timmons and him that I had heard about, about Prince's band and all that. I kind of felt a big burden had been lifted from me in quitting the band. I wouldn't need to think about that anymore. Good. Then, me and Monk had to figure out if there was something we could do for Mr. Mingus. Well, just as I was ready to bust out, Monk came busting in and nearly knocked me unconscious, busting into the band room, big as life, with Old Ben Webster trailing behind him, and said, all serious-like, "I've been looking for you everywhere. Come on, Kid, let's go."

Mary Jane

Dorothy Sterling

Chapter 6

Heads Up, Eyes Front

Mr. Jackson and Fred arrived at the Douglases' while Mary Jane was still eating breakfast. Tall Mr. Jackson making polite talk with Daddy while she spooned up her cereal, and Fred looking stiff and uncomfortable in a new suit and freshly shined shoes. Mary Jane almost wanted to giggle, to tell them all that it wouldn't hurt a bit. But she couldn't, because there was a lump in her throat, as if her tonsils had grown back.

Mamma had little frown lines on her forehead as she smoothed the lapels of Mary Jane's new blazer and straightened the bow on her pony tail and asked if she'd remembered to take a handkerchief.

"Now you be good and don't fret your teachers," she said. "Hear?"

It was the same thing she said every year on the first day of school. The same thing she used to tell Lou Ellen and James when they were little. Only people who knew Mamma well, like Mary Jane and Daddy, could have said there was anything different about her good-by kiss that showed this wasn't any ordinary first school day.

She stood on the porch, waving to them as they drove off. Mary Jane watched her through the back window of the car until she was only a blur. Fred, who had grown about a mile over the summer, was talking about basketball. He talked goals and fouls and dribbles steadily until Daddy parked the car across the street from school. Then Fred stopped—right in the middle of a sentence.

Mary Jane looked out to see what had made Fred stop talking. The fluttery feeling traveled from her stomach to her chest to her throat, and she clutched her schoolbag with a perspiring hand.

"Man!" Fred whistled through his teeth.

Because across the street, in front of Wilson, there was a row of green and white police cars. And behind the cars there were millions of people. Men and women and children sitting on the low stone wall, swarming over the big lawn and crowding the broad limestone steps. Men and women and children shouting and talking until Daddy and Mr. Jackson and Fred and Mary Jane got out of the car, then putting their voices together for a thundering "Boo-o-o!"

For a moment Mary Jane thought about Curly following her to school and how frightened he'd be by the noise. Then she stopped thinking about anything at all. With Daddy and Mr. Jackson on the outside and Fred and Mary Jane in the middle like a sandwich, the four of them marched across the street.

On the school sidewalk, two policemen joined them. The policemen went first, clearing a path through the crowd, leading the way. It was as if they were marching in a parade.

Heads up. Eyes front. One-two-three-four.

Only instead of drums to keep time to there were screams.

A man, angry. "Go back to Africa!"

Mary Jane turned her head, trying to see who it was. What did he mean?

A woman, high-pitched—could it have been a woman? "Pull her black curls out!"

Mary Jane's scalp tingled as if someone were tugging at it. Automatically her hand jerked up toward her forehead, toward the little fluff she'd combed so carefully at her new dressing table that morning. Then Daddy caught her hand, squeezing it in his own.

Heads up. Eyes front. Eyes on the broad blue backs of the policemen.

They were on the steps now, the white steps that led to the open school door. The crowd, not people, but a crazy Thing of faces and open mouths, was behind them, roaring in their ears. The Thing moved closer,

closer, until it seemed as if it were about to pounce. Mary Jane stifled a scream, and one of the policemen turned and shouted.

"Stand still. Move back!"

The Thing stood still, stepped back, turned into people again. In a way, that was worse, because the people were yelling at *her*, at Mary Jane Douglas, beloved daughter of Mamma and Daddy, baby sister of Lou Ellen and James. Mary Jane, who'd never had anything bad happen to her in her life, except to her tonsils, and even then the doctor didn't mean to hurt. They couldn't be screaming at her—but they were.

Daddy squeezed her hand again. Heads up. Eyes front. They were on the landing now, close to the door. A group of boys were chanting, for all the world as if they were at a football game:

"Two-four-six-eight
We ain't gonna integrate."

Two-four-six-eight. The four of them marched through the door and all the way down the corridor to the principal's office keeping time to the rhythm of the chant.

While they waited to meet Mrs. Davis, Daddy let go of her hand to give her a quick little hug. She looked up at him, her eyes round, black, startled. He looked down at her, straightening the bow on her pony tail, not neatly the way Mamma would do, but clumsily, like Dad. Mary Jane put down her schoolbag and straightened it all over again, as if fixing her bow was the most important thing in the whole world just then.

"Boy, that was rough," Fred whispered. "Look at my hand." When he held out his hand, it was trembling.

"Are you all right?" Daddy asked anxiously. "Should I take you home?"

Mary Jane shook her head. After the noise outside it was so quiet in the corridor that her ears buzzed. It was hard to speak around the lump in her throat. "I'm all right," she gulped. "You can go now."

But Daddy stayed until Mrs. Davis said "Hello" to all of them and introduced them to the other Negro children, three boys and a girl, who were entering the upper grades. When the warning bell rang, Daddy kissed her good-by and Mr. Jackson kissed Fred, who looked embarrassed but pleased just the same. After that it was definitely time for parents to leave and school to begin.

"Junior High Assembly," Mrs. Davis explained as she led them along winding corridors to the auditorium. "This is where you'll get your assignments to your home rooms."

In the big auditorium Mary Jane and Fred sat alone. Alone in the midst of a room full of boys and girls. Alone, as if they were on a desert island in the middle of the ocean.

Mrs. Davis gave a welcoming speech, saying how glad she was to greet all the new people and that she hoped everyone had had a restful summer so that they could buckle down to some good hard work this term. It was a nice speech. Mary Jane had heard Mrs. Buckley give one like it at Dunbar every fall.

After Mrs. Davis' talk, another teacher stood up to read the home-room assignments. She called boys and girls up to the front of the room, one after the other, to get their cards.

The A's, the B's, the C's. Fred looked down sympathetically as the teacher began on the D's. For a moment Mary Jane thought he was going to pat her hand. Only then he remembered that he was a boy and she was a girl and that patting hands just wasn't done, in school or out, first day or last, when you were twelve.

"Mary Jane Douglas." She shivered a little, even though she was still wearing her blazer. Slowly she stood up and walked down the aisle to the front of the room. Head up. Eyes front.

The room was so quiet that she could hear her own footsteps tapping on the floor, her new loafers with the good-luck pennies in them. Until, from somewhere behind her, there was a muffled chorus:

"We don't want her
You can have her.
She's too black for me."

Mary Jane flushed, faltered, kept on walking. Her cheeks were burning as Mrs. Davis jumped up from her seat on the stage and sternly rapped for order.

"Disgraceful . . . no more of that . . . rude . . . won't permit . . ."

Words. Words that Mary Jane scarcely heard as she took her assignment card and walked back to her seat. Head up, eyes front, not listening, not seeing anything. Not even reading the card until Fred came back with his and they compared them. He was in home-room 127, she in room 124. Her home-room teacher was Miss Rousseau, the card said.

After all the assignments had been given out and the junior high had pledged allegiance and sung "Oh, say can you see," the boys and girls shuffled through the auditorium doors to the crisscross of corridors beyond. Everyone seemed to know where to go except Fred and Mary Jane. They stood there looking uncertainly at each other, when something surprising happened. At least Mary Jane *thought* it happened. Puzzling over it later, she wasn't sure that it hadn't been a dream.

A girl came up to them, a little girl with bright red cheeks and pale blond hair, and said that she was sorry about the crowd outside. "Can I help you find your way?" she asked. "My sister used to go here, so I know where the rooms are, sort of. It's awfully confusing if you don't."

Instead of answering, they showed her their cards. She led them up a flight of stairs and down a hall to their home rooms. Then she disappeared without even saying "Good-by."

Room 124 was pleasant and sunny, with high windows and movable desks and a green blackboard behind the teacher's chair. Not much different from the classrooms at Dunbar except for the color of the blackboard, and the desks which were brand-new.

Even Miss Rousseau looked like the Dunbar teachers. Ageless, the way teachers always seemed to be, not exactly pretty, but not ugly either. Like the Dunbar teachers, except that Miss Rousseau's skin was fair instead of brown and she talked with a funny sort of accent. She rolled her *r*'s and did things with her *th*'s in a way that Mary Jane had never heard before.

"Good morning." She smiled as Mary Jane hesitated in the doorway, not sure of what to do next.

A bell rang and Miss Rousseau started to assign seats. Alphabetical order again, which put Douglas in the second row, with a window on one side and a girl named Duncan on the other.

Only the girl named Duncan didn't sit down. Instead she marched up to the teacher's desk and loudly announced, "My mother said I wasn't to sit by *her.*"

Miss Rousseau lifted her eyebrows. "In my class," she answered, "pupils sit where they are assigned." Calmly she continued to read out the names.

The girl named Duncan started to leave the room, then thought better of it. Without looking at Mary Jane, she slid her desk over until it was almost touching the one at her right. It stayed there until Miss Rousseau finished with her seating list.

"Now, Darlene." The teacher's voice was calm. "You can put your desk back in place."

Mumbling under her breath, Darlene obeyed. Through the entire period, however, she kept her head turned toward the door. If she *had* to sit next to Mary Jane, at least she wasn't going to look at her. For a crazy moment Mary Jane felt like giggling. Darlene was going to have an awful stiff neck by the end of the term.

The next minutes were busy ones. Miss Rousseau gave out schedule cards and locker numbers and explained about periods and bells and lunch and gym and not being late and bringing a note to the nurse if you were sick. Then the whole class trooped out to the hall to find their lockers and practice their combinations.

The combinations worked like the locks on safes. Two turns to the right. Stop at 27. One turn to the left. Stop at 14. Then right again until the lock clicked open when you reached 7. Mary Jane twirled and stopped and twirled and stopped until she knew her combination by heart. After she hung up her blazer on the hook inside the locker she went back to her home room.

There was another bell and still another, and regular classes began. Today was only a half day, so classes meant learning your teachers' names and getting your seat and your books. For first period Mary Jane stayed right where she was, alongside Darlene, because their class was French and Miss Rousseau taught it.

Miss Rousseau not only taught French, she *was* French, she told the class. Which explained the funny accent. At any other time Mary Jane, who had never met a person before who didn't come from North Carolina or Kentucky or Tennessee, would have been interested in someone from Paris, France, who said "ze" when she meant "the." But not today when her head ached and the back of her neck felt sore and she couldn't swallow the lump in her throat no matter how hard she tried.

After French and more bells came English and more bells, then Arithmetic, History, and Science. Only History was called Social Studies now, and Arithmetic was Math. All of the classrooms looked like her home room, except Science, which had tables instead of desks and a sink in the back of the room, and Social Studies, which had Fred.

Mary Jane had never realized before how much she liked Fred until she saw his friendly, dark face when she entered the Social Studies room. While people were still finding their seats, he leaned forward to whisper in her ear.

"Already I've been kicked in the shins and had my books knocked out of my arm. Score, Wilson two, Jackson nothing. This keeps up, I'll get a complex or something. I'll begin to think they don't like me," he chuck-led.

"Who did it?" Mary Jane's lips framed the words as the teacher called the class to order.

Fred shrugged his shoulders, the smile gone from his face. "Seems like all of them."

Mary Jane chewed her underlip as she copied the homework assign-ment from the board. "Columbus Finds a New World, pages 3–11." The next bell would mean Science, and then school would be over for the day. The bell after the next one would mean going outside to face that howl-ing, hating crowd. Maybe, she thought, they wouldn't be there. Maybe they had forgotten and gone away. But after she'd taken her blazer from her locker and found Fred and then Daddy in the noisy vestibule, she knew that the crowd was still outside, still waiting.

Down the steps and across the lawn she walked, with the policemen leading and the voices screaming. Mean, hate-filled voices screeching in her ears. She blinked at the white light from a photographer's flash gun. She ducked when a stick glanced off her shoulder. But she wasn't what you'd really call hurt. She was still putting one foot in front of the other and squeezing Daddy's hand and trying not to listen to the roar of the crowd.

One-two-three-four, and they had crossed the street. One-two-three-four, and they were in the car. With the doors closed and the windows rolled up to shut out the noise.

It was the end of Mary Jane's first day in junior high.

Chapter 7

Your Great Bravery

Driving home in the car with everybody sighing, sort of, and not talking, Mary Jane remembered her tonsils again. It had been like this after the op-eration when she left the hospital with Daddy. She'd been shaky still, kind of dopey from the medicine the doctor had given her to stop the hurt in her throat. And at home Mamma had been waiting on the front steps with a worried frown on her face.

Only now she was twelve instead of six and Mamma wasn't going to put her to bed with ice cream and coloring books and a promise that the pain would stop after a while. Now she was twelve and maybe this special going-to-an-integrated-school pain would never stop. Unless she stopped going to the school.

But she put. all thought of leaving Wilson out of her mind, because Mamma was hugging her as if she'd been away for a year instead of a few hours—and Mamma was starting to cry. All morning she had listened to radio reports about school. All morning she had pictures in her mind of Mary Jane being chased down the halls, bloody and maybe dying. Mamma practically never cried, and the sight of her red-rimmed eyes made Mary Jane say that everything was all right, just fine, over and over again.

Before they had finished lunch, reporters started ringing the doorbell. Ladies with notebooks and men with cameras, asking how old she was and what she wanted to be when she grew up and how she had felt that morning in school. Along with the reporters came phone calls. Lou Ellen, all the way from Philadelphia, almost crying like Mamma, and James from law school, and Grampa and the aunts. By the time she said to each of them, "It's all right," she had begun to believe it herself.

Grampa was the only one who didn't ask about school. Instead, he talked about Curly and Sophie and the chickens, until she wished it were summer and she were back on the farm. Then he chuckled his slow, deep chuckle and said, "Guess what I was doing when the man on the radio told about that mob outside Wilson this morning?"

Mary Jane couldn't guess. To tell truth, she was too tired even to try.

"Praying for rain, a regular cloudburst." As he chuckled again, Mary Jane pictured the people outside of school with the rain falling into their open mouths. She burst out laughing.

She was still giggling when Daddy took the receiver from her hand to find out what the joke was about. Standing next to the phone, she listened to his conversation.

"You'd have been real proud of her, Pa. Not a bit upset. She walked up those steps and into that school this morning with her head in the air. As if she were sniffing pies in Heaven."

"Not a bit upset." Mary Jane wandered into the kitchen to find some-thing to nibble on. Chewing on a carrot stick, she thought about what Daddy had said. He hadn't even noticed that she was scared. He was real proud of her, and so was Grampa. Pretty soon she got to feeling real proud of herself—and not a bit upset. Even when the other kind of phone call started.

The first time she picked up the receiver and it wasn't someone she knew, a man's voice said, "You take that black girl out of the white school or we'll kill her." There were others, women as well as men, calling mean names and threatening to blow up the house and Daddy's office. After that first call Daddy wouldn't let her answer the phone any more. By suppertime he had taken the receiver off the hook.

"Just talk," he said. "People talk like that, they don't do anything. But there's no need us listening to it."

When the paper boy tossed the *Evening Chronicle* on the porch, Mary Jane discovered that she was front-page news. There she was, more important even than the President today, with a picture of her walking up the school steps. Right behind her was a white girl, her mouth all twisted, face ugly with hate. Not just any strange white girl, either, but the girl named Duncan, Darlene Duncan, who sat next to her in home room and in French.

She stared at the picture for a long time, trying to understand it. Gosh, Darlene didn't even know her. How could she make a face like that? Of course, that's what Grampa had said. "They just don't know you." Probably when Darlene knew her, she'd change her mind.

Borrowing the scissors from her mother's sewing box, Mary Jane cut out the picture and put it in the bottom drawer of her desk, along with the baby tooth and the spelling papers and the graduation certificate from Dunbar. What in the world would her children think when they saw that picture? She'd have to tell them the whole story, the way Grampa told her about Red Anne.

Feeling proud of herself and pleased with all the excitement and with everyone at home acting so nice, she pushed out of her mind any thought of not going back to Wilson. Even when she was lying in bed at night and could still hear the women screaming and the men calling names.

The excitement didn't stop with that first day. Reporters kept coming and newspapers printed Mamma's picture and Daddy's and Fred's, newspapers all over the country. One man even wanted her to go to New York to be on a television show. Mary Jane's eyes lit up, but Mamma said of course not, she was supposed to be a student, not a star on television.

Then letters began to arrive, great big stacks of them every morning. A few were awful, calling her a "black baboon" and worse, words she didn't always understand. But most of the people who wrote said nice things and some sent little presents, handkerchiefs and dollar bills.

The letters came from every place you could think of, New York and Chicago and Los Angeles, and then faraway places like Paris and Berlin and Stockholm, Sweden. Weeks after school opened, the postman delivered one addressed "Miss Mary Jane Douglas, High Ridge, U.S.A." It had come all the way from Tokyo.

Mary Jane gave the stamps to Fred for his collection and stuck the letter from Japan in the mirror of her dressing table where she could read it, mornings, when she brushed her hair.

"Dear Miss Mary Jane," the letter said. "I am a schoolgirl in Tokyo, reading of your great bravery. From the top of my heart I wish luck come to you. Please excuse English. Your friend, Fuji Yanase."

"It's all right." Mary Jane repeated it to the reporters and the people who wrote letters and to Mamma and Aunt Ruth and Gwen and Peggy and Daddy. "It's all right," she kept on saying. Even when it wasn't.

Chapter 8

Sniffing Pies in Heaven
The second day at Wilson was a little better than the first. Now that she knew what to expect, Mary Jane concentrated on not listening to the shouts and screams. She marched up the steps with her head high, as if she were sniffing pies in Heaven. She marched up the steps like Joan of Arc and Red Anne and the Mary Jane who had said she was going to school to get an education, not to socialize.

Fred helped too. When the boys on the landing chanted:

"Two-four-six-eight
We ain't gonna integrate,"

Fred squared his shoulders and recited back:

"Eight-six-four-two
Ten to one, we bet you do."

Pretty soon Mary Jane joined in with him and they walked through the door and up to their home rooms, saying it in chorus, without breaking step except when they stopped to tell their fathers good-by.

Mary Jane kept on holding up her head and not listening all through home-room period and right into the middle of French. Only then she was so busy not listening that she couldn't answer when Miss Rousseau popped a question at her. Then she flushed and stammered until she could hear Darlene tittering. Then she didn't feel brave any more.

After French, other things went wrong. She took a left turn in the corridor when she should have turned right. She went down a flight of stairs when she should have gone up. By the time she reached English she was breathless and late and scared.

Wilson was so big, with so many stairways and halls and a new wing and an old one, that she was afraid she'd never learn her way around. Everyone else knew where to go. Everyone else walked in twosomes and threesomes, with their friends.

Lunch time was the scariest of all. When the first lunch bell rang, the seventh- and eighth-graders burst out of their classrooms. They slid across the shiny terrazzo floors, swinging books and pocketbooks and yelling at the tops of their lungs. It made Mary Jane think of a herd of cattle stampeding, running down anything that got in its way.

She flattened herself against a wall until everyone had passed, hoping that she'd be able to find Fred. When he came along, they got on the cafeteria line together. They slid their trays around the steam tables, choosing what they wanted to eat and paying the lady at the cashier's desk. Then they set out down the long center aisle to look for seats.

The cafeteria was an enormous room, as big as a football field, with row after row of long tables. Boys sitting at some tables, girls at others, and everyone shouting "Hi" and "Sit here"—only not to them.

Nobody paid attention to them at the steam tables or the cashier's desk, but when they walked down the aisle with their loaded trays there was a sudden hush. The big noisy room grew quiet as Mary Jane put down her sandwich and milk and Fred his hot plate and two desserts at a table near the door. It was so quiet that you could hear the scraping of a chair when the girl seated nearest Mary Jane got up and walked away. Quiet and then buzzing with sound, with everyone whispering and poking his neighbor to look.

Fred shook his head, meaning go-on-and-eat. He started right in on his hamburgers, but Mary Jane didn't feel hungry. She ate slowly, carefully, nibbling at her sandwich and wiping her mouth with her napkin after each sip of milk. She could almost hear Mamma saying, "Mind your manners. They'll be watching you."

They certainly were watching. After a few minutes of everybody staring and nobody at their table saying a word, Mary Jane whispered to Fred, "I feel as if I had two heads or something, the way they look at us."

"Likely they've never seen Negroes eating before," Fred said, right out loud. "Likely they think we'll pick up our meat in our paws and lick our plates."

Fred certainly was a help. One or two people at their table heard what he said and stopped staring. And by the time Mary Jane had watched him plow through his hamburgers and his two desserts she found her courage coming back. Of course it was that they didn't know any better, that they thought colored people were different. Once they got to know her, everything would be all right.

She didn't even get fussed when a boy blew the paper cover off his milk straw and it hit her on the cheek. At Dunbar, kids were always blowing the covers off their straws—when the teacher wasn't looking—and hitting kids with them. It didn't mean a thing. Maybe when she got used to Wilson she'd blow her straw cover at somebody too. These things just took time, that's all.

Time passed, and Mary Jane kept on going from brave to scared to brave again and from not listening to listening. She learned her way around the high school corridors and which stairs to take to English and to gym. She bought red and white Wilson covers for all of her schoolbooks and she saved her allowance until she had two dollars for a G.O. card so that she could go to all the school games. She was even getting used to the sudden hush when she sat down at a cafeteria table or walked into the noisy, crowded lavatory. Not liking it, of course, but getting used to it.

Time passed, and every morning there were fewer and fewer people standing in front of the school. Until finally there was only one police car at the curb and Daddy and Mr. Jackson said it would be all right, she and Fred could go to school alone.

At home the phone calls stopped—even the mean ones—and there was only a trickle of letters from faraway places. At home all the excitement had died down. The worry lines were fading from Mamma's forehead and she began to scold Mary Jane about picking up her room and helping with the dishes and making sure her homework was finished before she turned on the television. Daddy, working hard on a big case, was too tired to take her to the drive-in on Saturday night or to remember to pat her on the shoulder and tell her she was his big, brave girl.

It was as if the tonsils were out, the sore throat healed, and everything the way it had been other years. Only everything wasn't the way it had been other years.

Mornings, Fred called for her and the two of them walked to school together. The grownups were gone, but there was always a handful of boys and girls lounging on the school steps. Waiting to shout, "Why don't you go to your own school?" Waiting to call names and threaten to hurt them.

Mary Jane listened now and heard the things they said. She wasn't sniffing pies in Heaven any more. She was paying close attention when a boy bigger than Fred held up a water pistol and pointed it straight at her.

"It's full of acid," he called. "If you go into school, I'll shoot."

Of course it wasn't acid, only water that splashed Fred's pants and Mary Jane's socks. But all during French she shivered, not because her legs felt damp, but because it might have been acid after all. All during French she stared at Darlene, trying to figure out what made Darlene hate her so. Because she was still sniffing and sniggering and moving her desk away when Miss Rousseau wasn't watching.

Darlene wasn't the only one. On the way to lunch, people stepped on her heels or bumped into her, hard, in the corridor. And there was one boy in study hall who kept kicking the back of her seat.

When she complained about these things at home, Mamma looked unhappy. She tried to comfort her, saying, "Could be an accident," or "That's just school life." But even Mamma didn't say it was an accident the time she forgot to close her locker door and someone spilled red ink over her notebook and the composition she'd just recopied for English.

At first the people at school were blurred, like when you go to the eye doctor and he puts drops in your eyes. At first everyone looked alike, but after a while she was able to tell them apart. She could recognize the red-headed boy with the water pistol when he jabbed her with his elbow in the hall. She knew the tall girl with the pony tail who was good in English and the captain of the seventh-grade volleyball team. And the little girl in Science with pale blond hair and bangs who wore baby dresses and looked too young to be in high school.

Not all of them were mean. There were one or two girls who nodded when they passed her in the corridor. In classes some of them asked her for the home-work assignment if they had forgotten to copy it. There was even one girl, Sharon, who walked with her from Math to the cafeteria two days running. She acted so friendly that Mary Jane thought she might invite her to sit at her table at lunch.

Until the third day, when Sharon said, "Mary Jane, you can tell me.

Confidentially, weren't you born in New York? And aren't they paying you to come here to get Negroes into Wilson?"

Mary Jane widened her eyes, not understanding the question. "New York? Pay me? I've lived in High Ridge all my life. I was born here and—"

Sharon sighed. Mary Jane could see that she was disappointed. "Darn it," she said. "I had a bet with Elizabeth that you came from the North. The way you talk—" She went away, shaking her head.

Fred laughed when Mary Jane told him about it over lunch. "Don't you get it? You don't talk the way she thinks Negroes talk. You're supposed to say, 'Dis-here chile sho' nuff bawn in de Souf,' like Aunt Jemima or Old Black Joe or somebody."

"They've got this picture of a Negro in their minds," Grampa had said. And she had answered, so sure of herself then, "They'll learn. I'll be like some ambassador from a foreign country."

Only it wasn't easy being a foreign ambassador to people like Sharon who seemed nice but didn't really want to find out what you were like. It wasn't easy being a foreign ambassador when your only friend in school was Fred and he was busier and busier with basketball practice.

At Dunbar, Mary Jane had been busy too, acting in plays and on the Student Council and writing stories for *Dunbar Doings*. But here when she went to sign up for after-school things like cheerleading, the captain of the squad, one of the senior girls, stared at her, embarrassed. And then blurted out, "I'm afraid you wouldn't do. I mean, you wouldn't match— your color wouldn't match ours. You do see that, don't you? I mean, it's nothing personal."

Mary Jane saw lots of things. Like in gym, when she was the last one to be picked for volleyball every single period, even though there were other girls who were worse players. Or when they had folk dancing instead of volleyball and no one wanted to be her partner.

Even the gym teacher was uncomfortable then, not knowing what to do until Sally, the little girl from Science, came up and asked would she dance. Mary Jane wanted to say "No," but she couldn't, not with the teacher standing right there listening.

Sally's cheeks were scarlet and her hand shook as she took hold of Mary Jane's. She looked as if she were going to cry. Mary Jane felt like crying too, but she spread her lips in her best imitation of a smile and danced one turn around the room.

Before the second number was called, she murmured to Sally that her ankle hurt and left the floor. People didn't have to dance with her when they didn't want to, just because they felt sorry for her or something. To tell the truth, Mary Jane was feeling sorry enough for herself.

In Memoriam

Dorothy Sterling (1913–2008) was a major pioneer in the creation of an African American children's literature that was written with the intention of providing serious, complex, and nonstereotypical black characters for both a black and white reading audience, a challenge to what she called "confederate" thinking about the lives and character of black people. Born Dorothy Dannenberg in New York City, she graduated from Barnard College in 1934. She married Philip Sterling, a writer, whom she met while both wrote for the Federal Writers Project. In the 1940s, she worked as a researcher for *Life* magazine.

An active member of the NAACP, a communist during the 1940s, and a committed socialist throughout her life, she inevitably thought about the connection between literature and politics and the ways that history could inform and shape or reshape politics. She became what she called "an accidental historian." She found her true calling in the early 1950s when she began writing young adult black history books, joining the ranks of noted African American writers Shirley Graham Du Bois, second wife of W.E.B. Du Bois and author of *There Was Once a Slave: The Heroic Story of Frederick Douglass* (1947), *Your Most Humble Servant: The Amazing Story of Benjamin Banneker* (1949), and *Paul Robeson: Citizen of the World* (1946); and Langston Hughes, whose *The First Book of Negroes* appeared in 1952. Hughes would produce a spate of *First Books* about the Black Disapora and about black music throughout the 1950s.

Sterling's breakthrough occurred in the seminal year of 1954, when the Supreme Court desegregated public schools: a book entitled *Freedom Train: The Story of Harriet Tubman*, one of the earliest full-length books for young readers on the life of Tubman, preceding novelist Ann Petry's young person's biography of Tubman by a year. Sterling's book was published four years after another white writer, Elizabeth Yates, won the Newbery Medal, for her fictionalized biography, *Amos Fortune, Free Man*. (Yates would go on to write books about antebellum teacher Prudence Crandall, who, against popular sentiment of the time, operated a school for both black and white girls in Connecticut, and black theologian

Howard Thurman.) The cornerstone for African American children's literature as a historical and cultural corrective does predate postwar America, but its manifestation as a postwar movement was made up of both black and white writers. The author of *Freedom Train* was among the most prolific.

Sterling went on to write such black-themed books for young people as *Captain of the Planter: The Story of Robert Smalls* (1958), *Forever Free: The Story of the Emancipation Proclamation* (1963), *Tear Down the Walls: A History of the American Civil Rights Movement* (1969), and *The Making of an Afro-American: Martin Robison Delany 1812–1885* (1971). Her most famous book is *We Are Your Sisters: Black Women in the Nineteenth Century* (1984), an edited volume of letters, oral histories, and other primary documents that became a significant publication for black feminists.

Among her most important works is the 1959 novel *Mary Jane*. Based on interviews that Sterling conducted with black children who integrated southern schools, the novel is a powerfully moving story of a young black girl's determination to survive as one of the first black students in an all-white school. It was one of the few novels written by a white that Nancy Larrick (1910–2004) praised in her epochal essay, "The All-White World of Children's Literature," published in the *Saturday Review* in 1965.

The chapters from *Mary Jane* reprinted here, chapters 6 through 8, tell of the main character's and her friend Fred's dramatic first days at the previously all-white school, their fear, their isolation, and the harassment they endure.

Acknowledgments

I wish to thank my research assistant, Keya Kraft, for all her hard work in helping me find material for *Best African American Essays/Best African American Fiction* by culling through countless magazines, newspapers, and books. I also wish to extend my gratitude to the staff of the Center for the Humanities at Washington University for their assistance: Robbie Jones, our bookkeeper, and especially Barb Liebmann and Jian Leng, without whose help and organizational skills the book you hold in your hands would never have come into being. They are great people, and I owe them a lot.

Permissions and Credits

"The Torturer's Wife" by Thomas Glave. Copyright © 2008 by Thomas Glave. Originally published in the *Kenyon Review* 30, no. 4 (Fall 2008) 144–176. Reprinted by permission of the author.

"Prince Valiant Works the Black Seam" by W. David Hall. Copyright © 2009 by W. David Hall. Originally published in *Callaloo*, 30, no. 2 (pp. 454–460). Reprinted by permission of the author.

"Out of Body" by Glenville Lovell. Copyright © 2008 by Glenville Lovell. Originally published in *Queens Noir*, pp 270–280 (*Queens Noir*, ed. by Richard Knightly, published by Akashic Books, 2008). Reprinted by permission of the author.

"A Few Good Men" by David Nicholson. Copyright © 2008 by David Nicholson. Originally published in *Stress City: A Big Book of Fiction by 51 D.C. Guys*, pp. 376–387 (*Stress City*, ed. by Richard Peabody, published by Paycock Press, 2008). Reprinted by permission of the author.

Excerpt from *Yellow Moon* by Jewell Parker Rhodes. Copyright © 2008 by Jewell Parker Rhodes. Published by Atria, 2008. Reprinted by permission of the author and Atria, an imprint of Simon and Schuster.

"Microstories" by John Edgar Wideman. Copyright © 2008 by John Edgar Wideman. Originally published in *Harper's Magazine*, October 2008: 73–78. Reprinted by permission of the author.

"The Gangsters" by Colson Whitehead. Copyright © 2008 by Colson Whitehead. Originally published in *The New Yorker*, December 2, 2008. Reprinted by permission of the author and Aragi, Inc.

Excerpt from *Where the Line Bleeds* by Jesmyn Ward, pp. 1–27, published by Agate Boldon. Copyright © 2008 by Jesmyn Ward. Excerpt reprinted by permission of the publisher.

"Arrivederci, Aldo" by Kim Sykes. Copyright © 2008 by Kim Sykes. Originally published in *Queens Noir*, pp. 270–280 (*Queens Noir*, ed. by Richard Knightly, published by Akashic Books, 2008). Reprinted by permission of the author.

Young Adult Literature

Excerpt from *Chains* by Laurie Halse Anderson. Copyright © 2008 by Laurie Halse Anderson. Reprinted with the permission of Simon & Schuster Books for Young Readers, an imprint of Simon & Schuster Children's Publishing Division.

Excerpt from *Up for It: A Tale of the Underground* by L. F. Haines. Copyright © 2009 by L. F. Haines. Reprinted by permission of the author.

Excerpt from *Mary Jane* by Dorothy Sterling. Copyright © 1959 by Dorothy Sterling. First published by Doubleday, 1959. Reprinted by permission of the author's estate.

About the Editors

GERALD EARLY is a noted essayist and American culture critic. A professor of English, African and African American Studies, and American Culture Studies at Washington University in St. Louis, Early is the author of several books, including *The Culture of Bruising: Essays on Prizefighting, Literature, and Modern American Culture*, which won the 1994 National Book Critics Circle Award for criticism, and *This Is Where I Came In: Black America in the 1960s*. He is also editor of numerous volumes, including *The Muhammad Ali Reader* and *The Sammy Davis, Jr. Reader*. He served as a consultant on four of Ken Burns's documentary films, *Baseball, Jazz, Unforgivable Blackness: The Rise and Fall of Jack Johnson*, and *The War*, and appeared in the first three as on on-air analyst.

NIKKI GIOVANNI has written more than two dozen books, including volumes of poetry, illustrated children's books, and three collections of essays. She has received nineteen honorary doctorates, five NAACP Image awards, "Woman of the Year" awards from three different magazines, and Governors' Awards in the Arts from both Tennessee and Virginia. Her recent poetry anthology, *Hip Hop Speaks to Children*, was a critically acclaimed *New York Times* bestseller. Since 1987, she has taught writing and literature at Virginia Tech, where she is a university distinguished professor.

Best

african
2010
american
essays

GERALD EARLY, SERIES EDITOR

RANDALL KENNEDY, GUEST EDITOR